M J Johnson

Niedermayer & Hart

ODD DOG

PRESS

First published in 2012 by Odd Dog Press

British Library Cataloguing in Publication Data:
A catalogue record for this book is available from
the British Library.

ISBN - 13: 978-0-9562873-1-1

Printed and bound in the UK by
MPG Biddles Limited, Norfolk, PE30 4LS

www.odddogpress.com

Niedermayer & Hart

Acknowledgements

Extracts from the Authorized Version of the Bible (The King James Bible), the rights in which are vested in the Crown, are reproduced by permission of the Crown's Patentee, Cambridge University Press. They are as follows: Psalm 139:8; John 1:5; Matthew 26:50; Matthew 7:15.

The book's opening quote is taken from God's Love and Man's by Thomas Traherne. The poem Invictus, recited by the Thorpe sisters in this story, is the work of William Ernest Henley.

The Royal Observatory (Edinburgh) for their assistance with certain timings in the book.

My thanks also to the many kind people who have given so generously of their time and willingly shared with me their specific area of expertise.

I have to mention three people without whose help and support Niedermayer & Hart would never have seen (cliché or not, it's the truth) the light of day: my friend Peter Bolwell, for his patience, generosity and invariably good advice; my son Tom Johnson, for his abiding faith in the project, hard work on its behalf and beautiful artwork; my wife Judith, whose enormous contribution and her unwavering belief in the book and its author is impossible for me to put into words without sounding mawkishly sentimental.

'Tis Death my Soul to be Indifferent,
Set forth thy self unto thy whole Extent.

Thomas Traherne

Prologue

Shortly before 2am, a white Ford van was moving at a modest speed along a virtually empty carriageway. It might have been any one of a thousand places on the motorway network. Occasionally a lorry caught up and overtook.

The boy passenger felt extremely irritated by the driver's caution, at no time exceeding 55 mph.

'At least he's shut up though,' thought the boy, referring to the driver, who in fact had not shut up, but sang along with every song that came on the radio.

The boy recalled the question and answer session he'd been subjected to after first hitching the ride. It had posed no problem; he was sure his rehearsed answers sounded convincing: he was seventeen, and going to spend a few weeks with an older brother in London. He'd even been able to say what his brother's job was, his name and his girlfriend's name. The boy had invented a whole history for himself.

He was in fact only fifteen, a runaway; the background he'd escaped from told in his eyes, there was a fixed aggression about his features and a world-weariness that spoke volumes. He reckoned on at least a couple more hours before they arrived in London, maybe longer at the sluggish speed they were travelling. 'Perhaps it'll work out well for me,' he thought, 'No point getting there in the middle of the night.'

From the van's speakers the night-time DJ introduced, '*That all-time favourite about the Windy City, inimitably sung by no other than Ol' Blue Eyes.*'

The boy sighed inwardly as the squatly-proportioned driver joined Frank with gusto.

Despite the man's awful singing, the youth was finding it increasingly difficult to keep his eyelids open. He felt his head nod forward and jerked back into the seat. The driver's vocal accompaniment sounded far off, as if at the end of a long and echoing tunnel.

The driver smiled as he caught sight of his passenger falling asleep and immediately turned the radio off, the abruptness of which startled the boy momentarily.

"I'm stopping at these services … need a rest and a bite to eat. What about you?"

"I'll stay here if that's okay," replied the boy.

"No problem, I'll be about an hour."

As they came off the motorway and drew into the service area, the boy saw his all-singing all-driving companion more clearly as light spilled into the cab. The driver was in his late thirties. The boy reckoned he would be about the same height as himself when they were not seated, about 5'5", except the driver appeared to be as broad as he was high. He wore a woollen cap that covered the top of his head all the way down his forehead to just above the eyebrows. The cap was either black or blue, the light was insufficient to distinguish which, although he could make out the man's gingery hair, which sprouted in wiry curls about his ears and the back of his head, wherever the cap didn't reach.

The driver put the van into a parking space. "Sure you don't want anything?"

"No, I'm okay."

The driver got out and began to walk away. The boy was about to close his eyes when he saw the driver in the wing mirror come to an abrupt stop and turn around, as if he'd forgotten something. He returned to the passenger door and opened it.

"I just thought," he said amiably, "Look, get out and I'll show you."

"What?" the boy asked. The driver had already started walking to the back of the van. The boy released his safety belt and jumped down from the cab.

At the rear the driver had opened one of the double doors and had switched on a light, revealing the van's interior. There were half a dozen boxes marked 'Fragile'.

"What?" asked the boy.

The driver pointed to a mattress and some folded blankets that were piled on top of a box structure fitted across the width of the van at the driving cab end.

"You'll sleep better there."

The boy looked hesitant.

"It opens and locks from the inside," the driver said, demonstrating the door's locking mechanism, "You can get out if you need a pee," he laughed.

The bed looked very appealing. The boy nodded and stepped into the van's lit interior.

The driver immediately slammed the door and locked it with his key. He required nothing at the service area and went back to his cab.

He was about to start the engine when he felt the van shake. There was no sound. The van's interior was completely soundproofed; it must have been quite an impact. Another rocking motion followed a few seconds after the first, followed after a short interval by a third.

"Very spirited," the driver said.

Then with a contented smile he started the engine and pulled away.

He switched the radio back on.

BOOK ONE

BOOK ONE

Chapter One

Jim Latimer parked his car on the lane behind the bungalow then sauntered through the gate in the garden wall and along the path to the back door. The bright winter morning found him in an upbeat mood. It was ten to nine and he was in plenty of time for his appointment.

Erich Ledermann lived and worked from a small bungalow in Pett Village, a few miles inland from the coast. Jim and his wife Hannah had known him almost as long as they had kept a home in East Sussex; to their daughter Sophie he'd always been 'Uncle Erich'. And despite finding his interests in esoteric matters a bit cranky, Jim liked the man a great deal too; although he had been known to refer to him as the 'mystic pixie'.

Jim went straight in through the back door, where the aroma of fresh coffee pervaded the air. The kitchen doubled as a waiting room and clients were expected to entertain themselves here until Erich was ready to see them. Jim took a mug off a shelf, poured some coffee from an insulated jug and added milk from the refrigerator.

The mental association between the smell and taste of coffee and lighting a cigarette reminded Jim of his reason for being here. Erich practised hypnotherapy and was helping him to give up smoking. This was Jim's fourth visit.

Smoking wasn't the only thing Jim Latimer had relinquished during the past year. By this time, he'd also been free from alcohol for ten months. After Hannah had left with Sophie, his life had deteriorated rapidly; he'd thrown any pretence of normality away; stocked up at the nearest supermarket, where he regularly drove in alarming states, aiming to drink himself to death. At the end of the previous year, round the clock drinking had tolled heavily on his physical health and he'd spent six days in hospital with pleurisy. However, not even pleurisy and a stretch in hospital managed to reform him. Within an hour of getting home he was driving to the village store to replenish his stock of booze and cigarettes; the madness went on.

The reason why he stopped drinking had never been entirely clear to him. It had not come about through any sense of shame for harm done to his wife and child; at that point he was incapable of altruistic thought. It had nothing to do with realising he was alcoholic, he had known that fact for years; nor was it fear of premature death, in his view, unjustly long in coming.

The truth was, one morning he'd woken up sick and bleary-eyed, as usual; reached for the bottle, as usual, but had not taken the drink. Enough was somehow enough; what's more, and quite miraculously, he knew he need not go on. He admitted himself into an alcohol dependency unit and stayed six weeks.

The smoking continued; then, just over a month ago with the advent of cold weather, he had developed a rasping cough. Ruth, his neighbour, suggested he try Erich and hypnosis to help him stop. Ruth and Erich were close friends, and it had initially been through her that Jim and Hannah Latimer had come to know Erich. Ruth almost fell out of her armchair when Jim accepted the suggestion. In all the years she had known him, Jim had rarely been reticent in his disdain for alternative therapies. Considering his response to be something of a coup, she'd booked the first appointment for him there and then.

"This therapy will only work if you genuinely want to stop. As with any drug, staying stopped is invariably the hardest part," Erich had told him at their first session, the faint accent betraying his Austrian origin.

Jim hadn't smoked since that first session. He was convinced the hypnotherapy had considerably reduced the number of white-knuckle moments. Sometimes things might jolt his memory, like the coffee, but moments like these seemed to pass with increasing ease. During the twenty-five minute drive to Erich's on the first occasion he had chain-smoked the nine remaining cigarettes in a pack. Feeling a little nauseous on arrival, he'd confessed about it to Erich.

"Aha!" pronounced Erich, "Aversion therapy!"

Jim took a sip of coffee and browsed the magazine pile on the kitchen table. Unfortunately, Erich's selection hadn't altered much over recent weeks. At this time, Jim showed little interest in the world at large, however, the lack of less demanding stimuli forced him to pick up the daily newspaper: the beef crisis, the economy, credit card fraud, school standards falling, joy riding; more or less exactly the same stuff he recalled reading about the last time.

It was an insignificant column towards the middle of the paper; neither 'bizarre' nor 'suicide' would have enticed him; it was the word 'photographer' that grabbed his attention. Then as he ran his eye down the article and caught the name Loxton he let out a gasp of recognition.

John Loxton had taught at the school of printing where Jim had learned his craft. He checked the newspaper's date: 4 December, then began to read:

PHOTOGRAPHER IN BIZARRE SUICIDE

At 6.35pm yesterday evening, police were called to a location in Berwick Street in London's Soho. Local residents had alerted police to cries coming from a first floor apartment, home of photographer John Loxton. Police officers used force to enter the flat and discovered Mr Loxton severely wounded.

It appears his injuries were self-inflicted. Loxton had driven a Sabatier knife repeatedly into his groin, resulting in his emasculation.

A police officer later commented, "The pain must have been unbearable, he was still partly conscious when we got there."

Loxton lost consciousness in the ambulance and died later in the intensive care unit at UCH.

A colleague, and the executor of Loxton's estate, Robert Isherwood, rushed to the hospital to be with him when he died.

John Loxton enjoyed a flourishing international career throughout the 1950s, yet in later years became something of a recluse. He was never married. The police are satisfied the cause of death was suicide.

Jim looked up briefly when Erich entered the kitchen. Seeing him so absorbed, Erich leaned on Jim's shoulder and read along too.

Loxton had not figured in Jim's life for seventeen years; even so, he found the description shocking, "Emasculation ... that's another way of saying castration."

"You knew this man?" Erich asked, once he'd finished reading the piece.

Jim nodded.

"I see he was a photographer. Friend?"

"Hardly," replied Jim, "He taught at the place where I trained."

"A good teacher?"

Jim had to think about his answer before replying, "On a personal level Loxton was impossible. He'd stare down his nose at you with a really off-putting, supercilious air. I don't recall any student claiming to like him. Even so, his lectures were invariably full. He was really skilled with the use of light in portraiture; I suppose it allowed you to partially overlook the poison personality."

"If he was so talented and clearly disliked students so much, why did he teach?"

Jim shook his head, "I really couldn't say. It certainly wasn't vocational. John Loxton was very strange ... a really cold fish."

"But you looked surprised to discover he'd killed himself," said Erich.

It was true, Jim had indeed been shaken to learn of the man's death. He wondered if this was because he'd always credited suicides with a certain amount of introspection, a quality he had never detected even a trace of in Loxton. "I don't know why. Not wishing to speak ill of the dead or anything, but I found the man conceited to the point of repugnance."

Erich made a clicking sound at the back of his throat and tapped the paper with his finger, "Tch, what an awful way to go."

Jim considered the awfulness while he drained the last of his coffee.

"The genitals are central to our identity," postulated Erich, "Did he have problems with his sexuality?"

The question came out sounding like some dreadful cliché, particularly with the Austrian accent; Jim nearly laughed, but managed to maintain a straight face. "I've no idea," he said, "He wasn't someone you ever got to know. I recall he had a taste for expensive clothes, always wore a bow-tie. But he wasn't flamboyant. He was far too narcissistic for that, I think."

"The article doesn't say how old he was?"

"He must have been in his sixties. I finished my course in '79, and he was a good bit older then than I am now." Jim did some mental arithmetic, "Early sixties, I'd guess."

Erich consulted the paper, "It says someone was with him when he died ... Robert Isherwood."

"Bob runs a photographic library."

"A friend of Mr Loxton's?"

Jim smiled at the idea, "I doubt it. I can't imagine him and Loxton having much in common. Bob probably held pictures for him."

Erich looked at his watch. "We should get started. I have a full morning."

The paper was left open at the notice of Loxton's death as the two men exited the kitchen. Jim followed Erich into an L-shaped corridor that led on to his study. Erich had adorned this hallway with dozens of photographs and prints; here and there an occasional poem or a few lines expressing some spiritual message had been added to the gallery. To Jim it seemed incongruous to find, amidst charts of the chakras and mandalas of eastern wisdom, photographs of Erich at eighteen or nineteen taken with his commando unit during the final months of World War Two.

Erich Ledermann had fled to Britain from Austria as a twelve year old boy. Almost his entire family had perished in the Holocaust. Only one brother had survived the camps to become a Danish citizen after the war.

Erich was 5'6" tall, six inches shorter than Jim. He had kept himself fit, and on a good day looked twenty years younger than he was. Jim, on the other hand, looked considerably older than his thirty-seven years on even the best day. Erich had virtually no facial lines, his hair was still brown and full, immaculately brushed and regularly trimmed. Jim's hair by comparison was unkempt and streaked grey at the temples. As the two men entered the study it might not have been a great stretch of the imagination to think of them as contemporaries, though in truth, Erich was old enough to be Jim's father.

Within Erich's study a wall was devoted to family photographs, the lost childhood family from pre-war Austria, and his own small family as a man. There were several portraits of Erich with his wife and son. His wife had died some years earlier and had been much younger than him. Erich had married late; by this time he was seventy, yet his son, Danny, was only in his mid-twenties.

The room was very much a working space. A small pine desk was set against one wall, with bookshelves containing literature on various alternative therapies and healing techniques built into the space above. On the desk surface was a large lump of rock crystal and a framed photograph of Erich and Danny, looking like they were having a very good time sitting in a dinghy. Also in the room there was a couch, presumably for clients to lie down on, although Jim never had, and a couple of comfortable armchairs.

Jim sat with his back to the family pictures. The wall facing him bore an oil painting, a seascape. The artist had brought remarkable skill to the work; sea and sky merged, and at the painting's heart was a large setting sun, spilling rays of orange and crimson light onto the clouds and water. It was initialled R A, which Jim had recognised as soon as he clapped eyes on it for the first time four weeks ago, as the work of his neighbour and their mutual friend, Ruth Allinson.

"How have you been?" Erich asked from the other chair.

"I'm still not sleeping."

"Following the relaxation techniques I showed you?"

Jim shook his head sheepishly.

17

Erich smiled, nodding sagely, "Only you can alter it. Let go all the guilt you carry around. It's a waste of brain space. We can't change the past, but we can make a better future for ourselves by mastering the present."

Jim, who had clearly not been paying much attention to Erich's advice, went on to say, "I feel so ashamed of the damage I did ... all the crap I put Hannah and Sophie through."

"Going over and over it isn't dealing with it, you just give the past more power than it deserves. Addictions are like smokescreens, they conceal the real problem ... the tip of the iceberg."

"I don't want to be addicted to anything ever again," Jim said with feeling.

Erich paused, perhaps thinking about Jim's statement or maybe considering his next approach. "How are you feeling, now, at this moment?"

"Pretty good ... relaxed, comfortable."

"You're an excellent subject," observed Erich, "Hypnosis gets easier the more you practise it. I watched you let go the moment you entered the study. You've started doing my job for me."

Jim didn't appear to understand.

"You have begun to trust these techniques. As I've told you, all hypnosis is really self-hypnosis, inasmuch as we permit it. Hypnosis is rarely what people imagine it to be." Erich finished talking in a general way and told Jim to choose a point on Ruth's painting, "Release any thoughts you've brought in here with you ... let them go ..."

Jim felt himself sinking into the whirl of resplendent light at the painting's heart. As he listened to Erich's voice, calm, comforting, he merged with the sunlight. It was unimportant that Ruth had painted it; it no longer existed as a painting. He detached from the failed marriage and career; Erich's voice and the image before him were the foremost things he was conscious of.

Then, for just a split-second, the newspaper column about John Loxton sprang back into his mind.

"Become free of mental activity ..."

And Loxton too was forgotten.

Chapter Two

Wednesday, 4 December, 1996

Jim tried not to analyse the hypnotherapy sessions and why they appeared to be working. Erich's approach came down largely on the therapy side. It was the kind of stuff Jim traditionally sneered at and labelled 'psycho-babble'.

As Jim drove home after the session he was more relaxed than he could remember feeling in a very long time. For years, enslaved by the bottle and an increasingly negative mind-set, his eyes had been blinkered. His thoughts had grown increasingly bitter, like an anaerobe growing in some dim cavity of the brain, slowly poisoning its host. He had obsessed endlessly, cosseted old resentments, re-run ancient quarrels, and constantly scripted different outcomes.

For today, Jim's ghosts seemed laid to rest.

Normally, the sight of lights flashing and the barrier going down as he approached the level crossing in Robertsbridge would have made him irritable. But today, he waited contentedly as the fast train to London zoomed past; the gaps between carriages creating a kind of strobe effect against the winter sunlight. When the barrier went up again, Jim recognised one of the village postmen in the red van opposite and exchanged a wave as he drove by.

Jim lived about a mile and a half from here in a small cottage halfway between the villages of Robertsbridge and Brightling. He drove uphill, past the signs for the secondary school and the Hutterian community. A quarter mile on, the road forked; Jim kept to the left. From here on there were only occasional signs of habitation, the odd chimney stack puffing wood-smoke behind leafless trees.

He turned left into an unmade road without any sign to mark it; the car rattled along, bouncing and subsiding on the uneven surface. After about a hundred and fifty yards or so, two cottages, built together at the end of the nineteenth century, emerged from the woods. Both were uninhabited and all but derelict when Jim and Hannah had discovered them nine years ago. They had purchased the one nearest to the road as a retreat from London and its pressures.

Jim had been openly hostile when Ruth bought the adjoining property less than a year later; it wrecked a grandiose scheme he'd had of one day converting both cottages into one. Hannah, Sophie and Ruth had hit it off from the start. However, for many weeks Jim had sulked. He'd sometimes refused to visit the cottage at all.

"She's ruined it," was his sad refrain.

Eventually, feeling more than a bit dejected because everyone was getting on so well, he sullenly accepted the fact he'd gained a neighbour.

In the intervening years Jim and Ruth had become far closer than most friends, at times squabbling like sibling rivals. He probably wouldn't have survived the darkest booze-sodden months after his marriage break-up without her. Not that Ruth had become his caretaker, but she'd kept a watchful eye on him; rescued him when he'd collapsed unconscious in the garden on a night the temperature dropped to minus four; turned off the unlit cooker and opened the windows the time he filled the cottage with butane. Fortunately, on this occasion too he'd been unconscious; else as a chain-smoker, he would most likely have blown himself to kingdom come. Needless to say, she had received no thanks. In the final months he'd mostly ignored her, considering her to be in the enemy camp. Sometimes out of sheer loneliness he would deign to talk with her, inevitably twisting the conversation round to what a bitch Hannah was for abandoning him.

"You're lucky she stayed so long. Take a good look in the mirror, Jim. You're the problem." Ruth was rarely indirect.

At the end of the track an area had been cleared. Jim's car was the only one normally kept here, so he didn't concern himself with parking neatly. A footpath went down an incline towards the cottages, their boundaries marked with a picket fence. The location was idyllic, set amongst oak trees and hills.

As Jim got out of the car, he saw Ruth coming towards him, wheeling her bicycle along the footpath. She possessed no car and held strong views about the internal combustion engine and its destructive overuse. She was forty-six, 5'7" tall, and still a striking woman. She wore an army surplus jacket dyed a deep purple, and beneath the open jacket her grey sweatshirt and blue jeans were spattered with the obligatory patches of paint that adorned most of her clothing. She had thick brown hair tangled and trailing about her shoulders in customary unmanageability.

"You were up and gone early," she said.

"I had to see the pixie," he replied, coming to a stop before the bicycle.

"You were out before it was light."

Jim feigned a grand theatrical manner, "An irresistible urge to commune with nature!" It was true, he'd gone to visit the sea before Erich.

"Weirdo," she said with a smile, and wheeled by him. "Do you want anything from the village?" she called, not looking back as she glided alongside the bike with one foot on the pedal.

"Nope."

Once off the footpath, Ruth brought her leg over the moving bicycle and pedalled away, "See you!"

Jim went in through his gate. The gardens had to be fenced in order to prevent the deer that roamed the woods from causing havoc. Jim had learned the hard way how a couple of Bambi lookalikes could strip a garden bare in next to no time. There was more land to the front of the cottages than at the rear, so Jim had allocated his front garden to his passion for growing vegetables. There was little to be seen now; except leeks, the purple broccoli would be ready in a couple of months and the broad beans were overwintering beneath straw. Jim considered the restoration of his garden quite an achievement. It had gone wild after Hannah and Sophie left; an outer manifestation of his inner deterioration.

He went round the back and entered via the kitchen, removed his jacket, and threw it over a chair. He filled the kettle and spooned some tea into the pot ready for when it boiled.

Jim's study was entered directly from the kitchen. He checked his answerphone for messages. There were none; which was generally the case. In times past he might have expected half a dozen work enquiries a day, but life situations change. After Hannah and Sophie moved out and set themselves up at their London home, Jim had kept the answerphone on twenty-four hours a day. He wiped any messages without even listening to them. Consequently, Jim hadn't worked in two years. In his early career he'd presented himself as hedonistic and cultivated a reputation for unpredictability; already drinking heavily, but before alcohol had led him into an ever-decreasing spiral, he'd produced work of very high quality. Quite recently in a reflective moment shared with Ruth he'd said of himself, "The unpredictable genius became an undependable arsehole."

A small hallway led from the study. The staircase was here, and on the left a sitting room. Jim picked up two envelopes sitting on the front door mat and went back to the kitchen; they were both bills.

"They'll have to wait in line," he said, placing them for company amongst a pile of other bills.

But still, positive thoughts remained from the session with Erich. He placed slices of bread under the grill, scrambled two eggs, and had a late breakfast. Normally he left dishes and pans piled in the sink until the decision came to wash up or not eat; this, however, was a day for turning over new leaves; he not only washed up but ran a cloth across the work surfaces too.

He decided a walk in the winter sunshine would put him in the right mood for the dozen letters he intended to write that afternoon to various picture editors. It was time, he thought, to get back into the frame. He'd put his jacket on, and was reaching for the door latch, when the telephone rang.

"Jim Latimer," he said.

"Hullo Jim ..."

Loxton's suicide flashed back. The man's voice, immediately recognised, prompted a sensation at the back of his neck.

"... Jim ... it's Bob."

"Yes. Hello," Jim replied with some awkwardness. It was a shock hearing Bob Isherwood's voice after seeing his name in print so recently. Five years ago Jim had stormed out of Bob's office showering him with a string of expletives, and they had not spoken since. Bob had taken the liberty of telling Jim what a mess he was making of his life.

"Have I called at a bad time?"

Jim identified with Bob's diffidence. "No", he replied, trying to ease up. "I was just surprised to hear your voice."

"It's been a while."

"I read about Loxton this morning. It mentioned you."

"Christ, Jim, it was awful. You can't imagine what he did to himself."

"Stabbed himself it said ... 'emasculated' was the word used."

"His balls and dick were purée," the image expressed itself fully through Bob's tone. "For some strange reason he was carrying his will on him, so I got called to the hospital almost straightaway. I was down in it as the executor."

"I was surprised you knew Loxton that well."

"Christ no, course I didn't." Bob sounded shocked by the suggestion. "He breezed into my office about three weeks ago. 'I've decided to make a will', he declared, you know how he was, all sneery. 'Will you be my executor?' ... no foreplay like, 'How are you?' or any of that crap. I said, yes, okay, and thought no more about it. I didn't know he was planning to lop off his flamin' bollocks, did I? I used to see him round occasionally, he only lived a couple of streets from the office, and I held a few pictures for him. But as for knowing him, Loxton was a closed book far as I was concerned."

"It's seventeen years since I saw him," put in Jim.

"He hadn't changed much ... not at all. In fact ..." Bob broke off mid-sentence.

"What?"

"Just thinking about the way he was, always decked-up, bow tie, suit ... he must have been dyeing his hair."

"The police sounded definite it was suicide."

"No doubt there. He'd locked himself in. They had to break into the flat."

The conversation about Loxton gradually subsided and they started to crack up the years of accumulated ice, going on to discuss what had changed and was happening now in their lives.

"I was having lunch with a client last week when Hannah and a friend came into the restaurant. Do you see her and Sophie much?"

"Things have got better. I've been sober ten months."

"That's great," Bob sounded genuinely happy for him.

"I can see Soph anytime I like, and I pop by the house for a coffee and chat with Hannah."

"If you don't mind me saying, I can't think of two people better suited to each other than you and Hannah. Think you'll patch things up?"

"I don't know Bob, too early to say. I think she'd like me to have more time under my belt before committing herself."

"She told me you were doing well, a bit concerned though that you aren't working."

"I haven't worked in a couple of years. To be honest I'd have been incapable for most of that time."

Bob cleared his throat, "That's why I'm ringing, I may have something ... if you want it that is?"

Jim felt a judder, part excitement at the prospect of earning a living, part fear of returning to work after such a gap.

He made no reply, so Bob continued, "Actually, it's indirectly to do with John Loxton. He was supposed to start a job, today in fact, photographing porcelain for some catalogue. He'd worked for them before, it seems. Anyway, they have a deadline to meet and they rang me."

"Why you?"

"Christ knows, I told them I wasn't an agent. I spoke to a nice woman called Rosemary Hines. She said they were really sad to hear about Loxton and asked me if I could personally recommend someone. They're based not far from you, Brighton, and I remembered what Hannah said. Interested?"

"Yes. Thanks."

"Here's the number, ring up, find out what it entails. Can't hurt can it?"

"Okay, I've got a pen. Fire away."

"They're called Niedermayer & Hart ..."

*

It took Ruth an hour round trip to do her bits of shopping and chores in the village. The ride home was mostly uphill, and the general rule was ten minutes down, twenty back. However, she had been known to halve this when pushed for time, or feeling particularly vigorous. She navigated her bike off the main road onto the track that led to the cottages. There was no sense of urgency about Ruth that morning. She had enjoyed the exercise and the winter sunshine.

Almost the instant she turned off, long before the cottages came into view, she felt her perception of space and distance altering. She was only moderately breathless, and initially assumed over exertion was the reason why the trees and sky were shimmering. Her head was reeling, heart pounding, as she braked and brought the bike to a standstill. She felt more secure once both feet were planted on the ground.

The first explanation that sprang to mind was physiological, "Shit! I'm having a heart attack!"

But she was not having a heart attack, and realised this before imagination had time to develop the thought. Ruth grew calm again; actually, this was nothing new. She had never known it catch her quite like that, but then she had never been on a bicycle when it happened before, and each time was different. These 'events' had been part of her life as far back as she could remember, although it had taken years to come to terms with it. Erich Ledermann and the sisters had helped her to understand it, to use it beneficially without fearing it; she controlled it these days, unlike in the past when it had made her feel like she was mad. However, on this occasion her gift had caught her completely off guard. She knew there was nothing she could do, but keep calm and watch.

She felt a rigidity run through her body, her fingers clenching tight onto the rubber grips of the handlebars. The sky grew larger and the trees all around appeared to move further away, creating an expanse of air and light charged up with tiny flickering streams of electricity. The pressure in her head and neck was building, as though she were soaring up into the sky at some phenomenal rate of knots. Then everything exploded brilliant white, and for a moment nothing existed. She was not even aware of her own body, all pressures and restraints were gone and all was peaceful, pure bliss. Although the light had increased in its intensity it didn't hurt her eyes, but she knew that none of this was being witnessed with physical eyes. Once the brightness reached its zenith it suddenly vanished and all was exactly as before; the trees, the unmade road, the bright winter day.

Along the track a man was shuffling towards her. At first she failed to realise it was Jim. His movement was different, stiff, uncoordinated.

"Jim?" she called out uncertainly.

The man kept staggering towards her giving no outward sign that he had heard. Even when close enough to identify Jim's features, Ruth continued to feel unsure; something about him was wrong.

"Where are you going?" she asked, unable to think of anything better.

Again, no reply. He was now passing alongside, his intention was obviously to ignore her.

"Jim ... Hey! Jim! What's wrong?"

Only then did he seem to hear. He stopped in his tracks and turned to face her. The look he gave was chilling, as though she was nothing. During the final months of his drinking he had rarely shown her anything but contempt. Ruth thought she'd already seen Jim's worst side, but Jim's worst didn't come close to that look. The hate pouring out from the eyes was tangible. She knew whatever it was she was looking at, it wasn't Jim. Its mouth started moving. At first she thought it was trying to speak but then realised it was attempting to smile; a horrible vicious smile, a leer, a corrupted facsimile of that most human expression.

Ruth staggered backwards, suddenly very scared, vaguely aware of becoming entangled in something, losing her balance and crashing onto the dirt track.

Then came another flash of light and the alarming vision vanished.

For a few moments Ruth lay still, stunned by the realness of the encounter. She knew it was over; it always ended like that, with the flash. Once her heartbeat had normalised a little, she extricated a bootlace from the bicycle chain and pulled herself out from under its frame. She left the scattered debris that was her shopping where it had fallen and sat, shaking, on the grass verge.

She had no idea what the vision was supposed to convey to her. However, she had no doubt that it was both meaningful and significant. Only once before had she experienced anything quite so vivid.

Ruth had been six years old; far too young to put forward any rational argument, and with no understanding yet of the powerful gift in her possession. She had fallen back on the only resources a small child has when all else fails; begging, screaming, kicking.

"We are not going to put up with your tantrum. Daddy is driving us to the seaside, whether you want to go or not. You are being a very naughty girl, now be quiet!"

That was the last sentence Ruth remembered her mother making.

Two hours later, firemen cut her free of the car wreck and the carnage that had been her mother, father and baby brother.

Incredibly, Ruth emerged physically unharmed, but the mental scars she was left to carry had long outlived the child.

Chapter Three

Jim called the Niedermayer & Hart number as soon as he finished talking to Bob.

He spoke to Rosemary Hines. She thanked him for getting in touch promptly, stressed the urgency of their situation and suggested meeting to discuss requirements as soon as possible.

"I could drive over tomorrow."

"I'm afraid I shan't be here in the morning, and Mr Hart is currently away on a buying trip." Rosemary Hines spoke impeccably enunciated English. Jim pictured a woman in her sixties, the product of a ladies' finishing school that had trained its girls in the finest traditions. "The afternoon looks more promising. Would 2.30 be convenient?" she asked in the politest of tones.

"Yes, fine."

"Then I shall look forward to meeting you tomorrow, Mr Latimer."

He felt he had been regally dismissed.

Jim decided it was still a good idea to take a walk and get some fresh air. He was making to leave again, but on reaching the back door, he discovered Ruth peering through its glass.

"Are you going out?" she asked casually, "I was coming in for coffee."

Jim took off his coat and filled the kettle.

Ruth seemed pale considering her recent physical exertion, a bit distracted too. She was excited to hear the news that Jim might have landed a job, "That's great! When do you start?"

"I'm meeting them tomorrow, they're in a bit of a fix ... Loxton was supposed to have started today."

"Loxton?"

Jim explained; he told her about the newspaper at Erich's and the subsequent conversation with Bob Isherwood. She looked rather shaken by the account. Jim wondered if he had been a little too graphic in the re-telling of it.

"Horrible, isn't it?"

Ruth shook her head, "To mutilate yourself like that ... like torture ... like some vicious punishment. The pain would be unbearable. I can't believe it possible ... you'd pass out with the shock."

"He was a strange man. Perhaps in the end he wasn't quite playing with a full deck."

Ruth drained her coffee. "I must go," she said.

The speed of her departure was probably a record. Loxton's suicide certainly had the power to clear a room. Jim thought he might mention it the next time a Jehovah's Witness called.

*

Niedermayer & Hart were based in Hove; exactly where Hove became Brighton, or Brighton Hove, Jim had no idea. He found a parking meter in a nearby street and walked the remaining distance.

He entered Barnswick Square from its northern end. The square reflected the grace and refinement of its Regency period, black iron railings standing out against the cream facades of the houses, an inner perimeter of lawned garden at the square's centre, before a backdrop of sea and sky.

He climbed the steps to number sixty-seven. He was ten minutes early. A brass plaque assured him he was in the right place:

Niedermayer & Hart
Fine Porcelain
Est. 1957

He suddenly felt a bit jittery. He needed to work, but it would be a complete turn-off if he looked too hungry when he met Miss, Ms, Mrs Hines? He imagined her peering from behind bi-focal lenses, asking, 'And what has one been doing recently?' What could he say? 'Well, one has been pissed out of one's brains until quite recently, almost incapable of focusing one's pecker on the porcelain, in fact.'

In an attempt to calm down he looked around briefly. There was little to see, every window was fitted with blinds. He peeped over the railings down at the basement area; here, the windows were barred with wooden shutters inside. He wiped the sweat off his palms onto the legs of his jeans. It was such a long time since he had been an interviewee. Then, looking up he noticed a video camera peering down at him and wondered if his nervousness was being witnessed.

'To hell with it,' he thought, and pressed the doorbell.

He heard its ring announcing his arrival, and listened for the sound of approaching feet. Jim waited half a minute before deciding to try again; his finger hovering above the bell button just as the door opened.

Standing before him was a flimsily-built man, possibly in his late teens or early twenties. He was wearing a dark blue suit that looked about a size too big for him. The same could be said for his collar and tie, which failed to form any satisfactory union with his neck. The young man's sallow complexion and small, dark but alert eyes, didn't improve the presentation. As he smiled, a mouthful of widely-spaced teeth exposed themselves behind fleshy, crudely crafted lips.

"Hello. I've come to meet Rosemary Hines."

"She isn't here," replied the young man rather brusquely. "Were you expected?"

Jim gave an exasperated sigh, "I'd arranged to meet her at 2.30."

"Mr Latimer?" asked the man-boy, his eyes opening to maximum size, with an incredulity that was nearly insulting. "I'm sorry you were kept waiting, please come in."

Jim entered. The floors were carpeted in a sumptuous royal blue, discreetly patterned with a small grey fleur-de-lys design. At the hallway's farthest end a wide staircase rose in elegant progression to the floors above with polished brass rods holding its carpet in place. Various landscapes adorned the walls in large gilt frames. A semi-circular table accompanied on either side by two straight-backed chairs comprised the only furniture in the hallway; arranged in the centre of this table was a piece of Meissen.

Jim waited while the young man closed the front door.

"I'm Nicholas Cureton, Miss Hines' personal assistant. She's probably been held up in traffic. Do come through." He pointed towards the first door.

It was like entering a giant display case. Brightly lit glass cabinets adorned both chimney alcoves and several others had been placed around the room. The cabinets were arranged with porcelain figurines, plates and various commemorative cups, mugs, jugs etc. A white leather sofa was set along one of the walls, presumably to allow visitors an opportunity to relax and delight in this wonderland of fine china.

Nicholas Cureton gestured towards the sofa, "Please, take a seat. Can I get you anything, tea, coffee?"

"Some coffee would be great. Thanks."

The toothy grin returned and he left.

The room did what it set out to do, presented Niedermayer & Hart's wares in an atmosphere of refinement. Jim had never experienced the remotest flicker of interest in china of any description. In a glass cabinet to his right were some figures representing different kinds of cats. They were skilfully crafted, but porcelain, animal, human or vegetable, just didn't ring his bell.

He'd anticipated feeling wobbly; two years was a long time away from a career. Just being here was an achievement. At the end of the drinking he had needed a drink to steady his hand enough to brush his teeth. The anxiousness he felt approaching the house had now largely gone, but he still felt uncomfortable. Despite the obvious efforts that had gone into creating an attractive showroom, there was a stuffiness about the place Jim didn't like. Upon entering the house the cloying scent of air freshener had immediately assailed his nostrils. He had never liked the sickliness of those aerosol things. In bathrooms the world over, air fresheners overwhelmed a new occupant, while the inevitable, unmentionable, lingered beneath. It was akin to that here; beneath the smell of roses was a stale, slightly fetid odour.

'Must have drain trouble,' he thought, and consoled himself with, 'Think of the money.'

Nicholas soon returned carrying a tray. He placed it before Jim on a small glass-topped table. After he'd put it down, the unusual young man hovered about, closely observing Jim as he added a drop of milk from the jug provided and stirred his coffee.

"Thank you, it's very nice," Jim said, taking a sip, hoping it would encourage him to back off.

But Nicholas Cureton didn't move. After an awkward silence, he asked, "I understand you knew Mr Loxton?"

"John Loxton taught where I trained."

"His friend, Mr Isherwood, recommended you to us."

It didn't seem appropriate to point out Loxton had no friends. Jim nodded.

"Mr Isherwood was there when he died."

"I believe so."

"Does anyone know why he did it?"

Jim wanted to say, 'Why the hell should anyone have a clue what was going on in Loxton's head?' but instead he replied, "I've no idea. I haven't spoken to Bob since yesterday."

Nicholas Cureton was seriously encroaching upon Jim's space and beginning to creep under his skin. There was something intrusive about the young man's manner and the way he formed his questions.

Jim was rescued by what sounded like a lift arriving. Nicholas, clearly attuned to its sound, had already pricked up his ears before Jim first heard it, and immediately lost interest in him. The sound of a concertina door sliding across was reminiscent of old-fashioned department stores.

"Excuse me," Nicholas said curtly and left the room.

Jim detected a woman's voice in the whispered conversation that followed his exit. After a short time, the concertina doors were pulled across again followed by a gentle hum. A single set of footsteps, all but muted by the carpeting, approached along the hallway.

"I'm sorry to have kept you, Mr Latimer."

Rosemary Hines gave him quite a shock. Jim had pictured her the way she sounded, like women in old British movies, Celia Johnson in 'Brief Encounter'.

He rose and shook her hand.

Rosemary Hines was about twenty-seven years old, approximately 5'4" tall, with dark hair braided and raised about her head. Her face was finely-structured, her eyes deep blue, the lips full-blooded and sensuous. She wore a simple black dress to just above the knee, pulled into a tiny waist with a red belt. Rosemary Hines was one of the most striking women Jim had ever seen.

"Thursdays are always hectic ... payday for the staff."

Jim found it slightly unattractive the way she'd highlighted 'the staff'.

"Most of our business is through mail order. Our distribution centre is in Eastbourne. We try to maintain a family feel. Mr Hart and I always take the wages over together on a Thursday. Unfortunately, he's on a business trip to Amsterdam, so it all fell on my shoulders this week."

"Is Mr Niedermayer involved in the business too?"

"Mr Niedermayer passed away shortly before I joined the company." Inclining her head to one side, she gave Jim a smile accompanied by a girlish laugh and asked, "Would you like to come through?"

She led the way through the hall and into an office; here two desks sat face to face. The nearest desk had two TV monitors on it, one relaying pictures of the front steps, the other showing an alleyway. At the other end of the room, as far away from the other two as was physically possible, was a third desk. It was smaller, far less prestigious looking and Jim presumed that Nicholas, the office junior, was kept at bay over there. Rosemary Hines took up a position behind

31

the farthest of the two joined desks, gesturing for Jim to be seated in a chair beside it.

"We were deeply shocked by Mr Loxton's death. He had photographed our collection over the past few years. He was extremely professional and is a great loss to us."

"Your catalogue is produced annually?"

"Yes. Clients receive our catalogue in early February. We like all the photographic work completed by mid-December, in order to add text, allowing us time to proof read, check colour etc."

"How many pieces are involved?"

"Two hundred and thirty-seven. Only about a quarter is new, but as we're using a new photographer we'll re-shoot the whole collection."

"I think I should point out," Jim said, "that my own area of expertise is mainly in portraiture. There are people who do this kind of work all the time." Later he could hardly believe he had talked himself down like that.

Rosemary Hines opened a drawer and handed Jim an A5 brochure. He began leafing through it.

"Mr Loxton had never photographed porcelain before either."

"How many catalogues did he do for you?"

"I couldn't recall without checking, three or four."

"It is very straightforward."

"Mr Isherwood spoke highly of you and my instincts tell me you're the right man for us."

She made Jim a generous financial offer. Jim concluded from the size of the sum mentioned that they were desperate to find a replacement for Loxton. It was already the fifth of December, and because of the urgency of the situation it was arranged that he should make a start on Saturday. Tomorrow he would need to organise some equipment.

Rosemary Hines led him to a room on the first floor that he would be using for the shoot. It was the same room Loxton had used, sited directly above the office. It had been recently decorated and the smell of paint was fresh; the room itself was bare.

"Excuse the mess, we're having this floor re-decorated. We'll fix you up with something to sit on."

"Fine," replied Jim.

"When you come on Saturday, park at the rear, drive down through the mews." She opened the window blinds and pointed past the concreted area below in explanation. "There's an entry-phone by the gate. Nick will let you in."

A pair of solid steel gates was set in an eight foot high brick wall. While Jim watched, a plain white Ford van drove out into view from the right side of the house and stopped before the gates. Nicholas then rushed into view coming from the same trajectory as the van. He seemed to be angry about something; a driver emerged from the cab and followed Nicholas back to the house. Jim could only see the top of this other man's head. He wore a navy blue woollen hat with wisps of curly red hair sticking out at the sides. The driver returned almost immediately carrying a cardboard box marked 'Fragile'.

"We have four shops. We deliver directly from here. We like the hands on approach."

"Where are the shops?" Jim asked, without any real enthusiasm to know. He found watching the driver load the forgotten box more interesting.

"Bristol, Chester, Edinburgh and London," she replied.

The gates opened electronically, presumably operated by Nicholas somewhere out of sight, and the white van drove away.

Once all the details and arrangements were discussed and finalised, Rosemary Hines escorted Jim to the front door.

"We shall look forward to seeing you on Saturday, Mr Latimer," she said, shaking his hand again.

As he walked down the front steps into Barnswick Square, the air struck him as particularly fresh and exhilarating after being subjected for the past hour to the faint whiff of the house's drains.

*

When he got back, Jim dropped by next door. In Ruth's cottage, the study and sitting-room had been converted into one large studio. There were a dozen canvases, mainly landscapes, at various stages of development dotted about. Within the space were several tables without any uniformity of shape or size strewn with materials, brushes, bottles, and palettes with squeezed-out lines of paint blended and streaked in puddles of colour. The floor, walls, and even the ceiling here and there were flecked and speckled with paint. Ruth was working at a large canvas supported on an easel in the centre of the room.

"What's happening?" Jim called as he entered.

Ruth almost leapt out of her skin.

"Don't you ever knock?"

33

"I thought you heard me," he replied defensively, "You aren't usually that jumpy."

"Just bloody well knock next time."

"You never knock my door."

"That's because you were always pissed and I'd have been knocking till the cows came home."

At least one argument per week could be guaranteed between these two. The subject matter varied, and they were by no means one-sided, but regardless of how heated things became, they remained friends. Their fondness for each other ran deep; surprising considering how totally different they were.

Ruth had taught art until shortly before she became the Latimers' neighbour and started painting full-time. She met Erich through his son Danny, who had been a promising student of hers. Erich was the only subject Jim never broached, it was their taboo; he was not sure if their friendship was platonic or sexual. Hannah was never any use on the subject; undoubtedly she knew, women always did, at least so Jim believed. For all his pretence of worldliness there was something of the innocent about Jim and something of the prude too. Ruth generally stayed over at Erich's bungalow on evenings when they went to their healing group. Jim understood no more about what went on at these weekly meetings than the name suggested; he showed no interest in anything that came under the heading 'esoteric'.

"So how did you do?" Ruth asked, not in the mood for a good quarrel.

"I start Saturday," he replied excitedly.

Ruth paused almost imperceptibly. Jim failed to notice.

"Good. You must be pleased."

"It'll be great to have money again," he said. Then, remembering the bills on his kitchen table, added, "After the wolves at the door."

"How long will the job take?" she asked.

"I reckon four maybe five days. I'm off to London tomorrow to pick up some gear."

"Will you call in on Hannah and Soph?"

"Probably."

"Give them my love." She wiped the brush she was using on a rag and put it down on the nearest table, "Even though I'm busy I suppose you expect me to stop and make you coffee?"

"I made you coffee yesterday morning, even though I was on my way out for a walk. So the answer is yes, except I'll have tea, please."

Ruth smiled.

34

"It's okay," Jim said, "I'll make it."

Ruth made the tea. She felt like stopping; they chatted, drank tea and shared a pack of biscuits. Jim stayed about an hour.

Immediately after he'd gone, Ruth dialled Erich's number. It always surprised her how much stronger his accent sounded on the telephone.

"Erich. He's taken the job."

"Have you told him anything?"

"No, you know Jim, he wouldn't listen."

"Perhaps it's best, for the moment anyway. Let's face it, we don't understand it ourselves yet."

"I woke up terrified last night ... I was screaming ..."

Hugh's Tale

As narrated by Hugh Apsley to Brother Anselm at the Abbey of Valle Crucis during the month of December in the year 1202

I

After the passage of years even the most painful memories of childhood are apt to fade and thereby lose their poignancy, good Anselm. I still recall my mother's tearful eyes the day that I was taken screaming from her bosom. My father scolded me gently for my timidity, and assured me once again of my good fortune. I was six years old, and to become page to Gerbert Corviser, lord of a sizeable estate north of Chester.

"Let me be proud of you, Hugh," he said, as he hoisted me, still blubbering, into the arms of Gerbert's steward.

I caught a final glimpse of my mother's gentle face through milky eyes. The steward turned his horse about and cantered away from all that had been home.

Four months on, the same steward carried news to me of my mother's death. The next time I kissed that soft cheek, all warmth had left it as she lay before me cold as earth.

She had been with child, a fact that in my childish innocence I had no knowledge of. However, not even my ignorance of such matters could deny the howling presence of a baby girl, Melisend, my sister. Myself, I took no interest in the caterwauling bundle of misery my old nurse placed so joyously into my arms.

As Melisend grew she bore a striking resemblance to our mother. As transformation came about in her features, so too did feelings of brotherly affection in my heart. She was quicker-witted than I was, aided by a mischievous streak and determined will; my father doted on her, and his reprimands, usually meeting doleful eyes, often as not gave way to swift forgiveness.

Gerbert Corviser proved himself a fair and gentle master. I served at table as his page, and when a homesick look overtook my eyes, he

36

would give me leave to visit my family. I saw them at the fairs of Shrewsbury and Chester, which my father always attended with Melisend and sometimes my older brother Geoffrey too.

Gerbert grew fond of his reluctant page, and treated me as well as his own kin. At the age of thirteen I became his squire. The years passed comfortably, my master educating me in the knightly arts, whilst I continued to see my family at various times.

Gerbert Corviser had never been a man of much devotion in religious matters. He enjoyed hunting and good wine much more, and possessed a taste for women. However, as he progressed in years, he grew concerned for the state of his mortal soul. When news reached England that the Infidel had taken Jerusalem and men talked heatedly of the abomination, Gerbert I recall remained silent on the matter, which was not normally his way.

Whatever Gerbert's sins were, whether real or imagined, I knew him for a better man than most. However, the promise of absolution for setting foot upon Crusade brought comfort to him, and Gerbert was resolved to cleanse his soul in holy war.

When all the preparations for our departure had been made, I visited my home to bid farewell. Melisend was thirteen then, and on the eve of womanhood. Leaving my homeland brought to mind my earlier departure, and the sight of Melisend with tears on her cheek as I rode away forced me to choke back a tumult of emotions in my own breast.

We sailed with the fleet and met King Richard's army at Marseilles. We arrived later than expected, and the King had already departed. We sailed for Sicily, and met with Richard's forces outside Messina. We launched an assault on the city over a sum of money owed to the King. It was soon resolved, and I had received my first taste of battle.

We overwintered in Sicily before sailing for Cyprus. There was trouble here too, and Richard led his army against the island's fortresses. Within a few weeks the whole of Cyprus was ours; these victories intoxicated my youthful mind, and Gerbert seemed to grow younger with the thrill of battle.

Finally we reached Acre and joined the siege that had begun two years before. The bombardments started and our fleet blockaded the harbour cutting off their supplies. The city's surrender was only a matter of time.

King Richard himself was eager to reach Jerusalem. Saladin delayed payment of a ransom for the prisoners of Acre, and the King, impatient to move on, ordered they be taken outside the city walls and executed. The majority, about two and a half thousand, had been men of the garrison, yet a few hundred women and children were also put to the sword. I felt pity for them. Until then I had seen only glorious victory, but on that day I saw another side to war which did not glisten so brightly.

We marched south towards Joppa. At Arsuf, the rear of our column was attacked, and many horses were lost. Our knights charged too soon, but the King, seeing an advantage in this error, did not recall his men, and caught the Saracens off their guard. He ordered his knights to drive forward twice more, bearing down like a charging wall into the enemy. We won a great victory that day, handing us the prize of Joppa.

Gerbert had launched himself into each charge with great enthusiasm. I could see little from my position behind our lines with the other squires. Twice Gerbert rode back proudly, but after the third charge only his stallion returned. Taking no thought, I rashly mounted the beast and rode into the fray in the direction where I had last seen my master.

I found Gerbert propped against a rock, being comforted by a knight of the Temple, and knew at once that my master could not recover from the injuries he had sustained; his belly was split open, and much of his entrails had spilled out onto the dust. A short way from Gerbert lay the Saracen who had done him injury, himself dispatched by the Templar.

"Is this your master, boy?" the knight asked as I dismounted.

"Yes, sir," I answered.

Gerbert, seeing me, called out in a weak voice, "Hugh, you found your old master."

Tears filled my eyes as I knelt beside him; Gerbert took my hand and clasped it to his breast.

I said, "Don't try to speak. I'll take you back to our lines."

Gerbert shook his head, he spoke in short bursts, for his pain was great, "I will die where I am fallen. I shall not see the Holy City. Perhaps God will show mercy ... for the commitment I have shown to his great cause." Then Gerbert looked up at the Templar and said, "I would ask a favour of you, sir."

"If it is in my power to grant then it shall be given," the knight replied.

"This boy ... my charge ... take him into your order ... I have trained him well, he is obedient and dutiful ... I intended him to be a knight."

"I will speak to my order for your squire, if that is what both you and he desire."

Gerbert looked anxiously into my eyes; it was the look of a man desperate to conclude his affairs.

"I wish only to do your bidding, good master," I said.

A look of tranquillity came over his old face; he never spoke again. Then, a great wave of pain suddenly rose up and overtook him; he squeezed my wrists in his mailed hands as his body convulsed. He coughed, and a great issue of blood poured from his mouth. He gave out one last cry, then sighed, as though his soul had already fled from him. His painful grip on me released and I lowered his head gently to the rock.

The Templar recited a prayer as grief spilled from my eyes.

When the knight had finished, he said "We should leave this place, boy." The clamour of battle was still raging nearby, the combatants only visible to us as spectral shapes in the heat and dust. "I believe the day is ours, but we are still in the midst of a battlefield."

We lay Gerbert across the saddle of his horse; the Templar mounted his own steed and I followed behind leading my master.

When we were near to our lines, the Templar glanced back at me and said, "I will not hold you to the promise you made, to bring comfort to a dying man."

The knight's faithlessness caused me to speak angrily, "I gave my word. I will not go back on an oath I gave my master."

The knight turned his horse about, and looked down at me directly. I felt fearful of him for a moment, thinking the anger I had shown in my voice had overreached my station.

But the Templar only smiled, "If we are to be brother knights, then you had better learn my name. I am Reynald de Sauveterre."

Chapter Four

Jim caught the train to London; it was often easier when he had several ports of call as he did today. As he entered the station concourse at Charing Cross, he was aware that the run-up to Christmas had begun. Living where he did, in a semi-hermitlike existence, it was possible to let the festive season come and go virtually unnoticed. Not here, amidst the hurly-burly of the city; with Christmas trees arrayed with fairy-lights and tinsel, platoons of shoppers on reconnaissance missions bearing armfuls of well-known brands, and, '*The train now standing at platform three ...*' softly backed by the well-worn tunes of the season.

Whenever he could, Jim preferred to walk, but today his schedule was too tight for this, so he took the tube to Warren Street. Bob Isherwood was meeting him for lunch, and he was picking Sophie up from her school later. He'd phoned Bob the previous evening to let him know he'd taken the job.

"Great to know you're up and running again," Bob said.

Jim mentioned he was hiring a medium format camera. He normally worked in 35mm, but for catalogue work a larger negative was necessary. The photographic suppliers were based in Drummond Street, an area renowned for some of the best Indian food in London. They arranged to meet in a restaurant suggested by Bob at 1pm.

Drummond Street was only a short walk from the tube. They had his camera waiting to be picked up. Jim bought twenty rolls of 2¼ square film and four rolls of coloured paper: red, purple, and two shades of blue. Loxton had shot the porcelain against two backgrounds; Jim thought he would experiment with a couple more. When he realised how much there was to carry, he wished he'd brought the car. He arranged to pick the stuff up after lunch.

Jim got to the restaurant a bit early. He was pouring himself a glass of mineral water as Bob arrived.

"Now that's a sight to behold ... like watching a whore in a nunnery."

"Just shows you can get used to anything," said Jim, standing up and extending his hand towards Bob.

Bob flicked the hand away and the two men hugged.

"Christ, Jim, it's good to see you. I thought the next time I'd hear about you would be your funeral."

"I was headed that way. Anyway, how are you, how's the picture business?"

"Bloody great, bought a bigger house since I last saw you, which keeps the wife happy, and I just bought myself a fiftieth birthday present of a Mazda MX5, which the wife hates, but makes me happy!"

Bob looked greyer, balder, and a good bit wider around the middle. His laugh hadn't changed; it was the kind that made heads turn.

"How's Isla?" Jim asked.

"Yeah ... enemy's okay," Bob replied. 'The enemy' was the normal term he used for his wife. Bob and Isla had been married twenty-five years, had three daughters, and adored each other.

The Indian waiter came over and asked Bob if he wanted to order a drink. Bob cast a glance at Jim, "You mind?"

"Course not."

He ordered a beer; Bob had a prodigious capacity for beer. Jim had met Bob whilst still a photographic student. Bob had given a talk at his college and they had chatted over a few drinks in the bar afterwards. He had guided and encouraged Jim in the early years, introducing him to several influential people who had aided his career.

Bob was a New Zealander. He still retained a strong Kiwi accent, despite having moved to London in the late sixties, where he'd started out as a photographer. Bob had always possessed a fascination for native peoples, and by the time he arrived in Britain had amassed a large collection of photographs depicting Maori and Aborigine life. This had formed the basis of his library collection, which he'd built into one of the best picture libraries in Europe, representing native peoples from every corner of the earth. His company could supply an up to date photograph of a Laplander or an inhabitant of Borneo just as easily as a portrait of a nineteenth-century Cornish fisherman.

The restaurant offered a set buffet at lunchtimes. The food was excellent; Jim was slowing down on the second helping. Bob was ploughing through a third, when Jim brought up the subject of John Loxton.

Bob's face changed its demeanour immediately the name was mentioned. He tossed the naan bread he was about to attack back onto his plate.

"I got a visit from a friend this morning. Someone I play golf with, who as it happens is a Chief Inspector in the Vice Squad." Bob's face looked like thunder; Jim looked on perplexed as his friend continued, "Oh, it was okay, it was a friendly visit ... least I hope so. He wanted to know why Loxton had chosen me as his executor, were we good friends? Had I known him socially?"

"What was all that about, they don't suspect foul play?"

"No, no question of that ... definitely suicide. The body will most likely be released for funeral on Monday."

"So why the visit?"

"Loxton, it seems, mixed with some unsavoury types." The waiter passed by. "Could I have another beer?" The waiter nodded and continued on his way. Bob leaned across the table and said quietly, "They think Loxton was part of a paedophile ring."

Jim's eyes widened and his mouth fell open, "What?"

"Let's face it, Jim, everyone knew Loxton was weird, but Jesus, I was just as incredulous as you when I heard."

"They can't seriously think you're involved?"

"I don't believe so, least not any more, I told Ian in no uncertain terms," he saw Jim's confusion at the name, "Ian Rice ... the Vice Squad man. Actually, he was embarrassed too, kept apologising. To be fair, I think he was acting as a friend ... you know, clear my name, all that crap."

"You said paedophile ring, have they made arrests?"

"It seems not. Judging from what Ian said, they've had these people under surveillance for months. Loxton's suicide was a set-back. These sicko bastards are hyper-cautious and run to ground soon as they whiff any hint of the police. I tell you, if I find anything when I start going through Loxton's stuff, it'll give me the greatest pleasure ... they should have their balls mashed same as Loxton." He thought a moment before adding, "Yeah, and a stick of plastic explosive up the arse."

After this Bob's appetite recovered. He managed to finish his meal, drink a third beer and enjoy a helping of dessert washed down with coffee. Jim liked him a lot. It was good to bury the past.

The two men lost track of time trawling areas of mutual history, and were oblivious to the fact that they were the only diners left. Fortunately the waiter was watching the clock, and no doubt keen to put his feet up, was driven to place a stainless steel plate with the bill down on their table.

"Come by the office on Monday when you drop the film off," Bob shouted back at Jim as they set off in different directions.

42

Jim had forty minutes to pick up his gear and reach Sophie before she left school. They called him a cab from the photographic suppliers. Sophie's school was only a couple of miles north, but pre-Christmas traffic moved as slowly as hell. Fortunately, the taxi arrived just before the school bell. The cabbie grumbled miserably, but agreed to wait.

Jim watched Sophie coming along the school drive amongst a swathe of friends laughing and joking with each other. It had only been a couple of weeks, but he was sure she'd grown. She looked more like her mother every time. As a child she hadn't appeared to take after either of them much. Everyone agreed she was most like Jim in temperament, which used to flatter him, but more recently he'd worried she might be too much like him.

"Hi Dad."

"Hi."

The days of uninhibited displays of pleasure at the sight of him were long gone.

"Did you bring the car?" she asked.

"I've got a cab." Jim led Sophie to the taxi, amidst calls of "Bye Soph!", "Have a nice weekend!", "Give me a ring!", "See you Monday!"

Once away, without appearing to draw breath, Sophie filled her father in on what was happening in her life, "A boy in year eleven is a really good guitarist, he's in this band, and a record company want to sign them up ... I got the best mark in English and history this term ... there's a girl who left last year who moved in with her boyfriend and got pregnant, now she's having triplets, imagine that?" Occasionally she came up for air and asked him something like, "How are you, Dad?" or "How's Ruth?"

His answers needed to be concise.

The house where Hannah and Sophie lived ran behind Clapton Pond. They had bought it fourteen years ago. It felt odd returning to it, no longer as an inhabitant, but only an invited guest. Sophie opened the front door with her key and they piled the photographic equipment up in the hallway.

"Brought the kitchen sink I see," said Hannah, appearing on the staircase.

"I should be getting paid for this," joked Sophie, as she struggled awkwardly through the door with a metallic box.

"Shut up complaining kid, or I'll send you back to the chimney sweep," warned Jim smiling up at Hannah before going out to pay the taxi-man.

"Victorian Father!" Sophie shouted after him.

Hannah was standing just inside the doorway when he returned.

"Hello Jim," she greeted, "You look well."

"Thanks. You're looking good yourself." He meant it, she did; she had done something, the hair he thought was the most likely candidate, but couldn't be certain; the curse of being male.

They welcomed each other with a hug. They both felt uneasy when they touched, and greeting was best done swiftly.

"Can you stay to supper?" Hannah asked.

Jim suddenly had a flashback to pulao rice and chapattis.

"Go on Dad," encouraged Sophie.

"I had a late lunch with Bob Isherwood."

"It won't be ready for at least an hour."

"Go on Dad."

"Okay. Thanks."

"I'm going upstairs to take off the prison uniform. If the phone rings, don't pick it up, it's for me," Sophie instructed as she climbed the stairs.

Jim and Hannah exchanged eyebrow movements in mutual recognition as they watched their 'little girl' go off to change.

"She's right," Hannah said as they went down the short flight of stairs to the dining-room and kitchen, "If the phone rings there's a ninety-nine point six percent chance it'll be for her."

"What do they find to talk about?"

"God knows. They spend all day together and start ringing each other five minutes after they get home."

"Boys?" Jim asked, feeling an authentic attack of Victorian Fatherhood coming on.

"Not yet ... just talk."

The phone rang; it was picked up, the house's adult population was not required.

Hannah made a pot of Earl Grey; they sat and chatted at a large pine table in the kitchen. Talking had not been hard once Jim got sober. They shared the same liberal views on nearly every subject.

"So you met Bob, how was it?"

"Like old times, he hasn't changed much, just a bit wider round the girth."

"I saw him recently ... I was having lunch with Fleur."

"Yes, he told me. I believe I have you to thank for the job I'm doing."

"Me?"

"Bob put me up for it. The people Loxton was supposed to start work for got in touch with him."

"Loxton?" asked Hannah. The name rang a distant bell.

Jim reminded her who Loxton was.

"I remember, 'Pompous prick' you used to call him."

"He's dead."

Jim told her about his suicide, the piece in the paper at Erich's and how Bob had unwittingly become involved.

"What an appalling death, poor man."

"You might prefer to reserve judgement on the poor man bit." He explained all about Bob being visited by a friend from the Vice Squad.

Hannah was clearly horrified by it. "You read about these people but never expect them to be someone you know."

"Let's change the subject, what about you?" Jim asked.

"Things are fine. I'm picking up as much work as I can handle."

Hannah was a freelance journalist; she usually thought up an idea, got an editor interested in commissioning it, then researched it in more detail and wrote it up. She was good at her job, and enjoyed the work.

Before supper Jim was invited to hear Sophie's latest CD up in her room.

"Can I come to stay soon, Dad? I haven't been to the cottage for ages."

"Yes, of course you can. When?"

"What about next weekend?"

"Okay by me. I should have finished this job by Thursday at the latest. Talk it over with Mum, and we'll arrange it."

Shortly after supper, some friends called for Sophie to go ice-skating with them. Jim slipped a tenner into her hand as she hugged him.

"Thanks, Dad. I'll give you a ring."

Hannah and Jim chatted, mainly about Sophie, surrounded by the debris of the meal. After this Jim washed up and Hannah made coffee.

Jim rang for a cab to take him back to Charing Cross. It arrived just before 8pm.

"Soph asked if she could come to the cottage. I told her to discuss it with you."

"Fine, we'll arrange it."

"Thanks for the cannelloni, it was great. Blame Bob that I didn't quite do it the justice it deserved."

He gave her a quick peck on the cheek and began to struggle into the cab with the photographic equipment.

"Come for Christmas!" Hannah blurted out the invitation, as if it was a thing she'd wanted to say all evening but had found the words difficult to get out.

"What?" he asked, turning back to look at her.

"Would you like to spend Christmas with me and Soph?"

"Er ... yeah ... okay, thanks ... I'd love that."

The cabbie, different to the previous one but clearly weaned on the same rules of etiquette and good manners, growled with impatience, "Hurry up, mate, I'm losing fares while you piss about."

Hannah smiled at Jim's momentary confusion, one leg in one out of the cab.

"We'll speak next week," she said.

*

Jim recognised the waiter operating the buffet trolley along the aisle of the moving train. The man had clearly identified Jim too, and brought his trolley alongside him with a slightly unpleasant, rather knowing expression on his face.

"And what can I get you, sir?" he asked smugly, his hand hovering above a miniature of brandy.

"Nothing thanks," replied Jim chirpily.

"Oh," replied the trolley man, wheeling himself away slightly crestfallen.

All in all, it had been a good day. He was about to start work again, rekindled an old friendship and been invited for Christmas by the estranged wife he still loved.

The only blight on an otherwise perfect day was learning the unpalatable truth about Loxton. He immediately recalled Bob's justice for paedophiles, '... balls mashed ... stick of plastic explosive up the arse.'

Then, for no apparent reason, Ruth's reaction to Loxton's suicide floated up into his mind. 'To mutilate yourself like that ... like torture ... like some vicious punishment. The pain would be unbearable. I can't believe it possible, you'd pass out with the shock.'

Chapter Five

Close up, the gates looked even more impenetrable than they had appeared from the first floor. Jim stepped out of his warm car into the chilly morning and pressed the buzzer set into the wall at the gate's side. A camera peered down at him from the top of one of a pair of concrete monoliths that served as gate posts. A moment later a click was followed by an electronic whirring as the gates began to open; someone was alert.

He amused himself with the thought, 'It's a kind of Fort Knox for porcelain,' as he drove through the opening and parked beside a white Mercedes. Despite it being a rather gloomy morning, Jim felt bright and positive.

The gates vibrated and clicked as they joined together again. He found himself enclosed in a desert of brick and concrete. It was quite shockingly stark; no moss or lichen grew on any of the walls, and not even a solitary weed broke free at any point. The only relief in this hard-surfaced world was a series of small, square flower beds roughly formed in the concrete base of the car park, three on either side. Each bed supported a single rose-bush, dormant now and cut right back to the stem. They didn't look like happy plants but appeared frail, their surrounding soil light and thin. The constant squawks and banterings of seagulls didn't seem to add any life or colour, but somehow only contributed an element of eeriness.

The ground where Jim stood was level with the basement window, which like those at the front of the house, was barred and shuttered. There was a metal shuttered loading bay locked up tight, but next to it a normal sized door made of steel was opening.

"Good morning, Mr Latimer," Nicholas greeted with a toothy grin, his slight frame adorned as before in oversized clothing. Jim wondered if there had been a clearance sale at Oxfam. "May I help?"

"Thanks," Jim replied, opening the car's rear and sharing out some of the equipment he'd brought.

He followed Nicholas through the steel door into an area behind the docking-bay. Here there was a lift and two more metal doors, both bolted and padlocked; the one situated to the right of the lift bore the words 'Fire Escape' just legibly in peeling paint; the other, labelled 'Stockroom' was opposite the docking-bay. The lift was old-fashioned, with a varnished wooden outer door containing a small diamond shaped glass panel roughly at eye level and a sliding inner one that concertina'd across. The bad smell Jim had noticed when he'd visited on Thursday was far worse down here.

They made two journeys, piling the equipment at the back of the lift which left just enough space for them to stand.

"That's everything," Jim said.

Nicholas closed the outer doors. He activated the lift with a key which was kept on a chain attached to his belt. After he'd done this he drew the inner door across and pressed the button marked 'One'. As the ancient lift began its ascent, spontaneously and without warning, Jim's body gave an involuntary shiver.

Nicholas smiled. "Cold this morning," he said.

*

It took Jim just over an hour to get organised. Nicholas brought him a table, which he dressed with coloured paper to form a background for the items to be photographed. He used his own lighting equipment, setting up a soft box above the table, basically a black lampshade that held the flash and when operated threw the light down onto the object. The camera was set up a few feet away on its tripod and connected via a synch lead to the flash bulb.

Once everything was in place, the process would be straightforward. He would manually operate the flash in the soft box to get a light reading, and after focusing, take three photographs of each individual or group of items, the first exposure at the initial light reading, then by adjusting the aperture, one at half a stop above, providing more light, and another exposure half a stop below to give less. When the film was developed he could then choose the best shot from the three transparencies.

All ready, he went downstairs.

"I'm all set," Jim said as he entered the office.

He had not seen Rosemary Hines yet that morning. She and Nicholas were sat opposite each other behind the two joined desks.

"Good morning, Mr Latimer," she greeted.

48

"Good morning. I'm ready, but I don't have anything to photograph."

She giggled. "Nicky," there was something unattractive about the way she used the name, almost sexual, "Can you arrange whatever Mr Latimer needs?"

Nicholas Cureton stood up; his face carried a beaming smile.

"Can I help?" asked Jim.

"There's no need, Mr Latimer, it's just a matter of getting the items out of the stock-room. Nicky's very strong." She looked admiringly at the young man as she spoke.

'I feel like puking,' thought Jim, as he watched the smug youth go proudly off.

"Can I offer you some coffee, Mr Latimer?"

"That would be lovely, if it's no trouble."

"No trouble at all. I've just made some."

Rosemary Hines left the office and Jim took Nicholas' vacated chair. When she returned half a minute later with a tray she paused for a second as though surprised to find him sitting there. Jim, quite oblivious to this, was leafing through the previous year's catalogue which had been lying on the desk.

"I'd like to try some different backgrounds if it's okay with you?"

"Yes, of course, we trust your judgement entirely, Mr Latimer."

"Call me Jim."

"And I'm Rosemary."

They went on to discuss various details concerning presentation. Once all the pre-shoot planning was finalised, Rosemary somehow got on to the subject of John Loxton. Jim wished she hadn't; he was certainly not about to mention the man's alleged involvement with paedophiles.

"Does Mr Isherwood have any idea when the funeral might be?"

"I don't think so, not yet."

"Please let us know. I'm sure Mr Hart would wish to attend, as a representative of the firm."

"Yes, of course. Bob thinks the body may be released on Monday"

"As the executor I expect Mr Isherwood will be keen to get on and deal with the estate."

"Yes, I'd imagine so."

At this point Nicholas returned. He didn't look very pleased to find Jim Latimer sitting in his place. And for once, he wasn't grinning.

"Everything's ready," he grunted.

Nicholas led Jim back upstairs. He had delivered about ten large cardboard boxes, each one containing items individually packaged. Most of these belonged in sets, which varied in number but were generally around five or six pieces. Each box contained a small brochure showing other pieces in the series plus a certificate detailing its manufacture and authenticity.

Nicholas unpacked the first figures, a set of six, and presented them to Jim.

"What are these?"

"They're 'Stars of the Silent Era'."

The figure of a young woman seductively draped on a chaise longue made no impression on Jim, not even her name, Janet Gaynor, told him anything.

"They're collectors' items," Nicholas said sniffily, "This is our twelfth series."

"I see, so now you're left with the ones nobody living has heard of ... less stars, more comets ..." he raised another of the figures, its identity also a mystery to him "... asteroids even."

He could sense Nicholas' hackles rising. Jim was aware and not proud of the fact that one of his failings was the childish delight he could take in annoying people who lacked a sense of humour; Nicholas was irresistible.

"You should be able to manage. I've made it very straightforward for you," there was a touch of vitriol in Nicholas' voice as he left.

Jim became engrossed in his work, and over the next two hours photographed about twenty-five items both individually and in their sets. However, around 11.15am he noticed that he was slowing down. There was a point of pressure growing directly between his eyes.

"I hope I don't need bloody glasses."

He opened the window and took a few deep breaths. The fresh air helped, so he left the window open, even so, he couldn't seem to regain his former speed, and considered it possible that he was exhibiting early flu-like symptoms. By 12.30 he was feeling far worse, and decided to break for lunch.

There was a sandwich bar nearby where he bought an egg mayonnaise roll and a tea in a polystyrene cup. He walked down to the seafront and found a bench to sit on.

It was cold and grey, but the sea breeze was exhilarating, and the headache and eye tension soon dissolved away. He returned to the house just before 1.30pm.

He had intended working until four, but by 3.30 the headache had returned and was hampering his work again. He had done fairly well, and counted seventy items completed. He would get the film developed on Monday. Jim was extremely fussy about who did his developing, tending to use a firm in Clerkenwell, who did excellent colour work.

"I'd like to start a bit earlier on Monday," he told Rosemary. "I don't want to inconvenience you, but would eight be too early?"

"Eight is fine," she replied.

"You don't have far to travel to work then?"

Rosemary paused momentarily; Jim thought she registered a look of consternation, as if he was prying into her affairs. The next second she exhibited a large girlish grin, and said, "I don't travel. I live here."

"That's convenient."

Nicholas resumed his duty as lift man and took Jim down to the basement. It was pitch dark in the area outside the lift, Jim felt a shiver of discomfort as the damp air clung to his skin. Nicholas reached a hand around the side of the door and flicked on the light switch with the familiarity of habit, then unlocked the outer door and let him out. Jim thanked him and walked to his car with an unexpected feeling of relief.

*

Long before he arrived home, Jim's headache had cleared again.

'Perhaps there's something toxic oozing out of their drains?' he thought, briefly embracing a tendency for hypochondria. Common sense suggested that perhaps his eyes needed testing, 'I suppose getting to thirty-seven without needing specs is a decent run.'

When he got back, he found Ruth's house in darkness. She had put a note through his letterbox, which he discovered on the doormat in the company of two new bills.

> *Jim,*
>
> *Gone away, back tomorrow.*
>
> *Ruth*

He wondered why she bothered. Ruth's notes, succinct and to the point, lacked a little depth. Once, when they hadn't been to the cottage for several weeks, she'd left a note that just read:

Hi

He was disappointed she wasn't home. He felt a twinge of loneliness.

He ate, watched ten minutes of some utterly predictable detective series, then read for a bit. He managed two chapters, which was something of an achievement. His attention span had been about thirty seconds when he'd first left the treatment centre. Later he watched ten more minutes of television, and concluded from this that although quite possibly brain-damaged from alcohol abuse he was not yet brain-dead. He made some hot chocolate and went to bed.

Jim had slept badly since he'd stopped drinking. He rarely dreamed, or if he did, certainly had no recollection of doing so. Yet every morning he woke with the same grey feeling inside, as if all his failings and weaknesses had been re-run throughout the night like an old 'B' movie. As soon as he awoke, his conscious mind would be assailed by all the inconsistencies of his personality and a host of missed opportunities in his life. So catching up on sleep was not altogether an attractive prospect.

"Early nights are good for you," he told himself.

*

The sun's rays struggled to find the merest chink in a grey ocean of cloud being driven across a turbulent sky. The wind howled over the mountainous terrain, venting its spleen like a deranged beast. Only the barest tint of colour defined the features in this isolated place, sky and land almost indistinguishable, merging where they met into a grey and wavering obscurity.

Briefly, a shape on the horizon took on solid form, before dissolving once more into the haze. Then it appeared again, for only the briefest of moments; it came and went in this way for many minutes until, clear of the swirling backdrop, it propelled itself forward slowly. The shape gradually divided into two, which then became discernible as two hooded men, staggering through a barren land. Their faces were hidden beneath their white hoods. One man was taller than the other, and limped, the smaller man occasionally lent the other

52

assistance at the most difficult places. Yet they continued on with a grim determination.

Jim began to feel the emotions of these two. They were set upon a path of no return; advancing with singleness of purpose, resolved to do or to be damned. Then, as he watched the scene unfolding, he began to feel fearful; he had to warn them their plight was hopeless.

"Go back! For God's sake, go back! You'll be destroyed!" he cried.

It was just before 6am and still dark outside as Jim reached out a trembling hand and put on the bedside lamp. He leaned back against the headboard, T-shirt soaked in sweat, panting, waiting for his heart to stop thumping in his chest.

Hugh's Tale

II

The reluctant page became a reluctant Soldier of Christ. After a time of trial, at age twenty-one I became a knight and took lifelong vows of obedience to the order. In all honesty I cannot say that the monastic life held much appeal, yet I could hardly bemoan my fate, born second son to a house of good name, yet with neither land nor wealth to match.

Not being schooled in letters, a brother penned some words for me and dispatched them to my father. Two years passed before a reply came, which was read to me by the same good brother.

There was no longer an heir to my father's lands; my brother Geoffrey, never sturdy, had fallen sick and died. News of my sister Melisend was happier to bear; a woman now, and betrothed to wed. Here I observed cautiousness in my father as he explained, 'To a Welshman who answers to the name of Rhisiart ap Gruffydd.' However, he did go on to say, 'He appears honest and good-tempered, unlike many of his breed.' True to her nature, Melisend had rejected every suitor my father had presented. She would marry the Welshman she had met during the spring fair at Shrewsbury, or enter a nunnery.

You see, Anselm, I still bear the letter, the ink has run, and not even you could discern its words.

Sometimes I would lie on my pallet and stare at the paper. I made my scribe point to the mark that spelled Melisend, and as I gazed at the word I pictured her.

Over the next years I travelled a great deal. I visited many of the Mediterranean ports and cities, also the islands of Sicily and Cyprus on numerous occasions. These journeys were mostly undertaken on matters of commerce concerning my order. However, the business itself rarely involved me directly, being generally only part of an escort for more senior officials. All I can say is, the years passed; ten since leaving England, before I came to be stationed permanently at Acre, the jewel of our kingdom. Times had changed; Saladin was dead, as was his counterpart, the other giant of our age, Richard Coeur de Lion.

At Acre I became re-acquainted with the knight I met on the battlefield who had ministered to the dying Gerbert. I had disliked him at our first meeting; now we became friends. At Arsuf I had objected to Reynald's bluntness; this was but his way I found, for he possessed an ability to speak to every manner of man with the same directness of eye and tongue. He was a Frank by birth, and like myself came from a family of name but little wealth. "Was not our order created to accommodate the needs of younger sons?" I recall him jesting once.

I grew to love Reynald de Sauveterre like a brother. He was three years my senior, though at our first meeting, I had believed it more. His devotion to our Lord Jesus Christ ran deeper than my own, although he made no great show of piety. Reynald was the best man in Acre to have beside you in a skirmish, you could always depend on him to guard your back. Yet he avoided violence, being a peacemaker by nature, more often than not bringing words to calm boiling tempers; a man only prepared to draw his sword at the last resort when reason failed. But let me not deceive by portraying too perfect a saint, good Anselm, for he could always find an opportunity to snook a wink across the refectory table where we dined in silence.

Life in Acre was for the most part agreeable. It was a great city bursting with life, visitors of every race and tongue bustling through its narrow streets. I still recall the sounds and smells of its marketplace, traders and buyers haggling over the price of silks or muslin, the air pungent with aromatic spices rising from steaming cook-pots.

A great number of the visitors to Acre were pilgrims, and as you know, it is part of a Templar's duty to guide and protect. Many would have deposited funds with us for safekeeping before leaving their homelands; they were often targets for vagabonds and thieves, the dregs of our western cities attracted by the lure of easy gain. On every street beggars held out bowls for alms; some had travelled east driven by fantastic dreams of vast fortunes; others came as pilgrims, but had fallen prey to the worldly pursuit of dice, or the lewd calls of the fallen women who draped themselves lasciviously from the balcony windows where they plied their wares.

It was hot June, and the sound of all the church bells ringing told the city that a small fleet of a dozen ships had arrived. Their cargo was mainly wool, and five hundred pilgrims all told. Four of us were assigned the task of meeting the visitors, directing them to the inns and boarding-houses or to our Templar house if they had deposited money with us. Reynald accompanied me, as too did Robert de Frontignac, a knight from Normandy, who had recently arrived from Safed, in Galilee. The fourth man was a serjeant, a taciturn fellow who had served at Acre for more years than even Reynald had.

It took an hour before the ships had docked, and the pilgrims came ashore. A group of three men, indistinguishable by dress or manner from any others, walked along the quayside towards us. I saw a look of recognition enter Reynald's eye, and now as I recall it, one of the three shuffled to the far side of the group when he noticed the attention placed on him.

Reynald stepped before the man and called, "Hubert?"

"You are mistaken, sir," replied the pilgrim, "I do not answer to that name."

Reynald was surprised, "Then know sir, you bear the look of a boyhood friend of mine, who came from the lands nearby Toulouse."

"I am of Marseilles, sir," the man said, "Pray forgive me for denying you the pleasure of greeting an old friend."

"No matter," said Reynald. He stood aside to let the group pass, "God's speed to you, pilgrim."

"Thank you sir," replied the man, and the group hurried on their way.

However, so sure had Reynald been of his man that he would not let the matter rest, "He bore the very stamp of Hubert upon him, in voice, his whole manner."

"Let it be," I said.

He let the matter drop a while, before saying, "The Hubert I knew became a Cathar."

"A Cathar?" asked Robert.

"You know of them?" Reynald enquired.

I myself knew nothing of them.

"I have heard scant details," Robert said. "Do they not deny the death and resurrection of our Lord?"

"They hold many beliefs that seem a heresy to our church," answered Reynald, "Yet I never met a Cathar whose word I could not trust. And for all their strange beliefs, I never met more Christian folk. Indeed they call themselves 'true Christians'."

"Surely that in itself is a heresy," said Robert.

"Perhaps," said Reynald, "But I for one will neither judge nor condemn them."

After a time, Reynald accepted he had been mistaken and let the matter drop. The pilgrims had all disembarked, so we returned to our house and changed into our habits for vespers. I believed, as no doubt did Reynald, that the matter of Hubert the Cathar was done with.

Yet others it seemed were to credit this episode with far greater significance.

On my way to our chapel, I saw the serjeant who had accompanied us to the harbour talking in whispered conversation with Brother Ferdinand, the cellarer; during supper Ferdinand entered the refectory, his plump physique strutting with self-importance, and took obvious delight in informing Reynald and I that our marshal, Jerome, would see us directly we had finished eating.

I searched my mind for any crime I had committed. The marshal was a serious, aloof man, and being called before him was not a matter to be taken lightly. I had only spoken to him, briefly, on one previous occasion. He was an Englishman too, and had talked openly to me at first, only to lose all interest once he realised my family were neither rich nor powerful.

I felt some trepidation being ushered in by the cellarer before Marshal Jerome. Brother Ferdinand fussed around the powerful, imposing man, like a fat puppy about his heels.

"I hope Brother Ferdinand's summons did not in any way detract from the appreciation of your meal," said the marshal.

Reynald, in more control of himself than I, asked, "Sir, what required you to see us so urgently?"

The marshal threw an irritated look in Brother Ferdinand's direction, who was fussily flicking away a speck of dust from his master's habit. Ferdinand ceased the offending action immediately.

"It has come to my attention that you recognised a man today at the harbour."

"True," replied Reynald, "I mistook a pilgrim for someone I knew as a child. He bore a strong resemblance."

"This man denied knowing you?"

"Yes sir."

"Yet you were sure of him?"

"At first. I saw I was mistaken, it is a long time ..."

"Perhaps," interrupted Jerome, "I am informed the party your man travels with belong to the Catharist cult. I deem it wise to learn what brings them to this land."

"Perhaps they come to visit the holy sites," I volunteered, my fear of reprimand having abated.

"Cathars set no importance by material things," replied Brother Ferdinand testily, scorning my ignorance.

"What would you have us do?" asked Reynald.

"They leave tomorrow with a party of pilgrims for Jerusalem. Follow them. Keep out of sight, as best you can. See who meets them and where they are taken. Then bring word back to me."

*

Jerome's intelligence proved correct, for just after dawn our three left Acre in the company of two hundred other pilgrims. We kept our distance. The group moved slowly south at a pace acceptable to the elderly and infirm amongst them. The road followed the curve of the bay of Acre, skirting the base of the Mount Carmel headland and along the coastal plain. There are numerous inns and hostelries dotted along this well-worn route, and the pilgrims' nights were undoubtedly more comfortable than ours, spent under the stars amidst the olive groves.

For three days we pursued without event. The fourth morning brought the first surprise, when our pilgrims were met at the ford that crosses the river Auja a league or so north of Joppa. They were greeted as friends by two men dressed in the manner of the Saracen. These two had brought mares with them, and we were obliged to give our steeds full rein as the pace of travel increased.

South east of Joppa the road leads to Jerusalem. I had travelled these ways in the King's army. The party spent the first night camped near Lydda. At dawn next morning they were on their way once more. They led us on to Ramleh, and from here the group led us north-east into the foothills of Samaria.

It was certain by then that our three stray sheep were not bound for Jerusalem. For us, staying undetected became increasingly difficult amidst a rolling landscape.

Two hours before nightfall, we came to a community of about fifteen dwellings; the party was greeted warmly by its inhabitants. The people who lived there were well-served by streams that irrigated their valley, and farmed the lands thereabout. We tethered our horses beside a brook, a safe distance away, and took up a position on a hilltop nearer the houses.

"Why should men from your homeland journey to such a place as this?" I asked Reynald.

"Perhaps we shall learn in time," he answered, "Such a journey undoubtedly holds a purpose."

When night came, I took the first watch. Around the second hour, the people of the valley began to stir. I woke Reynald from sleep.

Torches were lit, and the whole community, men, women and children, congregated together, our pilgrims amongst them. At first they seemed to be climbing towards us, but our position was safe; the group, about fifty people, took a path that led north of us. We allowed them some distance start, before following on behind. They travelled in single file, a line of torches marking their progress through the hills.

The whole journey took, I suppose, an hour, and for the final quarter of that time we descended into a rocky gorge. Reynald and I took cover behind some rocks when we realised the crowd we were following had reached their journey's end.

The people gathered into a semi-circle around a flat stone in the gorge's midst, behind it lay the opening to a cave. Five men entered the cave; I recognised two of these as the Saracens who had met our pilgrims at Auja, and whilst they were inside the remainder waited in silence. The men returned dressed in white robes with cloths around their heads tied with gold thread; one of them walked ahead, carrying a wooden casket, whilst the other four came solemnly behind, two abreast. When the congregation, including our Cathars, saw the casket, all fell prostrate to the ground.

The high priest of the ceremony put the casket on the stone altar and raised his arms in adoration. He began with some words in a tongue that I did not understand. Then the people rose to their feet and when he spoke to them again it was in the Saracen language, which I understood well enough, having been so many years in their lands. He said, "We honour our Cathar brothers who have travelled far over many months. They are welcome here, as friends."

After this the priest reverted to the earlier tongue used, and a ceremony of sorts began; he prompted the congregation which responded in the form of chants.

At a particular point in the ceremony the Cathars drew forward and kneeled at the altar. The man who Reynald had identified as Hubert on one side, with the oldest-looking of the three taking up the central place; the priest raised the wooden casket and offered it to this man, who bowed solemnly in recognition. The priest then placed his hands upon the casket's lid and opened it. From my position I was unable to see what lay within, but thought I saw something glow. I supposed it a reflection from all the torches round about.

"I understood that Cathars set no store by relics," I whispered to Reynald.

"Perhaps it depends on the relic," he replied.

Our attention was captured once again by the scene before us. Then I saw Reynald out of the corner of my eye suddenly slump forward. I turned, just in time to witness the shaft of an unlit torch about to strike me. I felt a moment of pain as it crashed into my neck and heat and numbness rising through my skull. The curious tableau began to spin, all went black, and I saw no more.

Chapter Six

Although Jim considered his years of decline to be over and done with, in all honesty, the wreckage of the past was only ten months behind him. It was likely he considered himself more mentally resilient than he actually was; all the harm caused by years of destructive drinking could not be overturned in a matter of months.

Without a doubt, Jim at this time was not wholly in control of himself; and learning about Loxton, finding himself in that detestable man's shoes, was not a comfortable place for someone only recently restored to normal life. However, it was debatable whether events would have turned out any differently had Jim been more emotionally balanced, willing to see the darkness that was already swelling up around him, or ready to receive the counsel his friends were about to offer. As Erich Ledermann was often in the habit of saying, 'Nobody would be a fool if they could help it.'

Erich brought Ruth home around eleven. They knocked on Jim's door. He was feeling somewhat isolated, and was relieved at the sight of two friendly faces; although he would never have admitted this, especially not to them.

They were carrying a couple of shopping bags apiece. It was Erich who spoke, "We bought some provisions and thought we'd invite you to lunch."

Before Jim could reply, Ruth added, "Nothing to worry about, Erich's cooking. I swear I'll do no more than wash and peel veg." She licked a fingertip and crossed her heart, "Honest."

Jim was grateful for any company, and not even the infamy of Ruth's cooking would have kept him from accepting. Sundays were tough at the best of times, and the memory of last night's nightmare still clung on, all too vividly. It had not evaporated with the light of day as dreams are supposed to, but had left its mark like an indelible stain in his conscious mind. The experience had left him feeling dislocated and uneasy. He would probably have opted to work, had he not shot a good deal of film already and considered it prudent to see some results before ploughing on further.

Jim drove to the village, bought a bottle of wine and two bottles of sparkling water. It had become his mission in life that others should not be deprived of a drink because he himself had sworn off. He felt extremely vulnerable when people apologised for their own drinking, or abstained altogether when in his presence; the latter was by far the worst, like a large arrow was pointing down at him with the words Alky and Leper flashing up alternately in neon letters.

Lunch was good. Ruth had undoubtedly kept her word and only touched the vegetables. Jim was hardly chef of the year, but given a decent recipe could at least produce something fairly appetising. Sadly, Ruth, did not possess even this much ability. Past dinners at Ruth's were deeply embedded in the mind, to say nothing of the stomach wall, like grumbling war wounds.

Throughout lunch they asked him questions about the job in Hove; he assumed it was friendly interest. When they inquired how the lunch had gone with Bob, he changed the subject long before getting to Loxton; paedophilia was never a good subject, and he knew it would upset Ruth. Only once had she confided in him about the painfulness of her childhood after her parents' death. She'd attempted to tell her tale without emotion, which had made it all the more poignant.

"You are dispossessed of rights. I became a problem child. I fought against authority, fought everyone ... was moved constantly between orphanage and foster home. A few genuinely tried, most didn't seem to care at all - they were the most contemptible." She'd paused, excused the welling up of her emotions by brushing a strand of hair from her face with the back of a finger. "Some of my so called protectors were just sickos ... there for the sole purpose of abusing children."

Jim had a great deal of respect and admiration for Ruth, although he rarely showed it. For ten years she'd survived under the so called protection of the state, until her sixteenth birthday when the state relinquished all responsibility and left her to fend for herself. Through sheer will and determination, she'd got herself to art school and earned a degree. In reflective moments, when Jim considered how she had striven to overcome the odds, it made him slightly ashamed of his own inherent tendency to whinge.

"I've been invited for Christmas, Hannah asked me."

"That's wonderful," said Erich, "I know how much you miss your family. Isn't that great, Ruth?"

Ruth smiled her approval, but Jim could tell there was something not quite right. He'd found her unusually distracted over the past few days.

"If I'm lucky enough to get them back, I mean to do a better job as a husband and father this time."

"You weren't so bad ... least not for a man!" said Ruth, "The booze just took more and more control."

The main course completed, Ruth consigned its debris to the sink. It was agreed they'd take a pause before tackling the chocolate gateau, enthusiastically purchased by Erich, an admitted pudding fetishist. From now on the conversation flowed less freely.

Erich decided it was time to explain what was on their minds. After all, they had spent the previous evening, well into the early hours of the night discussing an approach. It was decided that although they had no deep grasp of Ruth's psychic experience or the frighteningly real dream that had followed, it was their duty to share, at least what they knew, with the friend whom they believed these matters concerned.

"Jim, there was a reason why we came here today," Erich began, "I'd like you to listen to Ruth. It probably won't make any sense to you, but we think it's important you hear it. Please, try to keep an open mind."

Jim's mind was already turning cartwheels.

"I've had these feelings," Ruth began, "Over the past few days ..."

"Hormones?" Jim chirped up.

"Since you told me about that man, Loxton ... no, before that ..." Ruth was expecting Jim to react angrily at any moment.

Jim certainly didn't like the way Loxton's name kept cropping up, especially during meal times.

Erich came in to help, "Jim, Ruth has experienced a series of 'events' that may concern you. We know your views on such matters, but we'd like you to hear us out."

Jim was a bit lost for words, but managed, "Okay, I'll give it a shot."

Ruth decided the best approach was to lay it out as straightforwardly as possible. The important thing was that he heard the whole story. "On Wednesday, after you arrived back from Erich's, I passed by you ... I was wheeling my bicycle?"

Jim nodded.

"Cycling back from the shops along the track, I saw you again ... but you weren't actually there. I saw an image of you coming towards me along the road ... your personality was changed."

63

"A daydream?" asked Jim, being deliberately annoying.

Ruth's eyelids flickered with irritation, but she went on, "It was a premonition. I believe it was you in a possible future. You no longer possessed your own mind, another ego was in control."

"Like Invasion of the Body Snatchers?" Jim responded; he could be incredibly cussed.

"I knew he'd be sceptical, you see?" Ruth directed these words to Erich. "I knew it would be a waste of bloody time!"

Erich nodded his head and made a placatory gesture with his hand. Tears of exasperation were collecting at the corners of Ruth's eyes. Jim was surprised by her reaction, he could not recall her being quite so riled by his irksomeness ever before.

"I'm sorry. I know you're sincere and must believe it's important. I'll shut up."

Ruth cast a quick glance at Erich and resumed, "I dropped in to see you, remember?"

"I'd just heard about the job. Yes."

"You mentioned the man who died. I immediately knew that somehow the premonition and his death were in some way related."

"I'm sorry, you've lost me. How can Loxton's suicide be related to my future?"

"Please Jim ... let Ruth explain best she can."

"If you remember, I left not long after you told me. I felt so uneasy about it."

"I remember you seemed to think he'd been tortured. The police, by the way, are absolutely certain it was suicide."

Ruth nodded, as though she was sure that was indeed what the police would think, but at the same time equally certain they were wrong. "That night I had a dream ... nightmare more like ..."

Jim found the word nightmare unsettling.

"... you weren't who you are now."

Erich came in here, "Dreams can be like that. You might recognise someone even though they look totally different, perhaps the opposite sex to how you experience them in waking life."

"So what happened to me in this other 'guise'?" Jim asked, a sardonic note underlining the word guise.

Ruth, detecting the sneer, replied curtly, "You died." The next instant she felt angry with herself for taking the bait.

"Death in dreams is rarely a premonition of actual death," said Erich, in an attempt to ease the growing tension.

"I'm pleased to hear it."

Ruth continued, "I saw you fall. You were dying. Something was coming after you, something dark, malign. You ran over the edge of something, a cliff, I think. It was night and I couldn't make it out that clearly." Ruth's eyes went into a soft focus. "You were relieved to be dying. It was better to die than face what was after you. You wore a hood I remember, like a monk. White, I think, Cistercian perhaps. I'm watching as you die, your body all smashed up ... your mouth moves ... you're making a confession, but I can't hear the words ... you're gripped by fear once again. You're watching a dark shape, as it slides down the cliff face towards you ... and you're praying for death before it reaches you ... it's black as ink, eating up everything in its path ..."

Jim had managed to look composed when the white hood was mentioned, but felt far less comfortable in the pit of his stomach. However, he could not hide his discomfort as Ruth described the dying man's sense of dread and foreboding. Although different in some ways, it was too close for comfort to his own night-time experience.

Ruth had broken off, distracted by the expression on Erich's face. He was staring intently at Jim, brows knitted together. Ruth turned her gaze onto Jim; saw his face drained white as ash, fear showing through his eyes.

"You know this ... you've dreamed it too?"

Jim, unnerved, fell back on an old standby - when scared, cover your tracks with aggression. "So what? It's only a dream for Christ's sake! You dream about a monk in a white habit and so do I, so what? You're the one with the hot-line to the 'other side'; tell me what it all means then? Come on. Give me the great benefit of your psychic powers!"

"I don't know ..."

"Exactly. You don't know, and nor do I!"

"I don't know, yet," she restated, "but I mean to find out. And I believe you're in danger."

"Christ. What danger then?" he spat back at her.

"That photographer ..."

"Who, Loxton?" he sneered.

"I sense he was involved in something ... something foul and debase ..."

Jim felt like an animal ensnared.

"... Loxton's death was murder, not suicide!" exclaimed Ruth.

"What proof do you have to make such an outlandish statement?"

"None. And I understand your scepticism, Jim. I want you to be careful, that's all. Doesn't it all strike you as rather too coincidental?

You read about Loxton, then, the same morning, a friend you haven't heard from in years offers you the job he'd been contracted to do?"

"I suppose you're about to tell me that Bob Isherwood murdered Loxton?"

"As I told you," put in Erich, "We don't know what to make of it ourselves yet. But what I know and trust from long experience is Ruth's gift."

Ruth spoke again, "What do you actually know about these people you're working for? Loxton had worked for them before, hadn't he?"

"For Christ's sake! They sell china ornaments, by mail order. Loxton did a few catalogues for them, they hardly knew him."

"And I suppose you know it's true because they told you it was?"

Jim decided not to reply to that sort of ridiculous question, and wished that Erich and Ruth would both just shut up. "Okay, you were right. Loxton was involved in something foul and debase. The police suspect he was a paedophile!"

It was calculated to shock Ruth into silence. Jim saw at once that it had worked, although he immediately regretted putting it so bluntly and felt he had exploited her confidence in him. Ashamed, he attempted to explain more calmly, "Loxton was a pervert. Bob told me about it when we met. He was visited by a friend of his who works for the Vice Squad."

Ruth made no reply.

Jim looked over at Erich, "The other day you asked me if Loxton had a problem with his sexuality. Well, it looks like he did. His suicide was most likely triggered by guilt ... self-disgust or something. Christ, I don't know!"

"That makes very little sense," Ruth said, staring calmly at him, "You see paedophiles don't suffer from guilt. They justify the acts they do. They believe what they do is acceptable, their right. The only thing that might drive one to suicide would be fear of getting caught. But even so, I'm sure most would choose a less painful means of self-destruction than Loxton did."

Jim remained speechless for a moment as though struck dumb; her words had an unsettling ring of truth about them.

She continued, "Loxton may have been a paedophile, but trust me, there's a lot more to this."

It was at this point that Jim lost control; he jumped to his feet and asked condescendingly, "For God's sake, Ruth, isn't paedophilia bad enough for you?"

Ruth got to her feet too, standing head to head with Jim, both red-faced and glaring at each other. "I think paedophiles are extremely bad," she mouthed with great conviction through taut lips. "Stop trying to be so bloody smart! Accept the warning of two friends who are really worried for you. I don't care if you think I'm some delusional bloody woman. Just watch out."

The warning seemed to hover in mid- air in the silence that followed.

"Okay, thanks." Jim said in a low-key voice, "Look, I don't want to talk about this anymore. It's just making me angry." He walked to Ruth's back door, "Thanks for lunch," he said, adding as he went without looking back, "It was nice."

Ruth sat down next to Erich and sighed. Both were silent for a few moments. Then she said in a casual tone loaded with irony, "That went well ... coffee?"

Chapter Seven

Monday, 9 December, 1996

The gates were almost invisible in the pre-dawn dark of the morning. Jim was about to step out of his car and press the buzzer as they began to open. He assumed they were opening for him, until he was suddenly blinded by a set of headlamps on full beam. He raised a hand to shield his eyes, making out the outline of a large van directly before him. Whoever was driving the other vehicle did not dip their beams, nor intend to give way. Jim cursed, swung his car to the left beyond the gates and out of the van's path.

Jim prepared his next manoeuvre by shoving the gearstick into reverse, and watched the white van emerge, lit up in his tail lights. The driver seemed to pay more attention to Jim than he did to negotiating the turn. It was the red haired man he'd witnessed being told off by Nicholas when Rosemary was pointing out the mews to him. His features were hardly well lit, but Jim recognised the cap and the distinctive way it was worn.

For a few seconds both men scrutinised each other, the van moving forward slowly. Jim, with his photographer's eye, framed the man's head and shoulders in his mind. On the left of this imaginary picture was a small round sticker on the window. Jim attempted to identify the logo, but it was too dark and far away. The red-haired man, having seen enough, and without acknowledgement or gesture, accelerated away. Jim backed up, and watched the white van's tail-lights disappear at the far end of the mews.

Jim was twenty minutes earlier than expected. He'd got there in under an hour. Rosemary showed him in. She made no comment, but he got the distinct impression his early arrival was an inconvenience. The steel door to the stockroom was closed but unlocked, weak light spilling faintly from its base. As he walked to the lift, a cold sensation rippled across his skin, causing him to shudder. It felt like a touch, an icy coldness slithering across the surface of his skin, with a speed and fluidity reminiscent of something reptilian.

'You don't want to set foot in there,' a voice inside his head warned; then the more acceptable voice of his rationale assured, 'Ruth and Erich have got you spooked!'

But try as he might, he had no explanation for the apprehension he felt whenever he passed the cellar door. Nor could he explain the feelings of exhaustion that dissipated as soon as he left the premises. He still held to the view that it must be the stale, slightly fetid air pervading the house that caused this debility; its source was without a doubt below ground level.

"We've had some orders from our shops," Rosemary explained as they ascended in the lift, "It always gets busy leading up to Christmas. You probably saw our van leaving."

"Do you always start so early?"

"Only at this time of year, and when we deliver to our shops farthest afield."

They arrived at the first floor and she slid the door across for Jim. He opened the outer door himself and stepped onto the landing.

"Nick has arranged everything you need. He's busy at present, but I'll get him to bring you some coffee when he's free."

"Thanks," Jim said shutting the lift door. Rosemary pulled the inner door across. He watched her descend through the diamond-shaped window. She was smiling, yet the eyes seemed completely vacant.

Jim got to work. The room was so cold he could see his breath. He tested the radiator; it was unexpectedly hot and his hand recoiled in pain, "Bad drains and bad insulation, just my frickin' luck." He kept his jacket on to keep warm, but soon afterwards he was able to remove it; the heating seemed to have taken effect by daybreak.

Nicholas brought coffee and exchanged a few brief words. He had it seemed taken exception to Jim, and was no longer capable of big toothy grins. Jim tried to be polite, thinking that perhaps he had been a little rude about 'Stars of the Silent Screen'.

By 10.30 Jim had taken over a hundred photographs, accounting for about thirty final stills for the catalogue. However, he had a blinding headache and was feeling sick. Same as before, his work had slowed right down. There was no point continuing like that, so he went downstairs and asked Rosemary if she had any aspirin.

"I'm afraid not. We're all healthy specimens and never have any call for medicines."

She let him out the front door and he set off to find a pharmacy. He had noticed one near the sandwich bar where he'd bought lunch on Saturday.

He reached the pharmacy in a couple of minutes and purchased some aspirin, but the walk in the fresh air had done the trick, and he found he had no need for them by then.

*

Jim was completely absorbed by the headache as he emerged from the front door of 67 Barnswick Square, shoulders hunched, brow furrowed with pain. If his frame of mind had been less introspective, he may possibly have spotted Ruth and Erich, crouching down in their car seats.

"He'll see us!" Ruth whispered anxiously to her co-conspirator. Jim was exchanging words with a young woman who held the door open for him. "He'll never speak to me again."

"It's okay," said Erich, "He's not looking over here. He's going the other way."

Erich had parked his car as near to Niedermayer & Hart's premises as he felt was safe, certainly beyond the range of their security camera. They had been watching the house for about ten minutes.

"Perhaps he's nipping round the shops for something," Erich added, once the threat of being seen had passed.

"We'd best not be here when he comes back."

"I think we're safe for a few minutes. It was certainly worthwhile coming."

Ruth nodded.

"The cellar is the source, no doubt," said Erich with authority, "I can feel the negativity ... but I also sense it's dormant at this moment."

"I can only see darkness. Could it be elemental, some kind of entity?"

"Difficult to say. It may have adopted a physical form. Otherwise, it must exercise its will entirely through others."

"I thought Jim looked tense. He wouldn't acknowledge it, but he must be feeling something with all that negativity about."

"I agree. It must have a paralysing effect on anyone inside those walls for any length of time." Erich clearly didn't relish what was running through his mind, and winced as he said, "We'd learn far more if we could get inside."

"No chance of that."

"I was thinking ..." Erich broke off, an idea was forming.

"What?"

"Hermann. I'm sure he'd help us."

Ruth needed to think for a moment to identify the name. "Hermann? How could Hermann help?"

Hermann was Erich's brother who lived in Denmark. Ruth had never met him, but she had heard Erich talk about him.

Erich started up the car. "I've got an idea," he said.

*

The lab would have Jim's transparencies processed in two hours, by 4.30pm. He took advantage of free parking and got a bus from Clerkenwell down to the West End. He would call in at Bob's office in Lexington Street.

"Global View," a woman announced over the entry-phone in a slightly affected tone.

"Hello Daphne, it's Jim Latimer."

"Come on up," the woman replied, followed by the buzz of the door latch. The main offices of Global View were one flight up, whilst the two floors above housed Bob Isherwood's collection of almost half a million transparencies.

"Hello stranger," Daphne said, as Jim entered the expansive open plan outer office. Daphne was a large woman, probably sixty or thereabouts, she had been working for Bob long before Jim met him. Daphne's sophisticated tone on the entry-phone, resembling royalty, was entirely put on. Daphne was a Londoner born and bred, possessed the keen wit of an East End native and dropped the affectation as soon as she realised who it was.

"You took a long time to get up the stairs," she said, rising to her feet, "You got effin' asthma or something?"

"Just heavy-hearted with my profound love for you, Daph," Jim said, holding out a box of chocolates.

"Flattery will get you everywhere," Daphne replied, taking the chocolates and tossing them onto her desk. She gave Jim a large welcoming hug, engulfing him in her capacious bosom.

"I understand you've been pissed rotten," she said.

"Haven't touched a drop for almost a year."

Daphne took him by the hand and introduced him around the office. There were five others, all busy at work behind computer screens. Jim didn't know any of them; Bob's business had grown considerably in five years. They seemed like a friendly lot, but then Bob's office always had a good atmosphere.

71

"His Lordship's in the inner sanctum," Daphne said, pointing at a door.

"Are you going to let him know I'm here?"

"Sod that for a lark," she replied, "Tell him yourself."

Jim and the others laughed, Daphne's eyes were twinkling, but she kept her face, as always, deadpan. Jim had in the past saved up the most ribald joke for this woman, but had yet to see her laugh. She possessed the most faultless comic timing, and generally had those around her in fits of laughter.

"What do you expect for a box of chocolates?"

"I was hoping to get my hands on your body later," Jim replied.

"You can't, it belongs to my husband," she said, "And after he's finished and I'm finished, medical science. You'll have to put your name down for what's left."

Jim walked through into Bob's office; he tapped on the door first.

"Jim," Bob said, looking up from a pile of papers, "I wondered who it was ... Daphne doesn't knock," making the last part of the sentence loud enough for her to hear.

"That's cos I'm considerate and don't want to wake him up," she shouted back.

"Come in and close the door," Bob said, "It's the only way I get any peace from her."

Jim closed the door and sat down before Bob's desk. It was good to visit that office again. Bob had set up the business, just him and Daphne initially; she was as much a part of its success as Bob, and although neither ever had a good word for each other person to person, publicly and privately they sang the praises of the other highly. Bob's business was a tight run ship, yet it had a family feel, and the non-stop banter of Bob and Daphne gave it a shambolic human touch.

Bob was excited about a set of photographs that had arrived that morning. They were of a tribe of rainforest people who had hitherto never been photographed. The set of over a hundred prints depicted their communal lives in great detail.

"Only one or two have ever made contact with the outside world. The majority had never seen a European before," explained Bob.

"That's not necessarily a disadvantage."

The photographer had captured some essential quality that words can never fully express.

"Are they in danger?" Jim asked.

"They're always in danger ... loggers, miners, and of course the multi-nationals. They've got about two years, four at most."

"Can't anything stop it?"

"Unlikely, their lives will inevitably change. These pictures may help. Now there's photographic evidence of their existence, the slashers and burners can't just go in and deny there was anyone there. Power lies where the money is. I'm afraid the cards are stacked against them."

"Christ, it's bloody awful."

Bob was holding a simple photograph of a young mother breastfeeding her baby sitting in the centre of a group of other young women, the child staring up into the mother's eyes as it fed. He said, "We've landed a man on the moon, sent probes to Mars, hard to believe there are still people hidden away in our own world."

Daphne brought some coffee in.

"Why can't you be nice to me when we haven't got guests?" Bob asked her.

"Cos I don't have to be," she replied.

"I could replace you with a lovely nubile young girl, malleable to my will in every way." He raised his eyebrows lasciviously.

"You'd be dead in six months," she responded, "Anyway you forget, I've still got the pictures."

"What pictures?" Bob asked.

"The ones with you in flagrante delicto with a hamster."

"Shhh," Bob pretended alarm, "You promised never to say if I let you stay."

Daphne stared at Jim, "Forget everything you've heard," she said, and left.

It was Jim who raised the subject of Loxton.

Bob sighed at the name. He took out a piece of paper from his briefcase and passed it to Jim. "Loxton's death certificate," he said.

Jim looked for the cause of death. Suicide. He felt relief.

"Notice something odd?"

"Self-inflicted injuries ... severe blood loss. No?"

"It didn't strike me immediately either. How old was Loxton, would you say?"

"Late fifties, early sixties?"

"Look at the date of birth."

It said place of birth, Havant, Hampshire, and there, next to it, February 23rd, 1905. According to the death certificate, John Loxton had been ninety-one years old.

Inexplicably, Jim felt sweat break out on his palms.

"It's a mistake."

"I checked. No mistake."

"Then the John Loxton we knew wasn't the man born in Havant in 1905."

"That's what I thought too, except nobody else agrees." Bob handed Jim another piece of paper, "Loxton's birth certificate. Same date, 1905."

*

"That's the place," Bob said, "Park over there."

Jim negotiated the space, and switched off the engine. How he wished he'd kept his mouth shut about taking a look at Loxton's body. He really had no idea why he'd even said it. After all, Bob had been with John Loxton at the moment of his death. However, Bob must have needed to satisfy some curiosity of his own, because he'd immediately suggested they could go together after work. Jim was reluctantly enlisted.

Loxton's body had been released from the morgue at UCH as soon as the coroner corroborated the verdict of suicide. Bob, as the executor, had employed a funeral director, who organised the removal of the corpse to a chapel of rest in Golders Green. They arranged to see the body at 6.30pm, giving Jim enough time to return to Clerkenwell, get the transparencies and pick Bob up from the office. The Christmas traffic was bad, and they were ten minutes late arriving.

Jim went to the boot of the car and took out an old Nikon he always kept there. It was one of his first cameras, a well-worn and trusty companion but not too valuable to risk leaving in a car. He stuffed the camera down into his jacket pocket and placed his hand on top of it. He didn't want the undertaker to think he was a sightseer.

They rang the bell on a highly polished Brazilian oak door, decked out in cheap-looking brass furniture. There was a window beside it dressed in purple velvet, a grim looking urn containing white artificial carnations as its centrepiece.

The door was opened promptly by a plumpish young woman, no more than twenty-two or three. She presented herself in a charcoal grey suit over a white blouse, a string of pearls at her neck, and hair neatly pulled back into a ponytail. Her manner of greeting was probably considered in the funeral trade to be the appropriate level of gravitas.

"Mr Isherwood?" she said softly, looking at Jim.

"That's me," Bob corrected, "This is my friend ... and Mr Loxton's, Mr Latimer."

"Please come in," she said, holding the door open for them.

"Please accept my condolences. Had you both known Mr Loxton for a long time?"

"Yes, quite a while," replied Bob.

"I know it's no consolation at this time but Mr Loxton did enjoy a very long life ..."

Bob and Jim threw a glance at each other.

"... but however old the departed one is, it doesn't lessen the sadness."

Bob seemed to feel they were in for at least half an hour's grief counselling. "Might we see our friend now?" he asked, slightly emphasising the now.

The girl nodded understandingly. She led them past a small office into a room dimly lit by four pinkish-coloured wall lights. The room was carpeted dark blue, and a coffin rested ahead of them on a trestle table draped in purple velvet like the window. A polished mahogany table was set before the light oak coffin, a Bible with a gold cross on its cover placed centrally upon it.

"Would you like me to leave you?" the girl asked.

"Yes. Yes please, we'd like a few minutes."

The young woman nodded compassionately and left them.

Jim had already moved alongside the coffin while Bob was dealing with Morticia Addams. If he had been told Loxton was seventy when he died he might have expressed surprise, but it would not have been outside the realms of possibility. But the idea of ninety-one was ludicrous.

Jim scrutinised the brown age spots on the corpse's hands, folded together in heavenly peace. The skin was almost transparent and the veins stuck out blue and bold. Before him was lying the body of a very old man.

It was not a disturbing picture in itself, except for the fact that this was indisputably John Loxton, the same arrogant, conceited man who had once instructed Jim on camera lighting. Without any doubt it was the same man that Bob Isherwood had sat beside and watched die less than a week ago.

"Jesus!" Bob said as he drew close.

John Loxton had aged thirty years in six days.

Hugh's Tale

III

It was after dawn when I awoke. A blurred Reynald spun before my eyes as he leaned over me. In confusion I attempted to raise myself.

"Come to your place slowly, my friend," he gently advised. "The spies it seems were themselves observed."

He gave me water to ease the dryness in my throat, and once my head had cleared I saw we were alone in the gorge where we had witnessed the strange rite.

"I recall our Cathars kneeling and the priest offering one of them a casket."

"Did you see what it contained?" asked Reynald.

"I saw something shining ... the light from the torches was reflected upon it."

Reynald looked pensive, "I thought the light came from the box itself ... but no matter."

We searched all around us and explored the cave, which proved to be shallow and bare, but found nothing whatsoever.

With some difficulty we sought out the path the previous night's procession had taken. The only water we had left was in Reynald's flask, and barely a mouthful each. So with parched throats and heads throbbing we made our way back to our horses.

"I would make him pay dearly who gave me this aching skull," I raged, as we trudged along.

"Perhaps you should thank him for sparing your life," put in Reynald, who had remained thoughtful since we had left the gorge, "They might easily have killed us."

As we descended into the valley where the community lived, the sight that met us took a moment to register. Smoke was rising from different points of the village, and as we began to comprehend it, we saw that many bodies were lying upon the ground, carrion birds feasting on their flesh.

76

"In the name of Christ, what has happened?" cried Reynald, rushing down the hillside. I followed close on his heels, our own infirmities vanishing at the sight before us.

We counted forty-seven bodies. Whatever had befallen these people had come upon them suddenly, most probably around dawn, for some were still in their beds when death had been dealt out to them.

"They approached by the same route we followed," said Reynald, pointing out the tracks, "Fifteen, maybe twenty men on horseback."

"They had no hope of escape."

None had been spared. Women bearing infants had been murdered as they ran to escape the persecution, no mercy shown either to them or the children they attempted to save, hacked down, their offspring trampled under hooves. There were some signs of resistance. The menfolk of the village, some ten in number, had died trying to protect their families. They had fought with scimitars, but the outcome was inevitable, outnumbered by heavily armed men who had attacked without warning.

I searched the dwellings in vain for signs of life. In one room I came upon a tiny child stabbed through the heart as it lay in its crib. As I went to leave my foot kicked a dagger that its killer had let drop as the baby's mother flew at him in her rage. The woman lay on the floor close by her child, a sword wound on her neck. But I recognised the knife, it was the kind I wore upon my own belt, as did Reynald and every Templar.

I tore from that house holding the weapon before me, "Men of our order brought this destruction. In the name of God, why?"

Reynald was equally appalled by the discovery, "I recognise signs that they searched for something. Yet I think they were unsuccessful. I cannot find our Cathars or the priests amongst the dead."

"You think they escaped?"

"More likely were already gone before the attack."

The extermination of the village had been thorough to the last detail, extending even to the livestock. We became concerned for our horses, but needlessly, for they remained undiscovered in the place where we had left them.

Reynald insisted that the bodies should not be left to the vultures. We gathered wood to build a funeral pyre, and disposed of them in this way.

"They spared our lives," he said, "This is the least we can do in return."

It was late in the day when we were ready to depart. We travelled swiftly, arriving back in Acre just before nightfall three days hence.

Brother Ferdinand, the Marshal's eyes and ears, was the first to witness our return and could not have exhibited more shock had two ghosts appeared. He hurried from our sight without word or welcome.

"Forgive the way I rushed off," the fat cellarer panted apologetically as he returned, "We had given you up for lost. I was so overjoyed at seeing you that I rushed to tell the Marshal. He wishes to see you immediately."

Whilst Ferdinand led the way, Reynald held me back a moment, and whispered, "Say nothing of the dagger."

Jerome was uncharacteristically ecstatic at the sight of us. We might easily have believed ourselves his greatest favourites, insisting we quench our thirst with a glass of wine before relating our story.

I left the storytelling to Reynald, for the marshal always brought a paralysing effect to my throat. Brother Ferdinand and Marshal Jerome listened patiently as Reynald told how the pilgrims had been met at Auja. They appeared to be genuinely interested by the account of our journey into the hills. However, the torchlit procession and the ritual that followed caused our Marshal and Brother Ferdinand to exchange some troubled glances; Jerome grew noticeably agitated when the casket was mentioned.

"When it was opened, did you see what lay within?" he asked anxiously.

"No," replied Reynald, "We saw nothing. The moment the box was opened we were struck down."

Jerome seemed almost relieved to hear this, "And I suppose that was the end of it … no matter …"

"But there is more," said Reynald.

"Pray tell us," said Jerome, looking somewhat perturbed again.

Marshal Jerome's expression of affability throughout the earlier account was transformed completely. When he heard tell of the massacre his face blanched with anger and he started to interrogate us on every detail. His former concern for our wellbeing was no longer evident.

"You have no idea who was behind this attack, no clue to their identity?"

"Nothing sir," said Reynald.

"None, sir," I concurred.

Finally satisfied, Jerome thanked us for the intelligence we had brought to him and granted us permission to leave. And although he presented a calm outer demeanour, it was not wholly convincing, for a rage burnt within his eyes.

A short while later, Robert de Frontignac, the knight who had accompanied us to the harbour the day our troubles began, sought us out.

"Good brothers, I am delighted to see you again. Only yesterday I returned myself from an errand to Safed. Everyone here seemed to think you had met your deaths. I asked Brother Ferdinand what had happened, but all he would tell me was that the Marshal was anxious for you."

"They must be glad then to have us returned to them," said Reynald.

"I fear that was not how the Marshal appeared to me when I saw him ride from our stables shortly after vespers in the company of three others. They were riding as if hell itself was at their heels and Marshal Jerome looked grave as thunder."

"What direction did they take?" asked Reynald.

"They took the road south, I think."

Chapter Eight

Monday, 9 December, 1996

The funeral director had soothing words for the two ashen-faced men as they emerged from the chapel of rest. What the young woman assumed to be grief was really dumbfounded shock. Bob found a phrase or two to express thanks, Jim didn't attempt to speak; both felt like travellers hopelessly lost in a foreign land.

Jim drove them back to the West End and parked near the British Museum. The two men said little.

Some food and comfort was found, amidst the liveliness and bustle of a Pizza Express. Jim had forgotten to remove the Nikon from his pocket; its weight kept unbalancing his jacket, causing it to slip from the back of the chair where it hung. He had taken a couple of shots of Loxton; however, the thought of looking at that corpse again, if only in monochrome, held no appeal.

"You remember my neighbour, Ruth?" Jim asked, as he stirred his coffee.

"Down at the cottage ... the artist?"

"Well remembered ... she claims to be psychic," Jim scoffed as he said this, anticipating an equally scornful reaction from his companion.

But no such response came back; Bob merely took a sip of his red wine.

"She had an unusual dream," Jim said, omitting to mention his own, "Ruth and a friend of hers, another so called psychic, gave me an ear-bashing yesterday," Jim laughed. "They warned me to be careful. Ruth claims that Loxton's death wasn't really suicide. She reckons he was involved in something sinister." Jim raised his eyebrows to suggest impending doom.

"You explained about the paedophile business?"

"Ruth claims it's something even worse."

"What, then?"

Jim smiled, uncomfortably, "That seems to be where the shutters come down on her mystic powers."

Bob failed to laugh as he was expected to. "Don't completely discount her advice, Jim."

"You can't be serious?"

"Jim, I've spent all of my adult life observing people who set great importance by dreams. All primitive cultures believe in the power of magic. Over the last couple of hundred years we've largely stopped believing such things in the West. We rationalise, place our faith in science. But do you think science has an answer for what we saw tonight?"

"What are you saying?" Jim asked incredulously, "that it was voodoo, black magic or something?"

Bob caressed the bowl of his wine-glass between the fingertips of both hands and stared into its liquid. "When I watched Loxton die last Tuesday night, he looked no different to when I first met him twenty-five years ago. You and I have changed considerably in that time, but Loxton didn't ... he stayed exactly the same. Strange, but it really didn't occur to me until I talked to you ... you hadn't seen him in years and assumed he'd be sixty-ish ... that got me thinking."

"I was just as shocked as you were when I looked into that coffin."

Bob looked up and smiled briefly at Jim before returning his gaze to the glass, "Every morning I look in the mirror and am surprised by the ageing man who's looking back at me. When I saw you again, the first thing I noticed was how you'd changed. In the same way you probably looked at me and thought, 'Christ, the old bastard's senile'. We re-appraise each other, constantly adjust the picture. But none of us is ever really sure about how much we've altered, or feels entirely comfortable about it. Perhaps that's why Loxton's youthfulness never struck me as odd. You added on twenty years to the Loxton you remembered, expecting to find someone about sixty. But if you'd seen him on Tuesday, Jim, you'd have seen a man who hadn't altered or aged an hour since your student days."

"Loxton had lost a lot of blood, perhaps that caused his skin to give the effect of ageing," Jim said. He knew he was fumbling for straws.

"Christ, the man was ninety-one, you've seen his birth certificate. What we saw at the funeral parlour was correct. John Loxton, born 1905 in Hampshire, died London, December 3rd 1996. Don't you see, it's the picture in our heads that's wrong."

"There has to be an explanation!"

"A rational one ... monkey glands and hair dye?"

"Jesus, Bob, you're not with Ruth and Erich are you? You can't seriously believe some mysterious force is at work?"

"I'm just saying that neither of us has the means of explaining Loxton."

Jim appeared to nod in assent. Really he just wanted the conversation to end.

Bob took a set of keys from his pocket and laid them on the table. Jim somehow understood from the significant way they were produced that the keys had belonged to John Loxton.

'Oh no,' he thought, 'I don't want to get involved.'

*

Loxton's flat was on the first floor of a building in Berwick Street. The front door opened directly onto the street. There were some other floors to the building, but their means of access must have been via another route; only Loxton's place was accessible through this door. A new lock had been fitted, a piece of plywood tacked over the original where it had been rammed by the emergency services. There was barely enough room for the door to open before the stairs rose steeply and it was necessary to stand free of the line of the door on the bottom step in order to shut it.

Bob went first, pressing in the light-timer as he began to climb. The stairway was shabby, the carpet threadbare on every tread. Jim could make out a faint blue pattern on the risers, but apart from this distant memory of colour, the carpet was a dull browny-grey from years of dirt and dust. The painted surfaces of the skirting, once white, had yellowed with age. The wallpaper, its design long faded, was torn and in places missing altogether.

By the time Jim had dealt with the front door and taken in his surroundings, Bob was at the top of the stairs. When he was only a few steps up, Bob disappeared from sight.

"What the hell am I doing here?" he asked himself. Jim sighed, proceeded up another two steps, heard a click and was instantly plunged into darkness. His left foot was in mid-air and he almost lost his balance on the steep slope of stairs. It was pitch black. He groped forward with a hand until he found a stair tread, and came to rest in an insecure state on fingers, knees and shoe tips.

"Bob!" he called lamely. He felt the Nikon in his pocket weighing against his thigh, and remembered Loxton's wizened corpse in its light oak coffin.

"Bob!" he tried again, a little louder and more plaintively this time.

Light spilled out from an unseen door on the landing above.

"Sorry old mate," came Bob's familiar voice, "The stair light's on one of those push in jobs. There you go … you alright?" he asked, gazing down at Jim's tentative form, poised like a nervous tom-cat.

"Yes," Jim replied curtly. He re-assumed a more suitable posture for Homo sapiens. "Lost my footing," he said.

Although difficult to comprehend, the flat itself was even less inviting than the stairwell. The air was stale and fusty, although Bob had partially remedied this by opening some of the windows whilst Jim was stuck on the stairs. The carpets and curtains, what could be seen of them for dust and grime, were old and threadbare. The room they were in, presumably the lounge, continued and developed the brown-grey theme.

Quite shocked on his own account but able to see the effect the grim flat was having on his friend, Bob said, "Loxton was badly in need of a home improvement manual."

"What an awful bloody mess!" Jim said, with deep revulsion.

"Hard to believe the dapper John Loxton, never seen without an expensive suit and bow-tie, lived in this shit-hole."

Shit-hole was right. Everything was worn out and filthy. Nothing it seemed had ever been renewed or replaced. An arm that had broken off an armchair was left to rot where it had fallen and years of dust had settled over and cocooned the shed limb. The room felt like a tomb. On every surface, the dust of years had accumulated in extravagant patterns; on sills and skirtings it had grown so high that it had collapsed in places, creating mousey-grey curving arcs like stalagmites.

For the second time in one evening, Jim Latimer was almost lost for words, "How … just how could anyone exist like this? I mean … what was going on in his head?"

"I think we can assume Loxton wasn't troubled by dust mite allergy," said Bob sardonically.

The room's furnishings were sparse, a three-piece suite, of which the broken chair was an item, a small table, a case of dust-laden books and a sideboard. The sofa, a Fifties design, was entombed beneath a fine unbroken layer of dust. The covering of dust was so comprehensive that it was easily possible to picture Loxton's routes in the well-worn trails where it had been disturbed. One end of the table was partly free of dust, presumably from Loxton's economic use of it. The intact chair residing opposite its arm-less comrade was mostly dust free too. It must have been in this 'good' chair that John Loxton was apt to sit in his habitual state of imperious grandeur.

Jim and Bob were magnetically drawn to a dark brown patch on the floor at the centre of the room. They stood just beyond its outer fringes transfixed in morbid fascination. The whole area was about six feet in diameter and very nearly circular in shape. Loxton had certainly lost a lot of blood.

The flat had been locked in a time warp. There was little to suggest anyone had actually lived there in years. Loxton possessed no friends, so nobody had ever visited. Some dust had been agitated by the police and ambulance-crew, leaving the area around the blood-stain looking as though a herd of buffalo had paused at a waterhole and drank it dry.

"Everything is fifties!" Bob exclaimed. "It must have been all new at the same time. Christ ... what could have made him give up like that?"

"You think something happened to him and he stopped making an effort?"

"He was one of our leading photographers. I've read interviews he gave back in the early fifties ... a globe trotter, highly in demand, urbane, successful ... celebrated even."

Jim began to see the flat differently. Bob was right, every furnishing and fitting had been acquired at the same time. As he looked closer, he realised that everything had been colour co-ordinated, perhaps the work of an interior designer. There was a television-set, state of the art in its day, bulkily encased in wood with a screen the size of a modern portable. Like everything else, its screen and casing were covered in dust; its operating knobs, long fallen off, lay half-buried on the floor in front of the sideboard where it rested. It could be safely assumed that Loxton was not a TV dinner man.

The rest of the flat told a similar story. In the kitchen there was an old radio set under the ubiquitous dust and debris. It reminded Bob of a set his father had owned when he had been a child in New Zealand. The kitchen units, originally olive green with handles of Bakelite, had like everything else been toned brown and grey over time. The cooker was unnerving to behold, filth and baked-on grease an inch thick had spread out glacier-like across its surface and was growing over the oven door.

Loxton's bedroom was as expected; a peek at the bed linen would have sent a rodent blushing; once-white sheets were greasy, grime-ridden rags, the colour of weathered tarmac. Bob opened the wardrobe, and here was the first surprise: hanging on its clothes rail, a dozen clean, sharp suits, wrapped up in cellophane; to the side of these, cleaned, pressed and neatly stacked on shelves, were about two dozen shirts, whilst numerous pairs of highly-polished shoes rested at the wardrobe's base.

It seemed inconceivable that a man existing in such a state of degeneration could have kept up the appearance of respectability. There was no hint about Loxton of the dire world he inhabited.

It was decided that Bob would search the bedroom and Jim would take on the lounge. The bathroom was next to the kitchen; they had given it little more than a cursory glance as they toured the flat. Jim decided to pay a visit here on his way to the living room, being in need of a pee. However, when he took in Loxton's bathroom, he decided that his need was not that pressing; bladder ache was distinctly preferable to exposing any part of one's anatomy in there. Loxton's personal hygiene had a far below zero rating.

Investigating a door that led off from the bathroom, Jim discovered himself in Loxton's darkroom. In marked contrast to every other room in the flat, it was spotlessly maintained. Here, Loxton had remained the consummate professional. Its normality amidst the wreck of John Loxton's home lent the space an eeriness all of its own. Jim opened a filing cabinet, only to find that all the files were missing. The vice squad it seemed had been there first.

Jim, taking advantage of the darkroom's cleanliness, availed himself of its sink. As he did so, smiling with relief, he said aloud, "Not a proper photographer until you've pissed in the sink."

The two men were soon searching the flat. Neither had any idea of what, if anything, they were looking for. Their aim was to shed more light on Loxton's life and death. Something that might explain the man's youthfulness was Bob's main motivation; nobody would ever convince him that he was simply mistaken and that on Tuesday night he had been present at the death of a youthful nonagenarian. As for Jim, he was secretly hoping to lay to rest the voodoo drum that had already started to beat faintly in his head.

Jim started with Loxton's books. There was just the one bookcase, hidden away in a corner of the lounge. The books were the same generation as everything else. The latest publishing date of any book in the Loxton library was 1956. The books were mainly photographic, journals and collections from the forties and fifties or books on art. Judging by what was there, he had not shown much interest in general reading; a Dennis Wheatley, an Ian Fleming, two Graham Greenes and a few other names long forgotten to the pantheon of literature.

Jim found that the dust irritated his eyes and he sneezed a lot. If Loxton had an appreciation for art then it had been a long time ago;

Jim's hands were the first to touch those books in decades. So consistent was the dust layer, there seemed little point in disturbing them, and little chance that books on a shelf for forty years would reveal anything. However, Jim went on, patiently flicking through each book for anything hidden in its pages. There was nothing, no letter or photograph used as a bookmark, not even a scrap of paper with a shopping list.

Jim spent an hour, breathing in and sneezing out Loxton's dust mites, and nothing had come to light. He didn't replace the books but left them on the floor in stacks.

It was just after 10pm and Jim had another early start in the morning. He looked about him; there was little else to do. He decided he would complete that room then head for home.

"I'm going to finish up in here and then I'll have to go," he called to Bob.

"Look at this lot," Bob replied, emerging with a small suitcase and an armful of small booklets, "Loxton didn't own that much, but he didn't throw anything out either."

"What are they?" Jim asked.

"Timetables, dozens of them," Bob replied. Jim was unimpressed until Bob added, "For Brighton ... train times to Brighton ... a full set back to 1957."

Jim was suddenly interested, "That's the year Niedermayer & Hart started. It says so on a plaque by the door."

"How many times did Loxton do their catalogue?"

"Only a few years, I was told."

"Maybe he had a maiden aunt he visited there."

"She'd have been very old."

"And Loxton must have adored her," said Bob, snapping open the locks of the suitcase, "Feast your eyes on this little lot!"

The suitcase contained rail tickets, hundreds of them, and every single one had the same destination, Brighton.

Jim felt a bead of sweat run down his spine.

"Do you think the people I'm working for could be part of Loxton's paedophile thing?"

"Christ Jim, I suppose anything's possible, especially with sick bastards like that."

"But if they were involved, why get in touch and ask you to recommend a photographer to replace Loxton?"

"Doesn't make any sense, does it? Why attract unnecessary attention? Perhaps Loxton went to Brighton for another reason altogether ... who knows, maybe he just adored the place."

The timetables and tickets were hardly any kind of proof. Even so, Jim was unable to stop thinking about them. They seemed somehow significant. Something happened to Loxton in the late fifties, around the time Niedermayer & Hart had become established. Jim began searching with renewed vigour.

He looked through the sideboard, which had clearly not been opened for many years. Here there were some wine glasses, a guarantee and operating manual for the TV dated 1955, a pile of magazines and newspapers from '55 and '56, and some unopened bottles of wine and spirits.

'At least he wasn't an alcoholic,' thought Jim darkly.

He had now looked everywhere in the room and was about to find Bob and offer him a lift home, when Loxton's armchair caught his eye. It was the only item in the room free of dust and sticking out like a sore thumb. He hesitated at first before raising the filthy seat cushion. The spring supports in the chair's base had been removed and a piece of board had been installed, a couple of holes had been drilled in it that fit two fingers for easy removal. Jim felt a tiny palpitation. He put his fingers into the unsavoury holes, smooth and greasy from use and lifted out the board. Stacked in the chair's base were four box files, sitting two abreast.

"Bob!" Jim cried out. His voice must have expressed urgency, because his friend appeared almost at once.

Neither man spoke as they removed the files, and only their gasps could be heard once their heinous contents were revealed. Neither man had ever seen anything so sickening. The material, mainly photographic, was pornographic, and confirmed the assertion of Bob's friend in Vice, that Loxton had indeed been a paedophile.

"Evil bastard," were the only words Bob could utter.

Jim felt physically sick.

On the top of one file there was a list. If it hadn't been on top Jim would not have found it, because he had stopped looking through the files, they were far too disturbing. It was a list of initials and telephone numbers, three pages long. Jim searched down the list and found himself looking for a link between Loxton and Niedermayer & Hart; there did not appear to be one, least not here; he recognised no initials, and none of the numbers were preceded by a Brighton telephone code; he sighed with relief.

"Your friend in Vice will want this," Jim said, passing the list to Bob.

Bob took out his mobile phone, pressed a couple of buttons, then stopped. "Look Jim, you don't need to get caught up in all of this. I'm Loxton's executor so I can't avoid it. But why don't you get off home? I'll sort it out with Ian Rice."

Jim considered the suggestion for a moment. It was now 10.40pm; it would already be well after midnight by the time he got back. "You sure?"

"I'll say I found them."

"Alright, if that's okay."

"Thanks for coming. I wouldn't have wanted to come in here and find this evil filth on my own."

Jim said he would come round to Bob's office tomorrow afternoon, after he'd dropped off the next batch of film.

"I won't be there," Bob replied, "I've got an appointment with Loxton's solicitor."

"What's that about?"

"No idea. He rang this morning."

Jim left Loxton's flat, making damn sure not to dawdle on the stairs.

*

The red-haired man hated telephone boxes, they were too public, so he turned his face towards the wall once he had dialled. Not that there was anyone about to see him at 3am, but staying anonymous was a habit. He felt comfortable in the night; it was his security, like being snugly wrapped up in an old familiar overcoat.

"It's me," he said.

"What is it, Picton?" Rosemary Hines asked.

"Isherwood must've found Loxton's collection. Two policemen came to the flat and took some stuff away."

"So?" she replied, clearly unimpressed.

"He went to see Loxton's body first ..."

Picton loved to surprise.

"... and he didn't go alone."

"Latimer? Latimer was with him?" Rosemary sounded furious.

Picton was grinning. He allowed the full picture to develop for her, before adding, "Nicky's idea wasn't it, to involve the photographer?"

"Shut your mouth, Picton."

"Sorry," said Picton, but unable to check himself he went on, "I just thought 'lover boy' had suggested it as a way of keeping tabs on Isherwood?"

Picton knew by the icy silence that he had overstepped the mark. Referring to Nicholas as lover boy was a bad mistake. He winced at the thought of his own stupidity.

"I'm sorry ma'am."

"Just keep your stupid mouth shut."

There was a discussion going on at the other end; Picton strained to hear but Rosemary must have had her hand partly over the mouthpiece. Picton could tell from the tone that it was heated, and he smiled to himself.

After a minute Rosemary came back onto the line. "Nicholas will take over from you. I want you to start watching Latimer."

"Why?"

"Because you do what I fucking say that's why!"

Picton made no further protest. He knew it would do him no good, no good at all, to argue with Rosemary.

Chapter Nine

Tuesday, 10 December, 1996

Jim could see the two men more closely this time. Heads bowed, eyes concentrated on the treacherous ground, faces shaded under cowls. They raised a hand from time to time, tugging at hoods to protect their eyes from exposure to the wind's bite. Occasionally Jim caught a glimpse of an eye, a cheek, a jaw-line, slowly assembling an impression of their faces.

Jim's role of observer frustrated him.

The taller man limped and he was partially crippled, the left arm hanging immobile and useless; the smaller man was attentive, often demonstrating concern for his companion. Yet it seemed to Jim that it was the injured man who set the pace; in fact, his whole demeanour spoke of urgency. Sometimes he paused to stare with deep misgivings at the sky, as though he feared their destination might be out of reach before nightfall. Both men grew increasingly disheartened as time wore on.

Then, late in the day, light fading fast, the smaller man stopped abruptly and pointed ahead. At last they had reached their journey's end. However, after all the hardship and bitter effort involved in getting there, arriving brought only an increased sense of dread. Before them was a single storey dwelling built of wood and stone which they cautiously approached.

The scenes that followed from this point were fleeting. The hooded men's journey had played to a soundtrack of howling winds and feet crunching on the icy surface of the land; from now on the tableaux were soundless, contributing a certain dislocation.

There was a woman, staring intently at a bundle of rags nestling in her arms. Jim saw some small movements coming from this object, then tiny fingers and the hands of a baby. The scene was like a parody of the Madonna with child, for here, the holy mother's sublime serenity was replaced by an all-consuming obsession; the woman's face did not merely adore, but burned with a maniacal zeal.

Jim sensed a familiarity about the woman. Now, just before the scene altered and her face started to blur, he realised that the demented Madonna was Rosemary Hines.

A new viewpoint: the taller man was kneeling before her and gently rolled down his hood. Jim saw his face clearly for the first time, his eyes had a fire in them too, smouldering; a strong but haggard face, handsome perhaps, if pain had not weighed so heavily upon it. He seemed to be hoping for some kind of recognition from the woman, but she threw him no more than a cursory glance before her gaze fell once again on the infant. Although the man was pleading, her eyes never wavered again from the small object of her passion. A fog descended and the scene was gone.

At first it looked as though the taller man was shouting, but as the picture cleared and focused, Jim saw he was screaming in agony, tears running down his cheeks; the absence of sound only adding to its grotesqueness. Jim felt compassion for his suffering.

The picture pulled out into a wider shot, and Jim suddenly felt extremely frightened. The man's pain had no natural cause; apart from his soundless screaming face, his entire body was wrapped in a living darkness, it was writhing over his body, holding him tightly as though he was mummified in its iron grip.

The scene shifted again: the smaller man was running blindly, like an animal that has sniffed blood at the abattoir door.

"Please God, let me wake up!" Jim cried out in his sleep.

Jim thought he had lost sight of the smaller man, before realising that he was now seeing everything directly through his eyes. Jim found himself running towards an oak door, heaved it open and immediately jumped back in alarm; standing just outside the doorway was a red-haired man, laughing at him like a madman. He appeared to have long hair hanging in streaks down his face, until Jim realised they were in fact streams of blood pouring from a wound on the man's head. His red hair encircled a bald patch, and in its centre was a gash many inches long from where the blood sprang.

Jim attempted to shake himself awake. He failed to come to, but succeeded in shifting his perspective back into the more comfortable role of observer again.

Time moved on: once again Jim was watching the shorter man; he was dying, his body smashed at the base of some rocks. He had no fear of dying, yet he remained fearful of the darkness that had already consumed his companion. He looked a pitiful sight, laying there, his warm blood trickling out onto the icy rocks that had smashed his young body. He was wracked with guilt; a hopeless coward, he had betrayed his friend by running away. His erratic breathing then came to an abrupt stop, and he lay still.

Then, as Jim observed the staring corpse, its face metamorphosed into his own.

Jim woke up clawing at his face, as though a mask of spider silk had been woven over it. He coughed and spat in a frenzied attempt to expel the dry fibres he imagined filled his mouth; sitting bolt upright when he came to his senses. He switched on the light, swung his legs out of the sweat-sodden sheets and sat at the bed's edge, head in hands. He was glad to be awake.

It was 5.30am, and he had enjoyed, if that was the right word, only a couple of hours rest. For ages while waiting for sleep to come, the sick, perverted existence of John Loxton had pervaded his mind; that vile portfolio flickering through his head. There had been so many thoughts, Loxton's youthfulness, the timetables and tickets to Brighton, all the ugliness and squalor of the man's life. Eventually sheer exhaustion won; but even sleep had robbed him of any peace of mind; one nightmare had simply been exchanged for another.

Jim switched off his alarm clock; it had been due to go off at 6am, there seemed little point in returning to bed and to be honest he had little or no enthusiasm for it. He took that most British of options when all is in turmoil, went downstairs and put on the kettle.

Ruth was the only person he wanted to see; he knew she would listen to him without reproach or ridicule, and he knocked for over a minute at her door. There was a thick frost on the ground, and by the time he returned to his own cottage his teeth were chattering. He found one of her ultra-concise notes at the front door which he'd failed to notice last night when he got home.

Gone to Erich's. Ring me anytime if you need to talk.

Love,

Ruth

Jim had wanted to talk to her when he got back, but it was very late and anyway her lights were out. He hadn't considered the possibility that perhaps she wasn't even home. He toyed with the idea of phoning her at Erich's, but it was very early and he was wide awake by then and already feeling a lot calmer; it was probably pride that got the better of him.

'I'll see her tonight,' he told himself.

The dream clung on in much the same way as its predecessor had done, and he felt reluctant about setting foot in Hove that morning, but after a shower and some breakfast his attitude changed.

'After all, what do I really think is happening? Their names weren't on Loxton's list. He was just someone they employed, like me.' He thought for a moment, 'I'm an ex-piss-head; but they don't know that. So why should they know what Loxton was up to?'

Looking in his shaving mirror, Jim was horrified to discover a deep scratch down the right side of his face - a sleeping injury. There were other marks too that had been caused by his clawing, but these were mostly just reddened skin that would soon subside.

'I'm going to need padded mitts every time I sleep, like a lunatic.'

The idea did not seem all that funny.

He phoned Rosemary Hines just before 7.30am to let her know that he would be late.

"I'm sorry about this. I've got the first transparencies. I think you'll be pleased," he said, giving an impression he'd actually looked at them.

"Great," she answered, "Don't worry about being late. We're here and don't intend going anywhere." She laughed chummily, "Did you have a late night?"

"No. I just overslept."

*

The aspirin Jim had bought previously failed to have any effect on the headache that had come upon him again by mid-morning. Just as before, only a walk in the fresh air away from the house brought relief. Rosemary seemed more upbeat than she'd been yesterday. Nicholas was not around, so it was Rosemary who fetched and carried the various items to be photographed.

"Sure I can't help you?" Jim asked.

"I understand our stock room. Thanks, but I can manage."

Jim was showing some signs of wear and tear. No doubt troubled by what had happened the previous night, he had cut himself shaving and missed a few bristles on his chin and below an ear. He was disorientated from lack of sleep, and all morning his thoughts kept returning to Loxton.

By 1.30pm, the headache had returned, but he had done enough by then to ensure he'd be able to complete the shoot tomorrow. He would then only need to return to Barnswick Square once more, to drop off the final transparencies and to pack up his equipment.

He went downstairs and stood in the hall leaning in the doorway to the office. Rosemary was facing him from behind her desk.

"I'll finish tomorrow," he said, "The equipment can stay until Thursday, just in case I need to re-shoot anything."

"No problems so far," Rosemary replied enthusiastically. "The different backgrounds work well. Mr Hart and I are delighted."

"Mr Hart's back from Amsterdam?"

"Of course, you two haven't met," she said, rising to her feet and gesturing over to her left, "I'm so sorry."

Jim stepped into the office; the open door had been obscuring his view of the right side of the room. Almost hidden from sight, sitting quietly behind the isolated corner desk, was Mr Hart. He was in the process of getting up when Jim first saw him, rising awkwardly, as though he was unused to introductions. His hair was white, and Jim noticed he used his right hand to lever himself out from behind the desk, while the other hand was kept out of sight in his jacket pocket. Mr Hart had a pronounced limp.

"How do you do?" Hart said as he shook Jim's hand, "The transparencies are excellent. You're giving us a first class catalogue, Mr Latimer."

Jim gave a faint smile and managed to squeeze out some mumbled words of thanks. He felt dizzy; the blood was rushing to his head, for a second he thought he might faint. Before him was Mr Hart: nothing exceptional or unusual about him, 5'10" tall, white-haired, dressed modestly in a business suit.

If Jim had met Mr Hart yesterday, there wouldn't have been a problem.

Although Jim had never met the co-founder of the porcelain business before, he had indeed seen him; but Mr Hart had been younger, possibly thirty years younger, and had seemed taller beside the hooded man in last night's dream.

94

Hugh's Tale

IV

Marshal Jerome had departed Acre in the company of two knights and a serjeant; the same taciturn fellow who had been with us at the harbour and witnessed the events when our pilgrims first arrived. Six days later I saw the Marshal return, his entourage much increased, by this time numbering thirteen in all. They appeared weary and battle-worn, and spoke of being attacked by bandits near Ascalon.

"I never thought bandits so foolish," remarked Reynald.

"What do you mean?" I asked.

"Attacking so many Templars? They must have had a small army to contemplate such an assault, else craved only death."

"You think these were the knights who murdered the villagers?" Although we were alone, I lowered my voice as I put this question.

Reynald considered it, and then shook his head, "Jerome was furious when he heard about the killing. I suspect that may have been the work of others."

"But for what purpose?"

"Perhaps it would be best not to know."

A truer word I never heard spoken, good Anselm, for discovering the truth has blighted my life. Let no man say to me we have nothing to fear of truth. For its revelation has violated everything I held dear.

Jerome became almost reclusive in the days that followed his return. Whenever I had the misfortune of seeing him, his face always bore a sour disposition. Brother Ferdinand scurried nervously about him, his corpulent body aquiver with the strain of serving so peevish a master.

But time passed, life for us returned to normal, or so it seemed.

Then one evening, as Reynald and I were patrolling the market area, we became active participants in events which until then we had only touched upon through ignorance.

95

Sometimes, Anselm, I wish we had been distracted at that moment, and failed to see the missile that struck the cobblestones at our feet. But fate I fear had already marked us.

The object was a piece of paper bound around a small stone with wool. It might have come from as many as twenty upper windows or even a rooftop. Reynald read out the message written there.

Your eyes did not deceive you.
If you can forgive me, then meet me at the place where I denied knowing you,
tomorrow at midnight.
I am in great need of a friend.
Hubert

The reason we were patrolling the market streets was because a number of pilgrims had recently been robbed in that district. Reynald suggested to our Officer a plan to catch the thieves if we might be allowed to lay in wait for them at night. His argument made sense, and we were granted permission to miss compline for the purpose of protecting honest pilgrims.

It was a while after midnight before Hubert revealed himself from the shadows of a warehouse, stepping out into the moonlight only long enough to be recognised before returning again to the darkness.

Reynald rushed to the man and embraced him.

"I am sorry I kept you waiting, my friend. I had to be certain you were not followed," said Hubert.

"You dog," laughed Reynald, "I am pleased to see you even if you do deny knowledge of old friends and lurk about in shadows. Let me introduce Hugh, he was with me at the harbour when I saw you first."

"I remember the good knight from that meeting. And I regret he was also in your company when my companions did you injury," said Hubert extending a hand towards me, "Friend, I hope you bear no grudge."

My hand fleetingly touched the back of my head in memory, "The hurt is healed," I said.

How swiftly wounds of the body heal, if only the same were true of scars borne in the mind and soul.

"When did you realise we were following you?" asked Reynald.

"Even though we were expecting it, you were only spotted at the end, just before you were assaulted."

"Then we made better spies than we credited ourselves for," said Reynald.

"Far better than they who sent you hoped. You were chosen as decoys and meant to be detected."

The statement was a bitter pill, yet somehow we knew it was the truth.

"Our Marshal sent us. And it would be true to say that he looked surprised when we returned," answered Reynald, "Word had already spread through our house that we were dead."

"Your Marshal is cunning and seeks enormous power for himself ... the greatest power in this world." Hubert broke off and paused a while before continuing, "I am glad you recovered from the harm we did you. I trust your journey home was less eventful?"

"Once we came round we returned to the village. You must have departed some time before the attack."

"Attack?"

Hubert had no knowledge of what had befallen the village. We told him of the massacre. He became distressed at the news that so many innocents had met such brutality. It struck him like a severe blow to the body and he needed to lean against the wall of a warehouse to support himself.

"How can any just man believe other than this world belongs to Sataniel? For Christ's love ..." he said, tears flowing down his cheeks, "... all perished you say?"

Reynald nodded.

We told him everything we knew, only omitting the discovery of the dagger which would have meant implicating and betraying men of our order. After a time Hubert grew somewhat calmer and went on to explain what had befallen him and his companions after they had left the village, "We left almost immediately after you were discovered. We had a ship waiting at Ascalon to bring us home. However, we were no less deceived than you had been, for the ship's master betrayed us. Men of your order lay in wait for us half a league from Ascalon. Yet our God protected us, the ship bore fifteen of our Cathar brothers who had come out to meet us. If they had not done so, then we must surely have perished, and our treasure been lost. Once we were ambushed, all we could do was flee, not to save our lives, but the gift we carried. Our brethren, poorly armed, held the Templars at bay whilst we escaped. I think it unlikely any survived."

"And the men from the village who accompanied you, did they meet their deaths at Ascalon too?" I asked.

"No. We knew the Templars could not be held off for long and so we split up. Our guides, those men from the village you speak of, attempted to lead them astray with false tracks."

"What made you return here?" asked Reynald.

"We had meant to go north to Tyre, but my companion had been injured in the fight. We meant to avoid Acre for it is full of deception and treachery, but by the time we had come this far, his wound had turned bad. He is at present being cared for by the Benedictines."

"Then he is in good hands," said Reynald, "What about you, were you hurt?"

"A few scratches, nothing serious. Our other comrade was struck down and killed at the onset of the fighting," replied Hubert sadly.

"I am sorry to learn what has befallen your friends. But tell me, what treasure can this be that men are prepared to murder innocents for it?" Reynald asked.

I will never forget the look on Hubert's face at that moment, for mention of the treasure made it suddenly light up with pure joy as he spoke, "By far the greatest treasure in the entire world. Yet in itself it is not an object of any material value ... for it is a thing of the spirit."

"The object in the box!" I exclaimed.

"Yes. And for your own safety do not question me further."

"Yet it is because of this treasure that so many have died?" asked Reynald.

Hubert nodded.

"And it remains safe?"

"Yes. For the time being, however I fear those who lust after it are close. I believe they already know I am in Acre." Hubert glanced about himself anxiously.

Reynald said, "Your message spoke of needing a friend. I was always so and will not forsake you in your hour of need. How may I help?"

"I would ask two favours. Firstly, I would have you inquire how my friend is. It is far too dangerous for me to visit him. Secondly, I need to get a message to the men of the village. They must be assured that I have survived, and that the treasure is here in Acre."

"Your first request can easily be attended to, however, the second is more difficult," said Reynald. "Our order imposes strict rules. It would be impossible for me to leave without permission for so long. It would mean severe punishment."

"I do not ask that you return to their village," replied Hubert, "Only to the ford at Auja, and the place where in all likelihood you saw us being met."

"That may be easier," replied Reynald, "Sometimes there are errands to run to Athlit or Joppa. However, I may need a few days to arrange it. How soon must it be?"

"If they still live then they will wait there every morning at dawn until they are certain our cause is either won or lost. Their leader's name is Aref."

"Who are they?" I asked.

"They come from a long line of men who have served mankind by keeping the gift I spoke of from the grasp of despots."

"Why are Cathars involved?" was Reynald's question.

"This land is no longer a safe haven for such a prize. Some years ago they sought us out. And when they were certain of our integrity, they asked us to become its new guardians. You see they had heard tell of us, how we are not dazzled by material things and know them to be the works of Sataniel, the evil one."

Hubert then broke off. We were suddenly aware of the sound of approaching feet. Hubert plunged himself into the shadows.

"If you can help, bring news to me at midnight. I will wait here every second night."

"Your friend ..." Reynald called softly to Hubert as he shrank away into the darkness, "... What name shall we ask for at the Benedictine hospice?"

"Jean ... his name is Jean."

We walked back alongside the harbour wall. A few moments later we came face to face with three men of our house. The most senior knight amongst them was Wilhelm. However, I recognised all of them as having been in the Marshal's company when he returned to Acre.

"What brings you here at this hour?" Wilhelm asked us in his strong Germanic voice.

"We watch for a gang of cut-throats who have been robbing pilgrims," answered Reynald.

"Everyone in Acre is in the business of robbing pilgrims," Wilhelm laughed, as was his way showing a little too much appreciation for his own voice. "We seek a fugitive. Have you seen anyone around the harbour tonight?"

"No," we replied, but perhaps a little too eagerly.

"We heard voices," put in one of Wilhelm's companions.

"It was our voices you heard," I answered.

"Sound carries well at night through empty streets. Strange, only two of you ... I could have sworn there were three voices," said the knight.

Chapter Ten

Tuesday, 10 December, 1996

"Mr and Mrs Ledermann?" Rosemary Hines asked the two people waiting on the doorstep.

"Thanks for seeing us," Erich replied. Ruth didn't try to speak; all her energy was going into keeping the smile on her face, which under the circumstances was no mean feat. Jim had smelled perfume masking a fetid undertone; for Ruth it was like standing in the path of a discharge pipe from an abattoir.

'Give me strength!' Ruth's mind was screaming, 'How can Erich be so relaxed?'

The young woman turned away from them briefly as she closed the door. Ruth found it necessary to swallow hard in response to what she was seeing. As Rosemary's hand touched the door latch it transformed into something withered and decayed, a crone's hand. Fortunately the shock was brief.

'Just your gift,' Ruth reassured herself, 'Pointing out something about this woman's true nature.'

Ruth managed to smile when the unnervingly affable woman returned to them, physically rejuvenated.

Ruth had agreed to hypnotherapy as a means of preparation for this visit; Erich had used self-hypnosis techniques on himself too. She'd gone along with the idea, but really considered it unnecessary. However, she had not expected to be assailed by phenomena quite so powerful. It was clear that she had totally underestimated the site's potency.

"I'm Rosemary Hines, Administrator."

"Erich Ledermann," said Erich, thrusting out a hand like he was really delighted.

"I received a fax from your brother's company in Copenhagen yesterday afternoon and spoke with his secretary this morning."

"Thanks again for seeing us at such short notice. This is my wife," Erich gestured towards Ruth.

'Shit,' thought Ruth, 'My turn,' and repeated the phrase, 'Keep smiling,' to herself as she tendered a hand. "Ruth Ledermann," she managed.

Thankfully Rosemary Hines underwent no physical degenerations when their hands met. Even so, the experience was not pleasant, the woman's hand was icy cold, the texture of her skin coarse but at the same time slimy.

"Pleased to meet you," Ruth managed, squirming inside.

"Please, come through to our showroom," Rosemary smiled, leading the way.

Erich followed, shooting back a concerned glance at Ruth. Ruth replied with a reassuring nod to let him know she was coping, and then took a last look around. A whole load of money had been spent creating a pretty picture; a veneer was all it was. She sensed that agony and pain had long occupied this house; at least for those thirty-nine years recorded on the name plate; its source and the fountain-head of all the despair she could feel, like a hammer blow to her solar-plexus, was undoubtedly below ground. Erich had been right, at times the energy lay dormant, indeed it was silent now; she shuddered at the thought of it at full strength.

Her eye then caught a footprint near the front door. It was deep and wet, and had oozed up from below rather than having been trampled in on shoes. The footprint was one of seven or eight that led from the door to where she was currently standing. Her only pair of court shoes stood in a pool of the same stuff, which appeared on the carpet at every step she'd made. From its stench and the way it looked, it was a mixture of excrement and blood.

'This is only phenomena,' she told herself, 'Stay calm.' The soggy exudation burped and squelched as she prised her feet out from the faecal matter and followed Erich.

Rosemary Hines was showing Erich work they had commissioned.

"Our plates are extremely popular. This was our first series, a bestseller."

Erich read the title card, "Seasons."

Ruth peered into the cabinet, attempting to look interested.

"I'm afraid I'm unable to answer technical questions. Mr Hart is our expert. If your brother has any questions about glazes or firing methods, he'd be more than happy to fax the information to him."

"I'll tell him that."

"Your brother owns a chain of stores?"

"Yes, gift items. He's done well for himself. He started with a shop in Copenhagen back in 1951, now he has nineteen throughout Scandinavia." Erich was telling the truth.

"How did he come to hear of us?"

"I've no idea."

Ruth was impressed by the ease Erich managed when he lied.

"We live up North, Leeds. I speak to Hermann regularly, and I mentioned we were taking a few days to visit friends in Worthing. He asked if we'd look in on you, being so near."

"We're glad you did," Rosemary replied warmly, "May I offer you some coffee?"

"I'd adore some," said Erich, sounding like he could easily have taken off his shoes and settled down for a nap.

"Er ... no ... no, thank you." Ruth answered, appalled at the idea of putting anything into her mouth in that stinking atmosphere. "We had a late lunch."

"I can always put away a cup of coffee," chuckled Erich.

Once alone, Erich allowed the strain of his performance to show. He took hold of Ruth's wrist and squeezed it reassuringly.

Ruth tried once again to feign an interest in the porcelain. It was no use, each time she focused her attention on one of the cabinets, it felt as though something was creeping up behind her.

As far as Ruth was concerned, there was no reason to remain. Everything they could learn, short of storming the basement, had been achieved. She was annoyed by Erich's decision to take coffee.

The negativity contained by that house was truly awesome. Within just ten minutes, Ruth had developed a pounding headache and blurred vision. There were less obvious symptoms too; her body movement seemed less co-ordinated, and her arms and legs felt like they were weighted down; also her speech sounded sluggish, at least it seemed so to her, as if her tongue had doubled in size and was all but filling her mouth. But the growing feeling of nausea welling up in her stomach was the physical item hardest to deal with.

'How can I stop myself from chucking up?' she thought.

Rosemary returned with a tray and some brochures and invited her guests to sit on the sofa. She had brought three cups. "Are you sure I can't entice you, Mrs Ledermann?"

"Honestly. Thanks."

Rosemary presented Erich with his coffee along with a copy of their most recent catalogue.

"Our trade prices," she said, passing him a printed list. "We're currently working on our new catalogue. It will be mailed out in February. I'll add your brother to our database."

Ruth felt her stomach turn over, managed to placate it, but suspected it was only a temporary reprieve. Only adding to her distress, Erich began asking questions about how the mail order system worked.

'In God's name, how can the man sound so bloody interested?'

Finally, Erich put down an empty cup. "Very nice," he said rising, "Thank you for letting us see your delightful porcelain."

"You're most welcome," Rosemary replied with exquisite politeness, and led them out.

The excrement on the hall carpet was gone, just as Ruth had expected. Erich shook hands with Rosemary over the threshold. Ruth escaped with a friendly wave.

"How do you feel?" Erich asked as they strolled away from the house.

"Awful."

Erich hadn't really needed to ask, her face was green. He caught under her arm to lend support.

The car was a few streets away. Ruth set a fearsome pace, like a guided missile locked on target. When they were only a few yards from the car, she broke away from Erich and directed her upper body towards the gutter.

A young man in his mid-twenties was sitting in the driving-seat of Erich's car. He had been watching their return through the mirror and got out immediately when he saw Ruth vomiting.

"What's wrong with Ruth, Dad?"

"She'll be okay, Danny," Erich replied, gently stroking her shoulder. "The house was a bit overwhelming."

*

When Hannah Latimer saw Jim her first reaction was to assume he'd started drinking again; although it only took a moment to dispel this view. He seemed quite changed from how he'd been on Friday. Sophie recognised something was wrong too; shooting a worried glance at her mother when she and Jim had come in. It occurred to Hannah that he might be ill, he certainly looked pale, and the scratch on his face failed to improve his appearance any.

"I hope you don't mind. I had to drop some film off. And I thought I'd catch you and Soph while it was being developed."

"That's okay."

Jim looked sheepish. "I know I should've rung. You hadn't got plans?"

Hannah shook her head, "It's okay."

He attempted an easy smile; only confirming to his wife and daughter how tense he was.

"It was a spur of the moment thing. Sorry."

"Stop apologising. Can you stay to supper?"

"Not really. I've got to pick up some transparencies from Clerkenwell by six."

"Come down to the kitchen, I'll make us a cup of tea."

"I'm going to change, see you later Dad," Sophie said, giving her Mum a look in feminine semaphore which read, 'God he looks awful, find out what's wrong'.

Jim followed Hannah down to the kitchen. She put the kettle on to boil. He sat at the table.

"Want a sandwich?"

"I'm fine, thanks."

"When did you eat?"

He hadn't, so didn't answer. Hannah started slicing bread.

"Well, are you going to tell me?"

Jim put up no resistance. He needed to get the whole sordid tale of John Loxton off his chest. He described going to the chapel of rest with Bob, the shock of seeing Loxton's corpse, told her all about the flat, and how he had discovered the disgusting portfolios and the list of initials.

Hannah listened open-mouthed with incredulity throughout. "How could both of you have been so wrong about the man's age?"

Jim shook his head, it seemed like he had been shaking his head all day.

"There's more, isn't there?"

Jim hadn't wanted to discuss the rest. He sighed, "Ruth claims to have had some kind of psychic 'thing' about it all. She believes Loxton didn't commit suicide. According to her he was involved in something even worse than the paedophile stuff."

"Worse, Christ, what could be worse?"

Jim hesitated, "Last night at Loxton's, Bob found some railway tickets for Brighton, not one or two, literally hundreds, dating back thirty years."

Hannah was not a journalist for nothing; she immediately saw the possibility of a link between Loxton and the people currently employing Jim, "You think your porcelain people are involved?"

"I looked for any of their initials on the list, but nothing. Telephone numbers don't match either."

"What are these people like?"

Jim thought about the question for a moment before replying. "If you'd asked me that a few days ago, I'd have said ordinary, mundane even. It's weird, they seem excessively security conscious, secretive too. You can tell they don't like it if you ask too many questions. You'd expect them to have gold in their stockroom, not just china." He shuffled uncomfortably on his chair, face colouring a little with embarrassment, "To be honest, I feel apprehensive about the place." He omitted to mention the drains which caused headaches; or the sensations he felt going past the stockroom door; or meeting Mr Hart only a short time after encountering him in a dream; in fact, he avoided the dreams altogether.

"Active paedophiles would most likely be highly secretive and security conscious. So what does Ruth think is going on there?"

Jim shook his head, "You know I don't have much time for that kind of stuff."

"You're open-minded on most subjects, but when it comes to anything esoteric or spiritual you're completely closed down."

"What?"

"Don't you have even the slightest doubt? Don't you ever wonder about the millions of people in the world who believe there's something beyond our physical lives? Are they deluding themselves? Or is it because you're afraid to believe?"

Jim smiled at Hannah's directness, he expected it of her; it was one of the things he loved about her. He recalled not always being sceptical, as a child he would look up at the stars and understand that something had put them there.

"I've never seen any evidence to convince me otherwise," he replied.

"Mmmm," she answered.

At the treatment centre many had seemed to share a view that alcoholism was an illness with a spiritual dimension. Jim had always baulked at the idea, not only considering it preposterous but delusional too; nothing more than a need to give purpose, absolution even, to lives foolishly squandered; wishful thinking, that all those years spent pissing your life away were actually important years of spiritual development. Even so, over the past months, and in spite of himself, Jim had experienced an occasional twinge, a yearning, sometimes triggered by a piece of art or music, or the words of a poem, which seemed to speak directly to an inner world that he had once found hard to credit with existence.

It was 5.15pm, and he had to leave if he was going to reach the lab before it closed. Hannah suspected that Jim had only told her part of the story, but knew better than to waste her time trying to squeeze any more out of him. Finding Loxton's portfolio had obviously been a horrible shock.

"I have to go now Soph," he shouted upstairs.

Sophie descended the stairs with her hand on the banister, taking two steps at a time. He realised as he watched her, that for all her affectation of adulthood, she was still at least in part a child, his little girl. And suddenly he wished he could stay, be close at hand, to protect her from all the sick bastards in the world. For the first time as a father he wanted her to be grown up, safe from Loxton and filth like him.

"I'll ring you Thursday evening Dad. I'll let you know what time to pick me up from the station."

He wondered if she would be safe making the train journey alone. "Okay my love," he said.

Sophie placed her hands on his shoulders. Jim bent down and kissed her cheek and with their arms around each other walked out to his car.

"Thanks for the tea and sandwich, Han, and for listening."

"You're welcome," she replied, hugging him without any feelings of awkwardness. "Look after yourself."

Sophie moved away to give her parents breathing space; she liked to see them showing each other affection.

"You can talk to Ruth, Jim. Trust her. She really is your friend."

Jim nodded. He got into the car and started the engine. As he drove away, Hannah had her arm around Sophie's waist; both remained waving until he turned at the end of the street.

Another car engine started up.

"Is Dad alright? Did you see that scratch?"

"I'm sure he will be. Ruth'll keep an eye on him for us."

A car went by, going in the same direction as Jim. Sophie turned away to go back indoors. Hannah glanced up at the car; its driver was unidentifiable in the dark. She didn't recognise the car, but assumed it must be a neighbour from the way he looked at her. Hannah thought she saw something on his head, a hat of some sort.

The traffic out of London had moved interminably slowly and it was 8.30pm by the time Jim reached home. He was disappointed to see no light on in Ruth's place again. He checked for mail and answer-phone messages, but there were neither. He was feeling tired, he'd been awake fifteen hours and needed a decent night's sleep. Unfortunately bed had not proved itself to be a very cosy place lately.

In fact, the thought of sleeping only seemed to bring last night's dream back to the forefront of his mind. Hart had been a good deal younger in the dream, but undeniably it was the same man.

"It has to be a trick of the mind ... like déjà vu. Somewhere I must have seen a photograph of him."

Jim was so tense he jumped when the telephone rang.

It was Bob Isherwood. One side of Jim wished to discover nothing else, but another part had to keep probing. The whole thing seemed to have grown out of all proportion, festering away like some unpleasant but fascinating boil.

"What happened last night after I left?" Jim asked.

"Ian Rice came over with two officers. They were very pleased with what we found ... you found, but of course, they think I did the finding."

"Pleased?"

"You know, pleased to get their hands on that list ... sixty-three in total. Ian reckons it'll put a lot of those bastards out of action. Some of them can be identified from the photographs."

Jim hated to think about those images.

"What time did you get away?"

"Christ, two-thirty. Ian gave me a lift home. I told him we'd gone to the chapel of rest together. I thought it best, seeing as the funeral director saw us."

"So I'm supposed to have left you after the funeral parlour?"

"Yes, I said I went to Loxton's place alone."

"What did Ian Rice have to say about Loxton's ageing?"

"What d'you expect him to say? We must've been mistaken. Some people look a lot younger than they really are ... all the usual crap ... same as you or I'd be saying if we hadn't known Loxton and seen him with our own eyes."

"Mmm," said Jim, eager to move the subject on from ninety-one year old cadavers. He asked, "What did the solicitor want?"

In response to this question Bob snorted with contempt, "Total load of bollocks … nothing … wasted two hours of my bloody afternoon! I even wore my best bib and tucker to go and see him. Stupid old fart had to call me into his office just to present me with a receipt. It's for something Loxton deposited in his bank a couple of weeks ago."

"Did he know what it was?"

"Not a clue."

"Do you think it might be more stuff like we found last night?"

"I suppose it might be, might well be. If it is I'll pass it straight on to Ian." Bob then returned to his favourite pet hate, the legal profession, "This solicitor must've been a contemporary of effin' Loxton's … older brother perhaps. This bloke was so old he was nearly ga-ga. I'm telling you no lie, he needed a care-nurse, not a bloody secretary. No bloody idea! Solicitors, typical! Useless bloody wankers, like the Pope's balls! He'll probably invoice for a couple of hundred, 'Services to the estate of J. effing Loxton Esquire'. Blood sucking bastards!"

It was always amusing to hear Bob engage his invective regarding the legal profession. However, Jim was not entertained by anything else Bob said.

"By the way, I did some digging for you … well, Daphne did. I asked her to find out what she could about Niedermayer & Hart."

"Yes. What?" Jim asked lamely. He felt his spine grow rigid.

"What date did you say they were established?"

Jim cleared his throat, "It says 1957 on the plaque."

"I thought I'd heard you right. That's weird."

"What?"

"People usually want to exploit it if they've been in business a long time."

Jim was beginning to squirm on his end of the line.

"According to the records at Company House, Niedermayer & Hart began trading back in 1894 …"

Jim intuitively knew there was more to come.

"Sorry, having trouble reading Daph's notes … oh yeah, the company was registered back in 1894. The directors were, J. Hart, R. Hines and …"

"N. Cureton."

108

Chapter Eleven

Tuesday, 10 December, 1996

Ruth came out onto the doorstep as soon as she heard Jim's car pull into the driveway. The arrival triggered a light on the garage wall, picking out Jim's features in its powerful halogen beam. He looked tired she thought; an air of disorientation about him. Ruth knew it could only have been desperation that had brought him there.

Whatever had happened to him since Sunday had certainly taken its toll. Ruth had felt the presence of an overwhelmingly malign force in the house in Barnswick Square; attempting to rationalise it, like Jim must have, would have got him nowhere; trying to apply common sense to such phenomena would simply amount to mental torture. Jim had done well, she thought, exposed for several days, alone, without any protection to the house's underbelly.

They exchanged guarded smiles as he stepped from the car. A truce between true friends needed no words of justification.

"I thought about taking a drink. I wanted to escape ... forget everything. I had an idea to drive off, find some hotel in the back of beyond, get drunk and never sober up. It scared me shitless!"

"But you didn't."

Jim managed a smile, "Hannah said to trust you."

"You told Hannah?"

"Not really, not everything. I felt too embarrassed. Nothing makes sense. If I told a shrink he'd probably have me locked away."

"Believe me, you aren't crazy. You'll be surprised to hear me say this, but I've always considered you one of the sanest people I know."

She was right, he was downright incredulous.

"Hannah asked me why I denied the existence of anything beyond the here and now."

"And?"

"The truth is I've always been frightened of anything I don't understand ... people, places, any new experience. Alcohol solved the problem. While the drink worked, I felt whole."

"We went to Barnswick Square today," Ruth said, deciding this was as good a time as any to broach the subject.

"You saw the house?"

"We went inside."

Jim's jaw dropped.

"Erich arranged it through his brother in Denmark. He sells giftware. We pretended we were there on his behalf."

Jim registered surprise but not the half-anticipated anger at their interference in his affairs.

"And?"

"I've never known anything like it. When the door opened there was this foul smell ... really disgusting. Imagine a mediaeval plague pit and you get the idea. After a couple of minutes inside my head was throbbing, my vision was starting to blur and I wanted to throw up."

Jim listened in amazement; to a lesser extent he'd experienced the same symptoms.

"There was phenomena too. I saw pools of blood and shit on the carpet, wherever I stepped ... as if it was bubbling up from the cellar."

"That's where it is, isn't it? Every time I walk past the cellar door I flinch."

"Erich and I agree the cellar is definitely the source." Ruth was shivering, mostly but not entirely due to the winter night. "We were on the ground floor, but it was like standing on ... I don't know, some kind of landing stage, and beneath, beneath where I stood there was something loathsome ... it felt like I was standing over a vast lake of blood."

*

Jim had never been in Erich's sitting-room before and immediately observed that it was far tidier than any room either he or Ruth possessed. In the fireplace there were logs burning, and alcoves on either side of the chimney breast were heavily laden with books. Just as in the hallway and study, all the walls bore framed photographs, mainly of Erich and Danny, but some of Ruth too. Erich quite clearly didn't believe in photograph albums. There was a whole series of school photographs, Danny's progression from kindergarten to sixth form, as well as photos of him rock-climbing, sailing, hang-gliding, surfing and swimming. About twenty trophies and certificates lined the top of a sideboard; Danny was clearly the outdoor type. There were also half a dozen photographs of father and son messing about in their dinghy. Jim was surprised by a picture of Erich firing a gun skywards; it seemed out of keeping with his passive image.

"Danny and I are sport nuts," said Erich, as he entered with a tray of sandwiches and wearing an 'I Love New York' apron. "I learned to shoot in the army and I love it. But I wouldn't like to kill anything. I shoot clay pigeons."

Erich passed out side plates, mugs of tea and offered the sandwiches around, "The best place to begin with defiant spirit forces is to keep the stomach full, so it weights your feet down to the ground," he chuckled, perhaps turning the Austrian accent up a bit for comic effect.

Jim was relieved to be in the company of friends. The point had been reached where he could go it alone no longer. He was hardly ready to suspend all his scepticism, but he was willing to listen. After all, he knew of nobody else who might have at least some of the answers to the questions beginning to dominate his every waking moment.

Jim started his story where it began, six days ago with the newspaper article. He gave a blow by blow account of his life, awake and asleep, since the hypnotherapy session.

Ruth and Erich only interrupted him at a couple of points, to elaborate or clarify a detail. They seemed as mystified as he and Bob had been by Loxton's rapidly ageing corpse.

When Jim finished, Ruth took over. She had made notes of her dreams and all the other experiences, visual and physical.

"How did you arrange for your brother to get you inside?" Jim asked once Ruth had completed her account.

"Danny owns a computer; he emailed his Uncle Hermann in Denmark. I didn't give him much detail, said a friend of mine was working there and experiencing some psychic phenomena. Not really the truth, but near enough. I didn't want to worry poor Hermann. Even though he's eighteen months younger than me, Hermann has always been concerned about my rash nature. Anyway, an hour or so later he faxed Niedermayer & Hart, requesting that his brother and sister-in-law might visit on his behalf."

"He's a devious old sod," said Ruth admiringly.

Erich chuckled, "Brother Hermann added a note of caution in his reply to Danny," He retrieved a folded piece of paper from the mantelpiece and began reading, "*Niedermayer & Hart will see Mr and Mrs Ledermann tomorrow afternoon at 2.30. Danny - Please remind father he is seventy and his commando days ended fifty years ago.*

Strongly advise you keep an eye on him. I fear he is still a little wild - Much love, Uncle Hermann."

"After that Danny insisted on driving us there," laughed Ruth.

Erich suddenly remembered something, "Crikey! I promised I'd ring Danny tonight to let him know how you were," he said to Ruth, and then looking down at his wristwatch, "No matter, only ten minutes past eleven ... still early evening for Danny!"

"What did you hope to achieve by going to Barnswick Square?"

Erich thought a moment before replying, "I wanted to double check. Ruth has a psychic power far beyond my own; even so, visions can be misleading. If Ruth was right, then we were dealing with something powerful. It was important to verify it, and get a fuller understanding."

"Were your experiences inside the house the same as Ruth's?"

"I didn't suffer any of the visual phenomena she had to deal with. The awful smell was there, but not so powerfully I think ... I too recognised the cellar as the source."

"Do you understand what it is? Can it be ..." Jim struggled for the right words, "... got rid of?"

"Since hearing about that photographer, I'm inclined to believe it takes some kind of physical form. It may partly possess the minds and bodies of those who serve it ... or it may possibly inhabit someone entirely." Erich glanced at Ruth; they looked extremely solemn, "We agreed it was dormant at the time we visited."

"What is it, some kind of supernatural evil?" asked Jim.

"That depends what you mean by the words supernatural and evil," replied Erich. "We give the label supernatural to anything that exists outside the bounds of our understanding. To my mind, it's merely universal law unfolding. As for evil, it is essentially the same whether practised here on earth or at a more ethereal level of existence. Where is evil found without ego ... a will driving it? Evil in itself has limited goals and a very shallow mind."

Jim was looking nonplussed. Ruth came in to help out, "At our level of existence, we experience division ... duality. Life on our earth is the most physical and therefore the most difficult. Yet the plains of existence nearest to us, although not quite as turbulent, are fairly similar and much the same goes on there as here. What we believe to be taking place in Hove is that an entity from one of these lower plains has built up some kind of power base ... effectively straddling both worlds."

"Like a sort of mini-god?" asked Jim, suddenly beginning to feel very doubtful about all this.

She nodded. "We think it physically manifests itself in some way, but like Erich said, we aren't sure."

"What about Loxton, any theories?"

Erich shook his head grimly, "I don't begin to understand. How could the ageing process be inhibited like that?"

Erich was convinced that both Ruth and Jim's dreams were of major significance. "This Hart, he was younger in your dream, you say?"

"That's right. In the dream … if it was the same man, he was late twenties, early thirties."

"You didn't doubt they were the same person before?" said Erich, thinking how insidiously doubt sheds its seed.

Jim was almost writhing in his chair, "But how … how could it be the same man?" His voice began to rise, "For Christ's sake, it appeared to be centuries ago!"

"Come on Jim, listen to yourself," Ruth interrupted. "A bit co-incidental don't you think, both of us dreaming about the same situation? Then a few hours after having your dream, you meet someone who was actually in it?"

Jim, acknowledging that he didn't possess an adequate riposte, slumped into his armchair with a sigh.

Erich spoke calmly, "You've probably heard of hypnotic regression. If you'll allow me, I'd like to guide you back to that place in your dream. I'm convinced this is a past life memory."

Although Jim was unsure about past lives, in truth the idea had already crossed his mind. And he was really desperate for some answers. Even so, Erich and Ruth were surprised when Jim replied with a flat but certain, "Okay … are we going to do it right away?"

"No," said Erich, "It's too late, and anyway it may not happen straight off."

"What shall I do in the morning?" asked Jim.

"Don't go anywhere near Niedermayer & Hart," advised Ruth.

"But I can't do that," he replied, "This is my first employment in two years. I have to complete the job."

They understood how important it was.

"Hart didn't suspect anything from the way you reacted to him?" asked Ruth.

"I'm sure he didn't. We alkies are accomplished liars."

"Then pretend everything's normal and finish off the catalogue," said Erich.

"Let me know as soon as you get home tomorrow, and make sure you get out of there before dark," warned Ruth.

"You don't have to remind me, not after Monday ... when I got there before it was light."

"Why not stay the night, there's a spare bed. It would save you driving back?" suggested Erich.

"That would've been great, but I left the transparencies at home. I'd only have to detour in the morning to get them."

"I'm coming with you," said Ruth, "Erich was going to bring me back anyway. He tried to tell you when you rang but you were in such a hurry and put the phone down before he got the chance."

The thought of Ruth coming back to the cottages with him was comforting. Jim held out his hand to Erich, "I can't honestly say that I believe everything I've heard, or even remotely understand it, but it was good to get everything off my chest. I'm grateful to you both for listening."

"A little healthy scepticism makes the world go round," said Erich.

Erich was about to show them out when Ruth reminded, "Don't forget to ring Danny!"

"Crikey!" said Erich, rushing over to the telephone, "I'd better do this straight away. Poor Danny, I don't like to let him down. I'm sorry, do you mind letting yourselves out?" Erich waved goodbye and began dialling his son's number. "We'll speak soon," he called after them.

*

A discreet distance away, a car was parked with a clear view of Erich's bungalow. Within its dark interior was the red haired man, Picton. He had been waiting patiently. He watched Jim and Ruth get into the car and drive away. He allowed a few moments before starting up his engine, then followed after them.

Hugh's Tale

V

Next morning we went to the Benedictine house and asked to see the injured pilgrim who had been brought to them. Unfortunately, the wound to his shoulder had become black and stinking with infection, and he had died the previous night. We were shown into the chapel to view Jean's corpse; he had been the eldest of the three Cathar travellers.

The brother who had cared for him was brought to us.

"Which of you is Reynald de Sauveterre?" he asked, much to our astonishment, for we had not offered our names.

"I am," answered Reynald.

"Please wait here," replied the brother. He left us for a few minutes only to return bearing a small bundle, saying, "The man who brought him here asked that the pilgrim's belongings be handed over to a Templar bearing your name."

Reynald unrolled the bundle. Jean the Cathar had allowed himself the meagrest of possessions. Some undergarments, a water flask, a piece of parchment bearing the Lord's Prayer, a small knife and the woollen blanket his belongings were wrapped in. The only object not entirely practical was a little beaker made of green glass that had been wrapped in a piece of muslin. The cup was smaller than half the span of a man's hand at its lip, and bore some writing about the rim.

"These letters are Greek I believe," said Reynald, "Good brother, is there anyone in this house who might tell us their meaning?"

"Let me look," replied the monk, "I spent some years in Antioch, and learned much of the Greek tongue there." The Benedictine took the glass and peered closely at it. "A fascinating object," he said, "An antiquity, I'll vouch." The brother began to mouth the letters silently to himself before saying, "Yes, a simple enough little phrase ... ἑταῖρε, ἐφ' ὅ πάρει ... an old drinking legend probably ... something akin to ... *Friend, what are you here for?*"

We thanked the brother and left. Reynald smuggled the bundle into our house beneath his cloak, and hid it behind his sleeping pallet in the dortoir.

Shortly before noon on the same day, an opportunity came to fulfil Hubert's second request. A rider brought dispatches from Joppa; the man had arrived in the early stages of a fever, and was taken to our infirmary. The papers he'd been carrying required a reply, and Reynald offered himself as a replacement.

"Then I must deliver the bundle to Hubert at the rendezvous tomorrow night," I said.

"Very well, but take care, Hugh" advised Reynald.

The following night I went to the harbour before midnight and waited until the one o'clock bell was long past, but Hubert did not come. I returned to our house, and hid the bundle behind my own pallet. The forty knights I shared the dortoir with were all sleeping, or so I thought, as I changed into the habit and took to my bed. Yet one of my companions could not have been asleep, covetously watching the dead man's possessions from behind slitted eyelids.

I must have fallen asleep the instant my head met the pillow.

When Brother Ferdinand shook me awake I recall having no idea of the time. He held a finger to his fat lips. "Say nothing," he whispered, "You must rise. Come."

Confused and half asleep, I did as instructed and followed him barefooted from the dortoir. Outside the sleeping room two brothers in uniform awaited us. One of the knights then went into the dortoir, whilst the other accompanied myself and Brother Ferdinand.

"What is this about?" I asked, suspecting full well that it concerned the Cathars and our deceptions.

"The Marshal will explain," said Ferdinand as he waddled down the staircase ahead of me, looking somewhat preposterous in his uniform. We observe a monastic tradition within the confines of our house, and I could not recall seeing Brother Ferdinand out of the habit before.

I assumed I was being taken to Marshal Jerome's chamber, but soon discovered that this was not to be the case. My apprehension grew as Brother Ferdinand led us into his personal domain, the cellars.

I had seldom had occasion to visit them, for Brother Ferdinand jealously guarded his office, and did not welcome intrusion.

He led us through a high vaulted room, the air pungent with the smells of salted fish and meat and the musky aroma of casks steeped in wine and ale, then entered a side room that served as his private office.

Here, Ferdinand drew open a small but stout door that lay concealed behind a curtain.

"There is more to my cellars than meets the eye," he said, lowering his head as he began to descend a flight of steep steps.

"These tunnels are the legacy of the Seljuks, who held the City before it was liberated by the armies of Christendom."

I hesitated a moment.

"Keep walking," said the knight behind me, poking his gauntlet into my ribs as encouragement.

At the base of many steps we went through a tunnel hewn out of rock and lit by torches. This corridor ran beyond the extent of the torchlight, fading away into darkness. A short distance along this tunnel was a door. Brother Ferdinand stopped here and drew it open.

When I saw within I knew that my growing trepidation had been justified.

The room was well-lit; seated upon two benches on either side were nine knights, all officers of our house. At the farthest wall was an altar, laid with a cloth of indigo and embroidered in gold; upon it were fine candelabra and a golden crucifix encrusted with jewels; before this altar, in a great chair, sat Marshal Jerome. He was gazing severely in my direction.

Brother Ferdinand, standing alongside the door and looking pleased with himself, now beckoned me to enter. I contemplated escape, but the knight covering my back had anticipated my thought and drawn his blade. Coming down the steps behind him I saw the knight who had entered the dortoir, holding Jean's bundle beneath his arm. There was no alternative but to go inside.

Having entered the chamber I learned immediately why Hubert had failed to meet me. He had been caught and was incarcerated there; the poor man was chained to the wall, his arms raised above his head in manacles. The serjeant that had been in our company when Reynald had first set eyes on Hubert was standing before him; he smiled cunningly as I entered. Hubert was stripped naked, his body cut and bleeding from the many punishments inflicted by the serjeant.

"I see we have at least one of the conspirators," Jerome said haughtily.

"Say nothing!" called out Hubert to me weakly, "Your silence will be rewarded in the hereafter!"

The serjeant responded to Hubert's outburst by jabbing a mailed fist into his cheek. The force of the blow drove the Cathar's head against the wall, knocking him half-senseless.

"Chain up our new prisoner beside his ally," ordered the Marshal.

I was manacled alongside the wretched Hubert.

"I found this bundle of rags behind his pallet," said the knight who had come from my dortoir.

"Set it before us," said Jerome.

"No!" cried Hubert imploringly, "You will serve only Sataniel. I beg you in the spirit of the nameless one, resist this temptation!"

"Silence the heretic," ordered Jerome.

The serjeant willingly obeyed the command by driving his fist again into Hubert's face. Blood issued from his nose, and his front teeth were shattered by the viciousness of the blow.

"This enemy of God would have us leave to him and his heretical religion the greatest gift in all Christendom. We see by his anguish that our acquisition greatly troubles him." The bundle had been placed on the floor before Jerome, who now rose to his feet.

"A new order has appeared in the world today. Christ's banner will once again be raised above Jerusalem. The prince of darkness and his unbelieving sons will be exterminated from the face of the earth. And our names will be praised forever more."

Upon hearing Jerome's words the congregation of knights raised fists and cheered, a great zeal burning within them.

"Never more will pilgrims beg permission from the spawn of Lucifer to visit the holy sites. With the sword of Christ in our hands we will wage eternal war against evil, here in the flesh and in the other world."

Jerome's speech had considerable impact upon his admirers. Yet much to his annoyance, not even the threat of being struck by the stout serjeant could silence Hubert.

"Fools, you are not dealing with a mere bauble. Its power is not of this world. In the spirit of the true God I beseech you! Only by renouncing material things can enlightenment be attained from the cup."

Only then did I understand. The glass beaker that had been in my possession was the prize, and I knew of only one cup that might be so bitterly sought: the holy cup, drunk from at the last supper, and in which Joseph of Arimathea had caught Christ's blood as He died upon the cross.

Jerome knelt and started to unwrap the bundle.

I recalled the words translated by the Benedictine, *Friend, what are you here for?* They suddenly began to reverberate within me with new meaning.

As Jerome uncovered the cup, I knew where I had heard similar words; they were very like those spoken by our saviour to his betrayer at Gethsemane.

Without thinking, I blurted out, "The cup of Christ!"

Jerome, holding up the beaker in his hand, glared angrily at me. The look of prideful conquest had vanished from his face, which was now consumed by hate and loathing.

"Fool," he scoffed, "You are easily deceived. Do you expect me to take this trinket for the holy vessel of the King of Kings?"

Then Hubert interrupted again, this time to laugh mockingly, "The fool is recognised by his actions. Did you think I would leave the holy cup where you might easily find it? And were it indeed the cup, it would prove no use - for vipers such as you can only remain as vipers."

Jerome, infuriated by the Cathar's contempt and insane with the knowledge that he had been tricked, rushed at Hubert and drawing the dagger from his belt slashed it across the Cathar's throat. Hubert's warm blood sprayed onto my cheek. I could do nothing to assist him, gurgling and choking as his life-blood gushed from his neck.

Jerome stared in a crazed leer at the dying man's contorted face. He said, "In your last moments watch me drink a toast in your heretical blood."

Then placing the beaker against the severed veins of Hubert's neck, he filled it with the Cathar's blood.

"In the name of God, no!" I cried.

Jerome scowled contemptuously at me as he drained the glass.

I could not bear to watch and began to recite the Lord's Prayer.

Jerome immediately refilled the cup with Hubert's blood and said to his knights, who stared at him in horrified silence, "The wine is flowing, which of you will join me?" Hubert's blood was smeared across his lips and teeth as he held the cup before him.

A chilled silence was at first the only response to the invitation.

"Not one of you? Come now, a sip of red wine?" He looked at Hubert, in his death spasms, "Quickly, the cask runs dry; you gutless dogs!"

"I'll share a cup," said Laszlo, a knight from the land of Hungary.

"I will join you," said Wilhelm, the same knight who had come upon Reynald and myself at the harbour.

"Then let me drink," joined in Cornelius, the Venetian.

These three alone came forward. Laszlo was about to take the beaker when, catching sight of the Marshal's face, he stepped back in terror. The beaker fell from Jerome's hand, and the glass smashed to pieces on the floor at my feet.

Jerome's face had drained of blood, and his eyes rolled white in their sockets. He fell to the ground, gripping around his throat and gasping for breath. All the knights were gaping in horror at the sight of their leader as he writhed about in agony.

Jerome's features bore a most hideous expression, as if every demon in hell tore into him. Then after a most violent convulsion, appalling to witness, his body fell still, and he breathed no more.

Chapter Twelve

Half an hour after dawn, Jim backed his car into the space between the Mercedes and the white van. Neither vehicle appeared to have been moved since yesterday. By the time he'd finished parking, the gates had shut. The sight of this brought on a twinge of claustrophobia and made his tongue feel thick and dry.

"Just get on and complete the shoot," he told himself.

He released his seat belt and stepped out of the car. The sticker on the white van's window, which he couldn't make out in the dark of Monday morning, caught his eye again. It was immediately identifiable; the red heart of the blood donor service and the words 'Give Blood'.

Jim was staring at it across the roof of his car when Rosemary's sudden, "Good morning Jim," made him jump. He hadn't heard her arrive.

"Oh. Good morning," he fumbled, "I, er ... I didn't hear you!"

Rosemary Hines said nothing, facial muscles implacable, as if her smile had been double baked like the pattern on a biscuit.

"Yesterday's transparencies," Jim said, handing her the box he was carrying. "I'm satisfied. I hope you agree."

"Judging by what we've seen already, I think that's very likely," she answered, with a soupcon of charm to garnish.

Rosemary led on to the house. A gloom descended on Jim as he followed, and as the outer door shut behind them with a resounding clang, for a split second he underwent a moment nearly bordering on despair. He took a deep breath and prepared himself for the walk past the cellar door; holding his breath as he crossed to the lift. Unconsciously his stride lengthened, like a child who avoids a certain spot because of the bogey-man.

It seemed to work, he had reached the lift without experiencing a shudder. He leaned against the lift wall and breathed a secret sigh of relief. In his hip he could feel the contours of his Nikon camera, still in the jacket pocket where it had remained since photographing Loxton; it showed how thoroughly distracted he'd been ever since.

Aboard, Rosemary swung the sliding door across and pressed the button marked one. There came the now familiar clunk of gears that preceded motion on the old machinery's part. Then, in the half second before they began to ascend, a delayed tremor ran through Jim's body. Rosemary made no comment, nor did her expression alter, but when Jim caught her eyes as the lift began its upward journey, he thought he glimpsed cold pleasure there.

*

Isla drove Bob the three miles to Epping tube station as she did every morning. The subject of conversation on these daily trips was usually to do with one or more of their three daughters. The two eldest girls were away at university, the youngest only fifteen was still at home.

"We'll have to take both cars. Dad can't drive all the way to the Lake District," Isla said.

She was talking about the family plans for Christmas. They were taking a large cottage in a beautiful setting overlooking Lake Windermere, just as they had done the previous year. As usual, Bob complained that he'd not been consulted and everything was arranged without his consent. His protests were invariably good-natured, something expected of him, and the four females in his life paid little attention. He liked to present himself as a gruff Antipodean bear, rather than the New Zealand lamb he really was.

This year the two eldest girls were bringing boyfriends along. Isla had already warned him against encouraging the boys to accompany him down the local pub too often.

"Rachel could pick your parents up!" Bob suggested. Rachel was the eldest with her own car.

"She's taking Robin," Isla answered.

"Why can't she take Robin and her Gran and Grandad?"

"Would you have wanted to spend six hours in a car with your new boyfriend and your grandparents when you were twenty-one?"

"Be lucky to do it in six with your parents. I swear, last year they had to relieve themselves at every services en route. I wondered if they were secretly compiling a book entitled, 'The Good Loo Guide'!"

Isla laughed. "I really ought to travel on ahead to get things ready."

"So you expect muggins here to do the bedpan run?"

Isla pulled into the kerb, a little way from the entrance to the station.

"You know my Mum and Dad adore you."

"Okay," he shrugged, a twinkle in his eye, "But I'll expect them both strictly 'nil by mouth' for the previous forty-eight hours." Bob reached across and planted a kiss on his wife's lips. "See you tonight," he said, getting out.

"Let me know if you're going to be late," she called after him.

Bob winked back at his wife and waved a hand before disappearing into the station.

Isla checked her rear view mirror before driving off. A young man of very slight build was getting out of a car in the distance; she'd noticed his car behind her once or twice on the route from home.

*

Jim began taking photographs immediately. Work helped relieve his uneasiness, at least to an extent; around 9.30am Rosemary brought him coffee.

"The transparencies are faultless," she complimented.

"Thanks," he replied, taking a sip of coffee. "No Nicholas today?"

For once Rosemary showed no hesitation about replying, as though it pleased her to say, "He's bringing some unfinished business to a close."

About forty pieces of porcelain remained to be photographed. Rosemary took any completed items away and returned with the outstanding ones.

"That's everything," she said, "When these are done you're finished."

Jim was already finding the throbbing pressure behind his eyeballs unbearable. His tolerance to the house had if anything diminished. The first twinges of headache had appeared after only about half an hour. He clung on until 10.30am, by which time his skull felt like it was splitting in two.

He walked along the seafront until his head cleared and returned to the house in under fifteen minutes. He possessed an almost manic urgency to finish, and under normal conditions he could easily have completed the remaining day's work by one o'clock. However, conditions were far from normal, and within no time at all his physical symptoms had returned.

Bob had checked the night before that he'd packed everything into his briefcase the bank would require; Loxton's death certificate, the necessary papers authorising him to act as Loxton's executor, sufficient identification, and of course the receipt itself. Bob had meant to pick up the package on his way to work, but the train was delayed. He had an appointment with a publisher in his office at 10am, so the Loxton business would have to wait until lunchtime.

Everyone was busy at their desks when he arrived at the office. He was greeted by a chorus of, "Hi Bob!" except for Daphne, who said "Glad you could join us!"

"I have to travel by train," he exclaimed, "Unlike you I don't possess my own personal broomstick!"

"Funny that," she replied without pausing, "From the way you sit around, I could've sworn you had one inserted up your backside."

Bob, unable to think of an appropriately rude reply, said, "Just get me some effin' coffee!" and disappeared into his office.

*

When Jim took a break for lunch at 12.30pm he'd been working so slowly there were still more than twenty pieces left.

He bought a sandwich and a tea, and walked about the streets until his head cleared again. He found himself in a part of Hove unknown to him and came upon a small church, which after a moment's hesitation he entered. He had never before gone into a religious building with any purpose other than sightseeing. Inside there were several people, and Jim recoiled momentarily. Two women and one man were seated individually at pews down by the altar rapt in thought, while two other women were quietly arranging flowers. Jim sat at a pew near the door.

The smell of damp and stone, wood and polish filled his head like incense. The idea of generations of people coming here to pray, at least attempting to think good thoughts, seemed like balm to his troubled mind. And when he left, he was surprised to learn that he had remained there for almost forty minutes. He heard no angels tuning harps, yet the stillness of the unremarkable little church had somehow reinvigorated him.

*

Bob's meeting with the publisher had gone well, and by 12.15 he'd completed his workload for the morning. Normally he broke for lunch round 1pm, usually taking a beer and sandwich with Daphne. The others generally took their lunch breaks earlier to ensure the office was always manned.

Loxton's bank was only ten minutes walk away on Tottenham Court Road. Bob went to the enquiries desk and presented the receipt to the clerk. The bank clerk returned in a couple of minutes holding a sealed brown package about six or seven inches thick. Bob thanked him, found a clear patch of counter and opened one end of it. He slipped the packet's contents out a couple of inches and peered inside. It contained a pile of thin glossy catalogues, and from the way each one bulged he could see a number of loose pages had been inserted into them.

Had Bob looked around at that moment he might have noticed the attention being paid to him by a scrawny young man in a badly fitting suit who was also displaying some anxiousness. The young man's expression relaxed once Bob had replaced the material back inside its wrapping.

Bob placed the package under his arm and left the bank.

Nicholas Cureton came out a few seconds after him, frustration written on his face as Bob successfully hailed and then leapt into a taxi. Nicholas looked furiously about him; then a moment later a car drew up and he got in.

"Follow that taxi, is it, Guv?" Picton said in his idea of a Cockney accent, smiling inanely.

Nicholas didn't bother to reply; it was blatantly obvious he despised his red-haired colleague.

In the back of the cab Bob opened up the package. On the cover of each catalogue in a fine copperplate script was printed *Niedermayer & Hart, Fine Porcelain*. Scrawled roughly across each one in marker pen, was the year's date. He didn't count, but there seemed to be one for every year, the top one marked '96, down to the one at the bottom inscribed with a large '57. They were everything anyone would expect of porcelain catalogues, except that interleaved between almost every page were several press cuttings, sometimes as many as a dozen. These were drawn from local newspapers from all over the country, and each article referred to a different missing person. Bob read the first one that came to hand. It had been taken from *The Hull Bugle* and was dated, 10 January, 1958:

Anthony Dawson, twenty years of age, an apprentice electrician, has been missing since last Tuesday. His parents, Mr and Mrs Jack Dawson of Hull, are deeply concerned about him. They ask anyone who may have information about their son's whereabouts to contact the local constabulary. Anthony left home wearing a light check jacket in the early evening, intending, he told his mother, to take a stroll. No-one has seen him since.

Bob flicked through the glossy pages that held, it seemed, a hundred or more of these sad tales. He stuffed them back into the package as the cab reached Lexington Street, paid the driver and buzzed Daphne to let him in.

Daphne could see he was troubled.

"Everything okay Bob?"

"I don't think so Daph. Could you get Ian Rice for me at the Met?"

"Yes, of course."

Bob disappeared into his office.

Daphne found the number of the Metropolitan police, picked up the telephone and was about to dial when the entry phone buzzed.

Bob had arranged some of the cuttings from the package onto his desk. There were so many, he quickly ran out of space.

He was about to examine them more closely when he heard a noise, a dull thud, from the outer office.

"Daph?" he called, and, receiving no answer he opened his office door to investigate.

Two grinning men were standing in the outer office on the far side of Daphne's desk. Daphne was nowhere to be seen. One of these men was physically quite unprepossessing, like someone in their early teens. The red-haired man with him was also rather short, although broad and thickset, and unlike his companion scruffily dressed.

"Who the hell are you? Where's my assistant?" asked Bob, immediately sensing something was very wrong.

"Had an accident," said the red-haired man, gesturing towards his feet.

"Fell over," said the other, grinning.

Bob had met danger in his life many times but only in that moment did he truly understand fear. He felt his legs weaken and begin to shake; cautiously he stepped forward and peered over Daphne's desk. She was lying on the floor beside the desk, head and neck twisted at an impossible angle, eyes staring blankly. Bob let out a short gasp and recoiled as her legs twitched in a post death spasm.

"Shame," said Picton. "What I'd call a victim of circumstance."

Bob side-stepped round the desk and smashed his fist into the red-haired man's face, who made no effort to defend himself. Bob had meant the punch to hurt, and although it brought blood to the man's lip, it had strangely little effect. His target was still standing and still smiling; Bob knew instinctively this was not the time to stand and fight. He ran for the door but Picton was too fast, he pounced on Bob and brought him crashing to the floor.

Bob was face to face with his attacker, completely helpless under the powerful man's weight.

"You've looked at things you ought not to see," said Picton, through his bloodied smiling teeth.

The small-framed man stepped into Bob's line of vision, grinning maliciously. But it was the long-bladed paper knife that he deliberately lifted off Daphne's desk that really seized Bob's attention.

The red-haired man placed a hand over Bob's mouth.

*

An hour after getting back from lunch, Jim rubbed his sore eyes and walked over to the window. He was halfway through the final set of twelve; a series entitled Canine Heroes. Number one in this series was the mythical she-wolf that succoured Romulus and Remus, along with White Fang, Lassie, and Rin-Tin-Tin amongst its cast of fictional four-legged heroes. The series' blurb presented Blackfriars Bobby and Gelert, billed as the loyal hound of Llywelyn the Great, as factional offerings, with Brave St Bernard as an unnamed generic specimen.

Jim's head was aching but he was determined to finish. As he looked down at the parking area he saw Mr Hart, whom he had not seen again since their unusual first meeting. Hart was kneeling beside one of the rose standards, busy loosening the earth at its roots with a small hoe, his left arm hanging limply at his side. Beside the redundant arm, resting on the concrete, was a small bucket filled with a greyish powder. From time to time Hart put down his gardening tool, reached for a handful of the powder and sprinkled it over the soil before working it in.

There was something solemn in the way he went about the task, as though he was performing some necessary rite. Jim was no expert on roses, but knew it was bad practice to feed them outside the growing season, December was way too late. He had been watching the man for a couple of minutes before Rosemary entered the picture; afraid she might look up he took a step back. She seemed quite agitated, pacing up and down, occasionally looking over at the gates as though wishing them to open. Jim saw her glance across at Hart and thought he caught a sneer on her face.

Realising he was now alone in the house, Jim recognised an opportunity. At various times he had wondered about the floors above. They were of course not as powerfully fascinating as the lowest floor, and he felt nothing like the same fear regarding them; but the basement was locked, and therefore outside the realms of possibility, however, the upper floors were suddenly available to him. Jim's heart raced as the idea overtook him; he took a final peep down at Rosemary and Hart before setting off. Stealth and speed, he told himself, were the main requirements needed for this venture.

'I know Rosemary lives here, what about the others?' he thought, as he came to the landing on the second floor. 'Perhaps they all do, like flies on shit!'

He decided to look through the rooms at the front of the house first. This allowed him an opportunity to check the rear windows last, that way he could be certain they were still outside before he proceeded any further. There were three rooms on each floor, two large rooms off each landing with a smaller room at the back facing the ascending staircase.

On the second floor there was literally nothing; the carpeting ceased at the top of the stairs and it looked abandoned. Jim found himself standing on pre-World War One linoleum, frayed, dog-eared at its corners and browned with age. It utterly contradicted the urbanity and comfort of the ground floor; it was as though he had time-warped into a derelict building. The plaster mouldings on the ceilings had collapsed, and splintered lathes protruded like the shattered ribcage of some extinct beast. Wherever ceilings or walls were decayed no effort had been made to put them right, and the floor bore mounds of fallen debris in places. The effect was all the more powerful on Jim, having recently viewed John Loxton's contending entry for 'Good Housekeeping'.

The room at the rear, once a bathroom, was now only fit for creatures who bathed in dust. Jim checked the window; yes, still there, Rosemary pacing, Hart attending his roses.

"Okay, next floor!" he said, dodging the piles of rubbish, careful not to make too much noise, yet trying to maintain a good pace.

The third floor, at first glance, seemed no different, same worn brown linoleum, same debris everywhere, only pushed aside in places where it was necessary to walk. The front room was almost a replica of its counterpart on the floor below; it was the next room, the larger of the two rooms at the rear that came as a surprise.

It was hardly a suite at the Ritz, but it had a kind of order, bearing visible signs of habitation and an unpleasantly cloying smell; Jim thought of body odours in a geriatric ward. There was a double mattress sited on the floor with drapes crudely arranged on poles and attached to the ceiling around it, like a DIY four-poster. The room's ceiling had been replaced with unfinished plasterboard, badly aligned nail heads trailing the lines of the joists.

Jim felt slightly queasy as he observed 'his' and 'her' clothes-rails against a wall, recognising some of the skirts and blouses as clothes he'd seen Rosemary wearing. The male suits were too small to fit anyone besides Nicholas. The room had a squalid, unwholesome feel; an unsavoury love nest. After this, it was with more reluctance that Jim went on.

The third room on this floor was again a bathroom, unused and in a similar condition to the one below; hygiene was certainly not an en-suite requisite. Jim checked the window, Rosemary still agitatedly pacing, Hart was only just visible now having moved to a rose bed nearer the house.

Jim took the stairs to the fourth floor. This floor was partially built out of the roof space, the rooms were lower in height, and its upper walls sloped. He took the rooms in the same order as below. The first and second rooms offered nothing new, but the third of these attic rooms had a different tale to tell.

The room contained no bed, and an armchair in a dilapidated state was the only furnishing that offered any sort of comfort. Bookshelves lined most of the walls and a couple of business suits and a few shirts were arranged on hangers hung on nails driven into the protruding lips of shelves. The book collection was eclectic and certainly not scholarly; however there was a book on every imaginable subject; although titles on ceramics and art were probably in the majority. There were books illustrating every type of car, dog, flower, tree and animal. There were illustrated magazines and guides to the movies and film stars, illustrated histories of the world, and guides to its peoples and tribes. It occurred to Jim that this library contained everything anyone would ever need to create infinite series in porcelain to satisfy every conceivable taste. The floor was laid with a carpet of sorts, old and worn, as if it had been salvaged from a dump. The door to the room itself had resisted opening as a result of several layers of underlay, visible beneath worn areas of carpet.

Yet one thing really set this room apart. Every square inch of wall and ceiling space not spoken for with books had been covered: with corrugated cardboard, bits of board, old magazines pinned up or taped; even polystyrene cups had been flattened out and attached. The back of the door too had been decked out in the same fashion, with carpet and felt overlapping the door frame, egg cartons, bits of bubble wrap, all contributing to the strange collage.

Jim was about to take a look outside, when he heard the rumble of machinery through the lift shaft next to the room.

"Oh Christ!" he cried out in panic. He quickly shut the door and began to race downstairs. Halfway between the third and second floor he missed the step, only managing to save himself from careering down the rest head first by lashing out an arm and catching the banister rail in the nick of time.

Thankfully there was no-one in the work room when he reached it. Panting and sweating profusely, he rushed to the window and looked outside. Rosemary was on her own in the parking area, she was standing before the gates which were beginning to open. Jim wiped the sweat from his face onto the arm of his sweater.

He was thinking his little subterfuge had provided him with quite enough adrenaline for one day, when he caught the sound of a footstep behind him. He spun about with an extremely inelegant jerk.

Mr Hart was just inside the doorway bearing a tray of coffee and biscuits. He supported the tray with his right hand; the other hand was out of sight inside the hip pocket of his jacket. "I didn't mean to startle you," he said, limping to the table and setting it down.

"I ... er ... was just taking a breather," Jim garbled, only too conscious of the tell-tale sweat on his face and inexplicable breathlessness of someone only photographing porcelain. "Must have been day dreaming ... didn't hear you."

"I'm sorry," Hart apologised again, "I always assume everyone has the same quality of hearing that I possess."

At this the muscles tensed in every part of Jim's anatomy.

Hart began pouring. "I find it hard to sleep, my hearing is so acute. Sometimes I'm certain I can hear mice in the attic from the ground floor."

Mr Hart looked up as he offered the filled coffee cup to Jim, who was experiencing a sudden rush of heat to his neck and face. "Cream?" he asked.

Chapter Thirteen

Jim was alone again with his imagination running on overtime. Hart's reference to mice in the attic had left him feeling extremely uncomfortable.

"What the hell was I thinking? Do I think I'm Sherlock Bloody Holmes?"

However, not even these personal remonstrations were enough to stop him taking another peek out of the window. The situation down below had changed; Nicholas and the driver had returned in a car Jim couldn't recall seeing before. The aforementioned Nicholas was being greeted by Rosemary like a returning hero. She held him in her arms as an adoring mother might; Jim found it strangely reminiscent of his dream. The woollen-capped man was walking in the direction of the house carrying a packet about seven or eight inches thick under his arm. He might just as well have been invisible as far as Nicholas and Rosemary were concerned, who had eyes only for each other.

It was at this point that Jim fetched the Nikon from his coat, adjusted its aperture, and took several photographs in rapid succession. The car engine had been left running, so he felt confident the sound from his camera would be drowned out. The red-haired man, having delivered his parcel, and without exchanging any words with the other two, took off in the car through the open gates.

Rosemary took a remote from her pocket and pointed it at the gates. As they began closing, she planted a kiss on Nicholas' fat lips and they strolled hand in hand towards the house. Jim's subversive activities complete, he resumed work, very much aware that the daylight was fading fast.

The debilitating effect the house seemed to bring on, and the general sluggishness that accompanied this, kept him there far longer than he'd anticipated. It was dusk by the time he was ready to leave.

Nicholas took Jim down in the lift. The odd young man no longer made any attempt at conversation and his brusque manner now bordered on the hostile. As they descended, Jim felt the temperature drop rapidly, and he was openly shivering by the time they reached the cellar. On this occasion, the journey past the stock-room door produced a sensation way beyond anything that had been experienced before. It was as if something had reached out through the steel plate of the door, something deathly cold and unmistakably malignant. The encounter with whatever it was, lasted no longer than a second, but it left Jim white-faced and shaken.

Nicholas said nothing but he seemed to understand Jim's discomfort and couldn't quite conceal his pleasure. He was grinning broadly as he unlocked the outer door. As Jim stepped outside, expressing relief with a heartfelt sigh, he heard the door slam shut behind him. "And a very good evening to you too!" he said, making for his car.

The Mercedes and Jim's car were now the only vehicles there. He hadn't heard the white van leave, but then his mind had been focused on those final pieces and the approaching night. He started the engine and drove a few yards before realising the gates were still locked. He looked back at the cellar door, now only faintly visible in the dimness. The office on the floor above was the only room in the whole house showing any light.

"Christ, come on. Open the friggin' gates!"

Jim banged the horn twice and was about to go for a third, when Nicholas appeared in the window behind its open blinds.

"Open the gates you ugly little bastard!"

Nicholas must have seen his predicament, yet he remained impassive in the window. Sweat broke out on Jim's upper lip. The relief he'd felt after finishing the shoot had been short-lived. He was trapped in his car in the grounds of that awful house, with darkness coming.

He punched the horn again. This time Nicholas grew more animated, and for a moment Jim was hopeful, only to have his hopes dashed when Nicholas gave a little wave at him then promptly closed the blinds.

Jim's anxiety level immediately shot up.

The car windows were steaming up; wild, outlandish thoughts were rushing through his mind; he considered scaling the walls. Then, when fear had almost reached fever pitch, there came the welcome click. Once the gates had made a space large enough to take his car, Jim was through them and away.

When he returned tomorrow with the final transparencies, he would drive around for hours if necessary, until he found a parking meter. He vowed never to set foot behind those gates again; and he most definitely wouldn't be going anywhere near that cellar.

*

It was after 7pm by the time he reached home, having stopped off to eat and to avoid cooking for one. He fumbled quickly through his pockets for the back door key when he heard the telephone ring and rushed through the kitchen, not pausing to turn on the light.

"Hello, Jim Latimer," he said, panting.

"You're out of condition," Ruth replied.

"Are you at Erich's?"

"No, but Erich's here too, we're at the Thorpe sisters' place."

"Who?"

"The sisters ... we meet at their house ... the healing group? You know, where I've gone every week since you first met me? But then, I've probably only mentioned them a couple of thousand times!"

"You never mentioned their surnames before," he said, "Is it healing tonight then?"

"Yes, we'll start in about an hour. Actually we've been here all day. Erich suggested we search the sisters' library. They have a huge book collection on phenomena of all kinds. Erich was hoping it might help us identify what we've got in Hove."

"And?"

"Not much. Apart from the odd account in, shall we say, less than authoritative works," she laughed and was clearly amused by the idea. "What about you?"

Jim launched into an account of all that had happened to him. Now safely away from the house, he felt rather proud of his little adventure exploring the upper floors.

But Ruth was concerned when he told her about Hart's comments about excellent hearing and mice in the attic.

"You shouldn't have taken the risk!"

"Hart's different," Jim said, "There's something about his eyes; they're sad, but not icy cold like the others."

"From your description of that room, it sounds to me like he's the one who dreams up the porcelain," she said.

"I can't explain really. The way he was working on those rose beds ... gentle, respectful almost. It's weird, he sits at a small desk in the corner of the office, like a mailing clerk," Jim thought about Hart's

133

status, "They don't seem very respectful, considering it's his name on the door-plate."

The incident with Nicholas and the car really had Ruth worried and she broke off to discuss what had happened with Erich. When she returned she said, "We'll be back at Erich's around 11.30. Why don't you come and stay the night?"

"I doubt I'll be awake by then. I really need an early night."

"Okay, if we don't see you, ring us first thing ... before you leave for London."

Jim put down the phone. He felt a twinge of loneliness as he thought about the evening spreading out before him; then he remembered the camera.

"Okay, let's see what we've got," he said, and climbed upstairs to his darkroom.

Jim checked that he had everything ready to hand. He switched off the light, and with an assured dexterity that came from years of practice, put the film onto a spool and loaded it into the tank. Then he turned the light back on, poured in the developer and inverted the tank a few times. He checked the temperature of the developer from time to time, pouring it away when seven and a half minutes had elapsed, replacing it with the stop bath.

Jim was more relaxed than he'd been in days as he concentrated on this familiar but invariably gratifying task. After one minute, he returned the stop bath to its bottle before pouring in the fix. He set the timer for a further two minutes, and when the time was up he poured this away.

In all the years of performing this procedure he had never been able to resist looking at the negatives at this point, it was still like magic to him. He removed the roll of negative from its spool, holding it up to the light like an alchemist seeking gold. Only the final twelve or so exposures had been used on Loxton and Co, the earlier negatives were mainly snapshots of Sophie and various friends at her last birthday party. He put the negatives back onto the spool, returned them to the developer tank and turned on the water.

The temperature in the cottage was a little too cool for comfort; there would most likely be a frost overnight. So while the negatives were washing, Jim built a log fire in the hearth of the sitting room and managed to get a good blaze going by the time he returned to the darkroom to clip the negatives up to dry.

134

Downstairs again, he had just boiled the kettle for some tea when the doorbell rang. Through the pane of frosted glass in the front door he saw the outline of a large man.

"Who is it?" he called. His recent experiences, searching sordid flats, viewing nonagenarian corpses, flinching past cellar doors, had left him jumpy.

Jim failed to catch the first part of the man's reply, but he definitely heard the last part, "... Metropolitan Police."

Jim opened up. The man standing before him was 6'4" tall, broad and grey-haired. He was somewhere around the fifty mark in years and his bearing suggested an athletic history.

"Mr Latimer?"

"Yes," answered Jim, somewhat uneasily. In that instant he forgot about Loxton, and everything to do with Niedermayer & Hart; he feared this visit was something far closer to home, to do with Sophie or Hannah perhaps.

"I'm Detective Chief Inspector Ian Rice," the man said, holding out an identity card.

There was a note of relief in Jim's voice as he said, "Bob's friend ..." then he stopped, there had been something odd about the way Rice had looked at the ground when he mentioned Bob.

"I'm very sorry to have to inform you ..."

After the word murder, Jim didn't hear the rest of the sentence.

"Are you alright, Mr Latimer?"

"Yes. Yes, I'm alright."

Jim led the Chief Inspector through to the kitchen. The two men sat opposite each other at the table.

"It happened around lunchtime. Their colleagues returned from lunch and found the bodies."

"Bodies?"

"Bob and his personal assistant, Mrs Mason."

"Christ no ... Daphne too?"

"You knew Mrs Mason?"

"Yes, a long time ... since my twenties. Daphne had worked with him for years. They were like a double act. Poor Isla ... and the girls? Christ!"

"My wife is with them." Rice said, "We're friends of the family."

"How did they die?"

Rice sighed, "Mrs Mason's neck was broken. She would have lost consciousness immediately." Rice paused, swallowing hard, "Bob died from stab wounds."

"How ... what stab wounds?"

Rice cleared his throat, "He was killed by a puncture wound to the brain ..." Rice felt Jim's eyes on him burning with intensity, "... stabbed through the eye." He hesitated, and then added, "His eyes had been removed with a paper knife."

Jim was speechless; he cupped his hands over his mouth and shook his head. After a moment he said, "I was with him two evenings ago."

"Yes, I know, you went to a chapel of rest in Golders Green together."

Jim looked up at Rice and without any hesitation said, "I was at Loxton's flat too. It was actually me, not Bob, who found the photographs."

Rice looked shaken by this revelation, "Why would he lie?"

"It wasn't really a lie, I mean, it wasn't meant to mislead. I found the photographs. It was late. I had to drive home here and get up early next morning. Bob suggested it. I think he felt guilty for roping me in."

"The murders are outside my jurisdiction," said Rice, "As you possibly know, I work for the Vice Squad. I came here as Bob's friend. I thought there might be a few areas a murder investigation might overlook. I'd like to make some notes if that's okay and I'd like you to tell me everything."

Jim didn't care anymore about how crazy his story would seem to a police officer's jaundiced eye. He told it from the start, and in order of event. Detective Chief Inspector Rice made copious notes, asking questions only when it seemed important to do so.

"So they kept asking you questions about Bob?"

"Yes, they seemed to take a really big interest in what he was up to as executor."

"Any thoughts about why they should have been so keen?"

"When I found the child pornography and the list of names I thought that might be it ... the reason for their interest, I mean. You know it's odd, but from then on they changed ... subtly ... not openly hostile, well not until Nicholas at the end of the shoot today. Come to think of it, after Monday, I didn't see Nicholas or the red-haired man again until this afternoon."

"You've no idea where they were?"

"Rosemary said something odd this morning. After I asked where Nicholas was, she said, 'He's bringing some unfinished business to a close.' The way she said it stuck in my mind."

"Why?"

"It was like she was deliberately pointing something up. And she looked sly as she spoke … like she knew something I didn't."

"What did you take it to mean?"

Jim shook his head, "Nothing at the time."

Loxton's connection with Jim's current employers seemed to interest Ian Rice a lot. He politely listened to an account of Jim's dreams and to Ruth and Erich's esoteric theories. Here he asked no questions, although he did make notes. Jim wasn't surprised; he was hardly presenting the man with hard facts. This slow meticulous process had already taken an hour by this point.

"Bob asked Daphne to do a spot of digging. The company was registered in 1894, not 1957 like it says on the door plaque. Can you think of any reason why any firm would want to look like they'd been in business for less time than they actually had been?"

Rice looked up from his notes and shook his head.

"Nor me," continued Jim, then something clicked, "The solicitor! Loxton's solicitor," it was the beginning of a revelation. "He passed on a receipt to Bob. Loxton left something at his bank."

"Any idea what it was?"

Jim was far away, his eyes wide as he recalled the homecoming scenes he'd witnessed that afternoon. "The red-haired man was carrying a package!"

"I'm sorry?"

"When Nicholas and the van driver came back today, the driver carried a mail packet into the house."

"What did it look like?"

"Brown paper packet, quite thick," he said using his hands to demonstrate its approximate length and breadth, "Open at one end I think."

"The solicitor will be able to identify the bank for us."

"I took some pictures, I was developing them when you arrived … unfortunately I didn't get any of the parcel."

"May I see them?" asked Rice.

"The negatives won't be dry yet," Jim said, consulting his watch, "I could speed it up a bit with a hairdryer?"

"It's not urgent, not if you're sure you didn't get the package. You're coming up to town tomorrow?"

"Yes, first thing."

"Then bring the photographs with you," Rice consulted his own watch, it was just after 11pm. "My wife will be wondering where I am." He produced a card and handed it to Jim, "Can you be there at ten?"

"Yes, no problem."

Rice got to his feet, "Thank you for talking so frankly," he said. His manner then became more serious, "It was wrong to mislead us about finding the list. Some of the bastards on it have the means to hire expensive barristers. They'll have a field day with this change in evidence."

"I'm sorry," said Jim, chastened by Rice's telling off, "Neither Bob nor I would have wanted to see the perpetrators of that filth getting any breaks."

"I know that, Mr Latimer," he said, placing a hand on Jim's shoulder, "And we've both lost a good friend."

"Do you believe Bob and Daphne's murders were tied up with the paedophile stuff?"

"I'm certain of it. I know the people you've been telling me about weren't on the list, but it seems likely they're involved. Don't worry, we'll be taking a very good look into everything they do."

Only yesterday Jim would have readily accepted Rice's conclusion that Niedermayer & Hart must be part of the paedophile network. Now, he wasn't so certain. He could hardly expect Rice to accept what only forty-eight hours earlier he would himself have referred to as 'the pixie reading'. Yet something deep down told him that Ruth and Erich, even though they possessed no solid answers, were somehow nearer to the truth.

"And Loxton?" Jim asked.

"What do you mean?"

"Bob and I both saw a man who had aged well beyond anything that might be rationally explained."

Rice shook his head. "Loxton lost a lot of blood and experienced an agonising death. Corpses deteriorate at different rates ... lots of factors might have affected his appearance."

"Except that isn't it at all. Only after Loxton was dead did he look like a man of ninety-one ought to. Twenty years ago he looked quite old to me, like a man of forty or forty-five looks to a very young man, but even then I recognised the difference between middle and old age. Bob was with him when he died and he said Loxton hadn't aged a single day in all the years he'd known him."

"I'm sorry Jim," said Rice, using his Christian name for the first time, "I haven't got an explanation for you, but let me assure you there will be one."

138

Jim nodded his head, but in truth he wasn't convinced.

"Thanks again for your help. I'll see you at ten tomorrow."

Jim walked Rice to the door. He switched on the outside light to help the policeman find his way back. "Please give Isla my condolences. Tell her ... you know ..."

"Of course," Rice said, offering his hand.

"Goodnight Chief Inspector," Jim said, shaking the bigger man's hand. It was easy to see why Bob and Rice had been friends, they were alike in many ways, solid, honest, both instantly likeable.

Once he'd passed through the garden gate Rice turned and waved a hand at Jim. "It's a cold one," he said, lifting the collar of his overcoat.

Jim raised a hand in response and closed the door. He went into the sitting room and placed a high-backed chair before the dying embers in the grate. Although he felt cold, he made no effort to put more logs on.

*

Ian Rice took a last look round at the woods all about him, the bare branches of trees silhouetted against a clear star-brilliant sky. In the suburb east of London where Rice and his family lived, there was too much spill from street lighting to ever view so dazzling a canopy of starlight.

Ian Rice had been a city dweller all his life. Sometimes he and his wife had discussed moving out to the countryside, what with retirement approaching and the fledglings having flown the nest, what was to stop them? Yet somehow he knew it could never be for him. All his life he had lived amidst the calls and cries, tears, shouts and laughter of other folk. He certainly would not miss the grime and pollution, sitting in a car for an hour to go three miles, or the human scumbags he dealt with in his daily work. Yet for all the bad things about the city and its many drawbacks, it would be its people he'd miss the most.

'There are always a few roses amongst the crap,' he thought as he got into his car.

He paused before starting the engine.

'Latimer's okay ... quite overwrought about Loxton. Maybe the birth certificate's wrong? Or maybe the corpses got mixed up at the mortuary and they saw the wrong body? Has happened.' Rice shrugged and fired the ignition, 'That package sounds promising though.'

139

No bank receipt or any kind of package had been found either on Bob's body or in his office. But why weren't Niedermayer & Hart on the list of paedophiles?

'I suppose they wouldn't be, not if they are the suppliers and the names on the list were clients. Loxton was possibly some kind of middle man.'

After serving thirty years in the police force, the last twenty in vice, there was not much in the way of greed and depravity that surprised Ian Rice.

He backed up, put the automatic into drive and moved off. When he came to the road junction he turned right towards the village of Robertsbridge. Seventy yards on from here there was a bend in the road, as Rice came up to it, he became aware of flashing hazard lights ahead. He slowed into the bend, braking in good time, a few yards from a stationary white Transit van that was blocking his path. He read the situation quickly; the van, judging from its angle, must have swerved to avoid the Mercedes that had come around the bend too far over. The van driver was leaning against the van door nursing his head in his hands. Ian Rice drew into the side, put on his hazard lights and climbed out from the car.

"You alright?" he asked, as he approached the man. He was close enough to make out the wisps of gingery hair frizzing out untidily beneath the man's cap. There was something surreal about the scene, lights from all three vehicles flashing out of synch. A woman, young and attractive, was sitting in the driving seat of the Mercedes and the flickering white and amber of the lights strangely accentuated the deceitful smile on her face.

Time suddenly slowed right down in Rice's mind; he acknowledged how well Jim Latimer had described Rosemary Hines. There had been no collision; both the vehicles were undamaged, merely arranged bumper to bumper.

"Gotcha!" said the red-haired man as he spun around, grinning like a game-show host.

Rice took a step back. He knew it was ineffectual to state the obvious, even so he said, "I'm a police officer. What's going on?"

The red-haired man drew in closer, this time Rice stood his ground. He'd clocked the man wasn't armed.

"You tell us, officer sir, what do you think is going on?" asked Picton.

Rice made a tight fist with his right hand and drove it hard into the van driver's face. There was the sound of cracking bone, Picton brought his hands up to his nose and shrieked in pain. Rice's hand hurt like hell, in fact he was surprised his target was still standing.

Only when Picton opened his hands as if he were playing a childhood peeping game, did Ian Rice truly recognise the danger he was in. The nose was indeed smashed; blood freely flowing from both nostrils onto his teeth, but the mouth was smiling. Picton cupped his fingers over his nose and grotesquely crunched the broken bone back and forth, performing what he saw as a hugely comic moment with great glee. "I dink you've doken dy dose," he said in mock concern to the accompanying click of the fractured bone.

"Police brutality!" exclaimed a voice somewhere behind Rice in a mean, sadistic tone.

Rice was in the process of turning when Picton brought a knee up into his crotch; the Chief Inspector doubled over, winded and retching in pain. Nicholas took Rice's neck in an iron grip, forcing him up again before he had time to regain his breath. He grabbed Rice's left arm and twisted it behind his back, with far more force than was necessary to restrain him. What was incredible was the small man's physical strength, which kept the policeman totally incapacitated.

Rice, who could do nothing but go where he was shunted, was propelled towards the back of the van. Picton stepped ahead to draw open one of its rear doors. The policeman was placed by Nicholas with his back against the opening like a stringed puppet. Then Nicholas released his victim and took up a position next to Picton. Rice, faced by this pair of oddities smiling inanely back at him, saw that he had only one chance. He would need to bring every ounce of his weight to bear if he was going to cover the twelve feet from the back of the van to his car.

Then, with an awful blinding flash, he realised the two men were not actually watching him at all, but something behind him. Fear and confusion seized Rice when he sensed the presence at his back.

In his peripheral vision he caught sight of grey fingers stretching out from the van's black belly, then fingernails like talons pressed into the soft skin of his neck. His two-man audience laughed appreciatively as he spluttered from the pressure on his windpipe.

In one economical and fluid movement the policeman's body rose from the ground, eyes bulging, desperate sounds gurgling from his mouth. A moment later, Rice was yanked backwards into the van's dark interior, like a side of bacon on a hook.

Hugh's Tale

VI

"I swear by God I'll kill the next man who attempts to leave!" threatened Laszlo, as he stood, blade ready, blocking the door.

Blind panic had seized the inhabitants of the cellar-room.

"Jerome choked. We all saw that. There is no mystery here!" he said.

"He drank a man's blood," answered one of the fearful knights who had been trying to flee.

"It is against the holy scripture."

"A sacrilege!"

"The man was a Cathar, an unbeliever. He denied the virgin birth, the death and resurrection of our Lord. I can assure you that Jerome's soul came to no harm by dispatching him. Jerome choked!" reassured Laszlo.

"I've seen men choke on their tongues in battle, the look on their faces very like Jerome's," said Wilhelm, taking up a position beside Laszlo.

"Wilhelm is right," joined Cornelius, "This talk of sacrilege is nonsense."

These three, who had been prepared to share a glass of Cathar blood, began to take control, utilising reason to calm fears of supernatural retribution.

Brother Ferdinand and the serjeant were the only ones who could be seen actively grieving for the Marshal; kneeling, like two bereft hounds, beside their dead master.

Laszlo left the fray then, and came to look upon the Marshal for himself. Jerome's features might have been set in stone. The muscles of his face were contorted into an appalling death mask, his expression terrifying, the eye pupils absent, blank, white, bulging from their sockets. And however much Laszlo was convinced by logic, I watched him swallow hard when he beheld that sight.

"Ferdinand," he said, "Fetch the altar-cloth and cover the Marshal's face."

Laszlo was an important knight, a skilled negotiator and adviser, who moved in circles far above my own station. He had also acquired a reputation for self-advancement. Reynald once jested to me, that if Laszlo offered his friendship and took your hand, it would be prudent to count the fingers when it was returned to you.

Concealing Jerome's face beneath the altar-cloth helped to ease the tension. Gradually the men's nerves steadied, and an emergency council of the secret chapter commenced. The knights began to debate their future. The serjeant and Ferdinand were present too, but remained apart, keeping vigil over their beloved master. Laszlo clearly regarded Jerome's departure as a platform to promote his own ambitions. Wilhelm and Cornelius were his rivals for the vacant post of master of this strange clan. They advocated ruling as a triumvirate, less out of altruism, I think, than fear that Laszlo had the most support.

"Our late master showed through his selfless efforts, the need for discipline and sacrifice. We must emulate the high ideals he set us by strong leadership," argued Laszlo passionately. He was a charismatic speaker.

"What you mean is you want to be Master," put in Wilhelm, mockingly.

"If any one is to be elected then it should be me," came Cornelius' peevish response, "I am the most senior." But seeing there was little support for this point of view, he immediately returned to the concept of a triumvirate, "However, I believe a council ruled by the three of us would serve all best."

"You only say that because you know you would lose a vote," laughed a dissenter.

"Laszlo is my choice!" put in a knight.

Seizing the moment, Laszlo rose to his feet, "Brothers, let us not argue amongst ourselves. Were matters not so pressing, I should prefer to mourn our dear master." Laszlo paused a moment to gain control of his emotions, it was impressive. "However, circumstances force us ... has it not been seen that others have knowledge of the Grail? Have they not demonstrated how avariciously they seek it by destroying the community where the guardians lived? Such men do not share our high ideals, else they would not have behaved so impetuously. We have diligently gathered our intelligence over many years to liberate the cup from the heathen brethren who possessed it. Now they have been alerted, and our task is made harder. The enemies of the true God still covet Christ's cup, and Jerome's efforts failed."

"Is it not possible," began a knight who still looked deeply troubled, "that Jerome was mistaken, that it was indeed the holy cup and that he perished through an act of blasphemy?"

Immediately there was uproar again.

"Come now," Laszlo laughed, gesturing the knights to be seated. "A vulgar little beaker is the Grail of the King of Kings? Where is your faith?" he asked, looking severe in his chastisement of their faithlessness. "The cup is eternal. We saw a worthless glass drop from Jerome's hand and smash into a thousand pieces. I ask again, where is your faith? The true Grail is indestructible."

"Laszlo is right," said Wilhelm, "A handful of these accursed 'guardians' escaped us at Ascalon and I'll vouch the Grail is still with them."

I recalled how horrified Hubert looked when Jean's belongings were brought before the Marshal. I searched about my feet for pieces of the broken glass, but all around me was awash in Hubert's blood, and I could discern no shards of the frail object.

Finally it was decided to cast a vote for the leadership, which Laszlo won by a sizeable majority. He took up his position with great satisfaction, occupying the seat recently vacated by Jerome.

"I make Wilhelm and Cornelius my deputies," he said, magnanimously. He then glanced across the chamber in my direction, "We must decide what to do with this irksome Englishman."

"Kill him!" shouted a chorus of knights.

"Agreed!" he replied, "But how exactly? His corpse will need disposing of, as will our late master's."

"I believe I may have a solution," said Brother Ferdinand, who until then had been too grief-stricken to play any part. "The Englishman has an ally, the Frank, Reynald de Sauveterre. He will most likely return to Acre tomorrow. Let them be caught plunging daggers into our late Master's heart, and summarily executed for treason. It can easily be demonstrated they were conspiring with heretics. We will be praised for uncovering a Cathar plot!"

"Excellent, Ferdinand, but how can we convince our house that Jerome was only recently killed if we must wait for de Sauveterre's return? The Marshal will be cold as stone by then."

"Nobody need attend him but myself. I'll kill a pig and smear its fresh blood upon his wounds."

So it was decided; Reynald and I were to become Jerome's killers.

My fate sealed, the knights departed. All except for Brother Ferdinand and the serjeant, who with great devotion prepared Jerome's corpse, which they stripped and washed down with water, then laid upon the altar. Once the ablutions were complete, Ferdinand sent the serjeant to the Marshal's chamber to fetch his habit.

It was while the serjeant was absent, as Ferdinand ministered to his master alone, that I observed the first movements in Jerome's body. I thought my eyes were deceiving me; until I saw the small but definite flexing of a finger joint.

All the torches were taken by the knights as they departed. The only light in the chamber came from the two altar candles.

I saw the hand move again, this time a different finger, and felt an icy sweat break out on the surface of my skin. I reasoned that these movements must only be the muscles easing after death. However, this did not explain why the room suddenly grew colder. I noticed that brother Ferdinand too had become aware of the deathly chill in the air. In response to the cold and fearful of what I was witnessing, my breathing had grown somewhat noisy and irregular. The cellarer turned and stared at me for a moment away from his prayers of devotion, he looked nervous and uncomfortable.

"Be silent," he commanded, "Else I'll not wait until tomorrow to despatch you."

The brother had his back to the altar as he offered these kindly words. I paid little attention to them; for the muscles of Jerome's body were rippling back into life. The dreadful vision I alone had beheld was suddenly communicated to Ferdinand, who spun about, in time to witness the awful resurrection.

"In the name of Ch-Christ ... wh-what is happening?" he stammered as he withdrew backwards, drawing his sword.

Jerome's eyeballs rolled back into position, yet he no longer saw with human eyes, for they smouldered, a sulphurous yellow in the flickering candlelight.

Speechless, Ferdinand staggered back, his blade trailing impotently on the floor at his side. Jerome, looking furtively about, expelled a growl, deep and low; no living creature could ever produce such a sound. He noticed the gold crucifix at his side, at first recoiling at the sight of it before casting the holy object to the ground with terrible ferocity. I saw too that the touch of his hand upon the cross brought pain, for there was anguish in the inhuman sound that came forth. Jerome then brought his legs about so that he sat upon the edge of the altar. The creature seemed stunned upon waking, and examined its own nakedness with those fell eyes as if seeing anew. Jerome rubbed a hand across his jaw as though he found discomfort there, then, placing some fingers into his mouth, plucked out some teeth and cast them to the ground.

Until then, Jerome had paid no attention to either of us. Ferdinand, however, captured his late master's attention by making the sign of the cross before him. The action enraged Jerome, who rose to his feet, glowering with malice.

"Heavenly Father, protect me!" implored Ferdinand raising his sword for protection.

This only served to anger Jerome further who expected the same loyalty from his underling in death as he had shown to him in life. Ferdinand cried out as he ran at the demon who had usurped the shape of his beloved master, plunging the sword into its belly, nearly to the hilt. Jerome gazed around about himself, as though surprised to see how the blade protruded from his back. Ferdinand let go the handle and stepped falteringly away, horrified that such a severe blow had caused so little injury.

Jerome's eyes burned ferociously as he came forward, the blade still through him; he lashed out an arm and grabbed Ferdinand's surcoat. The shocked cellarer began to weep, but he put up no resistance as Jerome drew him in. The dead Marshal then took Ferdinand's plump face into his shoulder as though embracing an old ally. I heard Ferdinand's sobs. I was not prepared for what I saw then. With only the barest effort, Jerome tore Ferdinand's head clean off its shoulders, and hurled it at the wall.

Spattered in blood, Jerome let the cellarer's torso drop to the ground. Then, to my uttermost despair, I became the object of attention for those dread eyes as he stepped across Ferdinand's headless body and came towards me. I cried out in my terror, pulling in vain at my chains; but then, quite suddenly, he stopped; I didn't understand why, but an inexplicable look of fear swept across those deathly features.

At the time I thought my reprieve was due to the serjeant's return. He had entered only a moment later bearing the habit he had gone to fetch. The man immediately let the garment fall when he beheld the carnage, collapsing to his knees in abject terror at the sight of the transformed Marshal.

Jerome withdrew Ferdinand's sword from his belly and offered its blade, stained darkly with his own blood to the man quivering at his feet. The serjeant seemed to instinctively know what was required, and to my abhorrence began to lick the blade. At first he did so tentatively, before developing a taste for it, then lapping the blood as though it provided all nourishment. I felt ready to vomit.

After this the serjeant stood before Jerome, no longer afraid; master and servant once again. Jerome, who was become more beast than man, had it seemed lost the human quality of speech. However, through forging this new bond with the serjeant, he had created a mouthpiece for himself. The serjeant listened a moment, responded with a nod as if in reply to a command and departed.

Once more I found myself alone with Jerome. He went to his chair of authority and sat there naked, composed no doubt in some evil reverie, from time to time distractedly placing a finger or two into his mouth to remove another tooth, or running a hand across his head, unperturbed by the clumps of hair that came away.

At moments, during that time which seemed an age to me, I was certain madness would take me. And all the while, the candles burned lower, one already flickering.

After a time the serjeant returned, Cornelius was with him.

"What nonsense is this?" I heard Cornelius say as he entered, "Who wishes to see ...?" He never completed the sentence. The serjeant slammed the door shut, then pushed the petrified man before Jerome, forcing him to his knees.

Cornelius flinched as Jerome's grey hand reached out and drew him screaming towards him. As Jerome opened his mouth I saw the removed teeth had been replaced, and that his new teeth drew themselves into points like a beast of prey's. And I was soon to learn what purpose they served, when they tore into Cornelius's throat. The Venetian knight writhed in pain as his blood was drawn from him; whilst I squirmed in my chains at the sight of such an abomination.

Jerome let Cornelius's bloodless body fall to the ground and sat quietly for a time as though in a state of rapture, his naked body diabolically baptised in the red blood of Cornelius and Ferdinand.

When this time of repose was done, he rose to his feet and the serjeant helped him dress. The cross pattee that Templars wear upon their surcoat and on the shoulder of our black capes was torn away by the serjeant before helping Jerome into them. Apart from the badges of our order he dressed as any other knight, except for the helm, which he took from the serjeant but then cast away.

When he was dressed, he viewed me again with malevolent eyes, but made no effort to draw nearer.

The serjeant lifted Cornelius's corpse onto the altar and when the task had been completed, he opened the door for his master who strode through it.

No doubt the serjeant understood something of my feelings, to be left hanging in chains in that cellar, for as he went he glanced at me and laughed mockingly.

And so I was left, with the corpses of three murdered men for companions.

The draught from the door extinguished the flickering candle, and I could but look on anxiously as the other one guttered.

Chapter Fourteen

Jim lost track of time as he stared impassively into the grey ash of the spent fire.

Over the course of thirty-seven years, he had met and mourned death before, but never without alcoholic back-up. In times past, emotional upheavals were steeped in a serendipitous blend of beer, wine and spirits; the murders of Bob and Daphne would have provided enough impetus to marinade himself for weeks.

He was experiencing powerful feelings of guilt. He'd been the one who suggested taking a look at Loxton's corpse which had led on to searching the flat and the discovery of the list.

'He's bringing some unfinished business to a close.'

Rosemary's words made something clench in the pit of his stomach.

Jim was convinced that whatever Loxton had deemed important enough to keep securely in a bank vault had also cost his friends their lives. He thought too that he may have glimpsed it, outwardly at least, in the form of the packet being carried into the house by the red-haired man. He tried to imagine its contents but couldn't conceive of anything more damning than the items already uncovered, and which Loxton had only seen fit to stow beneath the seat of an armchair.

Jim looked at his watch; it was ten minutes after midnight. Ruth and Erich would have already arrived back at the bungalow. He went through to his study and picked up the phone.

"Huh?"

He tapped the button where the handset rested, like an old movie cliché. It took a moment to register; no tone, the line was dead. In such a rural setting it was not unheard of for the telephone to go down from time to time; even so, a cold sweat broke out along his neck and spine. He had to get out, be with friends, talk stuff over; Ruth and Erich would understand. Jim picked up his coat and flung his arms into its sleeves on the way to the back door.

His hand touched the door handle and he was about to unlock it when he realised with a start that the face in the door pane was not his own reflection; beaming back at him was Nicholas Cureton.

A second or two passed, both men remained motionless, holding each other's gaze. Then Nicholas' eyes narrowed as he raised an elbow and drove it at the pane nearest to the lock. Glass cascaded down onto the tiles at Jim's feet. His first reaction was to turn tail and run, except he knew that his pursuer would not be far behind. Somehow Nicholas had to be slowed down or better still, stopped.

Jim's eyes fell upon the set of kitchen knives on the counter at his side. The small window was now mostly free of glass with just a few shards remaining around the edges. Nicholas' hand was already through, searching along the door frame for the lock. Jim withdrew the largest of the knives from its block base and raised it above his shoulder. Nicholas' fingers were splayed out feeling for the door catch, when Jim, with an intention to inflict harm he had hitherto never known, plunged the knife with every ounce of force he could muster through the back of the young man's hand, driving its steel blade an inch deep into the door's wooden frame. Nicholas shrieked from the pain, his hand writhing like a harpooned crab.

Then Jim ran. He sped through the study and into the hallway, heart thumping, frenetic with panic. He reached the front door, but stopped abruptly as it flew open before him.

"Stupid bastard," were Rosemary's words, delivered with contempt as she thrust her fist into his jaw.

The punch was unimaginably powerful, and Jim bit through his bottom lip as his face slammed into the wall, leaving a blood trail as he slid to the floor. He made a futile effort to raise himself, but his head was reeling and his legs buckled under him. While he lay on the ground, Nicholas arrived; he'd extricated himself from the back door and was wrapping a tea-towel around his hand.

"The bastard knifed me!" he said with brattish indignation, pointing at his hand, the cloth around it colouring red.

"You'll be alright, honey," Rosemary replied, stepping between Jim's splayed legs to drive her foot into his testicles.

Jim lurched forward screeching in agony, his face turning scarlet as he coughed and retched. But Rosemary didn't allow him any time to recover. She grabbed his hair and thrust his head back into the wall.

"Where's the woman?" she asked, shaking him. When only a confused look was returned, she shouted, "Where's the fucking bitch that paid us a visit?"

Jim, clear on the question now, still had no intention of answering. He drew back his head, mustered as much saliva and blood as he could and spat into her face. Rosemary turned white with anger. Jim immediately regretted his action. Her fist came down on his cheek like a club and sent him crashing to the ground.

Jim felt himself being raised by the lapels of his coat, everything was spinning. Rosemary and Nicholas were moving components in a shifting collage; a dozen Rosemarys, all equally terrifying with bared teeth, predatory, ferocious.

"Don't kill him, Rose!" exclaimed Nicholas.

"The bastard spat on me!" she raged.

"Do it later ... we'll make him really suffer then ... we can do it together!" Nicholas said; he sounded anxious.

But Rosemary's snarling hatred was unabated. Her fist was drawn back ready to deliver another vicious blow. If Nicholas hadn't become involved it's quite likely Jim would either have met his end or suffered some very serious injuries.

"Mr Niedermayer wants him alive!" Nicholas shouted.

Jim immediately felt Rosemary's hold on him release and he sank to the floor. He heard footsteps, indistinct words being spoken; something sharp jabbed into his arm, then everything switched off.

*

Ian Rice jerked back to consciousness with a start. His eyes opened into complete blackness and the terror he'd known during his abduction was immediately re-born.

He was lying on his side; every part of him was aching. His stomach and shoulder hurt like hell, but by far the worst was the soreness around his neck, which was in spasms of agony. His body movement was severely restricted, and he soon found that he was able to move little more than the muscles of his face. A piece of tape had been secured across his mouth; at least he assumed it was adhesive tape pulling on his stubble. He attempted to push it away with his tongue but the effort achieved nothing except discomfort.

The floor below him was hard and cold. There was a vibration and he sensed movement; but there was no sound, which greatly increased his disorientation.

Out of Rice's five senses, smell was the only one not mostly redundant in that silent darkness, though it might have been kinder to have lost this too.

The air was hot and sticky from the heat of his own body. From this he ascertained that his confines must be extremely cramped. In the air about him there was a putrescent stench that turned his stomach very nearly to retching, which he knew he had to avoid, for fear of choking. Then, without any visual aids to assist, he made an observation that drove him in one split second to the edge of sanity. The smell possessed a source, and that source lay right alongside him.

He felt a cold, dry exhalation of fetid breath on his face. Rice recoiled, but the effort was futile, and it only brought increased pain to his injured neck.

Until that moment he'd assumed he was tightly bound. Only then did the sickening reality of his plight hit home. His bonds were limbs, he could feel their boniness clamping like steel bands, arms and legs around his chest and thighs. Rice's captor, invisible in the dark, was closer than his own hands and feet, its stinking breath wafting in his face.

Screaming was a sensation previously unknown to Rice. Not that the noise he produced resembled anything remotely familiar, because his sealed mouth offered the sound no vent. It was merely a reflex action, having its inception in his guts and rising on a shock wave of unrestrained fear up through the organs of his body to its point of release. Rice actually expelled nothing more than a muffled whine, immediately followed by a lot of choking and spluttering.

His captor, sensing Rice's anguish, found the response gratifying and three gentle pats were communicated to the centre of the policeman's back. Rice's captor had become his tormentor too.

Detective Chief Inspector Ian Rice understood he was going to die.

He thought about his wife and three grown-up children. He'd always done his best and made ample provision for his family. Tears began to stream down his face, in that disgusting dark hole of a place. He recalled his wife's face the first time he'd ever set his eyes upon it.

Rice could feel himself being drawn irrevocably closer; resistance was useless; the stench grew far worse; his face touched an icy cheek. He felt something cold, rough and moist explore the contours of his neck, it followed the line of his pulse beat, trailing its course back and forth several times. Rice found himself expelling short, terror-stricken grunts in response to that dreadful tongue. Then he felt sharp teeth exploring his neck.

As Rice's warm blood began to flow he screamed out in agony. His executioner grew more and more excited, severing muscle and sinew, savouring each bite. Then unable to contain its voracious appetite, it bit into an artery and Rice's blood gushed into that insatiable mouth.

Ten seconds and Ian Rice's life was over.

*

Jim Latimer's re-entry into consciousness took a while. It felt like he was swimming up through a pool of deep water. Various noises resounded in his eardrums in a barking cacophony, while fractured images reeled before his eyes.

Gradually, the discordant sounds separated into growling speech many rpms too slow. A swirling kaleidoscope shimmered before him, anonymous body shapes, the undulating walls of unfamiliar surroundings. Jim was partially enjoying the experience; it was comfortable and painless, an alcoholic's heaven. The physical pain from his injuries had yet to kick in.

But as he shook off the anaesthetic, the sounds and pictures became far less pleasant, although everything still looked like it was happening behind a wall of steamed-up glass. Then he recalled Loxton's box files, Bob and Daphne and the violence he had suffered.

The world became a tangible, painful place again. His brain could not yet assimilate what was being said, but he could tell several voices around him were being raised in anger. He inwardly cringed, fearing himself the object of aggression, half expecting more beatings. Jim became aware of the red-haired man who was sitting on a chair about ten feet away, staring directly at him. When Picton realised Jim had seen him, he smiled and waved, as if greeting an old friend.

"Bastard," Jim mumbled.

Whether or not his first word had been at all intelligible, the argument in progress stopped abruptly and Jim became the main object of attention. For a moment his panic increased, before subsiding again; it seemed Jim's return to consciousness was not enough to sway Nicholas and Rosemary from the verbal attack they were subjecting Mr Hart to. The red-haired man seemed to be unconcerned by the row going on about him, preferring to leer in Jim's direction whenever he caught his eye.

Rosemary's temper, which Jim had already experienced to his own physical cost, was out of control. Her voice gave full vent to her anger as she shouted, "If you can't stand it, why don't you pin more fucking egg cartons to the wall!"

Hart replied softly, "It's just she was so young. Ever since I got back, all I seemed to be able to hear were her screams."

"You make it sound like the whole thing's new!" scoffed Nicholas.

"Sometimes it's worse ... but I didn't mean to kill her. I just wanted to stop her crying. I admit I gave her too much sedative."

"And you expect us to believe you, you piece of shit? Not exactly the first time, is it?" said Rosemary, looking disturbingly overheated.

"I'm sorry Rosemary, it was an accident. It won't happen again, I promise," Hart was pleading like a small child before an irate parent.

"You disgust me," she replied with contempt, "You've got no fucking balls!" Then she suddenly calmed herself and took an icy pleasure as she said, "Mr Niedermayer will be displeased."

"Please Rosemary, no ... please don't ..."

"It's not a matter of me telling him, is it? Let's face it, you were never exactly his blue-eyed boy," she mocked. "I wouldn't be surprised if he'll make you wait a month for your next ration!"

The suggestion sent Hart into a frenzy of despair, "Please Rosemary, no ... speak to him for me, beg him not to ..."

"Me, beg? You're having delusions. You know I'd never say a word for you."

"Nor me," said the grinning Nicholas, deriving great amusement from the older man's suffering. Hart, crestfallen and defeated, limped off into the poorly lit farthest reaches of the room.

Little of what Jim had heard made any sense. In fact he wondered if he was awake at all or whether the whole scene was just another dream, however, the aches and pains emerging in his face and groin said otherwise.

Hart out of the way, Nicholas began to pay Jim some unlooked for attention.

"Our photographer friend is awake!" he proclaimed.

Rosemary looked at Jim only long enough to scowl. "Picton," she commanded, "Dispose of that." She flicked her head in the direction of a long stout table, a few feet away on Jim's right. The red haired man got up at once and began attending to whatever was attached to it. Jim had a poor view from his hunched position on the floor, and was unable to make it out. Picton appeared to be loosening straps.

In fact it was hard to see quite a lot of the room because it was so dimly lit; its farthest reaches were in almost complete darkness. He'd observed that the surface behind his back was neither hard nor cold, and as he looked around he noticed the walls and ceilings, at least what he could see of them, were covered in a brownish hessian-like fabric, secured every twelve inches or so by one-time-white cotton rosettes. The room resembled a giant mattress; he had seen the same kind of thing before, the room was soundproofed.

When Picton raised up and threw the body of a girl across his shoulder, Jim let out a gasp in horror. The girl's long brown hair was trailing only inches from Jim's face as Picton went past him to the door. Jim glimpsed her profile and a staring pale blue eye; she had been young, perhaps seventeen or eighteen. He tried to connect the fragments of the argument he'd been listening to with this dead girl, but it made little sense.

Nicholas came close. "Now you'll have a bed all to yourself."

Jim knew it was a mistake but with Nicholas' mocking face so close, he couldn't resist aiming a punch directly at his teeth. Unfortunately, he'd colossally overestimated his capabilities. The fist moved in slow motion and Nicholas was out of range long before it landed. The exertion only succeeded in unbalancing Jim.

"Some people are incapable of even the commonest civility," said Nicholas, heaving Jim up to his feet, "Your friend Isherwood displayed the same flagrant disregard for good manners." He held Jim's face close to his; for Jim it was like looking into the mouth of a shark, "You should have heard him squeal when I dug his eyes out."

Jim wanted to vomit and wished he could have produced it there and then; to project it directly into Nicholas' face. Instead Nicholas, roaring with laughter, spun him around and effortlessly lifted him onto the vacant table top. When Jim saw that Nicholas was attaching a strap to his wrist, he resisted by flailing his arms about. Rosemary stepped into the picture and put an end to the rebellion by smacking a hand across his jaw. Jim's head went spinning off as he groaned in pain. By the time his vision returned to normal again his wrists and ankles were securely bound to the table.

"You'll love it here," said Nicholas, "We've entertained many satisfied customers."

"You ... you won't ... get ... get away with this," Jim mumbled defiantly.

"Oh please," said Nicholas, doing what he did best, scoffing, "Spare us the clichés. We already have got away with it. But I'm afraid, Mr Latimer, you're about to suffer quite considerably. And please don't over-excite yourself by imagining the police bursting in here to rescue you." He began to snigger, like he suddenly remembered he had a tremendous joke up his sleeve, "Picton!" he shouted through the open door, "Show Mr Latimer why he shouldn't expect a police rescue."

Jim was hardly at the peak of mental alertness. Even so, he suspected something bad was coming. Although he braced himself, he could never have been prepared for what followed.

Picton entered hands behind his back, with a look of choir boy innocence. "Have you seen anyone answering to this description?" he asked in an extremely stupid, almost cartoon voice.

With a flourish he produced Ian Rice's head. Jim had to gasp for breath. However, it failed to register immediately exactly who he was looking at. The severed head bore little resemblance to the alert human being he had recently spoken with. The eye pupils had disappeared above the eyelids with the sockets showing only white. The dead man's jaw had drooped open and was gaping horribly with a piece of adhesive tape partly torn off attached to the lower lip. The cheeks were sunk in, and the colour and texture of the skin was disgustingly reminiscent of supermarket chicken.

Picton was holding the head by a clump of hair, moving it from side to side to give Jim the full effect. "What you might call a top cop ... 'Head' of his own department."

As Picton made the severed head dance about, some of its hanging veins and sinews trailed onto Jim's chest. He managed to turn his face to the side just in time to throw up, mostly landing on the floor, thankfully missing himself and the table.

Rosemary, Nicholas and Picton seemed to find the moment hugely entertaining. Jim turned his head to the other side, spluttering and coughing to clear his throat and chest. Hart was sitting on a chair by the wall. He was looking away, as though he too found the sight as unpleasant as Jim had.

Then, something inexplicable began to happen. The temperature in the room suddenly plummeted, and the already insufficient lighting lost power and grew dimmer. Jim hadn't found the atmosphere exactly recreational before; however, from that moment the gloom deepened, as if an even darker cloud presided.

The three laughing amigos fell silent. Picton took Rice's head away but returned directly, closing the door behind him. Jim felt as though an oppressive weight was bearing down on him, his breathing grew more laboured and erratic.

Jim could hear sounds, loud rumbling sounds as though heavy stones were being moved. The noises seemed to be coming from a large shaded alcove left of a chimney breast on the opposite wall, but it was difficult to make out anything, so deep were the shadows.

He wanted to scream, "What the hell is happening?" but he was too terrified to even swallow the vomit-tasting spittle in his mouth.

The three standing members of the porcelain business had their heads bowed as if to show respect. Jim's eyes, which had begun to dart about everywhere, caught sight of Hart, who remained seated with his head buried in his hands.

The rumbling noises had stopped, Jim was straining every muscle to make out what was in the corner; he could see nothing, but sensed that something had arrived. Irrational though he knew it was, in a blind panic, he tugged at his restraints. He knew without any shadow of doubt that he didn't want to be here.

He caught a movement; his heart was drumming, blood ringing in his ears.

Jim Latimer was about to meet Mr Niedermayer.

Hugh's Tale

VII

The one remaining candle burned low for a time before it too flickered and died. Then all light was lost to me and I was cast into a pit of darkness, assailed by hopelessness and despair. My thoughts ran wild, wandering constantly into the realm of nightmare.

I relived through my mind's eye the brutal deaths of my three companions, and imagined their unshriven faces rising out of the darkness. I will spare you the details of my worst imaginings Anselm; suffice it to say, the evil I had witnessed in that cellar and its inception through an act of hideous sacrilege, utterly consumed me. Every creak and sound in my dungeon, whether caused by the earth in slumber or the mere scurryings of rats became magnified a hundred fold. Yet mostly I feared Jerome, or rather the demon Jerome had become, creeping unseen through the darkness to feast upon my blood and delivering my soul to hell. God forgive me, Anselm, but I wished that Laszlo had dispatched me to my grave before I lived to witness Jerome rise from his.

I learned later that I was incarcerated there for what remained of the night and most of the following day. When eventually I heard footsteps approaching I assumed my time was come; by then I was so overtaken by fear, so close to madness, that the release death promised was inviting. When the door opened I beheld three torches but my eyes were so enfeebled by the dark that I was forced to look away.

"In Christ's name, what evil work is here?" were the first words I heard.

"Hubert is dead," came another voice, using the inflections of a Saracen tongue.

"God be praised, you are alive!" said a third. This voice I recognised at once.

"Reynald, is it you?" I cried out in joy. The brightness of the torches was still unbearable, but I recognised his outline through slitted eyes. "How did you come here? They wait for your return!" I added anxiously, recalling the plan Ferdinand had invented to be rid of us.

"Robert came out to warn us there was danger and helped us enter the house unseen," explained Reynald.

I had by then recovered my sight sufficiently to identify Robert de Frontignac. The third man still remained a blur.

"I woke up when Brother Ferdinand fetched you from the dortoir," said Robert, "Then I saw one of the knights with him retrieve a bundle from behind your bed. I was troubled by this and followed the man to Ferdinand's room, though I did not dare venture on. Today, when there was no sign of you, I rode south hoping to come upon Reynald, and warn him that I feared for your safety."

"I owe you a debt of thanks," I answered, grateful indeed for Robert's actions.

"This is Aref," said Reynald, "I met him at the river Auja at poor Hubert's bidding."

I recognised the Saracen as the chief priest who had officiated in the strange ceremony we had clandestinely witnessed.

"We must free you," said Reynald. "Was there a key?"

"Search Ferdinand," I answered, "He kept many keys about him."

"This headless man is Ferdinand?" asked Reynald.

I nodded, his decapitation all too vivid in my mind.

Reynald stepped carefully around the cellarer's corpse avoiding the pool of congealed blood surrounding him and retrieved a large ring of keys from his belt. "Who did this to him?"

"Jerome."

"Jerome?" asked Reynald and Robert together in a mixture of amazement and disbelief.

"Then what became of Jerome?" said Reynald.

"He ... died ..." the ability to recall those diabolical events after my recent incarceration with only dead men and terror for companionship, made it hard to speak of, "... Jerome ..."

Robert seemed to be under the impression that it was Jerome who had been laid upon the altar. He had ventured across the room to gaze upon the dead man's features, "This is not Jerome but the Venetian, Cornelius. His throat is torn open."

"Jerome d-did th-that," I stammered.

The Saracen was beside me, silent, weighing up the dreadful place with his astute eyes.

"If Jerome is dead, where then is his corpse?" asked Reynald, inspecting the lock on the manacles and trying to match a key to it.

"He went away with the serjeant ..."

"But you told us Jerome had died?" said Robert suspiciously, as though beginning to question my sanity.

"You mean the serjeant took Jerome's body away?" suggested Reynald.

Somewhat hesitantly I replied, "Jerome died ... but then awoke."

Robert cast an unbelieving glance at Reynald.

Then the Saracen, Aref, addressed me directly for the first time. He spoke in a humble manner, yet with authority, he owned a great depth of voice. "How did this Jerome meet his end?"

"He slit Hubert's throat ... then ..." I could barely allow myself to say it, "... then he drank his blood ..."

The two Templars gasped at the sacreligiousness of such an act.

"How?" asked Aref earnestly, "Tell me friend, did he use a cup?"

"Yes. Jerome invited the others present to share in Hubert's blood ... most were too fearful. But three were prepared to drink ... that is, before Jerome started to choke. The cup fell and smashed when he collapsed ... terrified, clutching at his throat ... writhing in agony as he died."

"The cup was destroyed?" asked Robert anxiously.

Aref looked extremely troubled too as Robert voiced his fears.

"Ferdinand and the serjeant laid Jerome upon the altar. An hour or so later he rose ... but he was changed into a hellish creature ... Ferdinand drove a sword into his belly, yet he remained unharmed ... Jerome is dead, yet he lives ... possessed by a demon!"

"No, not so, not possessed," said Aref. "He has become that which he truly is, in his basest nature."

"You are able to make sense of this?" said Reynald to Aref.

"You must believe me!" I said in earnest.

"Calm yourself, Hugh. I have a key here that I think may release you. You will feel better away from here," said Reynald, placing a key into the lock.

"But you have to believe me," I implored again.

"I believe you," Reynald replied under his breath.

To my dismay, the key he had picked out did not work.

"This one then," Reynald said, choosing another.

"In what ways had Jerome changed when he arose?" asked Aref.

"He had new teeth growing in his mouth ... like a wolf's ... and possessed far greater strength. He tore Ferdinand's head from his shoulders with his bare hands. At first the serjeant was fearful of him, until Jerome let him drink his blood ... now the man serves him as a disciple. It was the serjeant who brought Cornelius here. Jerome bit through his neck and consumed his blood."

"Cornelius has a great lump of flesh torn from his neck," said Robert, bending low over Cornelius' corpse and peering at the wound.

The manacle holding my left wrist clicked open and I experienced the first moment of relief since I had arrived there.

"A few moments and I will have the other hand free," assured Reynald.

However, my elation had come too soon. Robert, suddenly let out a cry so bloodcurdling that the ring of keys fell from Reynald's hand.

Robert had dropped his torch, and all I could see at first was the sight of him careering backwards, like a man staggering under a great weight. Then to my horror I saw the reason. The altar had once again fallen vacant. Robert was indeed struggling beneath a burden; Cornelius, like Jerome before him, had returned from the dead, and taken hold of him. Robert attempted every ploy imaginable to shake himself free from the living corpse, yet it clung on. Cornelius' eyes glowed yellow, mad with the craving for living blood, snapping his teeth, which were not yet fully formed, at the exposed areas of Robert's face and neck.

Aref immediately drew his scimitar and rushed to aid Robert. Reynald remained beside me, terror-stricken, his eyes staring in disbelief.

Only as Robert cried out, "In God's name help me!" was the spell of Reynald's bewilderment broken. He too then drew his blade and ran to help.

Cornelius, snarling like a rabid beast, yet far more cunning, aware of the two men encircling him, stole the sword from Robert's belt, then hurled his would-be prey to the ground.

Aref rushed forward, and plunged his torch into the creature's face. Cornelius shrieked inhumanly with pain and fell backwards into the altar. He landed with such force that the altar slab itself was rent in two. The creature's face was charred black where the fire had met its skin, yet it remained unharmed. However the attack had greatly angered him, and his fell eyes burned deeply with malevolence.

In life Cornelius had been only moderately skilled with a sword, but in death his abilities were greatly improved. Reynald came at him with a blow to the head which he immediately blocked, although Reynald only managed to contain Cornelius' reply at his shoulder; and the force of the blow sent him sprawling to the floor. Aref came forth with the firebrand again, saving Reynald, who was momentarily dazed and thrown off guard. Cornelius, spitting and gnashing his teeth in rage, struck out at the handle shaft of the torch and sent it crashing to the ground. Then in demented fury he lashed out at Aref, who was forced to parry a succession of lethal attacks at a ferocious speed. The last stroke in the assault being so powerful it drove the Saracen to his knees.

However, Reynald had by then recovered, and re-entered the fray more prepared. Aref rolled out of the action for a moment to recover whilst Reynald took his share of the punishment. Both Reynald and Aref were excellent swordsmen but Cornelius' strength made him unassailable. I could only watch helplessly as the foul thing bore down on them with its dreadful countenance. I had seen Jerome, the archetype of these demonic creatures, shrug off what in all other cases would have been a fatal blow. So, as I helplessly watched my comrades bravely fight, I observed with much anguish the growing signs of exhaustion in them; whilst at the same time their foe only appeared to get stronger. In my heart I knew that Cornelius must ultimately win, and prayed for the means to be revealed to us whereby such a monster might be vanquished.

Robert, was by this time recovered and had risen to his feet, and seeing only hopelessness, made for the cellar door to escape.

"The cross!" I shouted, "Raise the cross ... upon the floor behind the altar!"

He hesitated, but then, and I must add that he did so bravely, found a path through the flashing blades; emerging from behind the broken altar holding the cross up before him.

When the creature saw the crucifix a look of terror seized him; momentarily transfixed before the symbol of our Lord. Then, beginning to control his fear, he growled low in contempt.

But Cornelius' courage had returned too late, turning his head with only enough time to express surprise as Aref's scimitar flew with strength and accuracy towards his neck. So precise was the blow and sharp the blade that a moment elapsed before the head fell, followed a second afterwards by the toppling of the body. Yet from the stump of Cornelius' neck came barely a trickle of blood, his flesh was like meat that had been hung and bled for tenderness.

Yet the horror was not over, for animation remained in the headless torso; arms and legs flailing about wildly, as though yearning to be re-united with their head.

Aref kicked the sword from Cornelius' hand. Robert immediately picked up his lost weapon and brought it forcefully down onto one of the arms, hacking it clean off.

"That is no good," cried Aref, appalled by the butchery that surrounded him, "Give me your knife," he told Robert.

"I do not possess one," replied Robert, "I recently lost it ... at Safed I think."

Reynald cast a look in my direction.

"Take my dagger," said Reynald, coming forward and handing it to Aref. "What is required here?"

"The creature is disabled but will recover. Its heart must be destroyed."

Reynald held the remaining arm pinned beneath his foot while Aref exposed Cornelius' chest by tearing open his habit. Then, using Reynald's dagger, Aref drove its blade deep into the creature's chest, severing the gristle that binds the ribcage. Prising open the ribs, he plunged in his hand and drew out the heart; then Aref set the heart upon the ground and put fire to it.

Unlike normal flesh, the heart burst immediately into flame and was utterly consumed in a few seconds, leaving but a smouldering lump of charcoal. Aref trampled this under his boot, the heart crumbled into black ash and Cornelius' torso finally lay still.

Reynald then, to my great relief, released me from my shackle. Aref in the meantime took Cornelius' head and burned this too.

"Do you know these cellars?" Aref asked.

We each replied that we did not.

"Why?" asked Reynald.

"I fear this Jerome is still in hiding here. He must be destroyed before others suffer this curse."

"That must not happen," I agreed.

Reynald nodded grimly.

"First to find the cup," said Aref, looking about the floor.

"It was smashed," I replied.

"No my friend," said Aref, "This cup can not be broken." The Saracen then cast his torch across the area where I had seen it fall, "Where are its pieces?" he asked.

Then he investigated the floor behind poor Hubert's legs and held up the small green beaker, completely intact. "See," he said.

"I now understand how I survived," I said, marvelling at the sight of the restored cup, "And the reason why Jerome looked somewhat fearful when he drew near me."

"Perhaps it would be best to leave the cup hidden for the time being. Would it not be a terrible disaster if Jerome was victorious over us and went on to possess such a prize too?" said Robert.

"I believe that you know more about this cup than you ought," replied Aref, looking sternly at Robert.

Reynald glanced at me as Aref spoke. When they entered he had propped his saddle-bag beside the door, and now he began to delve into one of its pockets.

I saw tension marking Robert's face. He said, "You yourself mentioned a cup with mystic powers. That was the first I heard of it. Indeed, after what you have said and what I have seen with my own eyes, I am inclined to believe that it is so. I only sought to help my friends. Remember, if it were not for me you would never have found Hugh. Is my assistance to be met by your mistrust?"

"This knife is of the same design as mine," Reynald said to Aref as he drew out the dagger discovered at the site of the massacre, "Hugh found it amongst your murdered kinfolk." Reynald cast the dagger upon the ground before Robert.

Aref's face grew dark; he glowered at Robert who grew uneasy.

"This is not mine. I told you I lost it at Safed. Will no-one believe me?"

"You must have followed us," I said, beginning to make sense of things. "You are part of the rival group that Jerome and Laszlo spoke of."

Robert, realising his subterfuge had been exposed, drew his sword. "I will dispatch the first man that reaches for a weapon. You, Saracen, bring me the cup and I will trouble the three of you no more."

I never saw avarice so defined in any man as it was written at that moment upon the face of Robert de Frontignac. "Come, what is it to be?" he asked with a nervous laugh.

"If you want the cup so badly, then here," said Aref, "catch it!" I saw the cup fly into the air and Robert rush forward to win it, but so dazzled was he by the object of his desire that he let his guard drop. In the blinking of an eye Aref drew his scimitar, had rushed upon the surprised Robert, disarmed him, and flung him to the ground.

Once again I saw the cup shatter into a thousand pieces. Aref had his quarry pinned to the floor, the point of his scimitar held unwaveringly to the man's eye. Then to my amazement I saw that the Saracen still held the beaker, and realised that what I had just seen was but an illusion.

"Finish it then," said de Frontignac to Aref, "Be certain I meant to rid the world of you, infidel, and these two fools."

"Hugh could make use of his clothes," said Reynald.

"Undress," commanded Aref.

"Of course, he would not care to wear this holy uniform if it were soiled with my blood," answered Robert with a sneer.

His uniform fit well, as we were roughly the same height and shape. Robert was manacled in the place where I had been restrained. We took down Hubert's body, covered him in my discarded habit, then laid him upon a bench.

Reynald and I stood at the cellar door. Aref remained standing before the captive, his eyes burning with hate. Robert de Frontignac looked fearful, as any man might, who anticipates his time is come.

"Will you allow an infidel to murder a fellow brother in Christ?" he appealed to us; there was not a hint of repentance about him.

"If you must, beg the Saracen to show you the mercy you denied his kinfolk," said Reynald. "As for myself, after the cruelty you inflicted upon innocent women and children, I care nothing for you."

Aref, filled with rage, bent down and lifted Robert's dagger from the ground. He was still holding the cup, but his eyes were fixed upon the knife. Robert cringed as Aref placed its blade against his neck.

Then the rightly vengeful man seemed to grow suddenly conscious of the cup, which he quickly put away inside his jerkin. I was amazed to notice that the cup, although small, brought no bulge whatsoever to his garment.

Aref dragged the dagger's point in a line down Robert's cheek from just beneath the eye to the chin. He said, "Were I not guardian of the cup, then vengeance would be mine. I leave you marked forever ... be sure that if I or any member of my clan ever set eyes upon you, that day will be your last. And I swear that even this holy cup will not stay my hand again."

Chapter Fifteen

Across from where he lay, swathed in shadow, two yellow eyes were watching, smouldering dimly; they were feral, relentless, callously assessing their prey, well-practised over long years of killing in the night. Jim Latimer could do nothing more than shift and squirm, pulling against his restraints in a hopeless bid to escape.

Rosemary, Nicholas and Picton waited patiently, eyes downcast, heads bowed, as solemn and as still as wax figures in an exhibition. Hart remained seated, forlorn and wretched, almost out of place there; like an object washed in by the sea; an oddity in the shape of a man. The room seemed to be suspended in time, as though all had become petrified; the only thing not motionless was Jim, his ribcage labouring hard to draw adequate breath.

Then, after what felt like a millennium, the watching was over, and the shadows were cast aside. Once he saw it emerge, that thing referred to as Mr Niedermayer, he fell to shaking, bedlam rampaging inside him. It covered the distance between them as swiftly as a reptile might, coming up close, boring into him with its terrible eyes. The hideous physique carried both the smell and look of death, and although the outer body resembled a human form in its proportions, a single look asserted that not one pinch of humanity remained. Mr Niedermayer was everything imaginable that is corrupt, and the effect of his presence upon a living mind was so overwhelming that Jim thought he would go mad or die of fright.

Niedermayer stood six feet tall but loomed larger, height exaggerated by his gauntness, the skin grey, cadaverous, stretched tautly like dried-out leather over a fleshless frame. The irises of the eyes were yellow and unnaturally large with no white visible, the pupils ovoid vertical slits. Such eyes had no difficulty seeing in the dark.

Underneath the sickening pallor of his skin were pronounced veins, brown in colour, most noticeable at the temples, neck and over the backs of the hands; the face and head were bald. He wore a tunic and leggings made of rusting chain mail beneath a torn and threadbare black cloak.

When Niedermayer stretched out a bony hand towards him, Jim automatically recoiled as far as his bonds would allow. In response to this effrontery, the pupils dilated and Niedermayer spat out a low snarl to express his displeasure. This action revealed a mouthful of pointed irregular teeth, sharp looking and darkly stained; a membrane of saliva, unpleasantly brownish, stretching in strings between the upper and lower jaw.

Jim was too terrified to move a muscle, except for his involuntary shaking, as Niedermayer's deathly fingers touched his cheek. The fingers themselves were elongated by filth-ridden nails, some broken off and cracked, some two inches long or more. Niedermayer traced a course from Jim's jaw down along the line of his jugular vein. Jim sensed the action brought something akin to pleasure in the creature. This unwanted insight became more fully realised when a long black tongue emerged from that appalling mouth and licked lasciviously around the teeth of its upper jaw and lip. Jim could do nothing but gape in horror at the sight.

With a sudden movement Niedermayer's head plunged towards Jim's face, drooling foul-smelling brown gobs of saliva onto his quivering cheek. Jim found it necessary to shut his eyes, convinced that he was about to die, repeating, 'Please God be quick! Please God make it quick!' over and over in his mind like a litany.

A few moments passed, and he realised that Niedermayer's disgusting breath had ceased pouring like excrement into his nostrils; he re-opened his eyes, not only surprised by the fact that he was still alive, but relieved to discover that Niedermayer had moved away. He was now about ten feet off from where he lay. Not that it brought any great feeling of safety; being a football pitch apart would not have lent much comfort.

*

Erich responded almost immediately when Ruth gently called his name.

"What is it?" he asked, rubbing at an eyelid.

"It's Jim. I woke up feeling extremely anxious. I've tried ringing his number – it's unobtainable."

Erich was suddenly wide awake. "You tried the operator?"

167

"Yes, disconnected," Ruth was shaking, "Something's terribly wrong."

Erich swung his legs out of bed, aware of more aches and pains than he generally experienced after a night's sleep.

"Should I call the police?"

"What would you tell them?" Erich replied fishing with his bare foot for a wayward slipper. "I'll go. If there's been trouble, then it will be time to call the police."

"I'm coming too," said Ruth.

"No," he replied without hesitation, immediately afterwards fumbling for a reason, "Someone should stay ... in case he tries to ring ... or maybe comes here."

Ruth made no protest. There were some areas where Erich would remain adamant; she concluded this would be the case here. He had grown up believing in a set of values, where women were treated respectfully at all times and protected from unpleasantness wherever possible. She fell in with it mainly because it would have used up valuable time to debate the issue.

Erich picked up his watch from the bedside table, strapped it onto his wrist and headed for the bathroom. It was 4.40am. He pictured his brother Hermann shaking a reproachful head at him.

"I'll make you a cup of coffee," Ruth said.

*

Niedermayer pulled up the mailed sleeve to expose his left arm, then with a long and putrid fingernail, sliced into the bulging vein on his inner forearm. Reddish-brown blood, the consistency of oil, oozed from the wound, down along the arm and hand onto the floor.

Rosemary came to life as though he had called to her, and she knelt at his feet as if the monstrous thing was her king. Then, to Jim's utter revulsion, she began to suck on the wound. Thirty seconds later she rose to her feet and returned to her place. Her eyes looked different now; they glistened, her face speaking of rapture.

Then Nicholas came forward and kneeled, avoiding the small pool of blood that had collected on the floor. However, as the youth eagerly bent down to drink from the arm, the creature bared its teeth and issued a warning growl. Nicholas, like a child fearful of correction cowered for a moment and said, "I am truly sorry for the misjudgements I made." Whatever the young man's transgressions were, Mr Niedermayer didn't look like the forgiving type. Nicholas seemed shaken as he got to his feet, quite desperate in fact; he went to stand beside Rosemary again who exchanged a brief look of commiseration with him.

The blood continued to drip from the creature's hand onto the ground with a plip every few seconds. Niedermayer eyed his captive, and his intention became crystal clear. Jim suddenly became insane with panic and fought the unyielding straps.

"Keep away from me! Keep away from me you bastard!" he screamed.

The cruel faces of Nicholas and Rosemary greeted Jim's eyes. Nicholas took hold of his head, whilst Rosemary gripped his nose with one hand and violently forced open his jaw with the other.

Time slowed to a near standstill, as the first drop fell from Niedermayer's arm into Jim's mouth; if decay, death and evil could be blended into a flavour, Jim would know its taste forevermore. He attempted not to swallow, but as the revolting liquid accumulated at the back of his throat, unable to breathe, he had no option.

He was made to drink three quantities. The blood was thick and cold as it ran down his throat; the desire to vomit was accompanied by a feeling of utter desolation.

So all-encompassing was his despair that he failed to notice when the source of the filth that had violated his mouth was gone. It was only when Rosemary released his nostrils, clamping his mouth shut with both hands to ensure every drop had been swallowed, that he glimpsed the back of Niedermayer's veined head and the flapping movement of his tattered cloak as it merged with the shadows again.

Rosemary sneered, "We all have to take our medicine Mr Latimer. See, Picton knows what's good for him."

She pointed to the red-haired man, on his hands and knees voraciously lapping up the pool of blood left for him on the floor. Jim's stomach contracted.

"Don't throw-up," she warned, "I'd only have to call Mr Niedermayer back. He may not be so good-natured and personable next time."

Jim turned his head away; he wouldn't allow her to see the tears collecting in his eyes.

With a violent jerk she grabbed his hair, twisting his head around so that he was looking directly into her face, and said, "Picton followed your every move for days. He recognised the stupid bitch that lives next door to you. I had my suspicions and showed him the video of your friends after they came spying on us."

Jim started sobbing. Why did he need to suffer any more of this, why couldn't they just kill him?

"Where are the old man and the bitch?"

One consolation remained, whatever they did to humiliate or hurt him, Jim would never betray his friends.

Then, to his uttermost despair he heard the words as they flowed out involuntarily from his own mouth, "Erich Ledermann, he lives in a bungalow at Pett ... Ruth's with him."

"I know the place," said Picton rising, replete from his à la carte dining. "Our Jim went there last night."

"Kill them," said Rosemary casually, "A fatal accident. I'll leave the details to you."

Picton smiled, the way people sometimes do when they find their work both challenging and rewarding; he left the room.

Rosemary returned her attention to the stupefied and weeping Jim. "Poor baby," she mocked, puckering her lips as though talking to a child, "Upset because we betrayed our friends?"

"Oh Christ ... Oh Christ no! No!" Jim cried helplessly.

"No good crying to him," she said, "He wouldn't be able to hear you in this place."

*

Erich turned into the ramshackle road that led on to the cottages; the heavy frost illuminated in headlights brought a spectral quality to the scene. The trees lining the route were dusted white along their boughs, branches eerily moving as the car rose and fell over the potholes in the road.

He saw as he emerged from the wooded avenue that both cottages were in darkness, and Jim's car was parked in its normal place cocooned beneath a layer of frost. Erich brought his car to a standstill beside Jim's but left its engine running, perhaps hoping that the noise might wake his friend. Half a minute later, after getting no response, Erich picked up a torch from the passenger seat. Then he switched off the car lights and engine.

There was a moment of hesitancy about him as he stepped from the car. Ruth had insisted he take his shotgun; considering it a piece of sporting equipment rather than a weapon he had not been enthusiastic, but her insistence eventually recommended the idea to him. However, it was still with some reluctance that he took the gun from the car boot.

He shone the torch down before his feet as he trekked along the footpath. The garden gate was the first thing that struck him as being out of place; it had been left wide open and Erich knew how jealously Jim guarded his vegetable plot. He shone the torch about; there had not been a clean view of the fronts of the cottages from the car. As its beam spilled light onto Jim's front door he realised with a jolt that it was wide open. Erich suddenly derived a sense of comfort from the weapon he held broken over his left arm, and slipped two cartridges into its barrels.

There was blood on the hallway carpet. Blood somehow evokes the most primitive response in the most phlegmatic of people; Erich felt his mouth turn dry and observed that his hands were trembling; the sight of blood on the wall seemed all the more disturbing in the dim, artificial light of a torch beam.

He considered using the mobile phone in his pocket. He could hear his brother Hermann's voice warning him. *That's far enough, call the police!*

He told himself that if Jim were dead then Ruth would probably have known. Precious time might be wasted if he called the police now, and after all, their opinions would undoubtedly be regarded with a large pinch of scepticism.

He decided that the shadows and unlit areas were too much to take, and anyway, his car had already proclaimed his arrival; so he turned on the lights in every room he entered, but kept his shotgun ready.

The sitting room had the remains of a log fire not quite cold in its hearth, but as far as he could tell nothing was out of place. Erich went back into the hall and walked through into Jim's study, here again there was no sign of disturbance.

The kitchen was a different matter; there had most certainly been violence here. The back door was open, and on the floor beside it lay a steel-bladed kitchen knife. The blade was stained with a blackish-brown substance which appeared to be as dry as dust.

"Better not touch anything," Erich told himself.

He noticed more of this dusty residue around the broken pane of glass, a great streak of it had run down the door frame. A small area of paint and wood had splintered away where something sharp, presumably the knife, had been driven in and then removed. On the floor there was another patch of the same dark stuff.

Erich thought the residue might have been blood, yet the assumption made no sense; it could only have been spilled around the same time as the blood in the hallway. Why, in that case, did it appear of have lain there for weeks, months even?

Erich took a deep breath before ascending the stairs.

It came as a relief to make no unpleasant discoveries in any of the upstairs rooms.

Erich went from room to room turning the lights off, intending to return downstairs again. It was at this point, as he came to Jim's darkroom once more, that the strip of negative hanging up caught his attention. He had seen it there when he first glanced into the room, but then he had been looking for things more sinister than a harmless piece of celluloid.

Erich was more than a little rusty when it came to film processing, having done an evening class in photography over ten years before. Danny had persuaded him to take something up during one of the many bad patches after his wife's death.

Jim's darkroom was well organised, which made the job easier, although Erich was surprised how readily the various processes came back to him. He cut up the negative into frames of six and placed them into the contact printer.

He ran through the routine. "Okay, twenty seconds under the enlarger, then a minute in the developer, swish under water then into the fix for ... er ... thirty seconds? Yes, I'm pretty sure ... then wash again."

He was about to take a piece of developing paper from its box before realising that the light was still on. "Crikey, fine photographer I am!" he exclaimed, switching to the red safety light.

He considered himself lucky when a few minutes later, the developing fluid worked its old black and white magic, and monochrome images bloomed before his eyes. About half the photographs were of Jim's daughter Sophie and her friends. As Erich scrutinised the contact sheet under a magnifying glass it was the photographs of Loxton at the chapel of rest that started to grab his attention. Finally, there was a set of photographs of some figures too far away to make out clearly from the contact sheet, so he decided to blow these up.

At first everything looked normal about the prints, but after a moment he began to notice unusual lines beneath the image depicted. He assumed the mistake was his, an error made at some point in the process, perhaps over-exposing the paper. As other prints took form in the developing fluid they each had the same inexplicable quality and appeared to hold another image beneath the surface. It took Erich a few minutes to comprehend exactly what he was seeing.

He'd recognised the Hines woman immediately; her clothing was more or less the same as it was when he'd met her with Ruth two days ago. However, the deeper Erich peered into her image the clearer the imprint grew that lay underneath her young face. The youthful Rosemary was superimposed over something a good deal older; a crone, at a more advanced age than any human being could rationally expect to reach. The eyes were deeply pitted and facial lines ran like a net across the skin, having long lost its elasticity and sagging in pouches on the cheeks and neck; her raven dark locks were shown here to be wisps of white on a balding head. In most of the pictures she and a companion, who was equally decrepit if you looked below the surface, were holding hands, and in one they were actually kissing; it was like a grotesque scene from a horror film; Erich assumed the man was Nicholas Cureton. In the final two photographs of the sequence another man appeared in the frame and here again an ancient face lay beneath the younger image imposed on top.

Erich clipped the photographs up then switched from the red safety light to the room's normal light to get a better look. Here there came a fresh surprise; under a standard room light the photographs looked completely normal, and the residual images disappeared altogether.

Contrary to whatever ideas Jim Latimer entertained about Erich, he did in fact have very few superstitious beliefs; but as he recalled the stuff he thought was dried blood on the back door, and for reasons he could not immediately explain, old superstitions, mostly from childhood, began running amok through his mind.

*

Shortly after Picton's departure, Hart left too. For some inexplicable reason, and in spite of his situation, Jim remained fascinated by Hart. He had never seen despair etched so vividly on a man's face before; it brought to mind the memory of him silently screaming in Jim's nightmare.

Rosemary was busying herself to Jim's right. At first he'd feared she was about to humiliate or injure him further, and he flinched when she went past. Nicholas, who was standing opposite her on Jim's left side, idly watching him, laughed at the sight of his nervousness.

"I don't have time to hurt you," she said brusquely, lifting off the floor a demijohn half-full of purplish-red liquid, instantly recognisable, and some heavily stained tubing. She removed these pieces of apparatus to a wash-basin a few feet away. The sight of the blood made Jim go cold and he could only watch through squinted eyes as the woman poured what appeared to be an enormous amount down the sink. His stomach turned over as the young girl's blood went glugging through a partially blocked U-bend.

"That Picton's a lazy bastard," she confided to Nicholas, whilst rinsing the plastic piping under the tap, the water running red through her hands. "If it's left it coagulates."

Nicholas appeared to be far away with his thoughts.

"He'll have to make a harvest soon, or else Mr N will not be happy."

But Nicholas was not interested in everyday business; he clearly felt bad about not getting his share of the blood and wanted to take it out on someone. "I think Mr Latimer is concerned about his fate," he wheedled, "How should I advise him, Rosemary?"

"I think you might suggest that he doesn't take up any long term projects."

"What, like a hobby, you mean?"

"Yes, that sort of thing, don't start knitting a long scarf."

Although Jim failed to appreciate the banter, he was long past the point where it mattered. After Mr Niedermayer their nasty humour was kids' stuff. But even so, Nicholas was an experienced pair of hands when it came to sadism, a crack shot.

"Don't imagine because you've tasted the blood that you will ever become one of us," said Nicholas, bringing his face close to Jim's, the eyes livid with malice.

The idea of being honoured with such a privilege had not occurred to Jim before.

But Nicholas had more cruelty up his sleeve, "Don't imagine you'll be filling Loxton's shoes on a permanent basis. And by the way, you ought to know that the blood you drank will make you entirely malleable to Mr Niedermayer's will. I suspect that a few days from now you'll find yourself somewhere ... very far from here, probably with your friend the Chief Inspector's torso by your side ... and when Mr Niedermayer tells you to, you'll kill yourself. I've no doubt it'll be something imaginative ... like Loxton."

Nicholas looked satisfied by Jim's reaction; he'd hit the mark beautifully, but there was more to do, "Of course your friends will already be dead by then ... a tragic accident. Imagine the shame your poor daughter will have to bear, learning that her father was part of a disgusting ring of paedophiles."

Rosemary had finished at the sink. She crossed the room and waited at the door for Nicholas.

He tapped a finger casually on Jim's shoulder. It was the hand that had been pinned to the kitchen door, yet there was no wound, not even a mark.

"We'll talk later," he said cheerily, as if to an old friend.

Rosemary went, but Nicholas turned back in the doorway for a parting shot, his hand hovering, much to Jim's unease, above the light switch.

"Have happy thoughts," he said, and with that Nicholas switched off the light and closed the door behind him.

Chapter Sixteen

Thursday, 12 December, 1996 approx 7am – 8.30am

Erich clipped the photographs up on a line above the darkroom sink. It was difficult to drag himself away from them. He felt like the witness to some terrible atrocity, appalled and horrified yet at the same time hideously fascinated. It was probably inexperience that had caused him to peer so keenly at the developing prints. A professional might easily have overlooked what lay beneath.

'What is it that could make an old man appear to be young?' he asked himself.

Erich was certain about one thing; they had woefully underestimated the force they were up against. Here before him was visual proof of something so powerful it could disrupt the very cycle of life. The swinging door of birth and death, that bedrock of universal law had somehow been side-stepped. Whatever the power source was, it had established an autonomy all of its own. The prints made him question things he had long taken for granted about the nature of the universe.

After a while, he came to his senses and remembered his reason for coming there.

'If I call the police, they'll see violence has taken place here. They'd have to investigate that at least …'

Of course, approaching the police would not provide answers to the metaphysical conundrum posed by the photographs, but practical help was urgently needed to search for Jim. Seeing no other option, he took the mobile phone from his pocket. Out of the corner of his eye he noticed the shotgun, still propped against the wall where he'd left it; he hesitated, finger poised.

Brother Hermann returned to mind. *What are you waiting for? Phone the police!*

"You are, of course, right as usual, dear Hermann," said Erich, replying aloud to the imaginary fraternal voice in his head, "But I somehow think I should check outside before I make the call … just in case."

176

Erich returned the mobile phone to his pocket and raised the shotgun.

Dummkopf!

*

Being strapped to a table in a pitch-black, soundproofed room has little to recommend itself. Especially knowing, as Jim did, that close by was something with excellent night vision and very sharp teeth. And although it was too dark to see the tip of his own nose, he was unable to remove his eyes from the point ahead where Niedermayer had first materialised. Those dreadful eyes glowing in the dark seemed the perfect incentive to stay alert.

After the sedative had worn off, various aches and pains had emerged throughout his body, particularly acute in his face and groin. It felt like he had a swelling around one eye, and also judging by the heat and sensitivity there, around the area of his crotch. Thanks to Rosemary's well aimed kick, he imagined his pants were hosting a pair of blue-black scrotal sacs the size of grapefruits. These injuries hadn't helped much in his battle to keep his head raised against the downward pull of the restraints holding him. Jim's constant surveillance of the alcove, which he of course knew to be utterly futile, was at the same time an unavoidable compulsion.

However, it occurred to him that for a while now, perhaps the last fifteen minutes or so, he had maintained his head and neck in that awkward position without much effort. In fact all his physical discomforts appeared to be rapidly diminishing. He reasoned this could only mean one thing; that the blood he'd been forced to drink was having an effect. Although he would probably have preferred not to, he made a connection between Loxton's youthfulness, the speedy recovery of Nicholas' hand, and his newly acquired obliviousness to pain.

It was torturous to recall what had happened only minutes after he'd swallowed that putrid filth; at the same moment as he was vowing never to give away his friends' whereabouts he'd betrayed them. This act, albeit involuntary, had devastated him. Nicholas was right to proclaim victory; they had indeed won. Soon Ruth and Erich would be two more victims of Niedermayer's ruthlessness, in a world oblivious to his very existence.

'How long before I become like them?' he thought, 'How long before they take off the straps and I won't think or want to run?'

Nicholas, the arch-sadist, had taken great pleasure forewarning him of his fate. As the darkness took root in his mind, Jim couldn't help picturing the ugliness he'd conjured up for him; how his name would be forever vilified alongside Loxton and the other paedophiles, and how his memory would be the cause of endless shame to his wife and daughter.

*

Erich stepped gingerly across the red bricked patio, treacherously glistening beneath his feet. The photographs with their hidden secrets had re-kindled all kinds of memories. The experience had left him feeling strangely disorientated. For some reason, his thoughts kept drawing him back to his place of origin, an Austrian village close to the border with Hungary. This in turn had triggered a plethora of half-forgotten stories, mostly involving long-held rural superstitions, folk tales and beliefs.

The grass was crunchy beneath his feet as he crossed the lawn. The garden shed he found unlocked. He checked inside and was relieved to find nothing unexpected, just tools and equipment. He shone the torch around the garden, and for the first time, he caught a glimpse of Ruth's back door through her kitchen window. The sight of which sent his blood pressure soaring through the ozone layer. He quickly cut through the gate into the adjoining garden. Unfortunately, it wasn't the optical illusion he found himself hoping for. Ruth's back door had been forced and left open to the freezing night like Jim's, its frame shattered where the lock was sited. It suddenly put a new complexion on everything. Erich began to chide himself for the time he'd wasted poring over the prints.

"What a fool I've been!" he remonstrated with himself.

The visit to Niedermayer & Hart's as husband and wife had not gone unnoticed. If Jim's activities were being watched, then Ruth too might easily have been recognised, not as the demure Mrs Ledermann, but as Jim Latimer's neighbour.

A terrible realisation struck Erich. If Jim had been followed, then he would have been seen visiting his bungalow last night.

"Dear God! I made Ruth stay there ... she's alone!"

*

Against every natural instinct he possessed, Jim started to fall asleep. At the same time his fearful state of mind abated.

The sound of his own voice jerked him back to waking as he whispered into the darkness, "This can't be right. I shouldn't feel comfortable. This isn't me. It's the influence of his ..."

He was not prepared to mention the B word, not out loud, not there.

'I told that evil bitch where to find Ruth and Erich. Next off, my aches and pains magically disappear and now I'm starting to feel like nothing's wrong ... like I ought to take a nap! Christ, who in their right mind could sleep here?'

It seemed ironic that when the door opened Jim had to turn his head away because the light hurt his eyes. He was aware of a back-lit silhouette, male he thought, framed within a blindingly bright rectangle. He assumed it was Nicholas, back to dispense more home-spun wisdom and kindly thoughts, an epilogue perhaps.

"I thought you might be thirsty." It came as a surprise and relief to identify Hart as the speaker. "I brought you some water. Let me know when you're ready for me to switch on the light."

"Go ahead," said Jim.

Hart closed the door behind him, limped over to Jim and waited for his eyes to adjust to the light before helping him to drink. Water had never tasted so clean and pure before, washing the acrid taste of Niedermayer's blood from his mouth, but unfortunately, not from the mind. Hart administered the water carefully. Jim's eyes, barely acclimatised to the light, returned to their surveillance of Niedermayer's alcove.

"Dawn has broken," Hart said.

"What?"

"Mr Niedermayer won't be troubling you."

"Until night-time?"

Hart made no reply. He hobbled back to the door and said, "I'll leave the light on for you."

"Mr Hart, I don't feel any pain."

Hart nodded. "You'll feel tired to begin with. It might be difficult to stay awake during the daytime, at least for the first few days."

Jim became agitated, tears of despair filled his eyes. "I have to fight it ... I can't let that evil bastard get inside my head," he sobbed.

Hart returned to the table-side and patted his good hand on Jim's shoulder. He performed the action tentatively, as though he could barely comprehend the thought processes that brought him to this show of compassion.

Jim bit on his lower lip, which was incidentally no longer painful, and glanced up at his comforter, "I won't give in to him."

Hart looked away, "Mr Latimer, it is useless fighting him," he said, emphasising the word 'him' by dropping his voice as he spoke it.

"What will happen to me?"

"I think you already know the answer," Hart replied. "Best not to think about it just now."

"I need to know. Please?"

Hart considered the request for a moment, gazing blankly into space; his face lost all expression. "The damage is done," he replied, flatly, without sentiment but without malice either.

Jim held his eyelids closed, peering into the abyss that had opened up before him.

"You'll notice changes, your eyesight and hearing will improve, even your sense of smell ... you'll understand why dogs suddenly begin to howl for no apparent reason ... I'm sorry."

Jim found that in some inexplicable way he trusted Hart, the man had a sincerity about him. He said, "It makes you stay young, doesn't it, like Loxton?"

"You'll never get a day older. Unless he decides you need punishing."

"I put a knife through Nicholas' hand ... there was nothing, not a mark."

"We heal rapidly."

When Hart spoke of healing he seemed like the most wounded person Jim had ever met. The stories told by his fellow inmates at the treatment centre had occasionally moved him to the point of tears; lives wrecked through the abuse of alcohol and drugs, often lives that had shown great potential dragged down to the gutter and beyond, any hopes, dreams and aspirations sold for a measure of alcohol or whatever substance turned you on and filled your own particular void. Hart reminded Jim of all the dependent people he had ever come across; except for one great difference, it was the thing Jim disliked most about his own personality; Hart lacked any self-pity.

"You're indestructible?"

"Not indestructible. You'll recall what became of Loxton?" Hart noticed that Jim was looking at his injured arm. "I probably did this before."

"Don't you remember?"

"When you've survived as long as I have, there's so much you can't recall."

"You aren't like the others," Jim said.

Hart looked unsettled by this observation, it seemed to fluster him. "Believe me, I'm really no different, Mr Latimer. I want exactly the same thing they do. All we do here is done to satisfy that need."

Jim noted that Hart trembled as he spoke of the object of his desire. Jim required no further description of the substance that evoked this craving.

As he observed him, Jim found Hart generated feelings of sadness in him; something which struck him as not only incomprehensible but quite absurd. Why on earth should he feel sympathy for one of his jailers?

Hart was well dressed outwardly, conveying success and affluence, but this struck Jim as wholly cosmetic. Jim had seen the man's private room, seen the egg boxes, bits of cardboard and magazines, strips of polystyrene covering the walls and ceiling. Not to insulate the room as he had originally thought, but to blot out the screams and cries that tormented him from five floors below. He had seen the library and could visualise Hart escaping the brutal reality of his life by burying himself in books. Something about him reminded Jim of the hurt he'd occasionally observed in the faces of the homeless. Hart seemed a wretched creature, inwardly derelict, caught in an endless web of despair.

"Why me?" Jim asked. There was nothing profound behind the question, he just needed to know.

Hart nodded; he seemed to understand. "Loxton kept a dossier … he probably imagined it would protect him if things got out of hand. Sooner or later, Loxton's executor was bound to come across it."

"Poor Bob."

"We needed a new catalogue. Nicholas suggested asking Mr Isherwood to recommend a friend. This he argued would be a good way of keeping an eye on Mr Isherwood." Hart's face expressed his low opinion for the scheme. "It was a mess from the start. I was in Holland. Rosemary tends to greet most of Nicholas' ideas favourably. It was very foolish, a stupid mistake. As you saw, Mr Niedermayer considered it a punishable offence … he won't tolerate anything that draws attention to us, thereby endangering his survival."

That it had boiled down to pot luck and bungling didn't make it any better. But it all fell into place; Jim could picture how the whole thing had come about; how he and Bob had been blissfully ignorant of the unimaginable truth.

"Was it the blood that made Loxton the way he was? I mean his interest in child pornography?" It was an important question for Jim.

The emphatic, "No," of Mr Hart's reply brought much relief. "We only employed John Loxton for our first catalogue because of his reputation. A prestigious photographer to get the mail order business launched." Hart paused, as if he was attempting to recall the past; 1957 was a long way back. "His sexual predilections were by then already established. Loxton sensed Mr Niedermayer's presence, as I'm sure you did too. The difference was that he found himself attracted, which I'm equally certain you did not. Mr Niedermayer decided he wanted to take Loxton on ... bring him into the firm so to speak. To begin with at least there was a mutual appreciation."

Hart looked edgy; he glanced around as if he feared being overheard. He dropped his voice to a whisper, "Mr Niedermayer found him entertaining." Hart seemed pained as he spoke, "But Loxton wasn't entirely a willing pair of hands ... he didn't like all the killing," adding with a look of disgust, "I suppose that at least wasn't part of his nature."

"He didn't commit suicide?"

Hart shook his head. "He was being investigated by the police. Loxton knew that Mr Niedermayer wouldn't tolerate his safety threatened. Perhaps he was always aware of how dangerous his compulsions were. Loxton had certainly tried to amass enough evidence to protect himself from his wrath."

"You don't strike me as a killer."

"I killed the girl," Hart replied, his anguish was quite visible. "Sometimes it can go on for weeks and she was so young, so very frightened ... she kept crying ... continually, day and night."

"He'd been feeding off her?" The idea of it turned Jim's stomach.

"He replaces the amount he loses to us."

"How often?"

"He 'harvests', that's our euphemistic term for murder, every seven to ten days. But we need to feed every second night ... which means there's generally someone imprisoned here in this room." The way he spoke suggested Hart found the practice almost as sickening as Jim did.

"What will happen to you and Nicholas now?" Jim asked. Hart didn't appear to understand the question, "Because you didn't feed tonight, will you die?"

Hart laughed ironically at the suggestion.

"If only ... if only," he said. Hart's whole physique shook as he reflected on what being denied the blood meant, "It's like an endless scream that goes on and on ... every nerve ending exposed ... every ounce of skin stripped away." Hart stared hauntedly as he considered the punishment, "If it goes on, after a few days, we'll slowly begin to age."

"Loxton aged rapidly?"

"That was because he died. While we're alive the process is far slower ... but believe me, very painful." He closed his eyes for a moment as if to blot out the idea.

"Has he made you go without before?"

Hart smiled grimly. There was so much pain in that face, Jim already knew the answer.

"I serve a purpose and because of that I am tolerated. You see I dreamed up the little charade we practise here."

"Is that why the porcelain business has your name in the title?"

Hart sighed. "I suspect he put my name with his so I can be constantly reminded that I belong to him."

"You hate him!"

"Hate? ... if only you could understand ..."

"Is there no way to escape?"

"Mr Latimer, to own something one hundred percent greatly diminishes the pleasure of exercising control upon it. I retain enough of my own mind to be totally repulsed by the business I am part of ... and all that I've become. He is entertained by the thoughts of rebellion I harbour. Death might seem attractive ... a way to achieve freedom ... but the idea of escaping him is an illusion ... just another of his taunts. You see, I possess no will of my own to stand against him. Just as you discovered when you betrayed your friends. I'm sure you had no such intention ... but don't blame yourself, you had no alternative, his mind is utterly compelling."

Now Jim understood why Hart was worthy of his compassion. "But the others seem to serve him willingly," he said.

"Because they are realists. I am a weak old fool, horrified by the very horror that gives me life. When I leave here, as I sometimes do on business, it's a relief to escape from all this obscenity. Yet, at the same time, it's an agony to be parted from my craving."

"But you go on resisting. You acted against his will when you gave that girl an overdose."

"And for what? The girl died sooner, that's all. A few days and Picton will have replaced her with someone else. At least the others

183

don't make any pretence about finding our activities hateful ... they accept it as reality. I go on, just as they do, day after day, craving the filth that pours from his arm ... and he continues to consume me."

"You can't help it," replied Jim, "But you are still human and he must hate you for that. Not because you're weak, but because after everything he still can't fully extinguish your humanity."

Something not evident before suddenly lit up Hart's face, bringing it to life for the briefest of moments; it was as though he recalled a distant memory of the man he had once been. It was fleeting, like the sudden appearance of a chink of blue sky in a whirling ocean of dark grey clouds; a second later and it was lost again.

"I dreamed about you. I saw you in my dream the night before I met you."

"I'm sorry?"

"It came as quite a shock ... when I met you. You'd actually been in my dream only a few hours before."

"Tell me what happened."

"Two men, monks I thought. They were on a journey. It was wintertime, the ground was frozen ... you were a lot younger. Rosemary was there, and now I think of it so was the red-haired man ... Picton? The fact they were in the dream didn't really surprise me, as I'd already seen them both before. But they looked exactly the same as they do now. Rosemary held a baby in her arms and you were kneeling in front of her. I couldn't hear what you said. She refused to look at you and ..."

"I'm sorry, I don't have time to listen to any more," said Hart. His face was ashen. He added, "I'm afraid I have to leave ... Rosemary and I must set off early ... I'm sorry ... I have to go."

"You recalled something?"

Hart made no reply. For a moment the two men held each other's gaze; it felt as if each of them held a different portion of the same picture.

Then Jim said, "Please, listen to the rest of it ..."

"Like I said ... I must go," Hart replied. "It's Thursday, Rosemary and I will set off soon. You see it's pay-day for our staff in Eastbourne, and we have to pretend to go carefully through the books. It's all a sham. Did you know we employ thirty-four people?" Then he added with a note of irony, "They fully believe our business is porcelain."

An image came into Jim's mind as he watched Hart shuffle towards the door; it was of Hart, moulded in clay, like an item photographed for their catalogue; something unusual, rare even, but irreparably damaged, a piece of cracked porcelain.

Then he was gone. The door was shut fast behind him, and only Jim remained.

He no longer considered it necessary to watch the alcove, since Hart had assured him he was safe in daylight hours.

Jim lay back and yawned; almost unexpectedly a large tear expelled itself from his left eye and proceeded to roll down his cheek. The light had been left on, but the cellar remained an exceedingly dark place.

Hugh's Tale

VIII

The steps and passageway that led from Ferdinand's private quarters to the underground chamber proved to be only a very small part of a much larger network of caves and tunnels. Whichever past rulers of Acre had made the discovery only needed to gain entry, for the real architect was nature itself.

After the encounter with Cornelius we began our exploration with no little sense of trepidation; and as our journey proceeded through that underground labyrinth, an ever deepening foreboding grew within us. Aref went first to light our way; I came next, with the crucifix from the desecrated altar in my arms and fear in my heart; then finally, at the rear was Reynald, bearing the other torch to keep watch over our backs.

The smallest sound might betray us; mere whispers were magnified tenfold in that echoing maze, therefore we spoke seldomly. Sometimes the tunnel forked, but Aref chose our path with unwavering certainty as if he possessed a nose for sniffing out the works of evil.

In some places we walked at full height through broad avenues; at other times the walls and roof closed in, forcing us to squeeze into holes upon our hands and knees, or travel through gaps only large enough to take a man sideways on. How long we journeyed I cannot say; fear makes for a bad timekeeper. I suspect we had gone about a quarter of one league when suddenly Reynald gripped my arm; I immediately communicated the warning to Aref; we held still and listened. Coming behind, I judged a good distance from us yet, were the unmistakable sounds of footsteps.

We increased in speed yet tried to maintain our stealth, for being discovered in such a tight spot would have offered us little opportunity to show much resistance. We reached a turn in the passageway and hurried forward. There was no way of telling that our subterranean journey had nearly reached its end. As we clambered around the final part of an extremely tight corner, Aref gestured us to be still. Our efforts had finally brought us to the mouth of a cavern which lay but a short distance ahead. Its walls were alive with moving shadows, projected into monstrous shapes by the effect of many torches.

Aref extinguished his flame and Reynald did the same. We crept forward in silence, marked only by breathing and the beating of our hearts in dread anticipation of what awaited us. Aref stole a glance within; he shook his head to say he could see nothing, then took a few paces more and positioned himself behind a boulder which lay to the right of the cave's entrance. From here he risked another look, and gestured us to join him. I heard voices, but could not distinguish the words being spoken. Yet our most pressing concern was the sound of approaching footsteps; we heard these distinctly enough, for they were rapidly closing in behind us. It was about a yard's distance from the boulder to a stone pillar that stretched up to the cave's roof. Aref, judging it safe, sent us across one at a time. I went first.

Here I received a first glimpse of a large cavern, which I had entered along a gallery running across one end of it. The gap we had needed to cross fell away into twenty or more roughly-hewn steps that led to a bowl-shaped arena at their base. I saw figures below but only fleetingly, my attention mostly concentrated on reaching the pillar unseen.

Once the three of us had crossed it was obvious that the pillar, although broad, would not obscure us from the eyes certain to emerge at any moment from the passageway. So, crouching behind a low wall that ran alongside the pillar, we followed the curve of the balcony until we felt sure of our concealment.

At first I thought the cavern must be a culmination of all the underground passages. Then as I looked about I saw that this was probably not so, for a little way behind us was a hole leading off into darkness beneath unstable looking rocks. This passageway had it seemed been investigated, for its opening was shored up with timbers, allowing a man bent double to enter.

I peered cautiously over the wall of rocks before me, counting eight men, all knights of Jerome's secret chapter. However, there appeared to be a problem with the group's unity, for four of these knights were bound-up, gagged and cast upon the ground; the remaining four sat freely on the rocks round about, laughing amongst themselves.

The lower level was well-lit with torches, with only one area hidden from our view, being concealed beneath an overhang of rock; most likely, I thought, the entrance to yet another chamber.

The four unbound knights were making much sport in tormenting their restrained brothers.

"Wait until you meet the master," one taunted.

"They thought he was dead!" scorned another.

"They were right there!" mocked a third.

The fourth knight merely laughed along with the others.

"Perhaps you won't find his looks too appealing, not quite as handsome as he was," put in the second man again, needling the captives who were already scared beyond their wits.

The others laughed uproariously.

The sound of feet echoing through the tunnel was now very loud indeed. Yet the four below, obviously hearing this approach, seemed unperturbed. From our position we could not see who entered, but from the cessation of footsteps and the response of the men below it was clear an expected party had emerged.

I recognised Wilhelm's voice and accent a moment before I saw him descending the staircase. Unlike the others, who were wearing military uniform, he was dressed only in his habit and was accompanied by the serjeant who was carrying a torch.

Wilhelm became immediately red with anger at the sight of the bound knights and the impudent faces of those awaiting him. "What is the meaning of this? Why are these brothers held prisoner?"

They responded to his questions with jeering and laughter.

"What is the matter with you? Fools!" he raged. "Release them immediately!"

Wilhelm was shocked to find his commands being openly scorned. Not one of them had ever dared show him such disrespect before. He turned to the serjeant for assistance, only to discover him smiling slyly. The German knight was starting to look distinctly unnerved.

"Where is Laszlo? You told me he had something to impart to me!" he shouted angrily in the man's face.

The serjeant gestured at the cave mouth below the overhang. We were as yet unable to see anything. However, it was clear that Wilhelm could, for his naturally sanguine features drained white, and he began to shake. The mocking knights immediately fell silent and lowered their eyes in what must have been an expression of deference.

"L-L-Laszlo ... wh-what has happened?" asked Wilhelm as he staggered backwards. The serjeant blocked the way and prevented him from retreating further. "Y-your eyes!"

An unnaturally deep voice came back from the shadows, "I have received the gift of new life."

I felt my stomach contract when Laszlo, or the thing he had become, entered the chamber. His eyes were smouldering yellow as though a sulphurous fire burned in them, whilst the light from the torches accentuated the hideous pallor of his grey dead skin. Unlike Jerome his progenitor, Laszlo had retained the power of speech; perhaps Cornelius had too, I thought, but during our battle had found no requirement to speak. Like Jerome, Laszlo wore his Templar uniform with the cross patee torn from it, and, also in keeping with his mentor, he wore no helm. A deep wound was visible upon his neck where sharp teeth had torn open the flesh. Yet apart from retaining the facility of speech, Laszlo possessed no more humanity than Jerome.

"Where is Cornelius?" Laszlo bellowed at the serjeant, producing a sound more like the growl of a beast than the speech of a man.

The serjeant shook his head.

"Fetch him!" Laszlo issued this command to the four knights. They immediately climbed the steps and departed into the tunnel we had entered by.

I exchanged anxious looks with Reynald and Aref. Our situation was extremely precarious. Soon Cornelius' destruction would be discovered. Then we would find ourselves in the unenviable position of being trapped and outnumbered with our escape route blocked.

"What do you want of me?" asked Wilhelm.

Laszlo made no answer; the serjeant laughed openly at the knight's question.

Wilhelm continued in a fearful voice, "P-perhaps I c-can help you leave Acre ... escape r-retribution ... I could a-arrange ..."

"Be silent, fool," growled Laszlo, his eyes flaming a deeper yellow. "We have no need of your assistance."

Wilhelm attempted to flee as Laszlo drew nearer, but the serjeant held him fast.

"Let us not argue, brother," said Laszlo, now face to face with the terrified Wilhelm. "Tomorrow we sail for Constantinople ... you amongst us."

"Me?" replied Wilhelm, horrified at the idea.

Laszlo gripped Wilhelm's shoulders as though intending to embrace a comrade. The German knight flinched at the deathly touch. "All is arranged," said Laszlo, "The Master has commanded it."

"Master?" asked Wilhelm weakly.

"See, he comes to watch as I impart his gift to you."

Wilhelm struggled desperately to free himself as Jerome emerged from the shadows. Jerome had degenerated a good deal since Wilhelm

189

had last seen him. His hair had now disappeared altogether and pointed canine teeth protruded over his lower lip, whilst brownish veins ran in a network below the surface of his corpse-like flesh.

Then a shout echoed along the passageway. The call, although indistinct, was clear to us by its urgency. A moment later it came again; this time its purpose was made clear to all.

"Cornelius is destroyed!" came the cry.

Jerome at once let out an inhuman howl, enraged to hear of a crime perpetrated against one of his disciples. And then he began to look suspiciously about, as though he detected something in the chamber was out of place; or perhaps he could sense the living blood coursing through our veins. His eyes roved across the rocks, and within a few moments alighted on the dimly lit area where we hid. He raised an arm and pointing a grey finger up at us, released a fearsome growl.

I doubt I could have done anything to save myself; I was rooted to the spot with terror. Reynald grabbed the crucifix from my hand and stood, holding it out before him.

"Let Wilhelm go," he shouted. Aref rose to his feet beside him, and I, partly returning to my senses, did the same.

Jerome spat a mouthful of foul brownish saliva onto a rock by means of a reply. Wilhelm looked hopefully towards us, but Laszlo did not release him. He opened his jaws, exposing a mouthful of pointed teeth and started to gorge on Wilhelm's neck. The German knight screamed out in agony for the few seconds of life that remained to him, as his blood gushed into Laszlo's mouth before falling limp and silent to the ground.

The serjeant drew his sword and rushed up the steps towards us. The three of us had drawn too, but the landing was only wide enough to take one pair of men in combat.

"Our masters do not take commands from their next supper," the serjeant said mockingly as he approached us.

Aref pushed me towards the mouth of the tunnel that lay behind. "Get in!" he shouted.

The ceiling was low and we had to stoop to enter. Reynald went ahead and I heard Aref exchanging some blows before clambering into the hole after me. We had to scramble and crawl inside for a good distance before the cave opened out, allowing us to stand at our full height. At first I thought we had achieved a strong position, for any attacker would be forced to travel along the cramped corridor, unable to protect themselves.

Several minutes went by. The four knights who had discovered Cornelius' remains returned, taking it in turns to peer at us.

"There is no way out of there!" one advised.

"You will have to come out sometime!" mocked another.

Then they disappeared for a few minutes. After a while, the serjeant returned and began to clamber into the hole towards us. At first we could not tell what his intention was. When he reached a point about halfway along he stopped besides a large central prop supporting the roof. Then, taking the end of a coiled rope carried on his belt, he began to attach it to the post.

Reynald, seeing the intention, sprang into the tunnel in an attempt to stop him; but the rope had been secured and the serjeant was fleeing the passageway before Reynald made half the distance.

"Come back!" exclaimed Aref.

Reynald ignored the call and went on.

At the cavern end the serjeant was being congratulated on his handiwork and helped from the tunnel by the knights. We heard the sound of the men as they heaved, and saw the line of the rope being pulled taut.

"For God's sake man, get out!" I called.

Dust and small stones were descending as the shoring on the ceiling started to give way. Reynald, struggling with the rope, saw there was no hope of untying it in time and began to crawl back towards us. The prop was beginning to move, another pull might easily bring it down and the roof with it. Reynald was just beyond an arm's reach when I recall seeing the post fall, and with it a great boulder crashed down at the farthest end blocking out the light. I reached in blindly, seeking for my friend, Aref doing the same. As we hauled him from the jaws of death, and jumped for safety into darkness, the ceiling all along the passageway fell with a cataclysmic roar.

Chapter Seventeen

Thursday, 12 December, 1996 approx 7.30am – 8am

Danny Ledermann sent an exploratory hand out from beneath the rumpled mound of blankets he was buried under to search out and destroy the ringing telephone. The quality mattress he had been asleep on, a birthday gift from his father, was stationed, without the complications of a bed-frame, on an area of his studio floor designated as sleeping space. He had been working on a piece of sculpture until the early hours; and although he had no idea what time it was, he found his internal body clock protesting wildly at the outrage of the ringing telephone.

"Yeah," he croaked.

"Danny, you awake?"

"I am now Dad, what time is it?"

"Ruth's on her own at the bungalow; she's alright, I've just spoken to her. Listen, she may be in danger, Danny. I'm too far away, but you could be there in a few minutes."

"What danger?" Danny asked, still bleary-eyed but already pulling on a pair of plaster-spattered jeans with his free hand.

"There's no knowing what they might do."

Danny could not recall his father sounding so troubled.

"Who? Not the people you and Ruth went to see on Tuesday?"

Danny recalled the sight of Ruth and Erich returning to the car at Hove; Ruth white as a sheet, his father looking unusually old and weary. They had said very little to him on the way home about their experience, and Danny wasn't given to prying. Unlike his father and Ruth, he was not entirely convinced about psychic phenomena.

"Everything is much worse than we thought. Please, will you fetch Ruth?"

"I'm nearly dressed," replied Danny, flicking a lump of dried plaster off the laces of a boot.

"Danny, please be careful. Get Ruth then leave. If anyone shows up, whatever you do don't confront them. Just get away from there as fast as you can. You understand, Danny? These people are not normal."

It was too early to ask exactly what 'not normal' meant.

"Shall I bring Ruth here?"

"No, go to the sisters'."

"Okay."

"Please, take care, Danny."

Danny drove fast and arrived at the bungalow seven minutes later. The roads although deserted were treacherous with ice, but he knew the route and which stretches to approach with caution. Although past dawn, the day seemed sluggish and reluctant to kick itself off the starting blocks.

He left the car facing downhill on the access road behind the bungalow and stepped out into the grey morning mist which clung low to the ground. He entered the back gate and pelted down the garden, tried the kitchen door to see if it was open before producing a set of keys from his pocket.

"Ruth?" he called tentatively on entering, "Ruth, you there?"

"In here," came the welcome response from the sitting-room. Danny's adrenal glands had been doing a bout of overtime ever since the wake-up call. He breathed a sigh of relief and felt the tension inside him ease. He began to suspect that his father, although it was unlike him, had exaggerated the imminent danger bit.

'Where the hell is he anyway?' he thought, feeling a tad crotchety. 'Why leave Ruth here and go off somewhere alone if she's in danger?' Danny found himself questioning the whole exercise.

He walked from the kitchen through the hall then into the sitting-room. Ruth was kneeling before the closed curtains, peering through a small gap at the road outside. She turned her head to glance up at Danny as he came in, the telephone in one hand to her ear, whilst in the other hand she grasped a sturdy wooden rolling-pin taken from the kitchen.

"He's got here. Yes, Erich, at the sisters' ... half an hour or so." Ruth put the telephone down and greeted Danny with a smile that failed to camouflage the worry on her face.

"Thanks for getting here so fast, Dan."

"Dad sounded worried. He seemed to think your life was in danger?"

Ruth decided it was not the time to debate that question, "We have to go. I just need a minute to collect my things. Would you keep an eye on the road?" She gestured to the gap in the curtains.

Ruth's nervousness was uncharacteristic; he'd known her for a good many years and had never seen her looking so troubled. In fact, Danny always thought of her as a phlegmatic type. The amount of tension she was exhibiting together with his father's dramatic phone call left Danny feeling quite confused.

"Yes sure," he replied, taking up a position in front of the curtains, adding as she brushed by him, "Of course, I have no idea what this is all about ... and why the hell should anybody start explaining anything to me?"

"I'll explain in the car ... I'm sorry Dan, is that alright?"

"Okay," he relented, half-smiling. Ruth went off to collect her stuff. Danny by temperament was easygoing, and any curmudgeonliness about him was mainly due to insufficient sleep.

Ruth's sense of urgency hadn't diminished by the time she returned. True to her word she had taken only a minute, perhaps less to get her things; Danny was surprised to see her back so soon. She had with her a small bag, and still in her possession but now cradled between the handle straps of the bag, was the rolling-pin.

Danny's attention was split between Ruth's return and the arrival of a white van slowly cruising along the front of the property. The driver was in shadow but Danny saw his outline clearly. He was certainly paying a good deal of attention to the bungalow as he drifted by.

"What is it?" Ruth asked, rushing beside him and catching a final glimpse as the van disappeared behind a hedge. "We have to get out!" she said anxiously.

"You recognised him?"

"No, but we don't want to tangle with him."

Danny didn't move and continued to stare through the gap in the curtain as though mesmerised. Looking out at an angle he saw the top of the van coming to a stop about twenty feet away behind the boundary hedge.

"We must go, Dan. Now!" exclaimed Ruth, heavily emphasising the now.

Ruth, who had spent much of the time since Erich's departure listening to the radio, had caught several reports about Bob and Daphne's murder. The news item also mentioned that a Detective Chief Inspector Ian Rice was also missing. Ruth remembered that Jim had made reference to someone called Rice as being a friend of Bob Isherwood's.

Armed with this knowledge, including everything they already suspected and what Erich had recently uncovered at Jim's cottage, she said with conviction, "Dan, two people are already dead, possibly three!"

Danny suddenly seemed to come round, remembering his father's explicit warning.

"Let's go," he said, and led the way out through the hall and kitchen.

As Danny closed the back door softly behind them they heard the sound of the doorbell ringing at the front. Danny fumbled in his pocket for the door key.

"Leave it!" Ruth whispered, tugging his arm away.

They hurried up the garden then exited through the gate. Ruth closed it behind them as quietly as she could.

"Don't start the engine. Get in and take the brake off. I'll push," she said, keeping her voice low.

Danny did as he was told. The car only needed a helping hand to get it rolling down the slope of the lane. Danny reaching across let Ruth into the passenger door.

She kept a vigilant watch over her shoulder out of the rear window. They had travelled about fifty yards, almost three-quarters the length of the lane, when Picton rushed through the gate. Ruth let out a short gasp as she saw him emerge. Danny caught sight of the stockily framed man in his rear view mirror.

Picton's face glowered darkly at the sight of them escaping, and he immediately broke into a run.

"Start up!" shouted Ruth.

Remarkably for one of Danny's ancient vehicles, the car started first time. Their pursuer stopped abruptly in his tracks when he heard the engine start, then swiftly altering course, disappeared once more into Erich's garden.

The white van was parked only a few yards from the mouth of the lane and Danny came to a stop beside it.

"Keep going," Ruth said anxiously, "Why are you stopping?"

Danny didn't reply as he stepped out, quickly taking a penknife from his pocket and jabbing its blade into the front and back tyres of the van along the side nearest to his car. He jumped back into his seat only a split second before the squat man rushed out of the bungalow's driveway.

Picton stopped abruptly and read the situation, his face scowling at the sound of escaping air. He stared directly at the car's occupants, baring his teeth as he cursed them.

Danny gave a smile of victory, but this proved to be extremely short-lived, a truly Pyrrhic experience. His composure started to evaporate when their pursuer started to sprint directly at the car. Danny plunged the gearstick into reverse, but not quite fast enough, and to his enormous surprise found that he had picked up an extra passenger when their assailant recklessly dived headlong onto the car bonnet.

"Christ!" spluttered Danny.

Picton lay flat across the car's front, one hand clutching the wing mirror.

Danny reversed with as much speed as he could muster. Then he applied the brakes suddenly. The man's body was flung a foot or so into the air, his face smacking into the windscreen with a bump. Amazingly, he still held onto the wing mirror, much to Danny's horror and fast growing realisation that this was all very unusual. The man's features were pressed tightly against the windscreen, the skin flattened white on the glass.

Danny's manoeuvre had largely served only to consolidate the red haired man's position on the front of the car; in fact, making things far worse, because Picton's head was now blocking his line of vision. The man's hair poked out in wiry profusion from the sides of his cap and he communicated an awareness of his improved tenure by grinning directly into Danny's face.

Pulling back his lips and offering Danny the most inane of smiles, Picton drove his fist at the windscreen. It cracked the glass directly in front of Ruth's face, who let out an involuntary shriek.

"Can't you shake him off?" she screamed in Danny's ear, almost deafening him.

A second blow caused the whole of the windscreen to shatter and become opaque.

"Oh hell. Hold on!" warned Danny as he ground the gearstick into first and took off.

He could only judge his position on the road by the distance from the kerb viewed through the side window. Fortunately he knew the road well. Two seconds later he put the car into second and then, as the revs and speed increased, up into third. Incredibly the man clung on although now slightly obscured to the car's occupants behind the frosted glass. It was like sitting inside a drum as Picton repeatedly punched at the windscreen.

As the car hit thirty mph and Danny judged that he would soon be meeting a bend in the road, he stepped hard on the brake. The car skidded over to the right on the icy surface but Danny corrected by steering into it. There was a sound of metal tearing as the wing mirror ripped away, the man's silhouette being played onto the windscreen as he was propelled backwards. Picton's acrobatic stunt was closely followed by a dull thud as the car, still moving forward, rammed into his body.

Danny's face instantly drained white and he began to tremble. He suddenly realised what had happened, and that the force of the impact might easily have killed him.

"Christ, what have I done?" he said, opening his door.

"Stay inside!" Ruth cried out, but Danny was too shocked to hear.

The red-haired man was lying face down in the road, his head only a few feet from the front wheel on the driver's side. His face had been skinned along its cheek and jawline, resembling ground beef, peppered black here and there with pieces of grit from the road. His cap had come off with the impact, and lay a few feet away. The man was completely bald in the centre of his head, and an old, deep, white scar ran from where the ring of red hair began just before the crown to the top of his forehead.

Danny squatted beside him; he was certainly seriously injured if not dead. Danny reached out and shook the man's shoulder tentatively. There was no response; he assumed the worst.

Then an eye in the bloody face flicked open, a look of consummate cunning contained in its pupil. Danny gasped with shock as a strong hand lunged out and grabbed him with a strength undiminished by all that had happened. Danny was thrown off balance and fell backwards, for the next few seconds floundering about like a beached turtle on its shell. The red-haired man clambered over him, the hideous grazed face smiling down.

Then a look altogether more sadistic came over his attacker's eyes. Danny felt his body become rigid with fear; as if deep within some instinct understood he was the defeated prey of an unmistakable predator.

Danny was aware of little more than the rush of blood in his ears, and completely oblivious to whatever caused the red-haired man to turn his head in response. It happened really fast, and Danny caught no more than a flurried glimpse of Ruth as she swung the rolling-pin.

Picton had to release his hold on Danny in an effort to protect his face. Ruth however proved too fast and too accurate as she smashed the solid kitchen utensil across the bridge of his nose. Picton yelped in pain and fell backwards, hands up holding his face, red exploding between his fingertips.

On the ground he recovered fast, but was momentarily blinded by the blood in his eyes. He scrambled onto all fours and started to scurry away like a rat. Ruth, however, was not about to let him off that lightly.

"Get into the car!" she shouted at Danny, who was looking up at her like a stunned animal. "Dan, get into the fucking car and start it up!" she screamed.

This time he was galvanised into action. As he made for the car, Ruth was wielding the implement in both hands over the back of Picton's head.

Danny heard the unpleasant sound of wood hitting bone as he took up his position behind the steering-wheel. He had stalled the engine in the braking manoeuvre, but once more, twice in a row being a minor miracle, it started first time. Beginning to get a hold on himself again, he pulled down the sleeve of his coat and smacked out the useless windscreen.

There was another cracking sound accompanied by a squeal of pain, then Ruth jumped in beside him, her face white; Danny was never quite sure whether this whiteness was caused by shock or fury. "Back up Dan," she said in a controlled voice.

Ruth was in command and Danny felt relieved just to do her bidding; not questioning for a moment the wisdom of his old art teacher, who had revealed herself to him that morning in a totally new light. He swiftly reversed down the road and then backed into his father's driveway. As he looked along the road to the violent scene of only a minute ago, he was surprised to see that the red-haired man was already back on his feet. Picton was shaking his head from side to side in response to the violent blows his skull had absorbed.

"That's ... that's just not possible," Danny said in open-mouthed amazement.

"Don't let's stop to debate it ... it's real, keep going," said Ruth, aware that the red-haired man was already focusing his attention on them again.

Danny did not hang about, taking the car left, the opposite direction to Picton. Nothing on earth could have induced him to go anywhere near that mad animal again.

Looking over her shoulder, Ruth saw Picton retrieve his cap and angrily plant the thing back on his head. A second later Danny took a turning to the right and he was gone.

"I thought ... he was going to kill me!" Danny was shaking as he spoke. "The way he looked at me ... Christ ... he would have killed me!" Danny shook his head like he was hoping he might wake up from the nightmare. "If it hadn't been for you ..."

"It was team work."

"Shit! You were amazing!" Danny remained stunned, the drama replaying itself in his head.

"I suppose an orphanage upbringing does give you an edge in some ways," she said, holding up the five surviving inches of the wooden rolling-pin.

Danny gulped, audibly.

"Your father's pastry cases will never be the same again."

Hugh's Tale

IX

Fortunately, by the time the dust settled and our coughing had abated, we found ourselves unharmed. We groped about in the pitch blackness, searching for some chink of light, but discovered nothing; where the tunnel had been, our hands met a barrier of immovable rocks. The serjeant's handiwork had thoroughly sealed off the passageway.

Reynald summed up our plight, "Jerome has won. We are discarded here to die ... the truth entombed with us."

Then, booming out of the darkness, came Aref's voice in reply, "We must survive."

"Christ's goodness, how?" I asked scornfully. "Would they have abandoned us here if a way out existed?"

"Aref is right, we are too knowledgeable to die," said Reynald. "We alone know how to destroy the demons, and must at least live long enough to pass on this knowledge."

"But even if there were a way, how could we ever discover it? Three blind men tripping about in the dark," I retorted.

"The nameless one gives His light to cast aside the darkness," Aref replied.

As he spoke he removed the cup from beneath his coat. It was exuding a greenish light, and as I watched this marvel, hope's flame rekindled within my soul. The cup's radiance grew in potency, transforming itself into a brilliant white glow that exposed every dingy nook of our intended grave.

"The cup will lead us," I said in awe.

"The cup will light our path. We must find the way," said Aref.

Words fail, Anselm, when they seek to convey the heavenly brilliance that poured from that holiest of vessels. Perhaps I risk blasphemy by my crude attempts to describe it, for its light was not of this world of shade; it illuminated our path entirely, and most marvellous of all, cast no shadow in its wake. Under its influence all injury and anguish seemed miraculously soothed.

The labyrinth meandered through interminable passageways into numerous caves; yet everything revealed through the cup's light was of an exquisite beauty. At times we explored vast caverns, the expanse and grandeur of Christendom's mightiest cathedrals, yet found nothing, no chink of light or wisp of air that might offer us hope. We had no food to sustain us but there was water in abundance, for some of the caverns contained great pools. After many hours of exploration, we found ourselves back in a place that we recognised, having gone full circle. Hungry and tired, we were forced to rest, settling upon some flat rocks in a large cavern beside an expanse of water the size of a small lake. How long we had explored or what time we took sleeping I cannot tell.

When I awoke, the cave was in darkness again and I felt despair race quickly back into my mind. But my fear was swiftly dispelled and my heart rejoiced to see the light rekindled within the cup at Aref's side.

"I see the cup has taught you something of faith," said Aref, who was observing me.

"Would that I possessed a good deal more of that quality," I replied.

"Its way is hard," he replied, "For the evil one is ever at our elbow whispering his doubts."

As I looked upon Aref's face lit by that divine light I became strangely unsettled. Here was a Saracen, my enemy, yet I could see no fault in the man; having already proven himself a faithful companion by assisting in my rescue from men of my own brotherhood. To say it bluntly, I felt no longer certain who my enemy was or who was my friend.

I knelt at the poolside and raised some water to my mouth in cupped hands, swallowing a large mouthful to quench my thirst on waking; only to find myself a moment later coughing and spluttering.

Reynald was wakened from sleep by the noise I made. "What is wrong?" he asked confusedly.

I was still choking on the water and incapable of making a reply. Aref stooped down beside me, dipped a finger into the pool and put it to his tongue to taste.

"Our friend may have discovered a way out," he said. "This is salt water! Beneath this pool there must be an outlet to the sea."

"I cannot swim," said Reynald.

"This might be a good time to learn," replied Aref.

Holding the cup aloft to give himself light, Aref waded into the pool, and then taking a deep breath, submerged beneath its waters.

Reynald and I watched the cup's light as it radiated from beneath the lake's surface. Aref was forced to re-emerge several times for air before he finally discovered something.

"There is a channel, quite narrow, but worth attempting. I will explore where it leads then return."

He took a large breath into his lungs and dived below again. I watched his feet break the surface and felt my heart sink as I saw the cup's light fade.

Once again darkness returned to the cavern. At the same time the seeds of doubt and suspicion began to find fertile soil in my mind. I asked myself why this Saracen, if he reached safety, should bother coming back, and risk losing his own life to save ours. After all, we were Templars, Christian Knights opposed to his race and creed; he possessed Christ's cup, that most precious object that all men sought. I wondered: in a different situation, would I have risked my life to save his?

I did not voice these doubts aloud; at least I do not believe I did, unless my previous incarceration and this new return to darkness conspired to bring madness upon me. Yet Reynald spoke as if in reply to me out of the dark, or as though he could read my thoughts; perhaps similar ideas were encroaching on his own mind.

"He will return," he vouched, "Else I never judged a man so wrong. If we are to die in this hole then it will be because Aref has perished too."

Time passed, at least a hundred times longer than any man could conceivably hold onto his breath for. Still we waited, hoping and watching for the light to return.

All was darkness.

Eventually I abandoned any hope of seeing man or cup again. I lay down upon my bed of rock and vowed that if death came I would not rail against it. I thought of home in a green, far off land, and remembered the family I had left there. I thought of my father, most likely white-haired by now if still alive, and sister Melisend, probably a mother long since.

It must have been an hour, perhaps more, that I lay so.

Then Reynald's voice burst through the darkness that felt as if it was slowly devouring me.

"Hugh, look! The light! The light returns! Aref has come back for us!"

The return of the light brought jubilation to our hearts. It was the only brightness I have ever known that brought no pain to the eyes after staying such a time in darkness.

Aref clambered out of the water and said breathlessly, "Forgive my being gone so long. There is very little swimming needed," he said pointedly to Reynald, at which the latter's face expressed much relief, "But it is a fair distance to the outlet from here. The reason I took so long was because I could not easily find the entrance back once I had escaped. You must have thought I'd perished, or deserted you."

"We knew you would return if you were able," answered Reynald.

I had to look away in shame.

The narrow underwater tunnel from the salty pool was indeed only a very short distance. Aref led, holding the cup ahead of him to light our way. Reynald held onto Aref's leg coping as best he could, and I followed behind. As we emerged, we found ourselves in a low-ceilinged channel with a pocket of air between the roof and the water's surface. Wading in chain mail, with icy water up to the neck, is no easy matter; but the lure of fresh air and freedom from those labyrinths kept our spirits up and lessened the burden of our clothing. We continued along this narrow gulley for perhaps a quarter of one hour before arriving at last before a wall of rock.

"This is it," said Aref, "Just beneath here there is a way through to the sea. Soon, my friends, you will find yourselves under the sky again."

We took deep breaths and followed Aref as he swam into a hole just below the water's surface. Weighed down by our mail, it was more a matter of crawling than swimming, the distance we needed to cover exhausting every ounce of breath; a moment came when I thought my lungs might burst for lack of air. Then came relief; I saw the tunnel end and Reynald's legs ascending. I kicked my way free of the entrance then dragged myself up on some rocks to the surface. The sound of the waves was like music to my ears. We coughed and spluttered for a time, but these were happy sounds interspersed with laughter; for we three, who had been intended to die in that underground prison, were set free again. The night air never smelled so sweet, and our lungs drank deeply of it.

For a time we rested. We had emerged about a league from the city.

"Will you return to Acre?" asked Aref.

"I wonder how wise that course should be," answered Reynald. "We are probably blamed for Jerome's disappearance, not to mention

Laszlo and Wilhelm's. And I do not doubt that Robert's allies would appreciate a talk with us."

"I doubt if any would believe the tale we have to tell," I said.

"Nor do I think that the Master of our house would show us much leniency for the way we have aided Cathars." Reynald paused, and smiling at Aref added, "Or Saracens for that matter."

"Jerome must be destroyed," I said. "By now they must already have departed for Constantinople."

"What are your plans?" Reynald asked Aref.

"As the last remnant of the old guardians it falls to us to bring the cup to France," he replied. "Yet I think we might assist you in the destruction of Jerome and his disciples, if we can reach Constantinople not too far behind them."

"I would esteem it an honour to ride with you," said Reynald. He looked to me for my response.

"Could you suffer the company of a man who has shown such lack of faith?" I asked.

"I would never have thought to go without you," replied Aref.

Chapter Eighteen

Thursday, 12 December, 1996 approx 8am – 11.40am

Niedermayer & Hart
Fine Porcelain
Est. 1957

Danny read the brass name plate from the pavement below. A week ago, Jim Latimer had stared up at 67 Barnswick Square from the same viewpoint, oblivious to the dangers awaiting him. Any hesitancy on Danny's part was understandable after meeting the firm's delivery man earlier, an introduction so memorable, it had taken him an hour to stop shaking.

At first, the vigilante approach proposed by his father and Ruth had seemed insane. Although he conceded it would be hard convincing the law of what he'd seen; he knew his early morning encounter with the red-haired man would sound totally implausible. He could imagine the reaction of some jaded desk sergeant to his account: *And so, your assailant was thrown off your windscreen, got hit by the front of the car, then he stood up and started fighting you ... fortunately, your old art teacher came along, and she hit him round the head a couple of times with a rolling-pin. Once again, he got up unharmed ... but you'd managed to escape by then ...*

Time was at a premium, and these difficult decisions, necessity being the mother of invention, took less time than Ruth, Erich and the sisters normally needed to organise a recreational walk. The unlikely war council had taken place over scrambled eggs, toast and tea, across the dining-table of the two elderly Thorpe sisters at their home in Herstmonceux, roughly halfway between Erich's bungalow at Pett and Niedermayer & Hart in Hove.

Danny arrived at the top step and put the two smallish boxes stacked beneath his chin down onto the floor. The long box he gripped under his right arm slipped in the process; he re-adjusted and clamped it more tightly beneath his armpit. The morning was cold; even so Danny was aware of the beads of sweat forming just below his hairline. He wiped his forehead on his sleeve, took a deep breath and pressed the doorbell.

He noticed the video camera, and like Jim a week earlier but for different reasons, a moment of uncertainty followed. What if, the door opened and he was confronted by the red-haired man wearing a big smug grin? At this point he actually thought about dropping the box and running. But instead Danny rang the bell again, picked up the boxes off the ground, and attempted a nonchalant air. It occurred to him that he had never even met Jim Latimer. 'I must be crazy!' he thought.

"How can we be sure he's still alive?" Danny had asked the group of friends.

"I just know it," said Ruth, apparently to the complete satisfaction of the others.

Jim's detailed account on Tuesday evening at Erich's proved essential in the formulation of a plan. It was decided a swift response was their only possibility of success.

Erich recalled, "When Jim met Rosemary Hines she told him Thursdays were pay-day for their distribution staff in Eastbourne. It's a routine she and Hart undertake together."

"Excuse me, but aren't we forgetting the driver?" put in Danny. "Surely he'll have warned them about what happened?"

Erich agreed, "Yes, we must assume he's contacted them."

"I suppose it depends on how big a threat they consider us?" Ruth thought for a moment, then added, "Not much I reckon."

"Let's hope that assessment isn't too accurate," said Erich. "We have to accept our limitations. We know we're dealing with something abnormal ... what exactly ... well, we might understand once we've seen inside the cellar. But we must agree, if we reach Hove and find everyone at home ... we call it off immediately!"

"No hope for Jim in that case," said Ruth darkly.

Danny came in to support his father, "We'd stand no chance against more than one. That red-haired maniac who attacked us ... his strength was incredible ... for a stocky little bloke he was really fast ... too fast. If he was in an athletics team they'd definitely want to test his urine!"

"We know they're after us," said Erich, pointing to himself and Ruth, "Possibly Danny too after this morning. It would be plain stupid to hand ourselves over on a plate ..."

Ruth nodded, she couldn't argue with anything said.

"If we can't get inside ... then we'll do our best to get the police to take us seriously."

"By then of course, it'll be too late."

Erich nodded; she was probably right.

"We'd best get started," said Ruth.

"I want you and the sisters to watch the distribution centre."

"No way," she replied, getting to her feet as if getting ready for a fight, "You're not stopping me from coming this time."

"Ruth, seriously, have you forgotten what it was like for you in that house?"

She could remember, and after this she made no further protests. Ruth and the Thorpe sisters went to Eastbourne to keep watch at the distribution centre; the telephone directory coughed up its address. If Rosemary and Hart arrived, they would contact Erich and Danny who would be watching the house in Hove to give them the green light.

Danny spent ten minutes organising some things he'd require; he found everything he needed by rummaging through the Thorpe sisters' garage; an Aladdin's cave for junk, unfortunately leaving no room for their car which was always kept outside. He found three suitable boxes and proceeded to arrange and weight them appropriately. The sisters possessed a typewriter, so he typed out labels for them, hoping they wouldn't be inspected too closely.

These parcels were mostly occupying Danny's thoughts when the front door was opened by a smallish man; Danny judged him about four or five years younger than himself.

"Yes?" Nicholas asked in his habitually condescending tone.

"Three parcels," Danny replied.

"We don't receive deliveries. They go to our distribution centre."

"I've got the right address," said Danny, concerned the ploy might not work.

"Yes," said the young man agitatedly, exposing his gappy teeth, "But all parcels go to Eastbourne."

"But it has this address. Look, 67, Barnswick Square, Hove ... it's printed clearly on the label."

Danny prayed Nicholas would not pay much attention to the label he was tapping with his finger, which bore no stamps or franking marks.

Fortunately, in Nicholas' eyes, the parcels together with their deliverer warranted nothing but disdain. "I don't care what it says on the label, it goes to Eastbourne. We don't take parcels!"

"I'm sorry mate," said Danny emphatically, "But I can't take it somewhere it isn't addressed to."

Nicholas was getting hot under the collar.

"That's your address isn't it?" continued Danny, deciding he might get further by being cussed.

"Yes, but," Nicholas Cureton raised his eyes as though he needed a better view of his eyebrows. "Alright, hand them over," he said with exasperation, reaching out his arms to take them.

This wasn't the way it was supposed to happen either; Danny's anxiety level started to climb. "I need a signature ... and I don't have a pen."

Nicholas glowered at him.

"Bring them in," he said, turning his back on Danny as he strode along the hallway. "Leave them there," he pointed to the floor beside the table with the piece of Meissen. Nicholas went on and disappeared into the office.

Danny, seizing the opportunity, dropped the two smaller boxes and rested the long box on the table. His fingers were trembling as they tore at the packaging. It seemed to take so long.

"Shit! Shit! Shit!"

The shotgun handle was being awkward. Danny had to rip a piece of cardboard to get it free. His fingers seemed to have lost the run of themselves and when he heard his father's footsteps behind, he was momentarily distracted. Nicholas' return from the office clutching a ballpoint pen more or less coincided with Erich's arrival.

Nicholas read the situation immediately and sprang into action. There was nothing ambiguous in his intentions, the eyes murderous, his speed just as surprising as Picton's had been. Having two targets posed no problem; Erich was unarmed, so all Nicholas' energy went into reaching Danny before he gained the advantage.

However, Danny had no intention of being overwhelmed twice in one morning, managing just in the nick of time to tear the shotgun loose and bring it into line with Nicholas' face. All Danny's hesitancy and nervousness were suddenly gone, as Nicholas came to a stop inches from the gun barrel.

Even so, Nicholas remained unnervingly calm, the eyes stock still, staring directly into Danny's, seeming to spell out how fatal it might be to look away or blink even. Offering a grin, he said, "I hope you've got a very good plan. Because you can't have any idea what you're mixed up in. This is an extremely dangerous place."

"Back away. Slowly!" ordered Danny.

Nicholas considered the instruction for a moment but didn't move a muscle.

Danny knew it would be a sign of weakness if he repeated himself. He firmed up pressure on the trigger.

Nicholas coolly complied.

"Slowly ... clasp your hands together behind your neck!"

Nicholas' hands paused at shoulder height for a split second. Danny remained focused, showing no sign of the churning-up going on inside.

"Turn around. Walk to the office."

Inside the office, Erich, who'd followed behind with one of Danny's boxes, placed a chair in the centre of the room, which Nicholas was ordered to sit on.

Danny cautiously handed the shotgun to Erich, "Watch him like a hawk, Dad ... he's quicker than he looks."

"A father and son team, how touching."

"You have nothing worth saying so keep your trap shut!" said Erich, the gun barrels closely trained on Nicholas' head.

Danny scored a line with his penknife along the adhesive tape that sealed the box Erich had brought in and lifted out a rope made of a synthetic material.

"I don't believe this," said Nicholas in his most condescending tone, "A boy scout!"

Danny said nothing as he secured Nicholas' hands to the back of the chair. Next he attended to his feet, taking great care to work from a position where he couldn't be kicked.

Nicholas chose to talk all the time he was being tied up. He would have made an excellent war propagandist; every word he uttered was intended either to misinform or lower morale.

"I wouldn't want to be in your shoes ... you can't seriously hope you'll get away with this? You do realise I'm not alone here, don't you? I'd think again if you've come for Jim Latimer ... I'll willingly volunteer the information of where he is though ... he's in the cellar ... but you may not be too pleased when you find him. You know that the others are already on their way back, don't you? And ..."

"And you shut up," said Danny, sticking a piece of adhesive tape over Nicholas' mouth, adding, "Wish I'd thought of doing that before."

"I'll be as quick as I can Danny," said Erich, returning the gun to him.

"You take it Dad. If he moves more than an eyebrow I'll whack him."

"No," said Erich, taking a peek through the window, "There's nobody else about. I'm sure he was lying. But even tied up ... whatever you do, don't take your eyes off him, not for a second."

Erich removed the set of keys from Nicholas' hip pocket, unhitching the chain that attached them to his belt.

"Be careful."

"You too," said Erich. He took a torch out of the equipment box and left.

Erich was somewhat reluctant about using the lift but remembered that Jim had described the fire escape as locked at the basement end. However the lift was not a problem, apart from the feeling of growing apprehension as he descended. Once in the cellar, it took far longer than it normally would have done to identify the correct key for the stockroom. Erich's mind had somehow undergone a strange obfuscation between the ground floor and basement. He needed to peer at each key for maybe half a minute before he could decide whether it was worth attempting in the lock; totally inappropriate keys, normally eliminated in fractions of a second, used up time this way.

When he finally made the correct choice, he unlocked the padlock and slid back the bolt. He anticipated there might be a disagreeable sensation when he opened the door, and here he wasn't wrong. Just as insects pass messages with pheromones, that cellar declared itself unhealthy for any creature dependent on light and air, although it wasn't the darkness in itself, but the deathly negativity of the place. Just to peer into its gloom seemed to bring harm to the mind. Erich's intention to venture forth alone took real courage. The torch, which he'd fitted with new batteries earlier that morning, cast its beam before him, but its brightness and efficiency was somehow diminished; the cellar seemed to resist light.

Erich remembered the myth of the angel Michael casting Lucifer down from heaven. As he plunged forward he said, "Help me bring light into this place of darkness."

Erich found himself shivering from the immediate effect of numbing coldness. An offensive sliminess infiltrated his clothing and seeped over his skin; it was like wading through a stagnant pool. A disgusting foulness pervaded his mouth and nostrils, like stinking breath. He felt malevolence seeping into his ears and eyes, its poison assaulting him, burrowing beneath fingernails, clinging to his skin. All he wanted to do was to turn and run; but if Jim was there, he had no option but to go on.

Erich found a light switch operating two bulbs that grudgingly illuminated either end of a long room running beneath the hallway on the floor above. Sparse though the lighting was it did allow him to see the whole room, right up to the window at the front where planks of wood had been nailed across it. Alongside the wall were boxes marked Fragile.

Twenty feet beyond its entrance, the room widened. In the centre of the wall to his right was a door, roughly coinciding with the showroom above. Erich noticed that he'd already missed a door; its entrance was tucked away in the recess where the cellar widened. He got an impression that the cellar's internal walls did not entirely correspond with those on the floor above.

Erich decided to take the door ahead first, and ran a hand along the wall beside the door frame in search of a light switch. The room's warmth surprised him; there was a smell in the darkness too that was different from the general stench, sweet and sickly. The poor lighting behind him barely managed to cast Erich's shadow onto the brick floor at his feet.

Erich's hand discovered the light-switch and simultaneously a sight that sent him reeling back, gasping for breath and needing to gain support against the door frame. With that first glimpse of the headless corpse, Erich believed he'd found Jim Latimer.

He took a few deep breaths and waited until his heartbeat slowed to an acceptable pace. Then, as prepared as he reckoned he ever would be for the sight awaiting him, re-entered the room.

He realised almost at once that it wasn't Jim Latimer but some other poor soul. The collar, tie and suit were the first give-away; in the years he'd known Jim, Erich had never seen him wear anything but jeans and t-shirts. As he looked closer, he realised it was the corpse of a much larger man that had been laid out minus his head on a sheet of black polythene. There appeared to be very little blood, only some dried bloodstains about the shoulders and around the crudely severed stump which was all that remained of a neck. The shirt had been ripped open to the waist, and the dead man's chest hacked open. It was far removed from precision surgery and looked like it had been performed with a cleaver and crowbar which both lay on the ground nearby. The fractured ribs stood up like protesting white fingers, highlighting the gaping hole in the corpse's chest. The heart was the only internal organ that had been removed and it lay alongside the torso on the polythene sheet.

Erich cast his eyes about the room and discovered yet another horrific surprise which made him jump and sent his blood pressure skyward once again. Propped against the wall behind him, alongside the open door and previously out of his line of vision, was another body, this time the corpse of a young woman; however, unlike the

211

body on the floor, she was physically intact. The girl was sitting in a chair; the man's missing head had been deliberately positioned between her thighs.

It was such a foul image that Erich had to turn away. Ruth had informed him of the news reports about the missing policeman. He found DCI Rice's ID card in a wallet in the dead man's jacket, which he immediately returned to the pocket where he'd found it.

The warmth of the room was explained by a great cast iron box, five feet tall, about four feet wide and six feet long. The contraption itself took up the whole centre of the room. There was a tiny view hole in the door, and Erich saw that its interior was red hot. There was a temperature gauge beside the door and the needle stood at a staggering five hundred degrees centigrade, although this was only about a third of the way towards its maximum heat. There was a pile of grey ash all around its base.

Erich found himself so transfixed by the terrible grisliness of the place that for a minute or so he lost track of time, able only to stare about him in a shocked state.

Then he remembered why he was there, "Jim!"

He left that awful room and returned to the door he'd initially missed. This room roughly corresponded with the office on the floor above.

The light was already on and Jim was the first thing he saw, straight in front of him. He had been laid out on a table, leather straps attached to his wrists and ankles and he appeared to be either asleep or unconscious.

Erich shook him gently, "Jim ... Jim, wake up!"

Jim stirred, and confused on waking, attempted to make sense of the familiar voice. Suddenly he was wide awake, craning up towards Erich, terror inhabiting every aspect of his face.

"Erich, get away from here! They're after you! For Christ's sake, please, get out!"

"It's alright Jim. I'm here to rescue you."

Erich's words didn't seem to bring the anticipated relief, if anything they only appeared to increase Jim's agitation.

"Don't. Please. You must go." he pleaded.

"It's alright Jim. Calm down."

Jim rested his head on the table and his breathing eased. Erich busied himself with the straps, and a minute later had him free. However, much to his surprise, by the time he'd completed the task, Jim was already sleeping again.

212

"Jim, wake up. Come on, you're free!" Erich shook him awake once more.

"What?"

"You're free. We must get out!"

"Erich? How did you get in?" Jim now seemed to be registering a more appropriate response.

"No time to explain. We've got a car outside. Did they give you something?" asked Erich, believing this the likely reason why Jim had returned to sleep.

"No! No, they didn't give me anything. What do you mean?" asked Jim, eyeing his rescuer suspiciously.

"Oh, nothing," replied Erich, surprised by Jim's reaction but trying to hide his own concern, "I thought they might've given you a sedative that's all."

"Yes ... that's right, they did. It probably hasn't worn off yet."

"Probably not," agreed Erich as he helped Jim to his feet. Strangely, Jim didn't appear to be physically weak, although he needed Erich's help to find the motivation to keep moving; his greatest desire seemed to be to sleep.

They reached the lift and Erich activated it with Nicholas' keys. As they ascended Erich felt the cellar's oppressiveness lifting off his shoulders. Then, just before they reached the first floor his mobile rang.

"Yes?"

It was Ruth.

"The red haired man finally showed up at the distribution place. He went inside for about two minutes then Rosemary and an older man, presumably Hart, rushed out with him. Rosemary looked furious, like she wanted to murder him. They left almost immediately ... I'm sorry Erich, it took ages to find a telephone box free."

"How long ago?"

"Probably about fifteen minutes."

"Okay, Ruth. We're almost finished."

"You got in okay?"

"Yes."

"And Jim?"

Erich looked at Jim. He was fast asleep again and leaning against the wall of the lift.

"Is Jim alright?" she asked anxiously.

"Yes, I have Jim with me," he said, "He's rather sleepy, that's all."

BOOK TWO

BOOK TWO

Chapter Nineteen

Thursday, 12 December, 1996 approx 1.20pm – 2pm

A uniformed policeman was stationed outside the gates that opened into the courtyard at the rear of 67 Barnswick Square. He viewed the approaching car suspiciously, but immediately waved it through once he recognised its passenger.

The Detective Constable driving took the only available parking space, which happened to be the spot normally reserved for Rosemary's white Mercedes.

"Thanks Steve," Harris said as she stepped from the car.

It seemed odd that forty minutes ago her brain had been entirely switched off regarding police matters. Detective Chief Inspector Susan Harris had managed two of the ten days leave coming to her when she was told she'd be leading a murder investigation. She hadn't even completed the first title on her book list. For Susan Harris, books and holidays were synonymous. It was sod's law too that she was on leave at the same time as her car was in the garage having some repairs done. The Deputy Chief Constable, not her greatest fan, seemed to consider it a feminine oversight to be vehicle-less at the very moment a murder investigation was about to start. He'd conceded to her request for a driver, albeit grudgingly.

'That bastard Markland wouldn't have minded if I'd rolled up in a frickin' mini-cab!'

Harris scanned her surroundings, observing the high walls and formidable gates which brought an immediate sense of claustrophobia.

'They certainly liked privacy.'

She observed how the concrete base of the car park had been laid right up to the perimeter walls. The only gaps were for a few straggly rose bushes. Just like Jim, she found these completely incongruous in such a Spartan environment.

There was a good deal of movement around the car park. A Mobile Incident Room had been set up, and there were several forensic officers in hooded overalls carrying boxes from the house to their vans.

Harris observed them keenly as they came and went; every head downcast.

'Grim!'

Detective Sergeant Frith climbed down the steps of the MIR. He was carrying a file with a clipboard attached. Dave Frith was in his early thirties and a safe pair of hands. Harris was relieved to find him there to guide her through the crime scene.

"Sorry about your leave, ma'am," he said smiling broadly as he arrived alongside her.

"An hour ago, Dave, I was in grunge mode with a Louis de Bernières."

Frith laughed, "We're all entitled to a little off-duty drink ma'am."

Harris didn't correct him.

"The Deputy Chief Constable sends his apologies for not being here."

"I suppose he had an important meeting to attend."

Dave Frith leaned forward conspiratorially, "Perhaps they're having a crisis at the golf club."

Harris allowed an economical smile to play on her face. "You'll have to brief me Dave, I know absolutely nothing. Who was the arresting officer?"

"Frank."

Harris nodded approvingly. DI Frank Wain was her best officer and a friend too.

"How did the arrest come about?"

"Tip-off. Anonymous. Called us from inside the house."

"From here!" exclaimed Harris.

"We've got video footage of two men entering. It must've been one of them who called us. He told us we'd find two bodies, DCI Ian Rice, Metropolitan Vice … went missing last night … and a young woman. They also left us a man bound up and gagged."

"Bloody hell! Who?"

Frith consulted his notes, "Nicholas Cureton, worked here. Frank's questioning him ... extremely violent by all accounts, broke young Grenfell's arm during his arrest."

"Christ!"

"Cureton's a nasty little sod."

"Sounds it. The bodies … DCI Rice and the girl?"

"The girl hasn't been ID'd yet."

"Any signs of sexual assault?"

"We're not sure yet, there aren't any marks on her to suggest it. DCI Rice's notebook was still on him. Last night he interviewed a photographer, name of Jim Latimer." Frith removed some photocopied pages from the file he was holding and passed them to Harris. He allowed her a minute to scan their contents. "DCI Rice was investigating the death of a friend ..."

"Isherwood," Harris replied, reading from Rice's notes.

"Isherwood ran a photographic library and was a close friend of Ian Rice's. Isherwood and his secretary were murdered yesterday."

"Who's this Loxton they mention?"

"Another photographer, Vice had been looking into his activities. They believe he was part of a paedophile network. Loxton topped himself last week ... no question of foul play apparently."

"Isherwood and Latimer seem to have been in a lot of confusion about his age."

"Yes, ma'am, I couldn't make much sense of all that."

Frith allowed her time to complete Rice's notes.

"Where does all this psychic nonsense come from?"

Frith shook his head, "According to DCI Rice's notes, Latimer had friends who believed an evil force was at work in the house."

Harris had no time for that sort of thing; she was a pragmatist. It was evil bastards, not evil forces, who committed murder, whilst detection and hard evidence brought them to justice.

"These people, Latimer's neighbour, er ... Allinson, and the other one ... Ledermann. Do we have them for questioning?"

"We're trying to locate them at the moment ... but we're only an hour or so ahead of you," said Frith, slightly defensively.

"I know that, Dave," she replied. Although Harris expected thoroughness from every member of her team, she nevertheless accepted the limitations imposed by time and lack of manpower. "What about these others? Latimer reckoned they all lived on the premises ..." Harris consulted Rice's notes again, "... Hines, Hart and some driver chap with red hair."

"No sign of any of them. We've got a team in Eastbourne interviewing the staff at their mail order place. Hines and Hart paid a visit over there this morning. The driver's name is Picton and he showed up there too, at about 11.30. Apparently the Hines woman went ballistic when he arrived. They all left at once and haven't been seen since."

"They probably saw our squad cars and drove on," said Harris, stating what was glaringly obvious to her. "They could easily be miles away by now. Do we have descriptions of their vehicles?"

"Yes ma'am, all divisions have been alerted."

"Good. What about the staff in Eastbourne, anything there?"

"At the mailing place?" Frith shook his head, "So far, it doesn't look promising ... just people doing a job. This bunch seems to have been extremely secretive."

"Okay, we have a suspect in custody and two corpses. Anything else I should know?"

Frith shuffled his feet; the question seemed to make him uncomfortable. "Two corpses for starters," he replied.

"More?"

"Not bodies. Forensic believe there are cremated remains in the cellar."

Harris was rarely caught off guard but at that point her jaw dropped. "You'd better show me," she said.

Frith nodded uneasily. As he led her across the car park, he warned, "It's the worst I've ever seen."

Harris felt an involuntary spasm in the pit of her stomach as they approached the back door. "What about the other one?" she asked, remembering her brief conversation on the telephone with the DCC. "I'm sure Markland said that there were two names in the firm's title?"

Frith considered the question a moment before replying, "Oh yes, Niedermayer & Hart ... if there was ever anyone called Niedermayer he doesn't appear to be around anymore."

*

Twenty-five miles or so east of Hove, near the village of Herstmonceux, was an eighteenth-century rectory. The house, long since fallen into secular hands, had, for reasons known only to its present occupants, been re-named 'The Grange'. Its owners were two retired school teachers, generically known as the Thorpe sisters. In the drawing-room of their house, Jim Latimer was asleep in an armchair and seemed altogether incapable of doing much else. Erich had shaken him awake when they'd arrived and Jim had staggered dreamily into the house with the aid of Danny and Erich. He'd managed to offer the limpest of hellos to Ruth only to promptly fall asleep the moment he was seated.

"What have they done to him?" Ruth asked Erich, she was noticeably concerned.

"It's not sedation," whispered Erich.

Ruth shook her head in agreement. "Any ideas?"

Erich's eyes communicated a sense of foreboding. He raised a finger to his lips and pointed to the door.

"Would you mind staying here, Danny?" he asked his son.

"Go ahead, Dad, I can do with a rest."

Erich laid the shotgun which he'd carried in from the car across Danny's lap. He nodded pointedly in Jim's direction, "You won't fall asleep, will you?" The way it was put suggested he didn't think it would be a wise thing to relax.

"I'll be careful," Danny quietly assured him.

The others adjourned to the kitchen. The sisters made a pot of herb tea, a blend recommended by them for its restorative properties. Erich commiserated with himself as he tasted the insipid brew; he would have much preferred a good unhealthy cup of coffee.

Erich recounted their story, how Danny had managed to get them inside and his own encounter with the cellar. It was almost as painful to recall as it had been to experience. Ruth and the sisters listened with shocked expressions as he delivered his account.

"When I saw how Jim was, I quickly suspected that he wasn't okay."

"I knew it, the moment you arrived. It's awful … just like when I saw him, in that vision." Ruth was anxious that despite their best efforts they had still failed to prevent whatever had happened to him.

"I think we'd all agree that the last thing he needs now is conventional medical help," said Erich. It was a view unanimously accepted by all.

There followed a brief lull in the conversation for reflection and tea-sipping; except for Erich that is, who was nurturing a secret hope that if he avoided the greenish liquid in his cup long enough it might magically evaporate. After a while he looked across at the Thorpe sisters and said, "I feel guilty. I suggested bringing him here. I'm sorry to have laid this at your door."

The sisters replied almost in unison, as was generally the way with them.

"You did the right thing."

"Definitely the best thing to do."

Ruth began to ask hesitantly, "Apart from the dreadful things you saw … that policeman and the girl … there was nothing else?" Erich had seen so much in that appalling cellar the question had been difficult to phrase.

But Erich understood what she meant. What had become of the negative presence they had both felt, and which they suspected was now exerting its influence over Jim? Erich shook his head. "The effect of the place was stupefying. It took an effort of will to get one leg to follow the other ... my mind was terribly confused. I searched all the cellar rooms, but I saw nothing."

"It just has to have a physical form. It's too strong to be wholly ethereal," Ruth looked agitated as she spoke.

"Perhaps it isn't bound to the house," and "Maybe it left with the others," the Thorpe sisters contributed.

Ruth looked across the kitchen table at Erich. He avoided her gaze. 'He's thinking something but isn't prepared to share it yet.'

Behind his outwardly fairly calm expression, Erich's mind was racing. Ever since he'd developed those negatives in Jim's dark room, outlandish ideas had been scurrying through his mind.

Why had Ian Rice been decapitated, with his heart ripped out? And there was something about the dead girl too that kept nudging him into some extremely unorthodox areas of thought; she had been exceptionally pale and anaemic looking, even for a corpse. Erich had seen various bits of equipment draining at the sink in the room where Jim had been kept, which at the time, confused as he was, had made little impression on him. However, on the way back to Herstmonceux he had become convinced it was some kind of apparatus for extracting blood. Which might possibly explain why there had been so little blood to accompany the terrible injuries inflicted on the policeman; although it didn't explain why the blood was extracted in the first place, or where it had actually gone?

*

There is inevitably a sombre atmosphere that pervades a murder scene; crimes of a sadistic nature involving children were undoubtedly the worst and had the most crushing effect on morale, but the death of a colleague always told heavily on everyone too. However, despite the fact that one of their own had been violently murdered there, Harris found that entering the cellar was in some inexplicable way entirely different to any investigation she had previously been involved with. Never before had she seen forensic officers looking quite so uncomfortable. The men who had been fingerprinting the porcelain objects in the boxes next to the cellar exit were ashen-faced. The word 'spooked' sprang unwanted to her mind.

She'd sensed a response in her own body the moment she entered the building. Her limbs had instantly become burdensome, as though the leaden atmosphere of the place was somehow draining her vitality. Harris could tell from the expression on Frith's face that he was experiencing this effect too. However, neither chose to mention how the place made them feel, after all, it had no bearing on the case. Everyone accepted that at times they did a tough job, but someone had to do it.

The bodies of DCI Rice and the girl were in the same macabre poses as when Erich had discovered them. Two forensic men were busy at work in the room. They looked up as Harris and Frith entered. Harris nodded to them.

"It's estimated the Chief Inspector was killed around midnight," Frith informed her, "and the girl we reckon an hour or so later."

"Not much blood," said Harris, examining Rice's headless torso, "Anything to suggest exactly where he was killed?"

"Nothing. He was decapitated and mutilated in here … but may have died somewhere else."

Harris nodded, the assessment seemed plausible. She turned her attention to the young woman; some sights one never got used to

"Sick bastards," contributed Frith.

Harris said nothing; her eyelids closed for a fraction of a second longer than it took her generally to blink and for a fleeting moment her lips became a taut line; this was all the emotion she allowed to tell on her face.

"They were using this as a crematorium." Frith pointed to the cast iron box in the centre of the room.

"A furnace."

"Kiln."

One of the forensic men was kneeling as he brushed ash into a plastic bag at the base of the large iron contraption. He had already filled about ten bags, which were piled up on a tray at his side. He stood up when he heard the kiln mentioned and pulled down his mask to speak, "It's a pottery kiln, gas fired … old, possibly turn of the century."

"What are you finding?" Harris asked.

"Huge amounts of ash … smallish particles of bone. We can't open the door yet, it has to cool down quite a bit."

"Could a pottery kiln cremate a human being?"

"Easily ma'am," the forensic man replied, "It's been customised. They certainly knew what they were doing. The optimum temperature for cremation is twelve hundred degrees centigrade. This thing can achieve heat way beyond that. It was designed for porcelain, which fires between twelve and fourteen hundred degrees. At that kind of temperature there would be very little smoke and only a few kilograms of ash left behind."

"They seem to have had a lot of practice," added Frith.

It was only then that Harris became aware of what the other forensic man working over in the room's farthest corner was actually doing. He was using a hand trowel to bag up the ash he was taking from one of eight large fertiliser sacks stacked against the wall. After weighing each bag on a set of scales it was labelled and recorded on his clipboard then placed in a black box.

"Is that all ash too?" Harris asked.

"Yes, ma'am," the forensic man replied staring up at her from his grim task.

Harris was dumbstruck for a moment. 'What in hell's name have we stumbled into?' she asked herself.

"An estimate?" she managed to croak out.

"Not possible yet," replied the first man, "Harry's only just started weighing it up into kilogram bags."

Harry lowered his mask to speak directly to Harris. "We contacted the crematorium to find what a body averages out at ... depending on body mass, between two and three kilograms they reckon. Each of these boxes takes twenty bags of a kilogram each. I've already filled four boxes."

Harris probably looked like she was doing a mathematical calculation. In fact, she was wondering why she'd declined her sister-in-law's invitation to join the family for a week's skiing in Austria.

224

Hugh's Tale

X

Aref's companions awaited him at a place previously arranged, some leagues east of the city. At first, they viewed us with suspicion, and understandably so, for they had good reason to despise the uniform we wore. For these five alone were all that remained of their community; not one left untouched by that terrible massacre. Even the youngest, Yusuf, a lad of but sixteen years, had suffered much, for his mother and father had been murdered, along with two younger siblings.

Yet through the relentless months ahead, mistrust between us fell away, a bond of friendship grew and we became as brothers. Indeed I credit it the greatest honour of my life to have ridden with such men as these.

Ayyub was the oldest, and probably the last to accept our friendship. He was an imposing man, broadly built, tall in stature, possessing abundant measures of strength in body, mind and spirit. Aref always paid close attention to any counsel that Ayyub offered. Reynald and he grew close, for they were both deep thinkers and alike in many ways.

It was Reynald who told me that the infant I had found murdered by Robert's hand had been Ayyub's grandson, and the child's mother his daughter. He said, "I doubt, even if I were guardian of the cup, I could have shown de Frontignac the restraint he received at Aref's hands ... these men are truly noble."

The final two of these guardians, Ibrahim and Salah, were brothers. They were in their early twenties, almost identical to look upon and by surviving together the only ones who retained an immediate relative. They were big-hearted and courageous, and an unshakeable bond linked them, as well as a degree of good-tempered rivalry. Ibrahim and Salah were without a doubt the most skilful swordsmen I have ever known. Over the months ahead they not only played a great part in our fight for survival, but also helped in our darkest hours to keep up our spirits.

Speed was essential if we hoped to rid the world of Jerome and his foul horde. To succeed, we believed it imperative to reach Constantinople soon after them. Our Templar uniforms, for the time being, were a source of danger, so we took Saracen overgarments to act as a disguise; and we were given mares for riding, which perhaps at the time seemed like the most effeminate and unjust imposition of all. Anyway, we headed north for Tyre, posing as a group of merchants. Our mission was well-funded, for the Cathars had entrusted a sum of gold to the guardians as a contingency plan; although I doubt anyone could have imagined the disaster which had befallen their venture.

At first, good fortune appeared to smile our way, for shortly after reaching Tyre we boarded a karrack bound for Cyprus. The ship's master complained bitterly about being robbed by the harbour authorities at Tyre, claiming they had taxed him too heavily on his incoming cargo, thereby making his venture unprofitable. He was prepared to give us and our beasts passage without requiring any explanation about our journey. However, he could not be pressed to deliver us quite as far as Constantinople; for it seemed that here too the harbour authorities were in the habit of victimising him. But, seduced by the sight and promise of an extortionate amount of Aref's gold, he agreed to set us down on the Byzantine coast, a day's ride from the great city.

"Speed is of great importance to us," said Aref.

"You will find no ship faster," boasted the ship's master, "I can have you there in twelve days."

"Make it in eight and I will give you half that amount promised again."

The master grinned at the prospect of such profit. "I cannot refuse a challenge," he replied, "for such a sum I will outrun the Templar fleet if need be!" And whether or not it was done deliberately, he appeared to glance in our direction as he spoke.

"Why should we have need to outrun Templar ships?" asked Reynald.

"Just a manner of speaking," he replied.

We sailed at dawn. A certain sadness overtook me, Anselm, as we drew away from the land that had for so many years been my home; perhaps knowing in my heart that I would never set eyes on it again.

Reynald stood beside me at the ship's bow and together we watched the coastline grow indistinct.

"We leave as traitors to the oaths we took," I said.

"We had little choice in the matter," answered Reynald.

226

Our guardian companions did not take well to water, for not one of them had ever sailed before. Aref and Ayyub sat uncertainly upon the deck throughout the first day, their faces green as the grass in spring. Ibrahim and Salah took turns at vomiting over the side, or so it seemed, for whenever I went by one or the other was in the process of doing so. The youthful Yusuf adjusted to this mode of travel best. By the third day all had recovered, apart from Ibrahim, who was still suffering from the effect of the waves, now much to the amusement of his brother Salah. We made good time, our journey aided by a fortuitous tail wind.

If memory serves aright, it was somewhere around the fifth day that I awoke from sleep to discover Reynald deep in conversation with Aref and Ayyub. They were seated but a little distance from where I lay and seeing I was awake, Reynald threw me a wink before resuming his discourse.

"You think that Constantinople in itself holds no purpose then?"

"I can see no particular reason why they should be lured there more than any other place," said Aref.

"Besides Rome it is the greatest centre of our Christian world," Reynald argued.

"Yes, but I do not believe this Jerome's motives to be in any way profound," replied Aref, "Evil owns no high ideals."

Then Ayyub spoke, "If as you observed they abhor and fear the symbols of your church, why endanger themselves by heading for Constantinople?"

"Exactly my argument," said Aref.

Ayyub continued, "Men often yearn for the land of their nativity when death approaches. These creatures have already gone beyond life. Perhaps they possess a yearning for their native soil ... maybe it is some instinct that drives them." Then he smiled darkly, adding, "But let us not conclude too much before we learn more about these monsters ... and let us never forget that our first priority is the cup's safety."

At this Aref and Reynald nodded in agreement.

We never truly understood the motive behind this journey of our adversaries. Was it indeed instinct or some unnatural law that drew the creatures home, or a wholly different reason altogether? We never knew. However, we were soon to realise that Aref had been correct; Constantinople itself was not their goal.

Eight days out from Tyre, we first glimpsed the Byzantine coast a long way distant. And some hours after this we sighted a galley flying a Venetian flag. Its oars were out of the water and the vessel was drifting precariously close to rocks.

Our ship's master, being distrustful of all things Venetian, was reluctant to go too near.

"Take us alongside," ordered Reynald, "We must board her."

The master was extremely fearful as were his sailors. "What if there is a plague aboard?" he asked.

"I do indeed believe a plague was carried on this ship," answered Reynald, "But I think its contagion is spent. I assure you no harm will come to either you or your crew. And, if as I think, this is the ship we seek, you may then set us down upon the land and depart about your business."

"Paid in full, with the extra promised?" enquired the master, wide-eyed with the thought of profit; yet in his defence, Anselm, there was an honest streak to the man's roguery that made him difficult to dislike.

"As agreed," said Aref.

No longer showing any hesitation, the ship's master brought us alongside the galley.

None of the crew wished to venture aboard. A creaking eeriness surrounded the deserted craft.

Nothing was out of place upon the deck, except for the dreadful stench which assailed our nostrils from below. We would soon uncover its hideous source; for on the lower deck, the fifty men who had manned the vessel had been slain, their bodies left to rot. There were signs that some had attempted to defend themselves when they saw they were under attack from those they had transported. However, this realisation had come too late, and by then their fate was sealed.

We undertook the grim task of inspecting each corpse for any corrupting marks left by the foul triumvirate of Jerome, Laszlo and Wilhelm. It was a relief to discover that all had died by the sword; that is, except for three bodies with their heads missing discovered in the ship's hold; their chests ripped open in much the same way as Cornelius' had been when Aref had torn his heart out.

We found some casks of oil aboard, and poured their contents liberally over the corpses and the galley's timbers before returning to our own ship.

Reynald took it upon himself to address the ship's master and crew, "Upon the Venetian boat, all are dead ... my friends, it would be wisest to forget you ever made this voyage. Give no thought to the passengers whom you brought here and who boarded this ship of death. Accept our reward and gratitude for transporting us, but never seek to understand the reasons for our coming ... die old men, content in the knowledge that some things are better not known."

We lit torches and threw them across the dividing water onto the galley. And by the time we were brought to land the Venetian ship was fully ablaze. Our ship's master knew the coastline well. He assured us that the spot where he set us down was the only safe landing place for men with horses for many leagues. Indeed, his words were borne out as truth by the fresh tracks we discovered there. Our horses were unloaded and Aref handed over the agreed sum.

"None shall ever learn of this venture from either myself or any of my men. Let your endeavours find fulfilment and may God's speed be with you!" shouted the master to us from aboard his deck.

The karrack began to sail quickly away from us, as if it was abandoning a group of lepers on the shore.

Then my eye was suddenly caught by a dark shape bobbing on the waves in the ship's wake. I waded a short distance into the water to reach it, transfixed by its shape, at once both familiar yet unrecognised. I reached forward drawing it towards me and as I did so the object rolled over, face upwards; immediately I recoiled, horrified by the blankness in those unseeing eyes. Unintentionally, I had propelled the head further out to sea, staring, uncomprehending, claimed by the waves and condemned to a watery grave.

Chapter Twenty

"It's soundproof," explained Frith as he introduced Harris to the room where Jim had been held prisoner.

It was a room that required little explanation. The awful stench of the place made every natural instinct flinch. Its filth-ridden walls and ceiling seemed charged with the cries and screams of the untold souls whose wretched pleadings they had absorbed.

A forensic man was working there alone. He was dusting for prints, taking scrapes and samples from the table top. He was grey-faced, the facial lines above the mask, particularly around the eyes and forehead, revealing an inner discomfort. The door to the room had been wedged open; Harris could easily appreciate his reluctance to be shut in there.

The table and its restraining devices drew Harris' eyes with hideous fascination. Its surface showed innumerable stains that had penetrated deep into the wood. An imprinted shape ran along its length, where over time the top had been polished smooth by the heads, shoulders and buttocks of its countless victims; just beneath the wrist straps agitated finger-nails had gouged out two rough trenches.

It was here that the real ugliness of the crime scene came alive for Harris. This room, even more so than the crematorium, drove home to her the scale of human misery and the depraved minds capable of conceiving such a place. Judging by the vast quantities of ash in the other room, the killings had gone on over several years. This was serial killing on a scale hitherto unknown to her.

"What do you have for me?" Harris inquired of the forensic man.

"I've taken some prints off the straps," he answered, pushing up his mask as he began to speak. "But it's odd, where I'd expect to find fingerprints there are only smears. The marks were made by fingers definitely, but I can't distinguish them ... certainly no good for our purposes."

"They wore gloves?" asked Frith.

The forensic man shook his head, "Doesn't look like gloves." He pointed to the equipment on the draining board. "Same with that, I just can't get anything positive off it."

"What's that stuff for?" Harris asked.

"Taking blood," he replied.

DCI Harris managed to conceal the horror she felt. "We'll need to check the drains," she told Frith.

A detective constable arrived at the door. He coughed once before he spoke to get their attention, "We've found something out in the corridor … would you care to take a look, ma'am?"

Harris thanked the forensic man and followed the constable out of the room.

What had been discovered was a large brown paper package. Frith and Harris immediately associated it with the one which Latimer had mentioned to Rice. The find looked promising. The opened package carried a bank stamp at each point where it was sealed.

Harris was passed some gloves by Frith and she retrieved the pile of catalogues from inside; '57 to '96, the dates scrawled in black marker pen on the front of every copy; interleaved were newspaper cuttings, each article referring to a different missing person.

"Where was it found?"

"Against that wall, behind those boxes," replied the man who'd discovered it.

"Good work! Get it dusted," she said, handing the package back to him. "Someone will have to work through those names, Dave," she said turning to Frith, who made a note on his clipboard.

Harris' house tour continued above ground level after that. The first thing she noticed was a marked difference in the demeanour of the people who were at work there. It was to some extent understandable, not being at the rock face so to speak like those below. Even so, at least half of them complained about the dreadful smell and said it had given them headaches. Although Harris had felt distinctly nauseous when subjected to the overpowering stench in the rooms below, she experienced nothing here.

"Can you smell anything Dave?"

Frith nodded. "Most definitely."

"What's it like?"

Frith didn't mince his words, "Like shit and rotten meat."

"Mmm, nicely put."

"My wife says I have a way with words."

"Wooed her with your love poems, did you?"

On the ground floor, the fingerprint people were experiencing the same problems as their counterparts below. Most of the prints they were taking were undefined, and so far only two distinct sets had been found, on one of the telephones and on the chair to which Nicholas Cureton had been tied.

"How can anyone live or work somewhere without leaving prints?" Harris asked Frith as they ascended the stairs to the first floor.

"Seems unlikely they'd wear gloves at all times."

"For Christ's sake, why bother? There's enough here without prints to put them away ten times over."

In the room Jim had used as his studio, the photographic equipment was just as he had left it; a St Bernard dog still in position against a blue paper background.

"This room hasn't been completely covered yet, but we've checked the gear out. The camera was hired by Latimer on Friday from a photographic supplier in London. Some of the equipment's his own and marked with his name."

The deterioration of the building as they climbed up through the house had a noticeable effect on Harris who was seeing it for the first time. "It's a facade," she said.

"Not remotely normal, is it?" replied Frith.

Apart from a lavatory with a hand basin on the first floor there was no other place to wash in the whole house. The two inhabited rooms on the third and fourth floors had not been examined yet, so they carefully avoided disturbing anything. What struck Harris was the number of personal effects that were noticeably absent.

"They possessed hardly anything belonging to themselves, as individuals."

"What do you mean?"

"Well, think of your own house. Aren't there items all over it that say something about you, where you picked them up, or when you got them?"

"My gaff's awash with kiddies toys ... Barbie and Lego everywhere."

"Exactly, a normal bloody home ... but look at this lot, Dave, and the room below." They were having the conversation in Hart's room at the very top of the house. "Apart from all these reference books, the clothes and that armchair there's nothing individual about it ... the bedroom downstairs is exactly the same ... there's the male and female clothing, and that curtain thing strung up around the bed, but that's it."

232

"What do you make of all this stuff on the walls and ceilings?" asked Frith.

"Insulation ... probably gets cold up here in the roof space."

Frith nodded. "Or maybe, do it yourself sound-proofing?"

"Why?"

Frith shrugged his shoulders, "Noisy seagulls?"

Once the recce had been completed, Harris paid a final visit to the men working in the cellar. It was more a gesture of solidarity, a morale booster than anything else. The bodies of the girl and DCI Rice had been removed for post mortem. The forensic man bagging up ash had now completed his seventh box.

Frith escorted Harris back to the MIR in the car park before leaving her.

"Thanks for the tour Dave."

"Welcome, ma'am."

Inside the mobile incident room two female uniformed constables wearing headsets were relaying messages back to headquarters. They gestured to Harris as she entered.

Sitting at a table in the centre of the van was DI Robson, another member of her team. He had various pieces of electronic equipment laid out on the table in front of him.

Robson looked up as Harris slid the door across. "Afternoon," he said, "Sorry about your leave."

"Did you have to remind me? What d'you have, Rob?"

Robson played Harris the call that Erich had made to the Hove Constabulary just before they had exited the house.

The message began with the responder saying 'Go ahead caller.'

'*I hope you're taping this message ... please pay it urgent attention.*'

'Can you identify yourself, please caller?'

'*Er ... no, no I can't do that. I have information about Detective Ian Rice. His body and the body of a girl are in the cellar of number 67, Barnswick Square, Hove. We've left a man tied up there for you. His name is Nicholas Cureton ... please, be very careful ... he is a killer. Be armed and extremely vigilant when you release him.*' After this there followed the sound of the telephone being put down and the line going dead.

"Slight accent," said Harris.

"German I thought ... but faint ... like he's lived here a long time."

"What time was the call made?"

233

"11.38am," replied Robson, consulting his notes, "We have visuals too." Robson slotted a VHS cassette into the machine before him and pressed play. "I made a copy from the footage off their security camera."

He talked Harris through the playback on the monitor before them, "A man, roughly mid-twenties, arrives with three parcels. Notice how he pauses for a moment before proceeding up to the door ... he looks nervous. He puts two of the boxes down and adjusts the one under his arm before reaching forward to ring the doorbell."

"That one looks heavy ... odd size and shape ... might easily conceal a weapon," commented Harris as she stared intensely at the screen.

Robson continued his commentary, "A conversation begins with someone out of picture ... it seems to go on for longer than you'd expect in a normal delivery situation."

"Do you lip read, Rob?"

"No. You?"

"'Fraid not."

"I've watched it through a good many times. I think there's some kind of argument going on about the parcels ... basically I think our man is trying to get in ... see, there ... he gives a sigh of relief before entering."

At this point Robson pressed the fast forward button on the video. "Thirty-two seconds later a small older man rushes up the steps and follows our delivery boy into the house."

"He looks a likely candidate for our anonymous caller," said Harris, "It isn't a young man's voice. How long before they come out again?"

"Twenty-three minutes," said Robson, "I've left a ten second delay on this copy."

The screen went blank before the picture resumed. Now the two men who had entered twenty-three minutes earlier were hurrying down the front steps supporting a third man between them.

"Three come out!" exclaimed Harris. "The one in the middle seems drowsy ... half asleep."

*

Mary and Millie Thorpe were in their late seventies, although they would never have admitted to being any age. When questioned on this subject they invariably replied, "You're as old as you feel," or "Age is all in the mind!" It was conceded however that Mary was the eldest of

234

the two by eighteen months. Neither of the sisters had married, and throughout their lives they had always shared a home.

Their parents had lived with them up until their deaths, 'passing over' only a few months apart, some thirty years ago now. Ma and Pa, as the sisters always referred to them, had been humble souls. Pa, through honest hard work and what might now be termed by business gurus 'a strong customer focus', had built up a small but successful greengrocery chain in south London. To Ma and Pa's eternal pride, their daughters had possessed brains, and had won scholarships to university. They had graduated with honours and had thereafter devoted their working lives to teaching children with learning difficulties. In those days, cruel terms like 'backward' and 'educationally sub-normal' had been used. The Thorpe sisters had been life-long campaigners against all such negative labels; at long last, the educational establishment had nearly caught up with them.

Even by Ruth and Erich's standards the sisters were eccentric; to be unkind, the Thorpe sisters were esoteric junkies. Their house was crammed to the gunwales with books on phenomena of every conceivable kind, from astrology to Zoroastrianism, the shelves in between covering such topics as astral projection, Atlantis, automatic writing, crop circles, Glastonbury and every conceivable kind of phenomena right the way down to UFOs; along with the collected works of Blavatsky, Castaneda, Gurdjieff, Rudolf Steiner, Carl Jung and others too numerous to mention. For Mary and Millie everything in life had its esoteric significance and their appetite for spiritual enlightenment had if anything only increased with age.

People sometimes asked the sisters why they chose to live in a five-bedroomed eighteenth-century rectory with two acres of land at their time in life. Wouldn't something smaller be more sensible now they were in the late autumn of their lives?

Such suggestions were considered by Mary and Millie as nothing more than negative thinking; replying politely that the house was put to excellent work in the service of humanity. For instance, the local choral society came there on Tuesdays to practise, usually on a Wednesday the healing circle met, on Friday it was yoga in the morning and Buddhist meditation in the evening, and on Saturday afternoons they taught an Ikebana class. Their house was frequently home to people they had befriended from much travelling abroad, often men and women in their twenties or thirties; the sisters showed a special interest in helping the young, having a particular rapport with them.

Erich, Ruth and Danny knew the Thorpe sisters well and adored them, even though an overdose of the sisters could occasionally make a saint weep. For they habitually finished each other's sentences, and to ask either Mary or Millie a question invariably warranted an in depth reply from both of them. Their relationship was symbiotic; once this was accepted and their kind natures were acknowledged, hardly anyone failed to be won over, eventually at least.

For lunch, the sisters, strict vegetarians, had made everyone soup served with warm rolls, that is except for Jim of course, who remained asleep in the armchair. It was decided that for the time being he should be allowed to sleep, and that no effort should be made to snap him out of it. Erich relieved Danny while lunch was being eaten, taking his on a tray in the drawing-room. Everybody was concerned for Jim, and the conversation around the dining table touched on little else.

Whilst eating they'd listened to the radio news. It stated that the police had discovered two bodies in a house in Hove; no names were given as yet. The announcer went on to say that the police were urging the people who had tipped them off to come forward.

In the drawing-room, Erich had put his tray of half-finished soup to one side. He was too troubled to eat. When Ruth and Danny came to join him, he seemed oblivious to them, often staring anxiously at Jim. Twenty minutes later, after they had tidied away the lunch things, the sisters came and sat with them too; there were still a couple of hours of daylight left but the afternoon light level was low, and the room seemed gloomy with everyone in semi-darkness, so they turned on some lamps to brighten it up.

The group of unlikely vigilantes sat silently, waiting for Jim Latimer to wake; a focused silence, each of them concentrating healing thoughts onto Jim. Danny possessed no such ability that he was aware of, even so he found himself somehow caught up in the peaceful atmosphere. And if the aura of tranquillity failed to reach Jim it certainly touched Danny, who felt his mind being gently soothed.

Time passed, it was just after 3.00pm; through the French doors of the drawing-room a miserable greyness had won the day. Inside, the drawing-room was lit by pools of yellowish light thrown off by the energy-saving bulbs in the standard lamps, and the only discernible sounds were those of the friends taking measured breaths, the tick of the grandfather clock and the occasional crackle from a log on the fire. Jim, who up until that point had done nothing more spectacular than flutter an eyelid, suddenly shook his head from side to side, sat bolt upright, and opened his eyes.

"Erich ... Ruth ... where am I?" he asked, confused by the strange surroundings and unrecognised faces.

The sisters were about to introduce themselves, but Erich quickly intervened as if he wanted nobody else to speak. "You're amongst friends. Do you remember what happened to you?"

The look of terror that shot through Jim's eyes made it instantly clear that he did.

"Rosemary and Nicholas broke into my house. I thought she was going to kill me!"

"Why, Jim? Why did they take you?"

"Bob found something, a file ..." Jim broke off for a moment, nursing his head in his hands as he reflected on what he'd been told about his friends' deaths. "Bob and Daphne were murdered by Nicholas and Picton," he said spitting out the last pair of names contemptuously.

"Did you know they also killed Bob's friend, the policeman, Ian Rice?"

"Yes." replied Jim, wincing to recall Picton's little late night presentation. "I ... I ... saw."

"Why did they kill Rice?"

"He came to see me ... last night?" Jim asked uncertainly, clearly confused about time.

"Yes, last night," assured Erich. "I expect he asked questions about Bob?"

Jim nodded, "They were watching my house." Only then did the penny seem to drop, and at once, seized with panic, he rose to his feet, "Christ, they're after you! They saw me at your bungalow! You've no idea ... you've got to hide ... they'll kill you!"

"It's alright, Jim ... we're safe here ... sit down," assured Erich.

"You don't understand ... you'll never be safe ... they won't stop, not until you're dead!"

Erich in a slightly raised voice, said more assertively, "Sit down."

To everyone's astonishment, Jim responded at once to the command.

"We're safe here," Erich repeated.

"You think you are, but you aren't ... you must leave, all of you ... go, go immediately ... please!" Jim implored them.

Each of the friends remembered the next moment slightly differently. The sisters thought they could recall Erich holding the silver medallion with a Star of David at its centre from the outset; Ruth was certain he had taken it out of his pocket the first time Rice's name

237

was mentioned; whilst Danny believed he first saw his father produce the Star of David at this point.

Danny had seen the charm many times before, his father kept it with him always. It had belonged to Erich's mother. She had given it to the young Erich on the day he had left his home for the last time. She had slipped it into the boy's palm, then held his small hand around it clasped tightly within hers, and with eyes sparkling trying to hold back her tears she had said, "Mein Liebchen, ich werde immer bei Dir sein." In Erich's memory that pure image of motherhood was fixed for all time, and not even the depravity of Auschwitz in all its hideousness could ever destroy it, as it had so efficiently eradicated the woman who had been his mother.

Danny had seen his father perform the simple yet skilful conjuror's trick many times, often entertaining him with it as a child. In fact, every child Erich met was introduced to the trick, but generally it was done with a coin; he rarely revealed this, his most precious heirloom. The trick involved moving the medallion back and forth along the base of his finger joints just above the knuckles, which gave the impression that the object was moving of its own accord. Erich's fingers were old but dextrous and as ever he performed the little trick with great aplomb.

He said, "Tell me about Mr Niedermayer, Jim."

Jim stiffened at the name. His eyes began to search from side to side like a panic-stricken creature.

"Tell me Jim ... I want to know everything ... tell me about Niedermayer."

Jim didn't reply, his eyes were roving, darting rapidly about. He began to shake. The effect the name had on him was so disturbing to witness that Ruth felt drawn to rush over and comfort him, but she resisted. She trusted Erich, who she suspected had been planning this moment throughout the long wait of the afternoon.

"Come on, Jim. Who is Niedermayer?" asked Erich insistently.

Jim's eyes focused with a maniacal stare on Erich. The shakes stopped and his eyes reduced themselves to slits burning with hate. Jim got to his feet; his lips were peeled back from his teeth as he snarled viciously at the man who had rescued him. It seemed extremely likely that at any moment Jim would fly across the short distance separating them and physically attack Erich. The others leaned forward involuntarily, immensely disturbed by the sight of this normally placid man who was clearly out of his wits; all ready to spring into action to prevent an assault on Erich.

Erich was the only one who seemed relaxed. He continued to sit impassively, speaking in measured tones, working the trick on the back of his hand. The movement of the medallion kept drawing Jim's attention. One second he looked set to pounce; then in the next, uncertain again.

"Tell me, Jim. Who is Mr Niedermayer?"

Jim's body went into a violent convulsion as he screamed, "Keep your stinking Jewboy nose out of my affairs you fucking cunt! I'll kill ..." Then he broke off, as if he had suddenly caught up with the words he was saying, aware of the abuse pouring out from his mouth. "Oh God!" he cried, raising his hands and clutching the hair at his temples, "I'm sorry Erich ... sorry ... I ... I ..." He started to weep.

"Easy, Jim ... just breathe and relax. I know you didn't mean what you said ... those words are someone else's, aren't they? We're still friends."

Jim grew calmer but he continued to look confused.

"Sit down Jim."

Jim sat.

"Take it easy for a moment. Let go of the pain and hate inside you. Concentrate on my hand ... keep watching the medallion ... see how the light plays on it. Let yourself merge with it ... feel peaceful again ... be at ease with yourself. Breathe deeply. Breathe. You're safe here. Amongst friends."

Jim began to look more relaxed, his breathing settled; for a minute or so nothing more was said.

"Now Jim ... now that you feel better, we can talk. I want you to remember that you're with friends. It's safe ... you do feel safe don't you?"

"Yes."

"Close your eyes."

Jim shut his eyes.

Erich left a space before speaking, "We're going to talk about the cellar in Barnswick Square."

At this, Jim's face contorted.

Erich hesitated, for a moment he seemed unsure about going on. Then he found his resolve again and said, "Tell me about Mr Niedermayer."

Sweat broke out and began pouring from Jim's forehead; his eyelids flickered as though he was trying to wake up; it was like watching a man engaged in a battle with himself.

"I … I can't," Jim squirmed, his voice was agonised; a plea to Erich to stop probing him.

"You must tell me Jim. I'm your friend. I can help you."

At this point an unnatural laugh came out of Jim's mouth. It was unexpected, hollow and mocking in its nature.

"Nobody can help me," replied Jim, in his own voice, though it sounded scared, like a small child.

"You're wrong, Jim, you have to believe me. Your friends who are gathered in this room will stand by you. We'll never desert you, no matter what."

Jim started to shake again. The sweat was running down his cheeks and he was whimpering.

Erich returned the medallion to his pocket; his body noticeably stiffened, he inhaled deeply, then he asked, "Mr Niedermayer … he's a vampire isn't he?"

The effect of this direct question on the hypnotised Jim was decidedly less marked than the open-jawed reaction it got from the others, who all stared at Erich as though he'd taken leave of his senses.

However their reaction was low-key compared to the shock on their faces, when, after a few moments spent resisting the question, Jim answered with a resounding, "Yes."

Erich didn't speak again immediately, he was unable to. He looked almost as stunned by the affirmative response as his friends did.

After a time, perhaps thirty seconds, he asked, "What did he do to you?"

"He ... he ..." Jim cried out the words, "... he made me drink his blood."

There was a collective gasp; Erich swallowed hard and was visibly struggling to maintain his composure.

"Where has Niedermayer gone?"

"He hasn't gone anywhere ... he's in the cellar."

Erich immediately looked up from where he sat, out through the French windows and off into the gloom beyond. Night was approaching fast.

"Oh my God! Those poor policemen!"

Chapter Twenty One

Thursday, 12 December, 1996 approx 3.20pm – 4.10pm

Before DCI Harris left Barnswick Square, a response came in from the two officers dispatched to contact Jim Latimer. They reported that Latimer's cottage, and the one next door belonging to his neighbour Ruth Allinson, showed signs of forced entry. There was also some compelling visual evidence to suggest a violent struggle had recently taken place in the Latimer home.

"Dave, I need forensic to cover those cottages."

"Everyone we've got is flat out here," replied Frith.

"I appreciate how difficult it is … but we'll have to rationalise … maybe call in some favours. And request a helicopter to get a team over there. I need whatever can be gleaned from those cottages as quickly as possible."

"I'll do my best."

"I know," she nodded. Then she thought of something else, "And Erich Ledermann … Latimer talked about him a lot to DCI Rice. Check him out too. Our caller had an accent … Ledermann sounds promising."

A squad car took Harris back to headquarters. Her office was on the first floor, just beyond a large open-plan area that served the twelve men in her team. It was unusual to see most of the desks empty; the office was normally teeming with activity.

There were only three people in the room when Harris arrived, even so she could sense the adrenaline. Two officers were at their workstations, speaking on telephones whilst at the same time tapping information into keyboards in front of them. They both gestured as she entered, Harris returned their greeting with a wave. The third man present was Detective Sergeant Bryce, the office manager, who was in the process of delivering a progress report to the empty desks.

"Sorry about your leave, Susan," he said, handing her a copy as she went by.

The two at their desks looked up and smiled at Bryce.

"Why has everyone got a smug grin on their face when they say that?" Harris asked.

"Was I grinning?" Bryce asked innocently, winking at the other two.

Harris smiled wryly. Enjoying the misfortunes of others, especially when the luck-lorn recipient was a senior officer, was part and parcel of working in a male-dominated environment. It wasn't personal and didn't have anything to do with her sex. Fourteen years in the force since leaving university had taught Harris a lot about men at work. They were not, she'd discovered, unsupportive; she knew that every one of her team, all males, would stand by her in a crisis. In the male psyche a holiday cut short simply came under the heading 'shit happens'.

"Where's Frank Wain, Stan?" Harris asked Bryce.

"He's settling our detained person into a cell."

"How's young Grenfell?"

Grenfell was a uniform and not part of Harris' team.

"He'll be alright. The bastard broke his arm in two places!" Bryce shook his head like he could hardly believe it, "Big lad like Grenfell too, and him a little runt of a chap ... wouldn't credit it possible to see him." Bryce suddenly remembered an instruction, and brought his voice down to a whisper, "By the way, Susan, DCC wants you ... asked if you'd 'drop by' when you got back."

Harris' eyes rolled ever so slightly. She would not normally be required to have too many direct dealings with the Deputy Chief Constable, but her immediate superior, a man she got along with, was away on sick leave. Deputy Chief Constable Stuart E Markland was generally considered to be more at ease in the boardroom than a squad room. He was notorious for pushing his nose into every nook and cranny and for impeding rather than aiding progress.

She replied under her breath, "If Ron doesn't come back soon I'll be getting a friggin' double hernia too ... in my backside." She nodded at the smiling Bryce, "Okay. But I need to see Frank first and take a look at our DP."

Inside her office Harris spent a moment reflecting on the hideous crimes being currently exposed at the house in Barnswick Square. Her mind kept returning to the forensic man steadily weighing out kilogram bags of ash; difficult to comprehend that every two or three bags accounted for a human being. Although Harris had no spiritual beliefs, mixing the last remains of all those people together in old fertiliser sacks seemed somehow deeply sacrilegious. She thought of her mother and the journey she made each week to sit for an hour by the plaque that marked the final resting place of Harris' late father.

'How could all this killing go unnoticed?' she thought, recalling the package and its newspaper accounts of missing persons. It was unlikely the two hundred odd names from those cuttings could ever be verified.

The light was dim in her office; it would be dark quite soon; she switched on a desk lamp and crossed to the window. Outside the town was a murky grey, the street below and the streets adjacent to it were decked out in Christmas lights in what seemed to Harris a last ditch attempt to raise the afternoon. The people scurrying along the pavements were hunched over against the cold, like refugees from a Brueghel painting. Harris drew the blinds, banishing what was left of the miserable afternoon.

Frank Wain rapped on the door before entering. He was just under six feet tall with brown thinning hair peppered grey throughout, already white at the temples. He was forty-two; Harris always knew Frank's age because there was the same age difference, seven years, between herself and her brother; Frank had always seemed a bit like a brother in fact. They had harmoniously worked together as DIs for over four years before Harris got promoted.

In Harris' opinion Frank Wain's experience and professionalism were second to none. He had probably been overlooked on the promotion front because he was too damn valuable to lose from exactly where he was. Frank was never the bitter type though, and the number of times he had failed to get a promotion had become a private joke between them. He occasionally bemoaned his lot in life, but Harris suspected he preferred working at a grass roots level.

"Stan said you'd arrived back."

"You heard about the cremated remains?"

"We've been getting reports."

Harris saw the same look of incomprehension on Wain's face that she'd been witnessing all afternoon in every pair of eyes connected with that dreadful cellar.

"You were told about Grenfell?"

"Yes. What exactly happened?"

"We underestimated him. I had a man with a pistol trained on him, Grenfell must've gotten into the line of fire and Cureton took his chance. For a moment he had us looking like the Keystone Cops. He had four men on the deck."

"But in the end you managed to restrain him."

"I shoved my pistol in his ear and he stopped. I don't know what kind of hormones he's on, Susan, but I've never seen anyone faster or more dangerous."

"I suppose Grenfell's arm got broken in the scrum?" Harris considered the strength needed to crack bone.

"He did it deliberately," Frank swallowed hard as he recalled the moment, "Grabbed Grenfell's arm and snapped it like a twig ... he enjoyed doing it too."

"I'm told he's been uncooperative?"

"You can say that again. We kept the cuffs on throughout the interrogation. Fat use interrogating him was! We got diddley shit. He hasn't said a single word ..." Frank broke off, screwing up his already well-lined face in disbelief, "Did Stan mention anything about prints?"

"No." Harris observed the uncertainty now entering her voice as she asked, "W-what?"

"We didn't get any. He looks normal enough ... ugly but normal ... but every time we tried to print him all we got were smudges."

*

Erich induced a deep trance state in Jim. He'd managed to calm him down with masterly flair, before ordering him to stand and follow. The hypnotised man was led across the hallway into the sisters' library where a sofa bed had been made up. Erich removed Jim's shoes, then instructed him to lie down and go to sleep.

"You have no reason to wake until the morning."

The Thorpe sisters volunteered to stay at Jim's bedside and keep an eye on him.

Ruth and Erich returned to the drawing-room; Erich looked exhausted. Ruth like everyone else was still partially in a state of shock. She lowered herself into an armchair; Erich chose to stare out of the bay window, gazing at the strip of road where he had seen Danny off ten minutes earlier.

"How long?" Ruth asked. It was unnecessary to phrase the question in more detail.

"About forty minutes I reckon. I told Danny to drive as far as he could in fifteen minutes, then to use my mobile."

"I'm a bit of a dunce when it comes to new technology ... but I didn't think it was possible to trace a mobile phone?"

"I'm not very sure about it myself ... I think they're difficult to pinpoint. If he can get outside the area it'll make it harder for the police to find us."

"You expect they will?"

"Yes, of course. They must already know we're involved in some way. But we need time for Jim."

"How long do you think he'll need?" she asked. Erich thought he discerned a sense of hopelessness in her tone.

"Your guess is as good as mine," he said, stealing a glance at Ruth before turning back to the window and the twilight. He gave an uncharacteristic sigh, not only expressing his concerns for Jim, but also the large number of policemen who would be on duty at Barnswick Square.

"He looked like he wanted to murder you, when you kept probing him about Niedermayer."

"What gives me hope is that after the outburst he managed to reconnect with his own feelings."

"I could sense the crisis going on inside."

"He has to reassert his own personality. We can't allow him to be swallowed up by that ... that ...thing!"

Ruth rested her head against the chair-back and began to contemplate the series of events that had led up to this point. Neither spoke for several more minutes; the darkness seemed to creep up faster through the silence.

"How did you come to realise what it was?"

Erich turned to face her, again emitting a deep sigh. "The negatives in Jim's darkroom started me off. They triggered all kinds of superstitious images from when I was a child. The village where I grew up was only a few miles from the border with Hungary; in those days amongst country folk, myths about such creatures were fairly commonplace. As a child I was terrified by the tales, usually related in lurid detail by older children. After I came to Britain, as I grew up, Nosferatu was dismissed as folklore."

"Was it after discovering Rice's body you knew for certain?"

Erich shook his head. "No, not really, I was too stunned at the time. If such an idea ran through my mind then I dismissed it. No, it was here ... once I began to relate what had happened to you and the sisters. When I discovered Rice there was hardly any blood, the girl was anaemic too ... even for a corpse ... and there was some bruising on her arms which I didn't quite take in at the time. In the room where

I found Jim there was some equipment draining. I realise now what it was for."

Ruth's eyes became overcast as Erich was speaking, and after he'd finished she remained deep in her reverie for a few moments before she spoke again. "When you said ... vampire," the word was still hard to give admission to, "I thought you were playing a trick ... some kind of mind game, to goad Jim into talking. I was astounded when he said yes."

"Me too. I had my suspicions, but once he'd confirmed it ... it was still a big shock."

"Incredible though it seems, it all ties in ... the vision I had, the dreams ... even the way we felt inside that house. It's insane, but somehow it all makes sense."

The true horror of the situation suddenly hit her like a tidal wave. "Oh God, it's still in there! How are we going to stop it?"

Neither of them spoke further; there seemed little more to say. Erich came across and sat on the arm of Ruth's chair. He clasped her hand tightly in his and together they looked out through the bay window as the last vestiges of daylight slowly faded.

*

"He's in the third one along, ma'am," the custody sergeant told Harris.

Wain had gone down to the cells with her, although he remained outside. After over two hours interrogating Nicholas Cureton and getting nowhere, he thought she might have more luck on her own, but he doubted it.

The custody sergeant took her through, unbolted the door grille and drew it down.

Nicholas Cureton showed not even the slightest curiosity about who was peering in at him. He was sitting at the end of a mattress pad as far from the door as the limited cell space allowed, his back upright, staring impassively at the wall in front of him. Even the most uncommunicative tended to register at least something when they were being observed; the flicker of an eyebrow, a few blinks, even an obscene remark, but not here; Nicholas Cureton didn't move a muscle.

Harris knew better than to think she'd succeed in getting him to open up where Frank had failed. Instinctively she thought it best to say nothing, not even to introduce herself.

It was certainly hard to comprehend how this puny specimen, a skinny, pallid young man, had nearly got the better of four burly

246

officers. Yet Wain clearly believed that if he'd failed to put a gun to the man's head, Nicholas Cureton might easily have won the day.

She noted how Nicholas' clothing was too large for him. It reminded her of her own childhood, when mostly clothing had been hand-me-downs. Occasionally she and her brother had been kitted out in brand new clothes purchased one size too big, for maximum wear.

'Perhaps he hopes to grow into them,' she thought.

She had seen clothes similar to the ones he was wearing hanging on the rail in the bedroom on the third floor of the house. The room had reeked of body odour. Latimer in his account to Rice had described Rosemary Hines as totally besotted with this man.

Harris considered him a moment from a purely feminine perspective. 'I know beauty's in the eye of the beholder, but he's no Harrison Ford.'

She found the look in Nicholas' eyes the most unnerving thing about him. There wasn't really any defiance in them; they were just blank and cold as ice. Harris had looked into the faces of killers before, but there was something different about Cureton, she couldn't quite define it. A detained person might exhibit every emotion, from despair and shame through every shade of anger to complete contempt. But Nicholas Cureton merely sat and waited.

'Christ, he believes he's going to escape, that's why he looks so damned surly!' The thought, irrational though it seemed, still disturbed her, 'It's as if he's convinced nothing will keep him here for long.'

Harris had seen enough. She straightened her back and began to raise the door flap. At that moment Nicholas turned his head to face her. He was grinning broadly, revealing the tombstones behind the blubbery lips. The look made its point clearly; he considered round one down to him.

Harris peered back at him through the opening in the cell door, holding his stare for a few seconds with her most inscrutable smile, before delivering a short but meaningful wink and slamming the door flap shut.

"Touché, you ugly bastard," she said under her breath as she made her way back to Frank, who was leaning against the outer door. "Iceman."

Wain nodded.

They thanked the custody sergeant and headed back through a labyrinth of pre-fabricated corridors to a set of stairs.

"We've got to up our search for the Mercedes and white Transit, they've already had a good head start on us," said Harris.

"They may have dumped them; everything suggests they're organised."

"We still need to find those vehicles."

"What do you make of the photographer, Latimer?"

"I don't know yet. If he was involved, why be so unguarded with Rice?"

"Do you think Niedermayer & Hart were behind this paedophile network?"

"I'm not sure ... looks that way," she replied. "I don't suppose you've seen the package with the press clippings yet?"

"I heard about it."

"If it's accurate, they didn't show any discrimination when it came to victims ... old, young ... either sex."

Harris and Wain were half way up the flight of stairs to the first floor when they heard footsteps behind them. They turned to find DS Bryce, flushed and breathless at the base of the staircase.

"I went down the cells after you ... must've missed you."

"What is it Stan?"

"Another phone message," Bryce said rushing up beside them, "In your office, Susan."

The three of them charged up the remaining stairs, through the outer office and into Harris' room. She pressed play on the cassette player now sitting on her desk.

'This is about Barnswick Square. I'm one of the two people who broke in and left Nicholas Cureton tied up for you ... we gave you the information about Detective Rice and the young woman.'

Danny, having offered up his credentials, began the real message. The three listeners were all struck by the urgency in his voice.

'I know this probably sounds crazy ... a crank call ... but please, you must listen. The house in Barnswick Square is dangerous. Nobody should remain inside it after dark.' Here Danny's voice seemed to implore them, the note of tension in it suddenly more marked than before, *'Please ... evacuate the house before it gets dark. You must believe what I'm telling you. Get your men out immediately, they're in great danger!'*

The message finished.

"He was right, it certainly does sound like a crank caller," said DCC Markland, who was standing in the doorway to Harris' office. "It seems I must come looking for you myself, Chief Inspector. Didn't DS Bryce pass on my message that I wished to see you?"

248

"He did indeed sir, and I was just on my way to you when this came in."

"Shall we go through into my office?" DCC Markland began to lead the way.

"I ... I think I should attend to this first, sir."

"Now, please, DCI Harris."

Harris, resigned to her fate, nodded gloomily. She followed Markland through the outer office then along a corridor to his room.

The Deputy Chief Constable positioned himself behind his desk, gesturing for Harris to be seated.

"With respect, sir," began Harris, who had remained on her feet, "I believe that message is important ..."

Harris felt herself momentarily distracted by the dim remnants of daylight she could see through Markland's windows.

"... I think the team working in that house might be in danger."

"Chief Inspector, there are over thirty police officers at the murder scene, a number of them armed, I can't possibly see ..."

"Sir, that message was from the people who tipped us off earlier."

"And exactly how can you be sure of that? I've heard the other message, the speaker had a European accent."

"He mentioned our prisoner and DCI Rice and the girl. We haven't released any precise details yet, sir."

"How can you be sure they aren't playing us for fools?"

"I can't, but I am directly in charge of this investigation, and the men in that house are my responsibility. My instincts tell me I should pay attention to that caller."

"I won't have this force made a laughing stock because of your feminine instincts, Chief Inspector. Can you imagine what the tabloids would have to say?"

"You won't allow me to withdraw the team then sir?" Harris could feel her hackles rising.

"Of course not," he answered dismissively.

But she could never allow a politician to endanger the lives of her colleagues.

"Then ..." Harris paused, her hands were trembling, her throat was dry, she tried again, "Then ... I'd like that in writing sir."

"What?" exclaimed Markland, immediately flushing dark red and looking like his head might be about to spontaneously combust.

"If anything should happen at the crime scene, I'd like to have it in writing that you overrode my judgement on the matter."

Markland pursed his lips. The dislike Harris had felt for him before was nothing compared to her contempt now.

Markland calmed himself, his speech was measured, although his eyes were glaring at her. "Do what you will. Be sure this incident will not go un-noted," he warned.

Harris pronounced "Sir" curtly, turned on her heels and sped out along the corridor back to her own office. Judging from the windows she passed en route, if it was not already dark then it very soon would be.

"Stan, Frank," she said breathlessly as she reached them, "Get them all out! Evacuate the building entirely ..."

Hugh's Tale

XI

"See. They made the journey several times," Ayyub told Reynald as we toiled up the steep cliff pathway before us, "They were travelling two abreast."

"And judging by the tracks," replied Reynald, "Bearing objects greater in length than width ... provisions perhaps?"

Ayyub shook his head, "Why carry such burdensome supplies?"

"Whatever it was must have been important. From reading their tracks, they went up and down three times before finally returning for their horses," said Reynald, panting as he spoke. "I am grateful I need only climb it once."

"The evil one distributes great strength amongst his followers," said Ayyub.

It was indeed an exhausting climb, made more tiresome by our horses, who having adjusted to the constant swaying of our time at sea, required more cajoling when confronted by firm land again. Finally, arriving at the cliff top, we cast ourselves onto the ground with much relief and rested for a time. Here, our enemies' tracks became easier to discern. They had brought with them a cart; however the ascent had been too steep to risk their cargo and so had dragged it unladen to the top. All told, we counted the hoofmarks of ten horses, the cart accounted for two beasts and along with its driver this allowed for eight men on horseback.

"Three missing," said Aref. "Jerome's party numbered twelve. I can only see nine sets of footprints ... unless the creatures themselves were the cargo?"

"They must have hidden away during the journey aboard the ship, but why transport them like this afterwards?" I asked.

"It is indeed strange," agreed Ibrahim, who had been restored to his former vigour the instant his feet touched land, "They murder a galley-full of men so none may tell of their escape, yet lose time and

251

advantage in making four hard climbs where only two at most were needed."

"They would not have engaged in such an effort unnecessarily," said Ayyub, shading his eyes from the midday sun as he spoke. "The sun is friend to all living things, but corruption and death are scorched and burned by its purity of light."

And so, Anselm, our pursuit continued throughout the lands of Byzantium. Days became weeks, the harshness of the journey and the severity of our purpose weighed heavily upon us, an unrelenting yoke. Even Yussuf seemed to lose his youthful bloom, and was no longer the carefree, happy lad of our sea voyage.

Our enemies travelled fast. I do not doubt the devil's power was assisting them. They skirted round whatever towns or villages were met en route, yet such a group could not move entirely unnoticed; for every third day, with a regularity we dreaded, gruesome finds were made. At these intervals they had paused to take sustenance in their abominable way, leaving in their wake decapitated corpses, the hearts plundered from their bosoms.

Aref had suspected from the outset that the creatures were aware of our pursuit. And as time passed he only became more certain of it.

Twenty-six days after landing we discovered the naked headless body of a girl. She had been strung up by her ankles from a tree and left for the carrion birds to feast on; her blood had been drained. She had been young, not more than fourteen judging from her youthfulness of limb and smoothness of skin. Yet there were bruises and marks upon her flesh that suggested her suffering prior to death had been great. Not content with robbing her blood to slake their dead masters' thirst, the poor child had been violated time and again by the living too. Ibrahim and Salah cut her down and covered the body. We dug a hole and buried her, except for the head and heart of course, which had to be burnt. I knew only rage inside me as we stood around her grave, while Aref offered a prayer for the unknown girl to his nameless god.

As we rode on from that ugly scene Aref said, "Each time the killings are more perverse and violent. These defilements are done to dishearten us and lower our morale."

"They succeed then," said Reynald, his face revealing much anguish. He had been deeply affected by the brutality shown to the girl.

"They have the strength of the evil one," said Aref, "But their horses are only beasts as ours are, and their cargo slows them down. In the spirit of the nameless one, let our resolve not weaken."

252

Each day we rode a little harder, yet always their stamina seemed to match our determination to rid the world of them. For whenever the distance between us narrowed, they threw us a corpse. It was much like a master may toss a bone at his dogs, thereby causing all confusion; knowing full well that we should be forced to attend to it. Yet in spite of these delays, we slowly gained on them, especially where the terrain was hard, for we could move the swifter. They changed direction only to avoid habitations or natural obstacles before returning to the same route, always travelling relentlessly northwards.

As our pursuit continued we left the lands of summer behind us. Every new day seemed to grow darker and shorter as we journeyed into harsher climes. By mid-October we judged ourselves to be no more than half a day's journey from our enemies. Low in spirit, we conversed with each other rarely, for the effort sapped our strength; hard riding and little sleep was our perpetual existence. Our hair and beards, except in Yussuf's case, had grown long; giving us the appearance of wild men, and any peasant who sighted us generally ran away in terror; but we no longer cared how the world regarded us.

At times, when my exhaustion was at its greatest and I doubted I had strength enough for another day, may God forgive me, but I cared not who won. I prayed only that the ordeal might finally be over.

One night I sat hunched beside Aref as we shared the first watch over our sleeping companions.

"Why have you always been so certain that they know of our pursuit?" I asked him.

"They can sense the cup. It comes like a scorpion's tail behind them. Remember how Jerome did not dare approach you in the cellar when the cup was nearby?"

"Yet it was the same cup that made him," I replied despondently.

For a moment I thought I saw anger flare up in Aref's eyes in response to the blasphemy he may have believed I had committed through my words. He appeared so fierce in the firelight that for a moment he looked ready to strike me. Whether this was truly the case or was only my imagination feeding on exhaustion, I do not know; if it was, he relented immediately.

Aref considered a moment, before attempting to convey something of the cup's mystery to me. "It is the crucible of all existence, the meeting between spirit and flesh. Jerome drank the blood of an innocent man of his own free will. He expected the holiest of cups to be the finest of all vessels, and seeing so humble an object before him he immediately perceived that he had been tricked. This, my friend, was but a reflection of his own grandiose and deceitful mind. He defiled the cup and became what he truly is; perhaps in his own eyes a king, but only a king of desolation and darkness."

"How can it be that he rose from the dead?" I asked.

Aref answered, "The cup is wholly creative ... the reason why it is so dangerous. It has been in existence since before the dawn of time and is the binding force for all matter. To drink of the cup requires purity of mind and spirit ... Christ came to his resurrection, the traitor Iscariot to despair and suicide."

"Have you drunk from the cup yourself?" I asked.

Aref shook his head disdainfully, "Only a fool or a saint might do so."

Then, reaching beneath his coat, he drew out the cup. I gazed at it in astonishment; for the simple green beaker transformed itself before my eyes into a fine chalice made of gold, encrusted with gems the like of which I never saw before, nor ever will again.

Aref allowed me a moment's adoration before returning the cup beneath his jerkin, as ever leaving no sign that anything lay concealed there.

"What did you see?" he asked.

I told him of the marvel I had witnessed. He replied, smiling, "A king's cup."

All the next day I could not remove the vision of the cup from my mind, or Aref's response to my description of it. However, as the day approached its end, I found myself alone with him again. I asked the question which had been burning on my tongue, "Last night, when you showed me the cup, how did it appear to you?"

Aref smiled and nodded, "I saw that which I have always seen, an everyday cup a carpenter might drink from, crudely fashioned on a village potter's wheel."

I have no doubt that it was only the beneficence of Christ's cup in our midst that gave us the strength to carry on. As winter approached our suffering increased greatly. We were beset by torrents of freezing rain that often transformed our route into a perilous quagmire, making progress interminably slow. We still gained on our enemies, for not even the devil's strength could entirely lighten their burden. Many times we saw from the deeply furrowed tracks of their cartwheels how they had been forced to unload their foul cargo and bear their masters across a sea of mud. Such hardships cost them time, and although we still had received no sight of them, we reckoned them no more than half a league ahead of us. We increased our effort, in the hope that our chase might finally reach its conclusion.

Since the sickening horror of the girl in the tree, we had experienced countless similar and infinitely worse sights. Beholding such butchery became a commonplace thing, like bread and water; their occurrence too numerous and their effect too distressing to burden your mind, good Anselm. It is hard to comprehend how inured to suffering the human heart will grow when constantly exposed to such abhorrence. However, through it all, we never lost sight of our purpose. The spirit of the cup and Aref's guidance helped us keep to our resolve. He reminded us always of the highest human virtues. We never failed to bury our enemy's victims, although on occasions it may have been advantageous to our purpose to have done so.

"Why must we forever delay?" asked Yussuf, the poor lad barely able to pronounce the words, his exhaustion was so great, and suffering bitterly from the wet and cold. "Every time we stop they gain ground. Why can we not allow a few corpses to bury themselves in the mire? We would save more lives if we could bring this business to an end."

"Expediency is cherished in the black heart of the evil one," replied Aref, "To do as, is to become that which we must ever despise."

Yussuf said nothing more on the matter. Ibrahim and Salah rode alongside him for the rest of that day, laughing and joking amongst themselves to help keep up the boy's flagging spirits.

One evening some hours after nightfall, the moon full and the sky clear for once, for the rain had stopped, our trail brought us to a poor run-down village. It was the first time that our foes had led us directly into any kind of habitation, and therefore we approached with trepidation. All the homes were barred and shuttered, and the sign of the cross was daubed upon every door. No light was visible, but we each felt that we were being watched by many eyes. Then as we grew closer to these hovels the sound of a lone voice wailing, in the way that I have heard women sometimes do in grief, assailed our ears. We dismounted and spread out to find the source of the despair.

The noise stopped abruptly, and for a moment silence reigned absolute over the group of ramshackle dwellings. Then the voice of the one who had been expressing her anguish rose into such a shriek that it froze the blood in my veins. Ibrahim and Salah, identifying the hut from whence the scream came, ran for its door. I was but a few steps behind them as a woman, screaming and deranged, burst out through the hovel door and collapsed in their arms. I drew my sword and rushed passed them.

Within, cast in shadow by the dim glow of an oil lamp, I beheld a terrible sight. Two girls, twins I believe, about nine or ten years of age, had been laid to rest whilst their mourning parents had kept vigil over them. The wailing had been a mother's grief, and the scream had come about when her beloved children had risen from death, utterly changed. For on the floor beside their funeral bed, I beheld these children voraciously gnawing at their father's throat whilst suckling on his blood.

As I tried to comprehend the diabolical scene, the two creatures looked up furtively, gazing upon me with their feverish yellow eyes, snarls like those of wild dogs being emitted out of their blood-stained mouths. One leapt at me with teeth bared; I blocked the assault with the mail of my forearm, and drawing back her head by its hair kept the snapping jaws at a distance. It had been necessary to twist my body in my defence, which offered the other sister an opportunity to jump upon my shoulder, thereby disabling my sword arm.

The strength of these two was incredible, attacking with the ferocity of beasts rather than small children. I lost my balance and went crashing to the floor, the child at my shoulder leaping away from me as I fell, and forcing me to relinquish my grip upon the other one. As I looked up I saw them gloating at my vulnerability and preparing to pounce again. I have no doubt that my life was only saved because of Ibrahim, who entering at that moment hurled himself at one sister, whilst Salah flew after him with his sword raised.

I scrambled to my feet and brought my sword into line with the other small adversary's neck. Then as I caught sight of her eyes my mind became suddenly thrown into confusion. What was I about to do? Had I been so overtaken by all the horror of my recent life that I was ready to execute a child? Before me stood no monster, but a tiny girl, a sweet child looking tearfully up at me. I cast my sword onto the ground and reached out my hand to her.

As soon as she saw the empty hand, a sly smile replaced the child's innocent features. Then she leapt, her yellow eyes fixed firmly on my throat, teeth gnashing in that bloody mouth.

The next moment passed as swiftly as it took the blade to sweep before my eyes; yet the image will continue to haunt my dreams forever, of that young head being cleft from its shoulders and cart-wheeling to the floor.

Reynald, a blood-stained sword in his hand, stood above the headless body of the wretched child, a look of revulsion upon his face; there was no knightly pride to be taken in this work of ours.

Ayyub came then, and putting his arms about our shoulders, gently led us from that squalid room out into the clean night air. As we left, I saw Ibrahim with his dagger poised above the other headless child's breast whilst his brother held down its struggling limbs; waiting for us to pass before doing what must be done.

Outside, the mother lay sobbing on the ground. Aref was beside her, patting her arm, attempting to lend some comfort. After a short time he left the woman with us and returned into the hut with Ayyub.

We set fire to the woman's home to cleanse it; and afterwards, Aref took her hand and placed a few gold coins into its palm. It would have been more wealth than she had ever known, enough to build ten such hovels; yet nothing could ever compensate for her loss that night.

As we mounted up, the grief-stricken woman was silhouetted against the flames of what until recently had been home to everything she treasured. When we started to ride away she called out to us in her foreign tongue that none amongst us understood. However, its meaning was plain to all. In the strange guttural words of her language which sounded to our ears like curses, she pointed out the direction our enemies and hers had taken. Aref nodded to her that he understood and led us away.

We had never been in any doubt where our foes had gone; as ever, the trail led north.

Chapter Twenty-Two

Although the house in Barnswick Square remained the primary crime scene, a number of personnel had been re-deployed to Jim and Ruth's cottages. This branch of the investigation had a high priority because DCI Rice had visited Jim shortly before his death. As a consequence, the Hove team were spread more thinly; in the cellar, only three forensic officers remained.

"Just our bleeding luck, hey Harry?" Joe Carter said pointedly as he brushed ash into a pile on the floor of the recently opened kiln, "We drew the short straw. The others get a nice break-in on the other side of the county, while we sweat it out here in the chamber of horrors!"

Harry responded with a vague gesture; he'd heard the tape before. Joe was a companionable workmate, however, there came a point on most jobs when he felt impelled to point out they'd drawn the short straw. However, on this one Harry was inclined to agree.

The conditions in the cellar's crematorium were extremely uncomfortable, nauseating in fact; an arid, unpleasantly sweet aroma pervaded the air. Both men had long since developed headaches and felt queasy; conditions no doubt exacerbated by the dust-laden air. Another side-effect, most likely caused by the oppressive warmth, was the drying of the membranes of the nose and eyes. Each time they blinked, tiny granulated air-borne particles, which neither man cared to think about, acted as an irritant.

"This is still too bloody hot!" exclaimed Joe, demonstrating the fact by waving a smouldering brush in the direction of his colleague.

"I told you it wouldn't work," Harry said, "Probably hours before it's cool enough!"

"I've done all I can then. I'll give you a hand," Joe replied, extinguishing the glowing tip of the brush beneath his boot.

Harry was on the final fertiliser sack. By then he had completed nineteen black boxes, amounting to 380 kilograms of ash, which by his own reckoning represented something in the region of a hundred and fifty people. The first samples had by now been analysed back at the forensic lab, their contents verified as human remains.

Both men working together made the laborious process go much faster. Joe filled and weighed whilst Harry recorded and labelled. Within fifteen minutes they had reduced the final sack by about two thirds.

"We need more bags," said Joe.

"How many you got left?"

"Two."

"Let's finish those two and then go pick up some more. I could do with a breath of air."

"Too right, my eyes are stinging and I've got a bastard headache. Must be the heat from that thing," Joe said gesturing at the kiln.

"Must be dark outside by now."

"Probably."

The third forensic man had been working alone for most of the afternoon in the room where Jim had been kept prisoner. His name was O'Malley, and Susan Harris had spoken to him briefly when Frith had given her a tour of the house. Like his counterparts next door, he was suffering in the hostile environment. However, O'Malley's problems were not caused through stuffiness and heat but because of the room's coldness. The lower half of his body was partially numb as a consequence of this, causing him to shift his legs and stamp his feet from time to time in order to improve his circulation.

He had spent most of his time taking specimens of the skin and hair samples found so abundantly on and near the torture table. However, so far, he had only managed to recover two sets of definite fingerprints; one on the table itself that he assumed most probably belonged to its most recent occupant, and another full set on the leather straps. Earlier in the afternoon, O'Malley had taken these up to the ground floor to be scanned into the computer which had been set up in the hallway.

"We're getting hardly anything in the way of prints," his senior officer said as they watched the computer match both sets with prints discovered elsewhere in the house.

"At least we've got something here," said O'Malley.

"You all okay down below?"

"Yeah," replied O'Malley, who was generally a bit ill looking anyway.

"I'd like to relieve you down there … but you're three of my most experienced men and we're really pushed."

"I know. We're alright, Ken," said O'Malley, never one to moan.

It was at this point that O'Malley noticed that the layout of walls on the ground floor was slightly different to those in the cellar. It was an observation that only struck him as peculiar at first. Weren't walls, certainly in properties of that age, designed to support the floors above them? It was something O'Malley's inquisitive mind kept coming back to over the next hour or so.

So, at the same time as Joe and Harry were finishing off their supply of polythene bags next door in the crematorium, O'Malley was pacing out the torture room's dimensions, heel to toe. After this, he went along the corridor measuring the basement's length from the steel door to front wall.

As O'Malley passed the room where his colleagues were working, Joe Carter called out to him, "What the bloody hell you up to, Barry? Finally entered the magical realm of the little people have we?"

O'Malley raised the middle finger on his right hand but kept focused on his count as he went by their open door. Twenty seconds later he returned and paid them a visit.

"Something odd here, lads," he said and began to pace out the crematorium. Joe and Harry, having completed their last available bag, watched rather bemusedly as Barry did this.

"Nineteen!" he announced when he got to the far wall. "I reckon there's about seven feet unaccounted for!"

"What?" exclaimed his two-man audience simultaneously.

"I noticed the walls upstairs are set out differently. Look at the alcoves each side of that kiln," said O'Malley pointing to them, "The one next to the dividing wall is half the size of the other. I paced out forty-nine steps in the corridor, but both these rooms only add up to forty-two!"

Following O'Malley's lead, all three began to rap on the dividing wall with their knuckles.

"Seems solid enough," said Harry, tapping half a dozen times in rapid succession, his ear pressed to the wall.

Joe and Harry, quite perplexed by the missing seven feet, began measuring for themselves. They arrived at roughly the same figure as O'Malley. Intrigued now, they went on to measure the corridor, and then returned to pace out the torture room, where, upon entering, Harry accidentally dislodged the door wedge. O'Malley hammered it back into place with the side of his boot.

"Blimey," Joe said, grimacing as he entered, "It's bloody freezing in here, and what a stench! Have you had to put up with that all afternoon?"

"Yeah. But, I don't know ..." O'Malley sniffed the air like a bloodhound, "... I'd say it's got worse."

They set to, pacing out the room. All three agreed a sizeable portion was missing.

"We'd better let someone know," said Joe. "Seven feet in a place like this has to be significant."

"Can I use your radio? Mine isn't working," said O'Malley.

"Ours neither," answered Harry. "It must be something to do with the cellar ... we switched it off ... just got static."

"We're going to fetch more bags. Come with us. Never know your luck, we might find a cup of tea," said Joe.

"No, I'll stay here. Ask Dave Frith to come take a look."

The two men left O'Malley at the end of the corridor near the exit door. As he began to walk back to the room where he'd been working, he stopped abruptly; he could hear a deep rumbling sound, its low pitch reverberating in his chest.

'Christ ... what the hell was that?' His heartbeat had suddenly accelerated and he felt a trickle of sweat on the back of his neck. 'Come on, Barry, you know what these old houses are ... probably the plumbing,' he assured himself.

When he reached the room, the door wedge Harry had kicked must have come out again. He flung open the door and kneeled down to re-insert it.

When a man's legs clad in what appeared to be metal links appeared before him, O'Malley emitted a gasp. He screamed when a bony hand gripped his hair and flung him across the room.

The door slammed shut. And after that, whatever sounds were expelled in terror and desperation by the unfortunate O'Malley would remain forever Mr Niedermayer's pleasure and the room's secret.

*

In the final minutes before nightfall, Frank Wain was driving Susan Harris back to the Square. A squad car sped along ahead of them, its lights flashing, siren deafening, carving a route through the congested town centre. Wain maintained the smallest gap he could safely manage between himself and the car ahead. In streets designed for the horse and carriage, cars and buses drew to the side as the police vehicles went through gaps with little more than a few generous licks of paint to spare. It felt to Wain like he was travelling on a fairground ride amidst a sea of faces. He hated this hot pursuit stuff and heaved a sigh of relief when their escort indicated left and led them down a side road. Here, away from the squall and mayhem of the Christmas-frenzied streets, the majority of cars were parked and there was only an occasional pedestrian to contend with.

For the first time since leaving the station he glanced over at Harris. She looked anxious. "Was my driving that bad?"

"Is this going to be a waste of time?" she asked.

Frank had guessed the exchange with Markland must have gone badly. "I think it's very likely the message came from the same people who left us Cureton." He paused for a moment as though considering whether or not to continue, "As for danger and insisting we get out before dark ... it's difficult to see why ... our people must have been all over that house by now."

"So I am an hysterical bloody woman!"

"Is that what Markland said?"

"Not quite ... condescending bastard!"

"Okay, so if nothing happens you get egg on your face ... the alternative is worse. If our people really are in danger and you'd ignored the warning, imagine how you'd feel then?"

"I don't know which is worse," said Harris with a wry grin, "Not being able to live with myself or having to look at Markland's smug face."

The car ahead turned into Barnswick Square. Barriers had been erected around the site and uniformed policemen were keeping onlookers, who always turned up like rent-a-crowd to any murder scene, a safe distance from the house. A constable opened a partition in the barrier to let the cars through.

Harris opened her window to speak to a uniformed sergeant as he approached their car.

"Everybody out, Mike?"

"Not quite ma'am, three men still in the basement ..."

At that moment the sergeant's radio crackled into life, and a voice said, '*They're coming out now,*' "Did you get that?"

Harris nodded. She didn't understand why the message brought with it such a distinct feeling of relief.

"What are we supposed to be looking out for, ma'am?"

Harris shook her head. "I don't know, Mike, we got a tip off ... hopefully it's nothing."

"Better safe than sorry."

Harris smiled. Thank God at least two men agreed with her.

"I'll be round the back if you need me."

At approximately 4.40pm DCI Susan Harris and DI Frank Wain arrived in the parking area at the rear of 67 Barnswick Square. The space itself was brightly lit, several arc lights had been established on stands, and the back of the house was well-defined against the night sky.

The first person Harris noticed was Robson. He was walking over to some parked vehicles with two of the forensic men she had spoken to earlier. There were only about six or seven police officers visible, mainly uniforms; all other personnel were sheltering from the cold in minibuses or cars.

As Frank was backing the car into a space, Harris watched Dave Frith enter the building through its rear door. "Where the hell is he going?" she said.

Robson left the forensic men and walked towards them.

"Where's Dave going?" Harris asked him as she emerged from the car.

"Their radio wasn't working... Dave and I were just going in to get them when those two came out ... but there's a third man inside."

Harris nodded.

"I was just talking to them. They reckon they've found something unusual."

Harris observed a tiny flicker in the nerve beneath her left eye, "Unusual?"

Frank exchanged a discomfited look with her. It was in fact Wain who spoke next, "What did they find?"

"They paced out the cellar ... reckon there's quite a lot of space unaccounted for ... maybe a hidden area between the two rooms."

"Call Frith up on his radio, tell him not to hang about ... find the man and get out!" Harris said with a sense of urgency.

Robson held the radio to his mouth. "Dave ... DI Frith ... It's Rob ... can you hear me?"

No reply only static came back.

"Try his mobile!" exclaimed Harris.

Wain was already there, accessing Frith's number. It wouldn't connect. Wain shook his head.

"Something must be blocking signals in there," put in Robson, who was a reliable man, but not always the brightest bulb on the Christmas tree.

For the next ten seconds everything was thrown into utter confusion, when all the spotlights trained onto the house were suddenly extinguished and the crime scene was plunged into darkness.

"What the hell?" shouted Harris.

"The lights were connected to the house's supply!" answered Robson.

"Lights! Get any headlamps on!" commanded Harris.

Robson rushed off issuing instruction to the drivers of the parked vehicles, which were unfortunately mostly facing away from the house and made little difference. Only the headlights of the MIR were pointing in exactly the right direction, trained directly onto the loading bay doors.

Excited voices rang through the air.

"Everybody quiet!" exclaimed Wain in a voice that expected and achieved absolute silence. The sound of traffic from the nearby streets could be heard; the town's seagull population had already put themselves to bed.

However, one sound dominated the scene: the droning of hydraulics as the docking bay doors began to rise.

"You armed, Frank?" Harris whispered.

But Wain already had his pistol out and at the ready.

Instinctively they sprinted to the side of the MIR. Robson appeared alongside them. He was armed too, handgun poised in the direction of the doors. Harris was unarmed; in fact she rarely chose to carry a weapon.

The doors had now risen about a yard, exposing a pair of legs that were visible to the knees. There was something odd about the feet, which looked as if they were in a ballet pose and up on points. The hum of the doors went on until a man's lower body became visible to the waist.

"That's Dave Frith ... I'm almost certain," whispered Robson.

Harris had recognised Detective Sergeant Frith too. What troubled her was the way he appeared to be standing; judging by his stance it seemed impossible that he could be supporting himself; but most disturbing was the red pool that had collected about his feet.

When the doors reached their limit, a clunk punctuated their arrival. The scene remained absolutely still for a moment, as the man, now clearly identifiable as DS Frith, suddenly leapt from the parapet. It was like watching puppet movements; the detective sergeant remained rigidly upright, legs failing to bend at all to negotiate the jump.

Frith's head lolled back and forth in response to the sudden movement, eyes staring, mouth hanging open. It was just possible to catch the outline of the figure keeping Frith upright. The man's clothing seemed to give off a dull reflectiveness.

Harris knew that a warning was not going to work but she had to try. "Release the Detective Sergeant. Step out where we can see you. You can't pass. There are armed officers all round!"

Nothing, no movement, no sound, no response, nothing; Dave Frith's body remained dangling in mid-air, a dark pool mushrooming around his shoe tips.

Then something did happen. Frith's body began to move. It was tilting sideways and performed half a cartwheel through mid air as it came forward, his assailant's clothing shimmering in the headlamps. This unnerving display came to a standstill halfway between the house and the MIR, when to everyone's disbelief; Frith's body was hurled directly at the lights. The distance Frith's body had to travel was at least five yards, and the lamp on the left side of the MIR was immediately extinguished when he smashed into it.

There was still enough light to glean a dim reflection off the assailant's clothing and see the grey, pale hands that were held up shielding his face. This hazy glimpse of Mr Niedermayer, a rare sight for those about to continue living, lasted no more than a second or two.

Both Wain and Robson fired. Niedermayer sprang away like a predatory cat amidst the blinding flash and smoke of their guns; gliding from sight into the protective cover of darkness.

There seemed to be a collective gasp before the scene exploded into frenetic activity; radios crackling into life; instructions shouted. In less than a minute a score of police sirens had cut through the sea town night.

Harris knelt beside Frith's lifeless form. The back of his head had been crushed and lay in a dark glistening pool of blood.

Wain and Robson had rushed off in pursuit of their colleague's killer. Wain re-appeared first; he was out of breath and like everyone else who had witnessed the strange escape, utterly confused.

"No sign of him ..." he said, breaking off when he saw Dave Frith, "Oh no!" He crouched down beside Harris. Wain, brought up Catholic, long ago lapsed, made the sign of the cross, "Dave!"

"Did you hit him Frank?"

"Yes ... no, I couldn't have ... hell, I don't know. I thought so, Susan ... I thought I'd got him ... I had him in my sights."

"I thought you hit him too." Harris knew of course that neither Frank nor Robson could have done so. In fact, she didn't understand why she'd even bothered saying it.

Hugh's Tale

XII

After the tragic encounter with the twin girls our foe adopted a wholly different tactic. They no longer rendered their victims harmless by removing their heads and hearts, but left the bloodless carcasses intact, ready and waiting to receive diabolical resurrection. We were now executioners.

On the next occasion we destroyed three of the fell creatures. The evil triumvirate led by Jerome had robbed but one soul; however, the contagion spread fast, and we had arrived too late to stay their victim from rising. He had gorged on the life-blood of his wife and of the priest he found there praying for his soul. Not even those in holy office are immune to this plague of evil, good Anselm.

Our violent work was misunderstood and we were hated and feared by the very people whose lives we came to save. For as soon as we had arrived in their community we immediately set to work mutilating their beloved dead. In their eyes we were the committers of sacrilege; defilers of the shape and form of God's creation.

Some days on, as we rode from yet another village, our grim work there done, I asked, "Why have they waited all these months to engender new creatures?"

"Because they wish to hinder us," said Ayyub. "Not that we pose much threat in ourselves."

"What they fear is the cup drawing too near them," said Aref.

"The cup will destroy them?" I asked in hopefulness.

Aref shrugged his shoulders, expressing uncertainty, "In truth none of us knows. I am the cup's guardian, but no man can truly understand its power. That knowledge resides solely in the mind of the nameless one."

Reynald spoke then, "If Jerome fears our approach, why does he not raise an army of monsters to defeat us?"

"He would not need an army," put in Ibrahim, "They are so powerful by night ... a mere handful might easily have done with us."

Then Ayyub spoke once more, "Jerome, through his violation of the cup, believes he has created an elite. But these latest creatures are wild and unfocused. Jerome and the others may not exercise any great amount of power over them."

"Why are these new creatures different? Neither Laszlo nor Wilhelm drank directly from the cup." I interjected.

"The pact had already been sealed with the evil one," said Ayyub. "Few men would be prepared to seal an oath with human blood, even if they were ignorant of the vessel they were about to drink from. Such a vow is forever sacrilegious."

Then Aref spoke once more, "Jerome is the archetype, a great master in his own eyes, the other two his vassals."

"Yet he is in some ways inferior," I responded, "For he has lost the power of speech, yet Laszlo his creation retains this faculty."

"He does not require words," said Aref, "For he can instruct his slaves through the power of his mind."

We rode on without more talk for a while. It was Reynald who broke the silence, "Yet the new creatures seem incapable of speech too. They awaken ravenous for blood, yet beyond an insatiable thirst seem to possess no other sense of purpose. In the daytime they hide in whatever place is free of sunlight. They lack intelligence enough to seek refuge somewhere they are not likely to be discovered."

It was an accurate observation. The new demons did not possess the cunning of their founders. However, they might easily prove lethal during the hours of darkness to anyone ignorant of their habits and desires. Yet armed with our knowledge of them, and with day inevitably following night, they had so far at least, always proved vulnerable to us.

"The original four were corrupt, power-driven men," said Aref. "Their victims are blameless. And although they are driven to madness with the hunger for blood, they do not possess the same mind that is in Jerome and his two surviving lords."

Ayyub agreed, "Remember, they only enslave these creatures to delay us. They know it robs us of time."

"They could never have embarked on such a journey as this without an intended destination," I said, "They cannot flee from us forever."

"Be certain they have already planned our end," replied Ayyub, "They keep us at bay, not intending to halt us altogether ... not yet at least. I do not doubt we are being led into a trap. They will want vengeance for the trouble we have caused them."

It was not Ayyub's way to speak rashly, which always lent power and weight to his words.

We continued to be led northwards, and in turn bequeathed new miseries to every place we were called upon to visit; our quarries were hell's plague and we were the purging fire that must come after.

November passed; weary from travel, sickened by our detestable work, we entered the year's final month. We found ourselves constantly under attack from freezing winds in a northerly clime, desolate and inhospitable. However, we continued to learn much about our enemies and how to dispose of them. The symbol of Christ we already knew was a potent deterrent for keeping the creatures at bay; a crucifix touching a creature's skin brought it agonising pain, searing its flesh like a hot brand.

Daylight was our best ally and the demons' greatest enemy, for the sun's rays acted like fire upon them, causing their skin to blister; in torment they would claw at themselves, tearing strips of flesh away with nails, screaming in a voice that had its inception in hell. After a time, flames would burst forth from the creatures' hearts, soon to consume them utterly; within a few minutes nothing remained but a pile of charred ash.

The greatest danger posed by this inferior third generation of creatures was to gaze directly at the eyes. I had learned this lesson during my encounter with the twins, which but for Reynald's timely intervention would undoubtedly have been to my eternal cost. It was possibly the only subtlety they had inherited from their creators, the ability to cast a spell of confusion over the mind of their intended victim, by conjuring an image of innocence.

As I have already said we forfeited a good deal of time hunting down and destroying these hideous progeny of our foes. Disagreeable though it was, we undertook to do our appalling work thoroughly; cautious always, forever wary that none had slipped through our net, thereby making all our efforts as nought; for this contagion would spread as easily as rats.

A simple trust in their nameless God sustained our five companions well. Their hardest burden proved to be the climate, for they had never known such harshness. Young Yussuf fared the worst. He had developed a cough that kept both him and us awake whenever opportunity came for sleep; Ibrahim and Salah remained as ever uncomplaining, their joyous spirits unbowed even in the face of adversity; Aref and Ayyub always solid and sound as rock to the task before us.

It was Reynald that I was most concerned for. He had been scarred deeply by the execution of the twin girls, and our work since had allowed him no opportunity to shake off this melancholy. The demoralising tactics employed by our enemy told on all of us, but Reynald, with his kind heart and generous spirit, suffered most of all. He found the endless delays intolerable, growing ever more desperate, reckless even, in his desire to eradicate the undead creatures; often rushing alone into a dark place that was thought to be its lair. I grew anxious for him, and saw that Aref and Ayyub shared my concern, yet there was nothing that could be done and the matter was never spoken of.

For eight days we pursued our foe along the eastern side of a great range of snow-capped mountains. The area itself was uninhabited except by wolves, and therefore, denied of their preference, the three had fed on the blood of these wild creatures. Our food supplies ran low, Yussuf grew weaker with every passing day, and we were all exhausted. When our enemies' trail took off west into the phalanx of mountains, we pursued them for two more bitter days, before finally admitting defeat.

"Our first duty is to bring the cup to safety," counselled Ayyub, "It would be a day of jubilation for Jerome and his lords if, along with us, it was buried deep in these mountains."

Aref sighed, nodding in agreement. Reynald said nothing; his head remaining downcast. Yet he knew it was the right action; we all did.

"Only the undead and their acolytes might survive such a place in winter," Aref said, "We must find shelter and provisions to sustain ourselves. Our intention still holds true. And be assured this matter is not finished."

We journeyed back over part of the route we had traversed the previous day. Then, as we looked down into the pass that we must travel through to be free of the mountains, we beheld a group of men encamped at its mouth; unlike us they had come equipped with tents and provisions. The Templar standard was raised above the tents, and I counted twenty horses. As we watched, our spirits low, we saw emerging from the centremost tent he who was despised by all, de Frontignac. True to his verminous nature, he had survived the cellar in Acre and now led a party in pursuit of us.

"We cannot hope to prevail against such numbers. Yet I swear I will take that bastard to hell with me," said Reynald, filled with hatred for him who had betrayed us.

"Let us not be hasty," said Aref. "We face the elements and possible death on one side or certain death upon the other. But to die here would mean surrendering the cup to him who has taken too much from us already."

"Then let us place ourselves in the hands of the nameless one," said Ayyub, "It seems we have no choice but to go on. If it be His will, then we shall survive whatever ills these mountains threaten."

Exhausted, half frozen and heavy hearted, we returned into the mountains; once again interpreting the tracks written in the snow made by the fell creatures' acolytes. The ascent was too severe to ride, forcing us to travel on foot, leading our beasts who suffered as equally as their masters. After a while, we came upon the cart that Jerome, Laszlo and Wilhelm had been transported on throughout the lands of Byzantium. Although it had been abandoned, much of its wooden carcass had been salvaged and three sledges had been made. This new method for transporting their dead masters left marks furrowed deep into the snowbound hillsides as they were pulled along.

The weather grew steadily worse and we took it in turns to aid Yussuf, who grew much sicker. For two days we climbed before finally arriving at the highest point of the range. As the clouds parted for a moment, we caught sight, for the first time in all our days of toil and hardship, of those we had relentlessly pursued for two hundred leagues and more; a moving group of men and horses the size of ants; their abominable cargo dragged behind in three long crates. They were about a hundred feet or so below us on a path that meandered over the adjacent hillside and went bending through the mountains like a horseshoe. Strange it may seem to you Anselm, but we viewed them with detachment; our more pressing needs were for food and warmth, the immediate enemy the cold. So far we had been fortunate, finding some crag or crevice large enough to huddle in at night on the leeside of the wind. It was past noon already and we needed to be far from the unprotected summit and under some kind of shelter before nightfall.

The gradient seemed imperceptibly small at first, and it was hard to believe that we were actually in descent. We passed an unusual formation of rocks a short distance from the summit, resembling a clenched hand with a solitary finger pointing skyward.

Progress was slow, and our weary horses grew more refractory and reluctant to continue. Then, half a league from the peak, with great apprehension we spied coming out of the west storm clouds; ominous, dark, boiling up and rushing at us, like steam escaping from the pit of hell.

"We are heading into a blizzard," warned Reynald, "If we do not reach cover before it strikes then we are lost."

The route before us offered little hope. The way was narrow and in places it ran alongside the edge of a precipice. Once the storm struck we would be staggering about as blind men, therefore in that direction only destruction seemed likely.

"There was an outcrop of rock just below the summit," said Ayyub, "All of you must have seen it ... a column pointing skyward. It would at least offer some protection."

It was agreed that Ayyub's suggestion was our best hope.

"Can we reach it before the blizzard is upon us?" I asked.

Reynald looking grave, replied, "Better at our backs than driving in our faces."

We wasted no time. We turned the horses about and started to retrace our steps up the mountainside, Reynald in the lead, Aref behind him, leading Yussuf's horse and his own; I was next, lending my assistance to Yussuf; after us, followed the brothers, Salah bringing my horse; and then finally came Ayyub. We had covered roughly half the distance back to the summit when the blizzard overtook us. The horses began shrieking as our party became engulfed; fearsome winds howling all about, the clamour filling our ears to bursting, ever rising in its power and malevolence.

I staggered on, my arm gripped tightly about Yussuf, half dragging him along, his face a blur in the swirling haze around us. I kept my eyes fixed ahead, hoping to at least keep sight of the horses' tails before me, but mostly seeing nothing but whiteness. An awful sense of aloneness grew inside me. Yet we trudged on, and without end it seemed; relying solely upon Reynald to deliver us from this snowbound hell to safety.

I knew that under such conditions we might easily come a hair's breadth from our intended destination and miss it entirely. For even the prominent feature we sought might be masked from our eyes by the turbulence about us.

The wind found every chink and gap in my clothes, numbing my flesh with its breath of ice. In my mind evil voices spoke of defeat, the hopelessness of our plight and futility of our venture. I yearned for the torture to stop, and considered taking my charge, the suffering child at my side, and stepping from the line; for he was weak and sick, dying probably, and I was too fatigued to go on - death was inevitable, let Jerome be damned, why must we suffer more?

Then I imagined Jerome's triumph, and a sort of madness overtook me which brought with it a renewed energy. I began to shout at the top of my voice, "Let us not be vanquished here! God in heaven, give me strength!" I recited this litany over and over, the blizzard my only witness, swallowing up my words in its rancour.

Then, Anselm my friend, came a miracle indeed. For the briefest of moments the clouds of swirling white before our eyes parted, and there, pointing like a monument to heaven, was the pillar Ayyub had remembered. It came and went, like a veil that is raised and immediately replaced; yet it was enough for us to find our mark.

Reynald led us to the base of the rocks and we felt our way about them onto the leeside of the wind. I could see Aref coaxing his horses just ahead of us as we entered a gully wide enough to house both men and beasts; well protected and better than anything we might have hoped for.

Yet our sanctuary was to prove far better still; for at the farthest end of this gully was a hollow deep enough to house every man in the party. In its midst was a chimney which ran inside the pillar of rock which had made the outer feature prominent; and, yet more blessings, for along its far wall we beheld with incredulous joy a modest but adequate supply of wood. It seemed that others had at times sought refuge in this place; judging by the animal droppings on the floor, not long since a refuge for goats and their herder.

Our horses could not enter the hollow, yet they were protected from the worst excesses of the wind by the gully walls. I lay Yussuf upon the ground and covered him with a blanket. He was barely conscious.

Salah entered behind me, immediately followed by his brother Ibrahim; then after a minute or so, we saw that no other came. Aref went and looked out from the entrance of the hollow; Ayyub's mare had followed Ibrahim's into the gully, seeking sanctuary for itself from the blizzard.

"Ayyub is not come," said Aref, his face showing great anguish.

Reynald, barely able to stand from weariness, staggered to the entrance. "I led us here, I will fetch Ayyub ... he is lost, and I must find him."

He started to leave, but Aref blocked the way.

"You must not leave, Reynald," he said quietly. "I cannot allow the evil god to claim another life this day. You stand little chance of finding Ayyub in this storm, and possess even less hope of reaching this sanctuary again."

"I must go for him! It was Ayyub's idea to come here ... it was he who saved us all!" answered Reynald in desperation, half-shouting the words and swaying unsteadily as he spoke.

The rest of us were crouched low, our heads resting on our chests; heavy with grief for our much-loved friend who we knew must be irrevocably lost.

Aref took Reynald's hand in his and led him gently back inside the hollow and sat down upon the floor beside him. "Let us stay here a while and consider what is the best for all. If after giving thought you still believe there is a chance of finding him, then I will join you ... Ayyub was my friend, and it grieves my heart to abandon him."

For a time we sat in silence; then Reynald, raising his hands about his face, heaved a sigh from the depths of his soul. The next instant he fell to weeping as a child.

The Guardians' nameless god had indeed performed a miracle by bringing us safely through the storm. Yet we had suffered a very great loss; Ayyub, ever wise in counsel, always constant in his friendship. The evil god had demanded a bitter tithe of us that day in return for our wretched lives.

Chapter Twenty-Three

Thursday, 12 December, 1996 approx 4.50pm – 6pm

Susan Harris knelt beside Detective Sergeant Frith holding his lifeless hand in hers. A film of frost was forming over the concrete base of the car park. Harris could feel its coldness creeping up into her spine.

Frank Wain was kneeling too. He was staring down at the dead man, intense, almost fierce in his grief, but at the same time, there was deep confusion in his eyes. Frank's body language invariably presented an accurate picture of what was going on inside the man; he would have made an exceptionally poor spy or wheedling mandarin. His face at that moment, as read by the ever observant Harris, was expressing not only shock but total disbelief at what had just occurred.

Robson arrived back. He stood beside Frank Wain, head down, hands clasped together uncertainly. He was wearing the same look of disorientation as Frank. Harris looked up at him inquiringly. Robson shook his head, "No sign … no sign of him at all," he said.

Harris made it her job to know everything she could about her personnel - background, strengths, weaknesses, service history. Both these men were first-class marksmen, yet they had failed to hit a target at a viable range. It was easily explained - the man was moving, the scene badly lit - but somehow, however plausible this seemed, it didn't hang together.

"Could you fetch something to cover DS Frith with?" Harris asked a young constable standing nearby; he moved away as if shell-shocked. A minute later he returned with a blanket, which Harris helped him lay across the body. Frith couldn't be moved yet, and although there wasn't any doubt, a doctor or coroner would need to pronounce him dead.

Harris knew that her personal need to mourn must come later and in private. "Frank," she said purposefully, "We still have a man in there. I think we've experienced what our caller wanted to warn us about … but we aren't taking any chances. You up for it?"

Wain nodded.

"Get six men armed and kitted out in flak jackets to accompany us."

Wain left; he was relieved to be doing something.

"Rob ... DI Robson!" she had to repeat name and rank because the man wasn't present.

Robson raised his eyes uncertainly from Frith's covered corpse.

"I need to see the two forensic men who came out. I'll be in the MIR."

Robson started to move off, then as if suddenly remembering something he turned back, "It could have been me ... I offered to go in and get O'Malley, but Dave said he would."

Harris clasped his arm, "It was bad luck ... nobody should have died tonight." She remembered Markland and bit hard on her lip. The Deputy Chief Constable had eaten up six or seven precious minutes of time, thereby delaying the evacuation, "Bring me the forensic men, Rob."

"Dave was a family friend ... If it's okay I'd like to break the news to his wife, Jackie."

"I'd appreciate that."

Inside the MIR the atmosphere was frenetic. All available cars were scouring the district, roadblocks were already being set up and every exit out of town was being watched.

One of the WPCs informed Harris, "A biker four streets away swerved and came off his bike to avoid a man who ran out in front of him ... said the man didn't even look round, just kept on running. He didn't see his face ... but thought he looked like he was off to a fancy dress party, dressed up as a knight or something."

"Did he see which way he went?"

"That's the oddest bit. The biker claims a car drew up and a woman got out of the driver's side and helped him climb into its boot."

Harris blinked. "The car ... make, colour?"

"It was a good way off, and our witness was a bit dazed."

"Keep combing the area. Warn all personnel to approach with extreme caution!"

Robson came in with Harry and Joe, the men from the cellar. They were understandably shaken by the events that had taken place so swiftly after their exit.

"I understand you may have found something in the cellar?"

"Not us, it was Barry, ma'am," said Joe.

"He noticed the walls downstairs didn't quite match the ones above," put in his colleague.

"We paced it out. Reckon there's about seven feet missing between the rooms."

Harris swiftly ascertained that the missing seven feet had to lie somewhere between the room with the customised kiln and the room that was soundproofed.

Five minutes later Wain came to fetch her. He was already wearing a flak jacket; he helped Harris into the one he was carrying and handed her a pistol.

Outside the MIR, screens had been erected around Frith's body. The atmosphere in the car park was sombre.

Six men all armed and protected were waiting for them. Each member of the team carried a flashlight as the house was still in darkness. They entered through the open delivery bay. The fuse boxes, which were set on the wall beside the lift, had had their circuits torn out.

"Have someone standing by to rewire the fuse boxes," whispered Harris into her radio.

The door to the cellar had been left open; they approached warily. Two went ahead, shining their beams through the opening and along the broad corridor in front of them. When they signalled that all was clear, two other officers rushed inside taking up squatting positions, pistols at the ready. They indicated for the others to come through.

The corridor was wide and they proceeded along it four abreast, eyes concentrated on the areas most deeply in shadow. They covered twenty feet, coming level with the end wall of the first room. Harris whispered instructions that four should go ahead to check out the crematorium; she, Wain and the two remaining men would enter the torture chamber.

Frank flung open the door, ensuring that he stayed low beside it and shone his flashlight inside. Only one side of the room was visible to him, nothing stirred, but he had a bad feeling about what lay ahead; you never forget the smell of fresh blood.

Wain rushed in, still keeping down, and took up a position beside the right hand wall. Harris went in directly after him.

"Oh Christ!" was all she could manage when confronted by the sight that met her eyes.

Harris felt certain the cellar no longer posed any danger and the threat their caller had been warning them about was already past. She put her pistol away in its holster.

They had reached Barnswick Square just a couple of minutes late to save the lives of two good officers. She had failed; Frith was dead and so too was O'Malley; she assumed it was forensic man Barry O'Malley that would be identified from the blood-spattered abattoir before her. One of the men who had entered after them rushed unsteadily back towards the door, a hand to his mouth, and a moment later came the sound of vomiting.

"Bad news," Harris said into her radio, "Get those electrical circuits repaired."

Harris sent the six men off to check that the floors above were secure, although she felt in little doubt they would be.

For a few minutes, Harris and Wain were left alone with O'Malley's dismembered remains and their flashlights.

"I don't understand," began Wain, "We watched Dave going inside as we arrived, the forensic men can only have come out a minute or so before ... then, a couple of minutes later the lights went out!"

"What are you saying, Frank?"

"Five minutes, Susan ... five minutes to kill O'Malley, kill Dave Frith and fuse all the lights. Just look at it," he said, gesturing at the carnage on the floor, "Imagine, a few minutes to do that! I reckon it would take ten minutes with a chain saw to do something like that to a man!"

Frank was right. What had been left was barely recognisable as a human form. The flesh, virtually flayed from its skeleton, was layed out like a mottled red carpet beneath the ribcage; the limbs appeared to have been torn apart at the joints and jumbled together in a mangled heap; the intestines seemed to have been deliberately draped over the head which was set on the ground a few feet away from the rest of him.

"What the fuck is happening?" asked Harris; alone with Frank she allowed her sense of desperation to show, it was a heartfelt plea.

Frank made no attempt at an answer.

The only sound came from the broad pool of blood that surrounded O'Malley's corpse, which gurgled occasionally, as it sluggishly drained between the gaps in the brick floor into the earth beneath.

*

Erich was waiting on the doorstep for Danny when he returned to the Grange.

"I managed about ten miles. I got as far as Beachy Head."

Danny followed his father into the drawing-room. The seventies ballad playing on the radio seemed out of place; Erich had been hoping for a news bulletin about the situation in Hove. Ruth was sitting bolt upright in one of the armchairs. Although her eyes were open she didn't respond in any way as they entered.

"What's up with Ruth?" Danny whispered to his father, "Is she hypnotised?"

"No," replied Erich, seeming somewhat amused by the suggestion, "She's been like it a while ... she's working."

Danny made no attempt to find out exactly what kind of work; it was no secret that Erich and his friends shared a fascination for all kinds of esoteric practices. However, until today, Danny had remained happily aloof from this area of his father's life. Within just half a day, he had survived a murderous assault, committed the criminal offence of breaking and entering with his own father, made an anonymous phone-call to the police, and discovered that vampires might actually exist. As far as Danny was concerned, the jury was still out on that one; very far out.

Danny Ledermann had done quite a lot of thinking during his car journey to and from Beachy Head. Taking up the seat next to Erich on one of the sofas, he began to formulate his thoughts into words. "How ... how might such a creature exist?" he asked.

Erich shook his head.

"Could something like that have evolved over time? I mean, man has no really effective predator ..."

"Man needs no predator," replied his father, "He rather too successfully fulfils that role himself. Look at the pages of human history – they are awash in blood."

"The ... thing ... in the cellar ...was it ever human do you think?"

"I think it was once."

Without warning, and giving Danny a start, Ruth suddenly entered the conversation. Her eyes had a strange translucency about them; Danny put that down, at least in part, to the glow from the log fire. However there was a tone to her voice that he'd never heard before. Her speech was flat and stultified, lacking its normal flow. "I've seen it," she pronounced with certainty, "Only the physical body is sustained on blood ... but it has a spirit form too ... which engulfs its victim's soul."

Ruth was expressing so much emotion through her eyes that Danny considered it possible she might be about to scream. It was disconcerting to see her like this; talking as if the horror she conceived was tangible. "I've seen it, it engorges itself on the fear of its victims ... it is utterly negative. There are souls, filled with light, who have attempted to disperse it ... but it's too strong, too powerful for us alone."

"Why?" asked Erich.

"Because its root lies with you ... the source of its perpetual existence in the next dimension is the blood of the living in your world."

"I think I understand," said Erich, "When the root is severed, the trunk and branch cannot be sustained."

"The imprisoned souls can then be freed ... and the beings of light will start to bring healing."

"What must we do?" asked Erich.

"Be vigilant, stand together ... help to rid your world of the blight."

"Us? What can we do? Three of us are too old to do very much and one of us is sick."

"There is always a way ... others will come to your aid ... have patience, much has been achieved already." At this Ruth's head sank down onto her chest as though she had just dropped off to sleep.

Erich turned to Danny and said in a matter-of-fact way that was typical of him, "Until today, Danny, we all believed such things were superstition, dark fairy tales, hobgoblins."

"How long do you think he has existed?" Danny asked, a bit uncertainly.

"For centuries," put in Ruth, much to Danny's relief she was talking normally again.

"But how could he go undetected for centuries?"

"People go missing every day," she replied. "They've been in business for a long time. I can imagine that red-haired brute we tangled with this morning cruising about in his van seeking out the lost and lonely. Some probably weren't even missed ... lost souls, disenfranchised by a society that turns a blind eye to its poor and weak. Sadly, it would be all too easy."

Danny was about to ask some more questions when a cry for help came to them from across the hallway. They exchanged anxious looks with each other before rushing out of the room.

In the library, Mary and Millie Thorpe were attempting to use their combined weight to restrain Jim. He was violently convulsing. Mary lay prostrate across the unconscious man's legs, and was being tossed like a most unlikely cowboy trying to tame a wild mustang. Millie lay on his chest, keeping down the arms to prevent him from scratching at his face, where his nails had already torn deep tram-lines marked in blood.

Danny and Erich immediately rushed to the aid of the sisters, who were valiantly losing the battle. Even with the two extra helpers, Jim's physical strength was incredible, each of them being buffeted by the wildly flailing limbs of his convulsive form.

Ruth, however, didn't join in. She stood apart from the others and appeared to be watching the frenzied scene with detachment. "Stop it!" she commanded powerfully, anger rising in her voice, "You've gorged long enough ... he doesn't belong to you!"

To everyone's amazement the storm almost immediately abated. Once again Jim lay calm. A little uncertainly at first, they relinquished their hold on him and one by one stood up.

"Mary, Millie, do you have some old sheets we could tear up? We'll need to tie him down to stop him hurting himself," said Ruth dispassionately.

"Yes, of course," said Millie, ashen-faced in shock.

"We'll get some right away, dear," answered her sister, equally as shaken.

They only had enough time to reply before Jim's face began twitching again. There was an unnatural quality about the way the facial muscles moved, as though a master puppeteer was manipulating them. Jim's eyelids sprang open, a sight which earned a joint gasp from the Thorpe sisters. The eyes were roving from side to side, the movements rapid and reminiscent of a lizard.

There followed a moment of hesitation about what next to do.

As they watched, mesmerised in horror, they saw the man's lips peel back from his teeth in a hideously contorted grimace.

Then Jim Latimer, or whatever was controlling him, released a growl. It was unimaginably deep; a sound owing no debt of origin to any human vocal cord.

*

It took Wain and Harris a few minutes to discover a panel that interrupted the continuity of the soundproofing. This was situated within the alcove on the far left of the door, at the darkest point in the room, so aptly referred to by Harris' team, as the torture chamber. However, Wain and Harris' efforts to move this panel by themselves were totally in vain.

Difficult questions were troubling Harris' naturally inquisitive mind. Why had Frith and O'Malley's killer waited until after dark to make his escape? The phone call had been specific, disturbingly

281

accurate in fact, that the house needed to be evacuated before the hours of darkness. Why? A get-away might have seemed strategically sound under the cloak of night, yet the assailant had in fact chosen almost the worst possible moment to make an escape bid with every available officer outside the building. How had that escape bid succeeded? And what had allowed Frith and O'Malley's killer to face gunfire with seeming indifference?

Frank was having similar thoughts. He'd refrain from shouting it from the rooftops, but he felt more and more certain that he'd hit his mark. Yet it made no sense; not even the best vest in the world could protect someone from the impact of being hit, especially at fifteen feet. He hoped ballistics might provide some answers when they dug the bullets out of the walls of the house.

After the lighting circuits were repaired, three men were drafted in to help them break into the hidden space. It was hard to work in an area where a colleague's remains so conspicuously covered about a fifth of the floor mass.

First they attempted to push on the panel's left side, but achieved nothing; then they moved over to the right, again with no results. A concerted push, which included the best efforts of Harris and Wain, caused it to budge a little. Ten minutes later they had moved the panel backwards about six inches, only just clearing the soundproofing and single brickwork. Harris shone her flashlight into the hard-earned opening, little more than a crack. However, all she could see at such an acute angle were the bricks and mortar on the wall behind.

It was at this juncture that Markland arrived. His jaw fell open when he beheld the macabre arrangement of the forensic man's body parts, in fact, his normally sanguine features drained quite white.

"Er ..." he spluttered, "... May I speak with you alone for a moment, Chief Inspector?"

"Yes sir," said Harris, just managing to sound respectful as she followed him into the corridor.

Markland turned to face her, glancing furtively about to ensure privacy. He was, she could tell by the look of him, extremely agitated.

"Why weren't these premises searched properly?"

Harris could hardly believe what she was hearing. "I beg your pardon, sir?"

"How could an attacker remain undetected for over five hours in a house under investigation with dozens of policemen swarming all over it?"

"The house was searched thoroughly, sir," asserted Harris. "The chamber we've uncovered in there was found only minutes before my two men were killed. With respect, sir, if we'd evacuated the house as soon as we received that warning, I doubt any fatalities would have occurred!"

Markland glared at Harris. He looked like he was about to strike her, and Harris found herself almost willing him to do it; at that moment she might have enjoyed taking him to the cleaners.

Markland regained control of himself, "I'll be waiting in the MIR, let me know when you've got the thing open!" he said and stormed off.

The men working at the panel had made some small progress during her absence, the gap was now about an inch off the brickwork. Harris exchanged a brief look with Frank, succinctly expressing their shared contempt for Markland.

"There's some kind of container in there ma'am. Look, down there on the left," pointed out one of the men who obligingly directed a light onto the object in question. "See it?"

"Yes. But I can't make it out very clearly … seems to be mounted up on bricks … dull looking ... metallic I think."

The entrance into the hidden space was gradually pushed back to its furthest point, and with a little more effort it began to pivot, relatively easily, to the left. When an opening almost wide enough to accommodate Harris was achieved, she radioed the incident room.

"Inform the Deputy Chief Constable we're almost ready to go in."

It was only after relaying this message and receiving back an acknowledgement that it occurred to her the radios were working efficiently. What had prevented messages from being transmitted in and out of the cellar earlier in the day?

By the time Markland returned, Wain and Harris were already inside the hidden chamber. They were alone. The space was approximately six feet wide and eighteen feet long. It contained no lighting and its walls were plain unadorned brickwork. A moment of shared excitement between those involved at the breakthrough point had immediately dissipated when it was seen what the room contained. No comments were made, not even one off the cuff remark, usually mandatory amongst policemen, even in the bleakest circumstances.

"Is there anything else you need us for ma'am?" one had asked.

"No. That's all, thank you … thanks for all your help," Harris said distractedly.

After being dismissed, they'd left fast.

In the corner of the room on a pile of stacked bricks lay a lead box, about two foot six inches wide and a little over six feet long. Its detachable lid was leaning upright against the wall behind it.

"What the ...?" blustered Markland, his words suddenly curtailed when he saw for himself what the space contained.

"It's a lead casket ... a coffin ... sir." said Harris.

Markland's eyes appeared to bulge. Harris watched the sinews in his neck at work, the saliva draining away, bringing on a sudden southern hemisphere drought to his mouth.

But she could hardly hold that against him. Everyone's reaction had been exactly the same.

Chapter Twenty-Four

Thursday, 12 December, 1996 approx 6pm – 10pm

After the seizure, culminating with that monstrous growl, Jim slumped over and lapsed into something resembling a catatonic state. The friends, deeply unnerved by the things they were witnessing, remained transfixed. They felt impotent; there was little to be done but stand by and watch.

Erich tried to communicate words of support to the seemingly unresponsive man, "Don't give in. At the moment you must feel like you're on your own ... this isn't so. We will never abandon you." And for the next fifteen minutes or so, Erich expressed supportive words like these in a kind of litany. The mesmeric quality of Erich's voice soothed and helped generate calm. Jim closed his eyes; it came as a relief to see that he was still responding to suggestion; his breathing eased and he became peaceful for a time.

Then, just as the company grew hopeful, once again Jim's condition darkened. His breathing deteriorated into erratic gulps and gasps, sweat began pouring out of him and he shivered feverishly as Niedermayer's venom raged within him.

Erich kept on, constantly reassuring, "Don't give in ... believe, his power must get weaker." But his influence over Jim was rapidly diminishing. For the friends this was plain to see, as was the note of growing anxiety in Erich's voice. Bit by bit, Mr Niedermayer was consolidating his gains.

The sisters remembered Ruth's request and went off to fetch some old bed linen, which was duly torn up and secured to the bed frame. Danny and his father attached the sheets to Jim's arms and legs, and across his chest and thighs in several wide bands.

The act of restraining Jim so soon after his imprisonment in the cellar, although necessary, did seem abhorrent. However, it was quickly shown to be the right approach and not undertaken a moment too soon. Jim, frustrated by the newly imposed restraints, began to thrash wildly, his arms and legs wrestling maniacally against the bonds.

Then a far more disturbing change began to take place in Jim which caused the friends to collectively gasp in open-mouthed horror and disgust. The flesh on Jim's face appeared to lose solidity and grew pliable, as though it was made of clay. The facial muscles were starting to bulge and twitch and underwent a series of contortions until another face was moulded in its place; a face only vaguely human. It was more like a sketch than a portrait of the conquering power, the cheeks gaunt and sunken, black spittle drooling from its mouth down onto the chin.

Jim's eyes sprang open, but now they belonged to Niedermayer. The dilated pupils were the colour of sulphur with licks of flame flickering through the irises. The eyeballs roved about in their sockets, but gave the impression they were not yet fully co-ordinated. The sight was an abomination, a sacrilegious icon sculpted in living flesh; a horrendous corruption of the human form by a despicable consciousness. The eyes slowly became steadier and more focused, falling upon each of the shocked witnesses in turn. There was a terrible promise in those frightful eyes for every one of them; Niedermayer would have vengeance for their meddling.

A sudden thought overtook Erich's mind as the eyes glared into him. He felt a strong impetus to rush off, fetch the shotgun from the other room, level it at the head and blow it away. For a moment this not only seemed like the rational thing to do, but also the only humane way of releasing Jim from his suffering. However, after he'd spent a few moments wrestling with such wholly uncharacteristic thoughts, Erich returned to his senses and affirmed he was there to heal, not destroy; it was Niedermayer's way, to obliterate what he could not control. Later on the friends admitted that each of them had experienced similar notions around this time.

It was Millie Thorpe, looking rather old and frail, who tentatively tottered forward and started to re-define the lines of engagement as she began quietly reciting the lines of a poem, learned half a century before.

"Out of the night that covers me,
   Black as the pit from pole to pole,
I thank whatever gods may be
   For my unconquerable soul."

Mary, never more than half a step from her sister, had joined in by the end of the first verse, and they went on together.

"In the fell clutch of circumstance
  I have not winced nor cried aloud.
Under the bludgeonings of chance
  My head is bloody, but unbowed.

Beyond this place of wrath and tears
  Looms but the Horror of the shade,
And yet the menace of the years
  Finds and shall find me unafraid."

By the time the sisters reached the closing lines of the third verse, Jim appeared to be undergoing a miraculous change. His eyes had closed and his face, although the skin was still quivering, had returned to normal. Jim's body was being hurled about on the bed in a series of agonising convulsions, and he cried out in pain, yet the sisters went on regardless, keeping up their concentration and the rhythm of their recitation, never stumbling once. During the final verse Jim let out a gut-wrenching scream, but the sisters continued undeterred.

"It matters not how strait the gate,
  How charged with punishments the scroll.
I am the master of my fate:
  I am the captain of my soul."

By the time the sisters had completed these simple heartfelt verses, Jim Latimer lay calmly asleep; he looked almost peaceful.

No-one deluded themselves that the battle was over and that the words of a little poem had won the day; but it brought hope and more optimism. The words the sisters had used contained no power in themselves and had merely acted as a catalyst. The real momentum had come from within Jim; the poem had somehow reached right inside him and spoken directly to his condition; had literally roused his soul.

It was agreed they'd each take a shift of two hours duration to sit with Jim throughout the night. The sisters would do their share, but chose to work their allotted times together.

As the others left the library, the sisters, on first watch, were discussing suitable material for reading aloud to Jim whilst he slept. They had an unshakeable determination to bombard the negative power with every weapon the forces of light held in its armoury.

287

"What about beginning with some Meister Eckhart?" Millie enquired of her sister.

"Dear old Meister Eckhart," replied Mary.

*

Morale amongst the police officers and forensic team working at Barnswick Square was understandably low. Security had been increased and the house was thoroughly searched. There were certainly no more hidden rooms; although Harris didn't rule out the possibility that some grim discoveries were yet to be made. However, she was satisfied that whatever the house had in store for them, was unlikely to prove directly life threatening to her team again.

Harris felt something had altered about the house. It was a strange observation for someone like her to make. She would have been unable to put it into words, and moreover would never have attempted to. Somehow, the leaden atmosphere, particularly in the cellar area, had dissipated. She noticed that her officers no longer complained of physical debility. No-one reported feeling nauseous or experienced headaches like they had earlier. Keeping the morale issue separate, it was as if Frith and O'Malley's killer had taken the dark cloud brooding over the house with him when he'd left.

After viewing the hidden room and its macabre single piece of furniture, Markland had been very nearly speechless; which was probably the one thing all evening that Harris and Wain were grateful for. Markland had only remained at the murder scene for a short while afterwards, and seemed glad to be leaving. However, before he went Harris got him to agree to extra personnel being drafted in. The house at 67 Barnswick Square, internally at least, must now be torn apart to discover whatever secrets lay hidden there. In something of a coup, she also got him to agree that more time would be needed with regards to their detained person, Nicholas Cureton, who had so far refused to speak. Under British Law only a police officer of the rank of Superintendent or above can extend the time someone is held in custody before a charge is made, and only then by twelve hours. If their DP continued to be uncooperative they would need to seek out a magistrate for a further extension. Harris certainly believed it was worth keeping up pressure on Cureton in the hope he'd start talking.

Shortly before 9pm Harris received a message that the post-mortems on DCI Rice and the girl were complete. Frank drove her across town to the pathology lab. They exchanged surprisingly few words together on the journey over. It was as though they were afraid to let slip some of the illogical notions rushing through their minds.

The post-mortem results didn't help any on this count.

Ashworth, the pathologist, greeted them with a lack of enthusiasm that was typical of him. Wain had once remarked that Ashworth owned a face that made the dead feel glad. He was a hulking giant of a man, with hands so large they seemed eminently suited to the work of plundering the internal workings of cadavers. It had always struck Harris that pathology was probably the only branch of medical science Ashworth was physically equipped for; the thought of him performing micro or any other kind of surgery on anything alive seemed to trouble the mind. He played golf and was on friendly terms with Markland, which as far as Harris and Wain were concerned was another black mark against him. He also shared the DCC's uncanny ability of avoiding too much graft, but somehow always made it to the front row when there were handshakes or awards. Also in common with Markland, Ashworth didn't appreciate women with personalities.

"What do you have for us?" said Harris, hoping to get this over and done with quickly.

"The girl died from an overdose of barbiturate. Time of death between midnight and 1am."

"What about the marks on her arm?"

"Please, bear with me, Chief Inspector," Ashworth replied haughtily.

Frank threw Harris a 'pompous prat' look.

"The girl was severely anaemic," continued Ashworth, "I counted five puncture marks in the left arm where blood had been drawn over a period of time, possibly ten days."

"Any idea about her age?" put in Wain.

"I'd say seventeen, possibly eighteen, but no older. No stomach contents, she clearly hadn't eaten in some time."

"Christ, poor kid, awful way to go, not only starved but systematically bled to death."

Ashworth, clearly uninterested in Wain's humanitarian views, went on, "The Chief Inspector died from sudden, acute blood loss ..."

"Because he was decapitated?" interrupted Wain again.

"No, Inspector," replied Ashworth testily, "The decapitation came afterwards, the carotid artery was severed previously ..."

Harris and Wain exchanged confused glances.

"The head was hacked off later ... probably with a cleaver or small axe."

"Time of death?" asked Harris.

"About the same as the girl, maybe a little earlier, closer to midnight perhaps."

"Why bother to remove his head and cut out his heart if he was already dead?" asked Wain.

"I couldn't possibly tell you, you'd better ask the murderer if you catch up with him," Ashworth replied sarcastically.

Wain's face gave the distinct impression that a bad taste had suddenly risen from his stomach to his mouth.

"So how exactly do you think DCI Rice was killed?" asked Harris.

"The carotid artery was bitten through."

"What?" came the simultaneous response from Harris and Wain.

"Something bit into his neck?" Harris tentatively enquired.

"Gnawed more like, judging from the amount of masticated tissue surrounding the artery."

Ashworth beckoned the two dumbfounded police officers to join him beside a covered corpse that was occupying a slab. He swept back the sheet with a nonchalant flourish that must only be common to pathologists. Rice's head, for the purpose of forensic science, had been re-united with its torso, although not totally lined-up; the corpse was crudely stitched from the neck to the abdomen where Ashworth's indelicate hands had recently gone exploring; the gaping hole where the man's heart had been was a disturbingly vivid void.

"See ..." Ashworth said, re-aligning the head with its neck so that the wounds met and matched. "A piece of flesh about three inches wide and an inch or so deep is missing. These marks were made by canine teeth."

"Some kind of animal?" asked Harris.

"But I'm damned if I know what species of animal has teeth to match these. The position and number resemble the human jaw-line, except for size and the increased number of canines."

Ashworth walked over to a counter that ran along one wall and picked up a cast that had been moulded in a grey rubbery substance; it looked like a small, abstract piece of sculpture.

"What's that?" asked Frank Wain.

"I had my assistant make it up. If you look closely, you can see the impression made by the teeth."

To an untrained eye it presented a very unclear picture of a jaw-line. Ashworth directed them to what they needed to be looking for; the six or seven details identifiable as teeth; canine teeth, pointed, irregular, but extremely sharp.

Danny had tuned the kitchen radio into a Brighton station and they listened attentively to each news bulletin. It was reported that the house in Barnswick Square had been evacuated shortly before a burst of gunfire was heard. No further details were yet available.

"Would a bullet stop it … I mean Niedermayer … or whatever its name is?" asked Danny earnestly.

"How could it?" Ruth answered, "He's already dead." A silence followed as they all tried to get their heads around this stark fact.

After a minute or so, Danny asked, "What about the others?"

"Picton went down when I hit him over the head."

"But not for long!"

"No, but they're alive and therefore still human. Niedermayer exercises control over them, like he's trying to do with Jim. His blood seems to inhibit ageing … like it did in the case of the photographer Loxton … it also seems to endow improved physical strength … but I don't think they'd survive a bullet, least not to any vital organ."

Erich listened as Ruth gave her opinion on Niedermayer's acolytes. It started a few bells ringing as he began to consider the reasons why Ian Rice had been mutilated. "Of course! Rice had to have his heart and head removed to stop him becoming like Niedermayer ... it wasn't necessary for the girl, because he didn't feed directly from her. If victims aren't de-commissioned they'd jeopardise his safety … Rice would have become like him ... they'd breed fast, and that could only make Niedermayer vulnerable … up till now it's been this careful ruthlessness, destroying every trace of his handiwork, that has protected him."

"So you think he's the only one of his kind?" asked Danny, a note of cautious hopefulness in his voice.

"There's no way of knowing, but I don't think he'd care for too much competition."

Everyone needed to eat, and Erich made a sauce for spaghetti while Danny and Ruth cut up vegetables for salad. Some of the food was put aside for the sisters when they finished their watch.

As they sat together around the kitchen table they began to unwind. However, when a news bulletin came on the radio they stopped eating immediately. The newsreader began by repeating what they already knew, but went on to mention Rice and the girl for the first time. The report also said that the remains of more victims had been discovered but that numbers could not be confirmed.

'*The murder scene was evacuated by Sussex Police after receiving a tip-off that a gang member might still be in hiding on the premises.*'

"I didn't say that," put in Danny.

'*A member of the forensic team working in the cellar had not been warned of the evacuation due to a fault on his radio. An officer returned to the house to inform him, and both men were attacked and killed. Road blocks have been set up and police are searching the Hove and Brighton areas for the killer and his accomplices. The names of the two deceased officers have not yet been released. We'll bring you more on this as soon as we have it ...*'

"Fat lot of difference my call made," said Danny, upset by what he had just heard and pushing away his half-eaten plate of spaghetti.

"You couldn't have done any more, Dan," sympathised Ruth, "You got the message across ... they must have been delayed for some reason. You heard what he said, they were evacuating the house." She shook her head in disbelief at the tragedy of it.

A few moments after Ruth finished speaking the telephone rang. There was a wall phone extension beside the kitchen door. Ruth, who was sitting nearest, raised its receiver to her ear but didn't speak.

"Who might I be speaking to?" said the woman on the other end of the line, in a brusque tone, with well-enunciated consonants.

Erich and Danny had never before seen a face drain to the colour of candle wax, as Ruth's did in an instant. Erich immediately rushed to her side, placing his ear next to the phone.

"It really doesn't matter ... you're probably too tongue-tied to introduce yourself just at the moment. I can understand your reticence ... who wouldn't be frightened in your shoes? Mr Niedermayer is hardly the forgiving sort ... and let me assure you, he is very, very angry. I'm afraid it's time to wake up. The nightmare is about to begin."

The line went dead.

"H-how ... h-how could they know?" Ruth stammered.

Erich made no reply, but dashed out of the kitchen through the hall and into the drawing-room. Danny followed him.

"Oh my God, how foolish I've been!" exclaimed Erich, bringing the side of his fist down in frustration onto the back of an armchair.

"I don't understand. What is it?" Danny asked.

"Everything Jim has seen, 'he' knows ... Niedermayer is reading his mind!"

Danny suddenly saw what Erich had been staring at. Alongside the armchair where Jim had been seated throughout the afternoon was a small table; innocuously residing there, a lamp, a telephone and a small cluster of mail. The dial telephone bore at its centre a disc with the sisters' number clearly marked, and sitting right at the top of the pile of envelopes was one neatly addressed to M and M Thorpe, The Grange, Herstmonceux.

Danny swallowed hard.

Hugh's Tale

XIII

The tempest endured for what remained of the day and on through the night, the incessant howling of the wind confounding the mind with its relentlessness. Occasionally a change of note broke the monotony of the tune, as the storm increased in strength or lost some potency, only to resume its interminable cant a moment later.

We divided the last of the rations between ourselves and the horses. Our long-suffering beasts were loyal friends, and had grumbled little considering the many deprivations imposed on them. They faced a worse night than we did, cold, hungry and insane with fear as the wind and snow rampaged around them.

Within the hollow we huddled together, shivering around a modest fire, silently mourning our lost companion. I drifted in and out of sleep, waking in fitful starts to the woeful sound of the blizzard.

Only Yussuf slept throughout the whole night. Reynald, who had become distraught when he realised Ayyub was lost, was granted a few hours of merciful release and when he awoke he was more like himself again. However, I feared that the joyous companion I had once known might be gone forever. The deeply etched lines upon his face could certainly never be wiped free again; his pain was deep and profound. And I noticed that the hair at his temples was turning white, where it had been black as jet only five months earlier in Acre.

During the final hour of the night the winds started to abate. We left our sanctuary shortly after dawn. The entrance leading from the gully was blocked with snow and we took turns to dig. It was hard work for exhausted men who had not eaten sufficiently for many days. Ibrahim tied Ayyub's mare behind his own, and we began our descent from the mountaintop, keenly watching for any sign of our lost companion. We passed the place where we had turned back on the previous day, and so gave up any hope of ever finding him. It was almost a quarter of a league on from here when Salah's sharp eyes sighted Ayyub's body.

294

He lay half-buried under snow at the base of a treacherous ravine. There was no hope of us retrieving him.

Aref said, "The evil god confused our brother Ayyub with his blizzard. We are greatly diminished, but the evil one has not triumphed. Ayyub's soul has flown already to the bosom of the nameless one, and because of his wisdom we ourselves are spared."

We stood for a time staring down into the ravine. Then Aref said, "Let our brother be at peace," and, taking up his horse's reins, led us on.

By midday we were descending more rapidly. The snow was deep, which checked our progress as too did hunger and exhaustion. Yussuf coughed incessantly, his brow was on fire, and he needed assistance to walk. It was certain we must find heat and shelter before nightfall else Yussuf, if not all of us, would perish.

As the afternoon progressed and the skies began to dim, we saw, nestled amongst the foothills, six wooden huts. Our hearts rejoiced at the thought of food and warmth. However, as we grew nearer and the daylight faded, we approached with a deepening sense of foreboding. The journey from first sighting to arrival took us about an hour, yet during this time we saw no movement or signs of life. It seemed strange indeed that the inhabitants of this mountain community should show no interest whatsoever in a party of men arriving out of the east.

I could only think of Jerome, and how his foul regiment must have already passed this way. The blizzard had swept clean their tracks but there was no alternative route. The closer we came to the huts the greater our trepidation grew.

Dusk was already upon us by the time we reached the settlement.

"Might they have travelled to warmer climes for winter?" I asked Aref as we approached the first hut.

"That would be an explanation," he answered unconvincingly.

The first cabin was empty; however the ash in its stone hearth still retained a little heat, though it had not been attended to for many hours.

"Salah, make Yussuf comfortable and keep watch over him," commanded Aref. "The rest of us must search the other huts to try and learn what has happened here. Work diligently, darkness comes upon us soon."

Behind the first hut, which was the largest, we came upon a large mound covered in snow, stained red at its base. We tentatively scraped at the layer of snow to discover the carcasses of the community's herd of goats; each creature had had its throat slit open.

"What was the point in this?" Ibrahim asked Aref.

"To prevent us from eating," he replied, "They know we would rather starve than eat what their hands have defiled."

We searched the remaining huts; they were all deserted.

"Perhaps the people fled," said Reynald.

Aref made no reply.

There were deep forebodings in my heart about this place. Our physical needs necessitated that we stay, but I feared it would not be a peaceful night.

We decided to make use of the first hut, it being the largest and sturdiest. There was room enough to house livestock, and so we brought the horses inside; we had no food for them but at least they should have warmth. Salah made a bed for Yussuf beside the fire, which he had raised by the time we returned.

"We'll need more wood," he said.

We left Yussuf asleep and went to collect fuel from a woodpile at the back of the hut. Salah had found a pail made of goatskin, which was filled with clean snow for our drinking water. We soon returned carrying armfuls of wood. It was nearly dark.

"One more journey should see us through until the morning," said Aref, "Then none of us need leave this hut again 'til dawn."

As we returned from our second visit to the woodpile, Ibrahim suddenly stopped in his tracks.

"What is wrong, brother?" asked Salah.

"The snow moved," Ibrahim replied, "See."

All around us the snow was coming to life.

"Get to the hut!" shouted Reynald.

We needed little urging as we sped towards the front of the building avoiding the mounds rapidly mushrooming around us. I had covered half the distance to the door when an ice-cold hand suddenly tore out from its shroud of snow and gripped my ankle. Its grasp was like iron and I fell headlong to the ground, shedding my cargo of wood before me. Painfully, I swivelled round, and tried to kick myself free. The creature was shaking the snow from its grim features as its head emerged; growling ferociously at my resistance, eyes gleaming and covetous as he dragged me towards him; so inhumanly strong that within a moment he had pulled me almost face to face with him, the yellow eyes on fire with lust for my warm blood. Beside him another creature broke out of the snow, the deathly countenance declaring the same intent as its companion; indeed, all around me creatures were dusting and shaking themselves free of their icy graves.

I punched a mailed fist into the monster's face as his slavering teeth were bared at me, but the blow did nothing to the undead thing, causing not the slightest hurt.

Mercifully, Ibrahim had seen me fall and rushed back to my aid. He took up two pieces of the wood that I had dropped and held them together forming a cross. The creature immediately let out a terrified scream covering his eyes with his hands as though fire scorched them, thereby letting go his hold.

"Get behind me," shouted Ibrahim as I scrambled awkwardly to my feet.

A dozen creatures had now arisen, snarling through bared teeth at us. As many again were rising from their undead sleep and more still were writhing beneath the surface of the snow.

As we moved back towards the dwelling, the others ran out, holding crucifixes before them. Reynald took my arm and helped me hobble through into the hut; Aref and Ibrahim came after, closely followed by Salah. The brothers slammed shut the door and placed a stout beam across it.

Inside there was mayhem. The mares, sensing predators all around, were agitated and began to rush about madly. Yussuf, recognising trouble, staggered from his sick bed to help Ibrahim and Salah tie up the horses.

The creatures could be heard tramping the snow outside, then they started pounding on the walls. The two windows, barred and shuttered, and the doorway were the hut's weakest points.

"I'll take the door," shouted Aref, "Keep watch on the windows!"

I knew I should prove little use in the forthcoming battle, for my ankle had been badly twisted and I was barely able to stand; I limped to the fireplace and tried to make myself useful by sharpening some of the wood into points. Judging by the clamour coming from without, a large number of stakes would be needed.

Before long the creatures started to attack the windows. Grey hands could be seen tearing at the shutters, ripping more pieces of wood away with each effort. Reynald placed his crucifix on the back of a probing hand which recoiled immediately, accompanied by the creature's scream and the hiss of boiling metal searing undead flesh. However, pain alone did not deter them long; lacking the ability to learn from experience, the same hand was soon back at work in its owner's frenzied search for blood. The shuttering was now so weakened that one creature launched its head straight through it. Reynald stepped closer to the foul thing, its jaws open, drooling saliva as it smelled the blood in his veins. Taunted in this way it rammed its fists through the remaining shutters and lunged at Reynald, who immediately jumped out of reach.

I had a stake ready, and passed it to my friend. The creature, maddened by the failure to reach its quarry, stretched further into the opening, unable to see the trap awaiting him. Once the creature's torso was wholly exposed, avoiding its flailing arms with incredible speed for a man who had endured many days of hardship, Reynald drove the stake directly into the vile thing's heart. The creature shrieked and fell limp onto the sill; Reynald drew his sword and smote off its head.

At the other window Ibrahim and Salah were employing similar tactics. Here, two monsters were seeking to find a way in. Salah enraged them by burning their hands and faces with a flaming torch, and when both heads had been enticed far enough into the window's opening, Ibrahim, scimitar poised, took them with one sweep of the blade. Yussuf, weak with fever, raised them by their hair, staggered to the fire and plunged them into its flames. The bodies had remained animated in the window frame, but as their heads flared up in the fire's heat and next moment crumbled to ash, both fell lifeless.

The door, guarded by Aref, still held, although its topmost hinge was loose, and the central plank had been torn out. I had returned to making stakes, Yussuf labouring beside me at the same task.

Then, abruptly and without any warning, the sound of the walls being struck and wood being ripped away ceased entirely. Only the growls and snarling of the creatures could be heard, along with the sound of their footsteps trailing away.

However, this retreat brought no relief, and only intensified our sense of dread.

"We have company," warned Aref, as he looked out through the broken door.

Our hearts sank as we saw six knights riding up the hillside towards us. The creatures had not risked coming themselves, but had charged some of their henchmen with the task of destroying us.

Suddenly I knew only weariness; the odds were insurmountable.

Aref, his face weathered and careworn, turned from the doorway and did what I understood to mean the end of hope. He knelt beside the fire and commenced in silent prayer with his nameless God.

The riders came to a standstill a distance away from the building, each man bearing a torch, shedding light enough for us to make out their leering faces. I recognised all of them from the underground chapel where Jerome had initiated the evil. The man giving the orders was the knight that had entered the dortoir after I was ousted from my bed and found the holy cup.

He addressed us in a sneering tone, "Long have you pursued us, but the time of reckoning is finally come. Only now do you see how puny your effort is against our masters' might."

Here the knight paused as if anticipating a reply; when he resumed there was annoyance in his voice, "Are you too fearful to speak?"

His companions encouraged him by mocking and jeering at us. "We are civilised men," he continued, "What times are these if civilised men cannot discourse together?" At each mention of the word civilised, his men were unable to contain their mirth.

None of us made reply, being too exhausted and having no desire to engage in this game. We looked to Aref for leadership, but he was still deep in meditation. I supposed it was indeed a good time to make peace with God, but my faith was never as Aref's, and I was unable to drag myself away from the door.

The next time the leader spoke, any pretence of affability was gone. "I intended to be reasonable. There can be no escape for you ... but had you been prepared to talk I might have let you die as men. However, your reticence has made me vengeful ..."

Approval spread through his fellow knights; vengeance appealed to them.

"I might allow our friends, the former inhabitants of this place, to show you their hospitality."

His men cheered at the suggestion.

"We can easily remove your Christian trinkets from you," he spat at the idea of the holy cross. "Do not imagine they will burn us. We will take your weapons and let our friends enjoy you. I will instruct them, for they heed my commands, to kill you slowly. Over many days of torture you will become like them, craving blood and shunning the day. Know that you will serve Jerome, who will place many torments in you for the effrontery you have shown him."

The knights liked these promises so much they could not contain themselves and began mocking and cursing at us.

Reynald had heard enough; taking his sword and stepping before the door he said, "I will go to my maker fighting, and perhaps I can dispatch some to victory in hell."

"I will die beside you," I said, drawing my sword.

Ibrahim, Salah and Yussuf looked to Aref, who was still absent in prayer.

Yussuf nodded in assent, his body trembling with fever.

"Come brother, let us slice necks before we die," said Ibrahim to Salah.

Salah smiling replied, "You will need to take a great many heads to match my tally, brother."

Then Reynald called out, "Aref, our time is upon us. We can listen no more to this fool's prattling. Will you die with us?"

"Stay!" cried Aref, rising from his knees, "Be not so hasty. Will you throw away your lives for a handful of Jerome's slaves?"

"There is no way to prevail, we are too greatly outnumbered," Reynald answered, his eyes welling with emotion.

"I do not mean to die, unless the nameless one asks it of me," said Aref.

"How then?" said Reynald.

"Put your swords away, they are no use," said Aref.

"What?" asked Reynald, taken aback by the reply.

"My brave friend," said Aref, touching Reynald's arm and looking deep into his eyes, "Faith alone can save us now. Put away your weapon."

The guardians responded immediately by putting up their swords. I hesitated, and saw that Reynald was uncertain too.

"Will you give your life for a few creatures Jerome can easily replace tomorrow? He expects us to die fighting, do you not see?"

"I will stand with you," said Reynald.

We both put up our swords.

"We wish to talk," called Aref through the broken door.

"Then come outside," replied the leader, to the sound of much sniggering amongst his men.

Aref removed the beam that lay across the door and stepped outside, the five of us beside him.

The undead creatures stood like hungry wolves in a semi-circle around us, a far greater number than any of us had realised, being at least fifty men, women and children; smelling our blood, they started towards us.

"Get back," yelled the spokesman, "You will not feed until I say." The creatures spat and snarled, and at first it seemed they would disobey. "I command you in the name of Jerome!" At the sound of his name they grew fearful, and began to retreat, though still gnashing their teeth.

They were in some ways pitiable; a short time before they had been goatherds living in community, possibly the same people who had stockpiled wood in the mountain shelter and saved us from dying in the blizzard. They ranged from children barely walking to white-haired grandmothers, wrinkled, but no longer toothless.

"As you see, friend, we are most reasonable," said the speaker, the facetious tone amusing his comrades.

"And as you see ... friend ... we are unafraid," replied Aref. The spokesman for the knights had not anticipated our response and clearly did not like hearing his sarcasm returned. Aref continued, "We stand before you, our arms put away. We do indeed come to reason, and not to fight, for you greatly outnumber us. It is hard to be boastful when so few, but it is easy to prate on when in large numbers."

The spokesman began to look uncertain.

"We do not come to ask for mercy ... for we do not beg favours from vipers, and certainly not of the slaves of vipers."

The knights were enraged by Aref's words, they started cursing lewdly and shaking fists at him.

Aref took no notice, dismissive of them as though they were an irrelevance. "We serve the good God, the nameless one ... heed my warning, for we are bound to Him. He will not forsake us in our time of need."

"Be silent," commanded the leader.

"Shut him up!" shouted one of the knights furiously at the speaker.

"I'll shut his mouth if you can't," said another.

The spokesman looked unsure about how to proceed. He had somehow been drawn in by Aref's words.

"We are the nameless one's free men, not slaves like you. We perform His will from choice, like all free men. We do not need an army of fell creatures to deal with a few brave men. If you wish to live beyond this night then ride from here now, else the nameless one will bring His retribution upon you. Be warned!"

"He dares to threaten us!" said an outraged knight.

"Let us end this," said another, reining in his horse and preparing to charge.

"God be merciful," I heard Reynald whisper at my side.

I braced myself for the coming onslaught.

However Aref did not waver even in the face of imminent attack. "If you attempt to harm us, the nameless one who binds us together will smite you down. You will be destroyed!"

One of the knights then broke rank, charging forward. Seeing their leader's hesitation, the other knights urged their steeds on and came galloping towards us. The undead creatures also broke free of the speaker's control and they too rushed at us.

301

My hand went to my sword hilt, but Reynald's hand stayed mine from drawing. He smiled and shook his head. I put my hand down by my side.

Aref stood his ground; then, reaching a hand inside his coat drew out the cup. It was as though he held the sun in his hand; the cup transformed into a brilliantly shining orb.

The first knight to charge was almost upon him, but when he saw the light, both he and his mount were instantly blinded. Terrified, he threw up his arms, the sword falling from his hand as man and beast crashed to the snowy ground. Panic-stricken, the other horses hurled their riders from their backs. For a time the speaker managed to stay seated, clutching onto his mount, which kicked and shrieked.

All about us the undead creatures were screaming in agony as their flesh began to burn and then burst into flame. Some of them tried to tunnel into the snow to spare themselves from the terrible light that seared them; the whole mountainside was lit up as if the sun had appeared in the middle of the night.

The last I saw of them, Jerome's knights were blind men crawling on the snow's surface tearing at their bleeding eye sockets with fingernails and screaming in pain.

Aref put the cup away and said, "The nameless one has delivered us, let Him finish His work."

He led us back inside the hut, barring what remained of the door.

Chapter Twenty-Five

Rosemary's call prompted Ruth and Erich to undertake some frantic research. However, on the subject of vampires, even the Thorpe sisters' large, eclectic book collection failed to deliver much. Hungary and Greece easily outstripped the rest of the world in such manifestations, yet even the most sensational authors on phenomena and the occult tended to give vampires a wide berth. Virtually every recorded account of vampirism could either be written off as peasant superstition or premature burial.

Even in modern times, people have been pronounced dead erroneously. Such terminal errors would have been far more common in centuries past. It is easy to imagine: sounds are heard coming from below the earth where a corpse has recently been interred, and by the time fearful hands have re-opened the grave, its tenant is incontrovertibly deceased. The poor unfortunate had probably been suffering from one of a handful of conditions that emulate the outward signs of death, only to revive too late to forgo a terrifying end. The corpse would be discovered still warm, its shroud and features stained with blood, drawn from finger nails that had clawed in desperation at the coffin lid, until its air supply was exhausted and death came through horrible and inevitable suffocation. The tragic victim, proclaimed a vampire, would then have a stake driven through its heart.

Some stories were less straightforward, but only a tiny number might justify further investigation. The most common means of eradication had always been staking and or decapitation; methods corroborated by the condition of Ian Rice's corpse. The symbol of the cross, so prevalent in vampire lore, could easily be put to the test. Mary and Millie possessed several crucifixes along with many other symbols from the world's multifarious belief systems; a silver chain bearing a simple cross was placed around Jim's neck. The physical reaction it caused was indisputable. The surrounding skin became almost instantly blistered and inflamed.

It was decided to make some crosses. It wasn't deemed wise to venture outside after dark, but fortunately the sisters kept a few tools under the kitchen sink. Ruth found some planks of wood in the attic along with several sets of old furniture legs that might be tapered into points. Danny was skilled with his hands and set to work. He made a cross for each external door and window on the ground floor. Ruth helped to hold the pieces steady as he worked them on the dining table.

"Do you think these will hold him back?" he asked Ruth as he held up the final cross to be completed.

"They might slow him down."

"I don't understand why they rang us ... surely it's cost them their advantage ... the element of surprise?"

"I've been wondering about that too," said Ruth. "Perhaps they thought we'd be so terror stricken we'd abandon Jim and run. It's impossible to know how something like that thinks."

"What about taking him somewhere else? We could blindfold him; that way he wouldn't be able to let on where we'd gone."

"He's too sick to be moved at the moment. Anyway, I wouldn't want to be trapped in a car with Jim in his present state. Would you?"

Danny winced, he clearly didn't like the idea much either.

Ruth continued, "He might be able to exercise a bit more control over himself during the day but at night he could easily become dangerous ... still, I've no doubt they'd find us ... Jim's like a radio transmitter for Niedermayer."

Danny thought for a moment, "You know, perhaps staying here isn't such a bad idea ... not if they're expecting us to run. The police must be searching all over for them. We might actually be less of a target here than we think."

"Could be ..." agreed Ruth, then after a moment, "... let's get started on those stakes."

*

The two days that followed passed slowly.

It was decided to divide the time into watches. At any hour, night or day, either Erich or Danny sat in the bay, a roughly made cross propped against the window's central bar, the shotgun resting across their thighs. A net curtain was pinned across the window frame during the day to hide the armed guard stationed there. At night the room was kept in darkness for improved vision.

Even an hour on guard duty seemed a long time. The strain on nerves from maintained concentration and sleep deprivation took its toll on Danny and especially on Erich. The layout of the sisters' house and garden made it improbable an attack would come from any area other than the front. The perimeter of the Grange was surrounded by an eight foot hedge of hawthorn and holly, so thick in parts it was possible to stand on it. Danny had scars that told of his acquaintance with the hedge, having subsidised his meagre earnings as a sculptor by doing some gardening for the sisters.

Nobody slept in their beds at night. They preferred to stay together, curled up under a blanket, gaining whatever comfort they could from the drawing-room. Ruth and the sisters, untrained in the use of a gun, shared the task of watching over Jim.

The Thorpe sisters kept up a vigorous assault on the negative force wrestling for Jim Latimer's soul, armed with spiritual bullets from their arsenal of esoteric wisdom. Ruth too spent time channelling positive energy and healing to her friend in the hope of increasing his resistance to the power assailing him.

Whatever duties were undertaken, it inevitably resulted in exhaustion. This told the most on Erich and the sisters, less resilient because of their ages. Ruth probably fared best of all. She possessed a natural ability that could direct any free moment into re-charging. At night, the time really dragged, unremitting fatigue and sheer dread bore down on everyone. The daytime was better and the shifts were longer, which allowed for longer rest periods. Often during these breaks they took to their beds.

Jim had slept almost entirely throughout Friday. And during those times when he was awake he was like a man in a dream state. He had no desire to eat; encouraged by Ruth he tried some soup but immediately threw it back up. However, he managed a few small sips of water the sisters had doctored with some flower essences. These they claimed would help combat outside influences and promote cleansing.

In one of his most lucid periods around mid-morning, Jim asked to see Erich. By the time he arrived, tears were streaming down his face. He was crying bitterly and begged forgiveness for the racist abuse he had dished out the day before.

"It wasn't you," Erich assured, "You think I don't know that?"

Jim shook his head as he wept, "It was only partly him ... I hated you, hated all of you ... you were in my way. It was more intense ...

but like being a drinker again ... you despise what you are, hate alcohol ... but all you can think about is that next drink."

"You told me at our last hypnotherapy session, that you never wanted to be addicted to anything again."

"I'm not doing too well then, am I?" Jim managed a smile. Erich took it as a good sign.

On a more serious note, Jim warned, "Don't untie me until you're sure." He indicated his bonds, "I know that I'd be capable of hurting all of you at times."

His words became prophetic. After midday on Friday his mood completely changed. It was as though a dark shadow had drifted over him.

"Why am I chained up like this?" he screamed ferociously, "You fucking bastards, let me go!" He ranted and raved, tearing at the sheets that bound him in outbursts lasting several minutes. Everyone came running when they first heard the hullabaloo. He shouted abuse at each of them, which was mostly childishly nasty and inane. The Thorpe sisters he insisted were not sisters at all, but mad old lesbians, and he referred to Ruth as 'Little Orphan Ruthie'. Erich and Danny, spared from most of the verbal onslaught because they were on guard duty, were referred to as 'the Jew boys', along with a whole host of other insults that might come trippingly off the tongue of any fascist bullyboy. It was mainly just tiresome, but it certainly added to the tension and exhaustion everyone was already feeling.

The sisters, polite and kindly to all, probably found Jim's abusiveness the most upsetting; but true to their natures they didn't complain or shirk their duties. They spent an hour on the phone on Friday morning cancelling all the groups due to meet at their home over the forthcoming week. The excuse they gave was that a niece in Lincolnshire had been taken ill and they were required to attend to her.

"We're becoming accomplished liars," Millie told her sister when they were about halfway through the list of people to be informed.

"Necessity, Mill ... the mother of invention," replied Mary. They laughed, forgetting their predicament for a moment.

At dusk before the second night, Erich, on guard duty, answered the telephone when it rang. He had a good idea who it was, and considered not answering, but decided to get it over with, rather than let it ring all night. He didn't speak.

After a longish silence Rosemary said, "Still there? I'm surprised you didn't take my warning more seriously. Be assured, we'll be meeting again very shortly."

The phone went dead and Erich replaced the receiver. He wondered if it was true or whether the point was just to drive them to despair. 'They're succeeding!' he thought.

Mary Thorpe had entered a moment later. "Erich, Jim is much worse. Perhaps I could keep guard for a moment while you take a look at him?"

"Yes ... er, okay," he replied uncertainly.

"Just show me which button to press," she said, pointing at the shotgun.

"Perhaps it would be better if you woke Danny, I'm sure he wouldn't mind," he replied, coming to his senses.

"Yes," agreed Mary, as she left the room.

Danny had taken the last opportunity that day of resting on a bed, as had Ruth. They both came downstairs simultaneously in response to Mary's call. Danny took on the responsibility of guarding the house, which he would, as it turned out, maintain single-handedly for the next twelve hours.

A winter night, alone and fearful of what may be lurking in the darkness, is a long time passing.

*

The man tied to the bed in the library was barely recognisable. Jim had become a ranting lunatic, what one might imagine locked away in a rambling Gothic asylum. Alternately he either chanted or raged in gibberish, his body soaked in sweat, his skin red, on fire with the fever raging unassuaged within. The skin on his chest around the crucifix had broken out into watery pustules resembling chicken pox. His breathing grated on the ear, like the rasping breath of the dying.

Erich tried hypnotic suggestion, but to no effect. Ruth attempted to reach him as a friend, but here again there was no response. The four friends could only stand by, helpless, as Jim began to convulse so violently it seemed plausible he might break his own back. His condition was growing worse by the minute and it seemed increasingly unlikely that he'd survive until the morning. They were witnessing a man fighting for the autonomy of his soul against a tyrant determined to usurp that God-given right; Niedermayer would destroy rather than lose what he could not possess.

A crushing sense of hopelessness crept through the friends; gloom descended and spread over them like the legs of a spider, despair its venom. Defeat drowned every heart and mind; it was all over.

They each felt the failure was personal. What idiots they had been, a bunch of backwater healers who had lost the run of themselves, egoists. They had deluded themselves into believing they were capable of pitting their wits against a force immeasurably more powerful, fools. It would be over soon, for Jim, and probably them too. They were like rabbits caught in headlights; they could see destruction looming but were powerless to act.

Erich's thoughts drew him back to childhood, picturing the faces of his parents and the sister who had perished. He revisited the guilt and irrational shame he'd carried throughout the years. Why had his life been allowed to go on when theirs had been extinguished? He was loathsome, an unworthy survivor, who only existed because of the sacrifice of others.

Ruth saw how she had always failed at relationships, forming bonds with men who had seemed the perfect partner, capable of providing the love and companionship she desperately sought, only to discover that she had deluded herself yet again. Erich was the only man she had ever forged a lasting intimate relationship with, and he was old enough to be her father.

Mary and Millie too were confronted by their innermost regrets. The sisters had spent their lives right up to and beyond their middle years being dutiful. They had responsibly looked after the children in their charge, and when their parents had grown infirm they had lovingly cared for them. Yet there remained something inside each of them that yearned for the personal fulfilment lives spent in the service of others can never wholly satisfy.

It was not only Jim's life energy that was being leeched out of him. Niedermayer had launched a coup; Jim Latimer would be destroyed and he would also send these insects scurrying away from him in fear for themselves.

Then something quite unextraordinary happened; but it started off a process that brought about miraculous results.

Jim cried out in agony. It was the first definite sound he'd made since the others had assembled. Almost with a jolt they reconnected with the suffering man before them, enabling their minds to break free from the fog of despondency clouding their judgement. Jim muttered something in a voice too frail to understand. They each crouched closer to hear him. He pleaded in a croaking whisper, "Help me ... please. Please help me!"

Mary Thorpe immediately raised her head and said, "'If I make my bed in hell, behold, thou art there.'"

Millie Thorpe added, "'And the light shineth in darkness; and the darkness comprehended it not.'"

Then Ruth, taking Erich's hand, linked up with the sisters and led them in a mantra they had used many times in healing and meditation: an Aramaic word, in the language spoken by Christ, which meant simply 'Come Lord'.

"Maranatha," Ruth began and then they all took it up.

Spontaneously they spread out, two each side of Jim, their hands joined in a circle over him. They repeated the word aloud for ten minutes or so before falling silent, keeping the image of the word alive within them.

Jim's survival had become a matter of faith.

*

Just after 2am on Saturday morning, Danny was pleased to see his father again after spending so many hours alone.

"How is Jim?"

"It looked bad Danny, but I believe he's now over the worst."

"That's great."

"I'll take over for a bit, you take a rest ... you've had a hard night."

"And you've been partying," said Danny. "I'm a bit younger than you are. You rest."

Erich conceded to his son. 'It's no good me being stubborn,' he thought, 'Anyway, I'd probably fall asleep on duty.'

Erich curled up beneath a blanket on the sofa. Danny had his back to him, unaware of the proud eyes watching. It was good to think how well his son had turned out, in those flickering moments before sleep came.

*

Around 4am, Jim asked weakly for some water, which Ruth gladly helped him to. The fever had passed. The blistered skin around the crucifix had healed, although Jim looked extremely frail after surviving the frenzy of the night. Ruth had volunteered to stay with him until dawn while the others took a rest.

He whispered something she didn't quite catch.

"What did you say?"

"Thank you," he murmured.

She patted his hand affectionately, tears welling up in her eyes.

Saturday was a less traumatic day than those that had preceded it. Once again Jim mostly slept, but it was considered a restorative sleep and not induced by an outside force. He managed to eat, albeit lightly, but at least succeeded in keeping it down. Erich wanted to release him from his bonds, but Jim insisted they should remain until it was certain Niedermayer had gone for good.

The sisters read aloud to Jim from Marcus Aurelius, and he listened as keenly as his physical weakness allowed. Around midday a shadow passed over him and he grew slightly morose, but he hurled no verbal abuse. After dark his temperature rose slightly, and he appeared to be suffering some discomfort occasionally in his sleep, but nothing compared with the first two nights.

The privilege of answering the telephone fell to Danny when it rang at dusk on Saturday evening. He was expecting it; their nightly call had become obligatory.

This time it was a man's voice. Danny assumed it was Picton, the maniac who had almost killed him.

However Picton chose not to speak. He delivered a warning about their impending doom in the form of a song, "Your end is near ... you're going to die ... I guarantee it ..."

"Eat shit!" Danny shouted into the mouthpiece before slamming down the phone.

But the message had got through. So far Niedermayer had been foiled, but they all knew his wrath was undiminished. Perhaps tonight, perhaps tomorrow, perhaps one night next week or even a year from now; at some point Mr Niedermayer would definitely come calling, to claim the reparations due to him.

Hugh's Tale

XIV

"No-one may leave this hut until dawn," warned Aref.

The three headless corpses entangled in the shuttering were pushed outside, and we blocked the holes they had vacated. Indeed it was a relief to have some work to take our minds off the terrible cries reaching us from outside.

I have known the piteous sounds of the maimed and dying on battlefields, yet this was infinitely worse. Although the six knights had been our enemies, no man of compassion could hear and be unmoved. Their torment went on into the third hour of the night, when suddenly all fell silent and we were able to rest.

We took turns to care for Yussuf, whose condition had grown far worse. When dawn came we made ready to leave; men on the edge of starvation, horses too weak to bear us far, lost in an alien land.

We left the hut in the morning prepared to be met by a harrowing sight. Yet to our surprise, there was little to witness. More snow had fallen during the night, and there were strange undulations on its surface, where the creatures had fallen in flames and melted into the icy ground.

Our only task before departing was to dispose of the three corpses. We retrieved them from the snow and placed them inside the hut, which we set on fire. As for Jerome's knights and their steeds, nothing remained, no foot or hoof print, nor mark of any kind.

Our progress was slow. The snow came up to our waists in parts, and at times we faced some steep descents. Yussuf was barely conscious and had to be secured to his mare. I had become a burden too, for my ankle was swollen and it was an agony to walk. Ibrahim fashioned a crutch out of some wood to aid me, for many places proved too treacherous to ride. At such times, my companions not only assisted me but coaxed our weary mares and bore along Yussuf. By noon we had reached a plain where the snow was lighter, and might have increased our pace were it not for hunger, exhaustion and the cold.

If Jerome and his remnant had gone before us we saw no signs; it seemed we had achieved nothing. As Aref had said, Jerome's knights were a renewable resource, easily replaced whenever he wished. Our loss was far greater; the destruction of the six knights no consolation for Ayyub's life. Without food, warmth and healing care, Yussuf would soon be lost too, and our own chances of survival looked bleak. The guardians' nameless God had not made the way easy for his loyal followers.

Yet I suppose some God must have taken a hand in our survival; whether it was the God of Abraham and Isaac, Aref's nameless God or the Good God of the Cathars, I know not. However, by late afternoon we noticed spires of smoke rising above the leafless oaks whose company we kept.

We entered a village, and at first things went badly. The peasants, suspicious and fearful gathered around us in large numbers. They brandished staves and axes and were shouting at us in their incomprehensible tongue, gesticulating for us to leave. However, fortune once again took a hand in events. An old man, dressed in much finery, appeared before us and began speaking to us in our own language.

"Since when have knights of the Temple ridden beside the Saracen?" the old man asked, standing proudly before us. He had recognised our black cloaks, which we once again wore as protection from the cold.

"When united by a common purpose," Reynald answered.

"What do you want here?"

"Shelter and food, and help for our sick companion. We come in peace and will pay for these things we ask," Reynald replied.

"Then give weight to your words and offer up your weapons," said the old man.

Reynald hesitated, then drew his sword. The peasants, not understanding, instantly fell back in fear, but grew calmer when they saw him offer up its hilt to their spokesman. The tension was eased further when they saw each of us follow Reynald's example.

"Put your swords away," the old man said courteously, "I have not lived this long and learned nothing of how to judge a man's character. I am Gezce."

The old man led us to his house and showed us many kindnesses. Our horses were fed and stabled and Yussuf was laid in a bed of clean linen. We dined on good food and wine, served at Gezce's table by his three daughters. These girls were younger than might have been expected of a father so advanced in years, the youngest being but fourteen and the eldest only four years her senior. All three were fair of face and temperament and took much pity on Yussuf, taking turns to attend on him through night and day. They possessed great skill in the healing arts for ones so young, as I discovered myself when they bathed my ankle with herbs. They found my coyness amusing, for I had not known the touch of a female hand since the days of childhood. These daughters we learned were the offspring of a third marriage, for Gezce had outlived three wives in his seventy-eight years.

Our host enjoyed our company and loved to talk, particularly with such mysterious guests. During our first meal with him he told us of his life. He had been taken by his father on pilgrimage to Jerusalem as a lad of fifteen, which was how he had learned something of our tongue. Gezce talked much about his wives and recited the names of his eighteen surviving children enthusiastically.

"The ten oldest are white-haired and have grandchildren themselves," he laughed.

It concerned him that in his final years he was again without a wife. On this subject he confided to us, once his daughters were out of earshot and with a glint in his eye, "I am much taken with a young widow in the village. I caught her making doe-eyes at me recently. She is not the fairest woman I have ever known of face, but her hips are well endowed for bearing children, and I may marry her in the spring. I believe it unhealthy and indecent for a man to remain wifeless, do you not agree?" He suddenly remembered that as Templars we had taken oaths of chastity, "Pray forgive me brother knights, I meant no offence."

"None taken," we answered smiling.

The old man then went on to ask us questions that could not be answered with smiling faces.

"You crossed the Carpathians in winter?" he asked with incredulity when we described our route. "What drove you to such recklessness?"

We hesitated to reply, exchanging awkward glances between us.

"I see you do not trust me yet," said Gezce.

"You have shown us great kindness ..." began Reynald.

"Friend," interrupted Gezce, "There is no need to explain your reticence. If Templar and Saracen ride together, it is certain they are engaged in an endeavour of some importance. When you have rested and had time to judge your host's nature you may choose to tell your story, or what you will of it."

We thanked him for his courtesy and understanding.

"However, I may possess some information for you," Gezce continued. "I see the look of both hunter and quarry in each of you. Perhaps I can help shed light on what the hunter seeks. The night before last a woodcutter from this village was caught in the storm. He was a league south of here, and found shelter amidst the overhanging roots of a great oak. I generally pay little attention to the man, for he drinks and is unreliable, loving to prattle on and make up stories. However on this occasion something about his manner made me listen attentively to what he said. He told of six riders, dressed similarly to yourselves; three of their horses pulled sledges, each bearing a large crate ... the woodcutter thought they resembled coffins!" Here the old man laughed, but checked himself when he saw our grim expressions.

"Did the woodcutter see which way they went?" asked Aref.

"Four went west and the remaining pair rode north. I see this story holds some significance. I had a feeling it might. The woodcutter has not drunk a drop since his return, spending much of his time on his knees thanking God for his deliverance. He said that three of these riders bore the features of demons."

Aref considered for a moment, then said, "I cannot tell all the details of our tale, much of it must remain our secret. However, your generosity and kindness deserve our thanks, and you should know something of our foe, for your own protection. Six months ago in Acre, a group of knights indulged in an act of appalling sacrilege. Their leader, a man named Jerome, drank a toast in the blood of an innocent man and immediately choked and died. However, this was not the end, for his action unleashed a curse, and this Jerome rose up again. He had been transformed into one of the demons seen by your woodcutter. Jerome lives on in death ... in daylight he is confined to a coffin, lifeless as any dead thing, but at night he rises and requires the blood of the living for sustenance. He can pass on this curse to his victims, and has taken two others, who stand beside him as his lords."

Gezce looked so incredulous at Aref's account I assumed he did not believe a word of it. Then, indistinctly, the old man said, "Vampir." He shook his head from side to side and repeated the word again, but this time with more voice, "They are Vampir."

"We do not know this term," said Reynald.

"It is a Magyar word, from legend, before our race was Christian. Warriors who had died without honour took the shapes of wolves or demons after death to torment and haunt the living. A vampir could sap the strength of even the strongest warrior."

"They are very like the vampir of your land," agreed Aref. Avoiding all mention of the cup, he then proceeded to give an account of our pursuit of Jerome and his horde.

Gezce was much saddened to learn of the goat-herders' fate. "Every spring they came, trading animals, buying salt and provisions, for as long as I can remember ... all perished?"

We lowered our heads.

Gezce continued, "I do not understand how so few as you are could have defeated so many, but I will not seek the answer, for I know you will not tell me. I believe you carry a good deal more about you than you would have me think."

Gezce was not only a fine host but he was also a man to be trusted. Never again did he attempt to get any more information from us on these matters.

For two days and nights Yussuf's sickness looked as though it would get the better of him, but on the third day, with the care he received from Gezce's daughters, the fever departed. However, his travails had left him weak, and the daughters informed us that it would be at least two months before he was fit to travel.

"We cannot wait so long," said Aref, "The cup is safer on the move. Robert de Frontignac and his Templars may yet find a way through the mountains."

"What about Jerome's party?" asked Salah.

"The cup itself stops us from coming unseen upon them," Ibrahim replied to his brother.

"Before he died Ayyub reminded us that our first duty was to bring the cup to safety," said Aref. "We became obsessed with Jerome and his fellow creatures and almost perished in our effort to destroy them. Let us deliver the cup to safety, then deal with our enemies. I doubt we have a trail to follow anyway."

"The Cathars will lend men to help in their destruction," said Reynald.

"Who knows what evils they will do whilst we delay," said Aref, "Yet I see no other course open to us."

"But Yussuf cannot leave yet," I said, "And surely he is too young to travel alone."

Aref lowered his eyes sheepishly and said, "I hoped, friend Hugh, that as your ankle is still painful and cannot take weight, you might stay behind with Yussuf and be his guardian."

The idea of being separated from my comrades filled me with sadness, yet I knew this was the best solution. My ankle was indeed slow to mend; it was not only Yussuf who would delay them.

So it was that our company broke up. Aref, Reynald, Ibrahim and Salah were to deliver the cup to the Cathars whilst Yussuf and I would follow on later. Yussuf wept when he was told that he was to be left behind. We did our best to console him.

Aref offered Gezce recompense for his hospitality, but he would take nothing.

"It has been an honour to welcome such men beneath my roof. May God's blessing go with you, for I believe you carry something of his light in your midst," he said.

Ibrahim and Salah held me to their bosoms as though I too were their brother. Bidding farewell to Reynald after our long association was hard; his hair had grown even whiter, as though he had aged ten or more years, yet the rest and kindness shown us at Gezce's house had restored him partly to his former self.

"Soon, Hugh, we shall be together again. Seek me in the town of Albi. If I am gone from there I will leave word," he said. "It grieves me to be separated from you after such a long friendship. I feel I am saying goodbye to my own kin."

The four guardians of the cup got up onto their mares, waving back at us before urging them on, and were soon gone from sight.

Aref's last words have resonated within me ever since. Holding my hands in his and looking deep into my eyes, he said, "Be certain we shall meet again, friend Hugh, when the nameless one ordains it ... if not in this world then through the cup of life in countless others."

*

Yussuf made excellent progress. Gezce's daughters had judged well the time it would take him to regain his strength, and almost exactly eight weeks after the others' departure we too took our leave. My ankle was as healed as it would ever be, for the vampir's grip had left me with a permanent limp.

We had grown fond of Gezce and his daughters, and bade farewell to them with sadness.

"I hoped you might stay for my wedding, Hugh," said Gezce, who had already proposed to the young widow and been accepted, "If you and your friend Reynald venture back this way when your work is done and want to renounce your vows I have two beautiful daughters for you. I would be proud to call you both my sons. As for my youngest child I think she has eyes only for Yussuf here."

Yussuf blushed at the mention, although none could fail to notice the girl's attentiveness. When we rode away the girl waved to him in tears and was comforted by her sisters.

"I think you've broken a heart in this village," I said.

Yussuf shifted about in his saddle and blushed again. I saw that the feelings between the youthful pair were at least in some part reciprocated, and so I teased no more.

We grew close during the long journey ahead. The horror of our previous travels seemed far behind us, although we could never entirely forget. We travelled west, throughout the late spring and summer, following the great Danube along its course through Austria and Germany. By the start of autumn we had come to the lands of France, when once again fate took a hand in our affairs.

We lodged for a night at an inn just south of Nancy, and whilst taking supper overheard a conversation between a group of merchants.

"I tell you, his skin was grey," the first man said.

"I am not surprised," replied one of his companions, "If all the blood had been drained from him."

"Not a drop left," continued the first merchant, "He was like a hung pig."

"Then he had been murdered somewhere else?" asked one of the group.

"His wife was with him only minutes before he was discovered."

"How can a man be murdered, his head and heart stolen, with no drop of blood left in him, within but a few minutes?" asked the disbelieving companion.

The first merchant shuddered at the memory, "What times, when a man cannot expect to die with his head on his shoulders and the heart in his chest. It was not as if he was rich and worth murdering."

"Excuse me sir," I interrupted, "I could not help overhearing your story ..."

"No story, friend," replied the first merchant in a surly tone.

"Forgive me, I meant no offence," I assured him. "When did this killing take place?"

"Two days ago in Nancy, avoid the place if you can, friend," advised the merchant.

"Go south like us," laughed one of his companions.

How sound that advice was, Anselm. How vain and foolish to think that together with a boy just turned seventeen, I might succeed where seven before had failed.

We found the trail we sought, and again became obsessed.

We pieced together a picture of those we sought from their tracks, and from eye witnesses who had seen a man driving a covered wagon. One of those we questioned saw two men travelling at night, one of them masked beneath a hooded cloak.

"What do you think became of the other creatures?" asked Yussuf.

"Perhaps they returned to the lands of their birth as Aref and Ayyub thought," I said, "If that is the case then this must be Jerome's trail."

From Nancy they had taken the road to Reims then North West for Calais. We gained on them each day, but once again they had the devil on their side. We reached Calais early one morning in mid-November; by my reckoning they were only an hour or so ahead of us, and we hoped they would fail to find a boat immediately or that the tide would prevent them from sailing. We had forgotten the devil and his luck.

Yussuf and I secured the horses and searched an end of the harbour each. We knew that if we found them in daylight then we should only have to fight the serving acolyte, the creature itself would be at our mercy. Surprise was our best weapon; for we were no longer in the company of the holy cup. Jerome, for I was certain it was him, could not have sensed our approach.

As I reached the furthest end of the harbour wall, I saw directly ahead of me a boat pulling out to sea. It could not have been more than a hundred feet away from me. Standing beside a long box in the ship's stern was the serjeant. He had removed his helm, and the autumn sunlight was reflected on the bald centre of his red hair.

I let out a dispirited sigh and slumped against the wall beside me. It was only then that he looked up and saw me. I could do nothing but watch him laugh uproariously at my failure.

And from then on, all hope of catching them unawares was gone.

Chapter Twenty-Six

The Hove investigation: Friday, 13 December 1996

5.40am. Susan Harris was at her desk, sifting through a two inch pile of paperwork the case had already generated.

Frank arrived in the office only a few minutes after her. "Thought I'd find you here. I couldn't sleep either," he said.

"Seen this?" she replied tersely, holding up the front page of a tabloid. Its headline read, *The Sussex Vampire*.

As a boy Frank had read all the Sherlock Holmes stories. "I'd no idea these people had any literary taste. I'm impressed."

"Markland will go apeshit!"

"Let him."

"He'll probably take me off the case."

"I doubt that. What happened last night was partly his fault for not listening to you. He won't want to risk making that public knowledge."

The events of the previous evening were almost too painful to recall. Frank knew that Susan would have thought about little else. She'd probably lain awake throughout the night, mentally replaying those horrific scenes, just as he had done.

"Anyway, you're the best he's got. He'll make a fuss, of course, the man can't help it, he's a moron! But he does know which side his bread is buttered. The tabloids were bound to get hold of the coffin angle. Dozens of people, not all of them ours, were going in and out of that house yesterday. We're lucky nothing's leaked yet about the cremations."

The official statement to the press quoted only four dead: Rice, Frith, O'Malley and the unidentified girl '... *Possibly more to be announced after forensic officers have completed their investigations* ...'

Harris nodded, Frank was right. When the real death toll was announced, the press would indeed have a field day. She knew it was only possible to contain information for a limited period; eventually all the details would emerge, no matter how good the propaganda machine. Experience and instinct told her that working from a basis of

319

truth always proved the firmest ground, otherwise lies multiplied like a virus no amount of treatment could cure.

Markland asked to see her before she briefed her team. He looked agitated, as expected. But his expression was somehow more intense than she'd ever known before. There was an acute nervousness about him, his eyes showing a lot more white than usual; the way people look when they're traumatised. Markland's office door was open, but he was too deeply engrossed in what he was reading to notice her arrival. She tapped on the door to get his attention. He seemed flustered for a moment, before placing the book, a copy of the Bible, into a drawer.

Markland's religious beliefs were common knowledge, and the butt of many jokes amongst the lower ranks. As for Harris, she knew little and cared even less about where or how Deputy Chief Constable Stuart E Markland sought salvation. She'd heard he was a lay preacher and belonged to the kind of church that promised transgressors death by a hundred tortures. Markland had apparently been warned in the past by those above, the ranks above that was, against proselytising for the souls of his fellow policemen. Harris was convinced that he considered her absence of faith in a divine being, her belief in the advancement of women, and above all her brain to be the works of Satan.

Markland was certainly an odd creature; for all his protestations of living in the light of Jesus, there lingered about him the whiff of double standards. The Deputy Chief Constable possessed the instinct of a politician, and tended to support only issues that aided his self-advancement. It was uncanny how he seemed to know instinctively when to back away from a lost cause. He signed his name Stuart E Markland. Once, when drunk, Harris and Wain had tried to guess what the E stood for; Harris had proffered 'Expediency'.

She observed that his hand was shaking slightly as he passed a press statement across the desk to her. As she began to read, she noticed his face smugly observing her. He looked like he was complimenting himself on a piece of writing he no doubt considered to be admirably bland and imprecise.

Halfway through the piece Harris began to wonder if the statement actually referred to the case she was working on. It read: ... *Ash was discovered in one of the cellar rooms, which on further analysis contained traces of human remains. Wood ash and other debris were also found to be present, making an exact figure difficult to ascertain ... it is thought possible that as many as fifteen or twenty victims may have been cremated in the cellar...*

"Surely the figure is way too low, sir!" exclaimed Harris. She expected the estimate to be conservative but this was minimalist. "Add a nought and the body count might still be short of the truth."

"The numbers were assessed by Dr Ashworth. We have to go along with the scientific information, and after all, we aren't in the business of alarming the public unduly. I acknowledge the figures may have to be increased slightly, depending on what we find during our excavations."

Harris understood perfectly; the art of damage limitation was being practised. Neither Ashworth nor Markland would have dared produce such figures without a nod and wink from the grey heads above. The powers that be knew that the two hundred plus names in Loxton's package could never be verified as victims of Barnswick Square. Everything was being kept cynically in line with what the public consciousness deemed acceptable as far as serial killers were concerned. A trace of wood ash had been found, which offered a perfect opportunity to massage the figures; bodies would have been far trickier; the kiln had cut them a break. And after all, twenty corpses might easily fall into line with what the public had grown to expect as the legacy of a serial killer.

*

By 8am Harris had briefed her team and allocated them various tasks.

"We have a long way to go," she said in summing up, "Two separate groups of people have disappeared into thin air. We've identified Erich Ledermann and his son Danny as our anonymous callers. Unlikely as it seems, they may have been acting as vigilantes. It is possible they came to rescue their friend, the photographer Jim Latimer. Latimer may have been taken hostage. His blood and prints on the bench in the cellar would certainly support this ..."

"You don't think that Latimer and the Ledermanns were involved in the murders then?" someone asked.

"We definitely can't rule it out," Harris replied, "Especially as DCI Rice met Latimer shortly before he died. It's possible that Latimer set him up. However, that wouldn't explain why Latimer was taken hostage or why he spoke so unguardedly to DCI Rice."

"Do you think these people were linked with Loxton and the paedophile network?" asked another officer.

Harris paused for a moment before replying, "It's a possibility. However, the package we found yesterday that was retrieved by

Isherwood from Loxton's bank shortly before he died, suggests they had other motives besides harming children."

"But some of those newspaper cuttings referred to people who went missing forty years back. Surely that can't be relevant to what's been going on at the square?" responded the same man.

"I admit it does seem improbable ... even so, each case will need to be investigated."

There was a collective groan around the room.

Harris continued, "We also need to liaise closely with Metropolitan Vice. They've arrested the sixty-three names on the list that Isherwood and Latimer discovered in Loxton's flat. We need to find out whatever they knew about Loxton and his involvement with Niedermayer & Hart."

"What about DS Frith's killer, ma'am?" The question caused a commotion in the room. Harris had been expecting it; Frith was highly regarded.

"I'm afraid we still have very little," Harris said. A flurry of murmurings and questions followed her insubstantial reply. It was a tough moment; she had never lost a member of her team before. She recognised that the men's anger was not directed at her personally, and that it was born out of a sense of injustice and frustration. "So far, the rather vague description we have of DS Frith's killer from the biker who caught a glimpse of him is the best we have to go on. We've launched a nationwide search to find the white Mercedes and the Transit. We have full descriptions of all the other suspects and their details have been passed on to air and sea ports. It should only be a matter of time."

Harris spoke with more conviction than she truly felt.

*

After the briefing, while Frank Wain went to his desk and attempted to liaise and piece together information from the many disparate strands of the investigation, Harris visited their detained person. For the best part of the next hour she was eyed with contemptuous disregard by Nicholas Cureton. Because of his violent tendencies, a safety procedure had been put in place and was carefully adhered to. Before anyone entered his cell, Nicholas was instructed to kneel on the floor.

Harris was quite surprised when he immediately complied with the instruction.

'Maybe he's just keen to get out of the cell,' she thought, 'Research for a future escape bid, perhaps?' After the ordeal at the Square last night, this rather preposterous notion seemed distinctly unfunny.

Nicholas was told to face away from the door with his hands clearly visible behind his back. Once the cell door was opened, two armed officers went in and took up positions inside, cautiously marking their man. Harris put the cuffs on Nicholas herself. She helped him to his feet and led him out. The custody sergeant unlocked the outer door when they reached it and the group then proceeded the short distance to an interview room.

Harris began the recording and went through the standard procedure - date, time etc. She went on to explain, "As you have already been informed, you are entitled to free legal advice ..."

To the look of ferocious enmity that came her way, she responded, "Mr Cureton, are you willing to proceed without a solicitor present?"

Harris received another withering look from Nicholas.

"Your silence will be taken to mean that you do not intend to engage any legal help at this stage."

After this Harris proceeded to give the formal caution, reminding him of his right to remain silent etcetera, then went on to state the reasons for his arrest. Because it was her first official meeting with Cureton, she laid out her own credentials too, "I'm Detective Chief Inspector Harris. I am in charge of this investigation. I don't think I need to point out to you the seriousness of the crimes being uncovered at Barnswick Square. Perhaps you'd like to tell us what's been happening there?"

No response.

"You violently resisted arrest yesterday and assaulted and injured a police officer ... a very serious offence. However, you're implicated in far graver crimes than this. Perhaps you'd care to explain why you considered it necessary to attack the police officers who untied you?"

No response.

"How long have you lived at 67 Barnswick Square?"

Nothing.

"Why did you live on site?"

Harris changed tack several times. She tried to engage him in more personal ways; asked him about the porcelain business, about their involvement with John Loxton, about Isherwood and Latimer; asked him about his background, "Did you grow up around here ... are you from the Brighton area?"

Still nothing. There wasn't the remotest flicker of response to any of her questions, which were all followed by an interminably long silence. Nicholas Cureton glowered directly into her face as she spoke. The hate message transmitted was unambiguous.

It was quite a strain, and after about twenty minutes of this one-way conversation, Harris felt her tongue drying up. She poured out a glass of water, feigning an expression of relaxed disinterest as she sipped. Never before had she needed to conduct the interview of a DP with armed officers standing by. Cureton looked like someone who enjoyed inflicting pain. Harris wasn't about to let him see how disturbed she truly was by this whole case. The tension in the room was tangible. He gave her the creeps.

Harris went on, "We know you weren't the only one who lived on site. Can you tell us about the others?"

No response.

"We've discovered cremated human remains in the cellar. Would you like to tell us about this?"

Nothing.

For forty minutes Harris made absolutely no headway whatsoever and the only voice recorded during the whole session was hers.

She decided it was time to wind things up, "Last night two of my colleagues were killed by a man escaping from the house ..."

For the only time during the interview Nicholas' expression of complete disinterest wavered. He was trying not to show it of course, but Harris could tell; his eyes for a fraction of a second had betrayed him; he was anxious about something, keen to get more information.

Harris could exploit this; she'd keep the vindictive little sod hungry for the thing he sought. "It seems he was met by one of your accomplices, probably Rosemary Hines. She must have considered him very important to risk being caught ... would you like to tell us who he is?"

Nothing.

Harris brought the interview to an end.

*

Shortly afterwards she met up with Frank. He drove her round to the garage to pick up her car. He quickly filled her in on the work he'd been doing in her absence. Once she was up to date, he asked, "How did you get on?"

Harris rolled her eyes, "Evil little bastard doesn't respond … like I'm too far beneath him to even sneer at!"

"Not normal is he?"

Harris didn't like the way the hairs on the back of her neck prickled at the suggestion that Nicholas Cureton wasn't 'normal'. "The custody sergeant reckoned he hasn't slept a wink since he came in. Just keeps sitting there … like he's waiting for something."

"For what?"

"You know, Frank, I think he honestly believed his chums were going to spring him."

"Out of police custody?" Wain asked incredulously. "What makes you think that?"

"I don't know. It occurred to me the first time I saw him, something about his manner, his arrogance … the sheer contempt he has for us."

"I'd have to agree there. He certainly doesn't hold us in high regard."

"But something happened during the interview. He didn't know Frith and O'Malley's killer had got away. I saw something strike him when he heard, like he thought it was all going to be alright up till then … as if, all of a sudden the reality of his situation hit him."

Frank looked confused.

"Don't worry," laughed Harris, "Just more feminine intuition."

He smiled. "Would you like me to have another go at him?"

"No. I think it would just be a waste of time. Let him stew a bit longer."

Frank pulled into the garage.

Harris made to get out but thought of something, "Get on to Stan Bryce … tell him we'll need to obtain a warrant sometime this afternoon from a magistrate for the further detention of Cureton. He'll need to stress the seriousness of the case and how uncooperative our DP is being. We'll need to apply for the full thirty-six hours."

"Okay, done. I'll meet you at the house in half an hour," he said.

*

At Barnswick Square some archaeological equipment had been brought in that utilised sound waves to expose what lay underneath the cellar's brick floors. The analysed data depicted pockets of what were believed to be skeletal remains.

"We're standing on a frigging cemetery," the officer in charge of forensics confided to Harris and Wain.

"How long before you can start excavating?" Harris asked him.

"We can't get on with the dig until the plotting has been completed … not for a good few hours yet."

Harris and Wain didn't stay long; they wanted to take a look at Jim Latimer's cottage. Wain left his car behind and Harris drove.

The two cottages on their southerly wooded slope came as a welcome relief from the chamber of horrors in Hove. Two of Harris' men, Patterson and Thorn, were already there, and showed them around.

Erich Ledermann's fingerprints had been discovered all over Jim's cottage, most profusely in the darkroom. Indeed, the only prints found there belonged to either Ledermann or Latimer. There was no evidence of anyone else, except for the very real physical signs of forced entry and violence. The dark residue on the door and along the knife blade found on the kitchen floor had been analysed and was discovered to be blood. However, its presence was an enigma, as this blood was estimated to be a good deal older than the cottage itself. In the hallway the blood stains were less than thirty-six hours old and corresponded with Jim Latimer's medical records. They also perfectly matched tissue samples taken from the torture chamber.

Upstairs in the darkroom, the film being developed had, according to Rice's notes, been started by Latimer. However, the processing was almost certainly completed by Erich Ledermann, who'd left his fingerprints everywhere.

"He kept making copies of the same prints," said Wain, peering at the series of photographs Jim had taken from the upstairs window in Hove, "What did he find so fascinating about them?"

The truth about the prints was hidden as they studied them in ordinary light, and in fact, had they switched over to the safety light, it would have made no difference. The underlying images disappeared entirely once the photographic emulsions dried.

Ruth's cottage had been broken into but forensic failed to find anything of interest. Harris and Wain together with Patterson and Thorn moved on to Pett village and went over Ledermann's bungalow. Someone had tried to telephone Jim Latimer's cottage from there at 4.30am on Thursday morning and reported a fault to the operator. But there was no fault on the line. The number was unobtainable because the cable had been cut.

Ledermann had a licence for a shotgun which was missing from the place in the study where it was normally kept locked away and bolted to the wall.

"The son had it in the box he was carrying when he entered and left the house," asserted Harris.

An elderly neighbour who lived in the bungalow opposite Ledermann's had been woken just after dawn by the sound of a screeching car. From behind the safety of her net curtains, she had watched an angry red-haired man with blood on his face stomp off to find a mechanic to replace two flat tyres on his white van.

Danny's studio was the next port of call. He had been captured on the security camera at Barnswick Square and was later identified from his father's picture collection. A girlfriend of Danny's had also recognised his voice as that of the second caller.

Around lunchtime word reached them that the Mercedes and the Transit van had been found abandoned on the Sussex University campus in Falmer, north east of Brighton. A forensic team had already begun work on them by the time Harris and Wain arrived.

There was enough of Latimer's blood in the boot of the Mercedes to explain how he had been transported from his home to Barnswick Square. The white Transit told tales that were altogether more disturbing. There was a broad wooden box across the width of the vehicle situated directly behind the driver's cab. The interior of this lidded box had been lined with lead and was darkly stained with human body fluids. It required a strong stomach just to peer into it. The freshest traces of blood found here belonged to DCI Rice.

"Where's the rest?" asked Wain.

"The rest of what?" responded Harris.

"His blood. What happened to the rest of it?"

*

Hannah Latimer had been contacted and interviewed by one of Harris' team on Thursday evening. However Harris felt that Mrs Latimer and the daughter might help her build up a profile of her husband and the group of vigilantes, referred to by Sussex Police as Group B.

Hannah struck Wain and Harris as a woman with nothing to hide. She was direct, and Harris found her likeable and intelligent.

"You told the officer your husband was anxious the last time he came here ... er, on?" Harris pretended to lose her place in the notes.

"On Tuesday evening, he'd brought Sophie home from school."

"Was he in the habit of picking her up?"

"Not without ringing first. Jim's generally considerate about not interfering with our plans."

327

"You get on well?" chipped in Wain.

"We're still fond of each other."

"Do you think you might reconcile your differences?" asked Harris.

"I hope so. And I know Jim would like that too."

"If you don't mind me asking ... why ..."

"His drinking," Hannah replied without hesitation, "Drink took away his best qualities. I left because I couldn't bear to see the man I cared about being destroyed."

"Did his personality change much when he drank?"

"Yes."

"Was he ever violent?" asked Wain.

"Never, though he could be verbally abusive. But in the last few years he was generally too comatose even for that while the bender lasted ... followed by the inevitable remorse, 'never again'; all that crap. But as soon as he felt better he'd be back out."

"He found some child pornography on Monday evening."

"Yes, with Bob Isherwood. I think that was the real reason why he came here on Tuesday. It upset him a lot."

"He told you about it?"

"Perhaps not everything ... he mentioned Ruth had experienced some kind of vision ... warning about the people in Hove ... Ruth is psychic."

"And do you believe in psychic phenomena, Mrs Latimer?" asked Harris, her face impassive.

"I believe there are more things to life than we credit it with. And I know Ruth wouldn't invent a story. Neither Ruth nor Erich Ledermann is the melodramatic type. They don't broadcast the things they believe in. Jim was sceptical but I told him to trust them. I think those were about the last words I said to him."

"Mrs Latimer, I have to ask you this, do you think there's any possibility ..."

Once again Hannah anticipated Harris' question, "I know what you're about to ask. No, Chief Inspector, my husband isn't mixed up with paedophiles, nor is Ruth or Erich. If they've gone into hiding it's because they're in some sort of danger."

"In that case why not come to us for protection?"

"Perhaps you aren't able to offer them the kind of protection they need."

*

328

During the journey back to Hove Harris and Wain compared their impressions of Latimer's wife and daughter. They had managed to talk to Sophie independently of Hannah. The girl was understandably upset by her father's disappearance.

"She clearly adores her dad," said Harris. "Have someone keep an eye on her. Latimer was very attached to her too, who knows, he may attempt to contact her."

By the time they returned to Barnswick Square it was after 8pm. The building was all lit up and still bustling with activity. The press had set up camp outside, and they had to push their way through a scrum of reporters firing questions at them.

Harris calmly stated, "I have no further comment to make at this time. However, a statement will be forthcoming in due course which will detail any recent findings at this site."

In the cellar a pit had been dug and the bones of three skeletons exhumed. It was reckoned that there were plenty more to come. They were met by DI Robson, who led them to the burial site.

Three skeletons had been laid out on sheets of plastic in the cellar hallway. In each case the skull had been severed from its body and the ribs had been prised open.

"Forensic reckon these must have been in the ground a very long time," said Robson, looking distinctly uncomfortable at the idea, "Quite possibly since the late nineteenth century."

Chapter Twenty-Seven

The Hove investigation: Saturday, 14 December, 1996

Harris didn't sleep very soundly but managed to get a couple of hours at least. Before checking in at the station, she made Barnswick Square her first point of call. Three teams were now working there around the clock. By 6am, when Harris arrived, the body count had jumped to fifteen, the legacy of just three pits, two dug in the crematorium and one in the torture chamber. The graves, their contents removed, had been shored up with timber. Consistent with earlier finds, in each case the victim's skull had been separated from its skeleton, and the ribcage had been torn open.

The scanning equipment was remarkably accurate. It identified forty-seven burial sites in the cellar and outside in the car park. There seemed to be no end to the horror of the place; even the soil in the rose beds was found to contain human ash.

A terrifying picture was beginning to emerge. The sheer scale and longevity of the murderous practices that had taken place at the Hove site were truly stupefying. The original three skeletons were of two females and a male, all in their twenties when they died. It would be a while before tests could produce an accurate date, but it was believed they had lain in the ground for approximately a hundred years. It seemed inconceivable that such mass killing could have gone undetected throughout an entire century. It was also patently clear that these finds couldn't be the sole legacy of N Cureton and Co, unless the bones were somehow misleading them. The murders in Hove had spanned three, or possibly four generations.

It was impossible to remain untouched by the sordidness of the place. Morale was generally pretty low, which was only to be expected after the deaths of colleagues. Susan Harris toured the house just to let everyone know their efforts were valued. From the group digging in the cellar to the teams at work on the upper floors, raising floorboards, chipping away plaster, and exposing wall back to its laths, she communicated her personal thanks and solidarity. It was an action greatly appreciated by those working there. This ability to empathise, her capacity for clear, concise thought and a reputation for good decision-making was probably why Harris engendered so much loyalty.

As a habitable dwelling the house was finished. Over the days and weeks ahead, its internal structure would be torn apart. The cellar area and car park would become a maze of walkways around its forty-seven open graves. The long charade of the house at 67 Barnswick Square was finally over.

*

After the morning briefing, Harris went through the painful ordeal of interrogating Nicholas again. Despite his total lack of cooperation so far, she thought it worth a try to see if he was prepared to talk about the graves and skeletal remains. They had been in the ground long before Cureton was born, so he wasn't implicated in exactly how or why they had got there. Even so, Harris thought he might be able to throw some light on how such a grisly legacy could have been handed down over several generations. She even considered it a possibility that Cureton might be cajoled into offering some help now that he'd had time to digest the seriousness of his situation.

Harris was of course entirely wrong about this; two nights detained in police custody hadn't in any way improved Nicholas' communication skills. The interview had been almost a complete re-enactment of the previous morning's fiasco. The same procedure had been adhered to for getting him from the cell to interview room, the outcome exactly the same with absolutely nothing achieved. Nicholas still refused to speak.

However, there had certainly been a change in the man since yesterday. His physical condition had noticeably deteriorated. It had also been noted with increasing concern that Nicholas hadn't eaten or drunk anything since his arrest on Thursday. This, together with the fact that he hadn't been seen to take any sleep for forty-eight hours, was assumed to be the reason why he looked so drawn and haggard.

It was assumed dehydration and loss of sleep were telling on his mental wellbeing. Harris observed a growing uneasiness in the man, and although he continued to glare at her, he seemed less sure of himself. Even so, despite the obvious deterioration, Harris began to wonder if the warrant of further detention had really been worth applying for. There was always a hope Nicholas might open up, but quite frankly, within the time frame allowed, she doubted it.

"Isherwood reckoned Loxton hadn't aged at all since he first met him," Wain said to Harris.

They were eating lunch whilst discussing DCI Rice's notes across a pale blue laminated table in the police canteen.

Harris propped her fork against the unappetising mound of grey mashed potato on her plate, "I'll talk to Markland. I'm going to request that Loxton has a full post mortem."

"I thought they'd already done one."

"An obvious suicide … they wouldn't have looked too far."

"How far are we prepared to look, Susan?" asked Wain, in a tone pregnant with meaning.

Harris gazed at Frank. Since the discovery of the coffins she was seeing that look on a lot of faces. Officially the coffin found in the Transit van was referred to as 'a rectangular crate lined in lead'. However, it had already derived the nickname 'meals on wheels' in the squad room. There was a fair smattering of vampire jokes being exchanged, which was par for the course. Yet for all the black humour, a discernible apprehensiveness had settled around the inquiry.

After lunch, Harris went straight to Markland and requested a fresh post mortem on Loxton. The DCC was his usual obstructive self. His anxiety level was clearly running high, no doubt exacerbated by the copious numbers of human bones surfacing at Barnswick Square.

"I fail to see any reason to question the coroner's findings. Dr Ashworth won't welcome unnecessary work for his already overstretched department."

"Sir, two men independently admitted to DCI Rice that they believed Loxton had aged significantly after his death. Robert Isherwood was actually with him when he died."

"Yes, Chief Inspector, and the other witness is the main suspect in our murder inquiry. I think it's extremely likely that Latimer and Isherwood were more involved than you seem ready to acknowledge."

"I've found nothing to suggest that either man had any dealings with Niedermayer & Hart prior to John Loxton's death. If I might add, sir, another post mortem might be the only way to rule out any confusion arising from Isherwood and Latimer's testimony."

Markland shook his head from side to side, which she assumed was a negative. In fact he was probably responding to the constant headache the case had given him. Grudgingly he conceded.

An hour later, he sought out Harris in the bustling incident room.

"You were a day late, Chief Inspector," he announced, loud enough for all to hear.

"Sir?"

"John Loxton. He was cremated yesterday. If there was any evidence, you missed it. It's all gone up in smoke!"

Markland turned his back and sauntered off in the direction of his office.

As they watched him go, Frank muttered under his breath, "You pompous arsehole."

*

Throughout the afternoon, Nicholas Cureton's behaviour and physical condition became increasingly a cause for concern.

Harris was watching him through the flap in the cell door. He was sitting in exactly the same position on the bed as he'd been on every other occasion. He was staring blankly ahead just as he'd done before but now he was shaking and there were beads of sweat on his forehead. Of course it couldn't be ruled out that he was withdrawing from a drug of some kind, and that was certainly what it seemed like. But more significantly perhaps, Harris thought he looked like a man who'd suddenly become conscious of his own fallibility.

"What's wrong, Nicholas?" she called to him, not anticipating any reply would come back. "Let me know when you decide to talk."

"You're so stupid ..."

"Who, me ... me personally?" she was taken aback by the response, but careful not to show it.

He had turned his head and was staring directly up at her. His coarse blubbery lips were peeled back from the ugly tombstones of his teeth. At the moment he spoke for the first time, Harris had felt a shockwave jolt her spine. Nicholas was a good deal more palatable when his eyes weren't boring into you. Their malevolence was unquestionable, but even so, Harris' own eyes never wavered from his.

"You've no idea ..." he said, shivering as he spoke. He looked dreadful.

"About what? You're the one behind bars," she said, hoping to goad him into developing his thoughts. "Have you been 'using' something, Nicholas?" she asked.

Nicholas smiled sourly to himself but said nothing more. He turned away and resumed his visual encounter with the wall.

After their brief exchange Harris left the detention-block. She instructed the custody sergeant to keep a close eye on him and to contact her immediately if his condition deteriorated.

"He looks quite ill. We may need to arrange a doctor for him."

*

By late afternoon on Saturday, a total of forty-one skeletons had been exhumed from the cellar.

Frank had taken a trip across town to the forensic lab. He wanted to know what progress had been made by ballistics on the shots fired by himself and Robson. So far, no bullet casings had been recovered. It was as if the shots had never been loosed at all. Of course if they weren't found, then they must have been absorbed by the target. Which begged the question, how could Frith's killer have possibly remained standing?

Harris in the meantime had received a call from Robson over at the square.

"They've uncovered something in the attic ... beneath the lath and plaster. You might care to take a look at it."

"What?" she asked hesitantly, unable to meet surprises in this case with anything other than dread.

"It's a manuscript ... in Latin."

Harris drove over immediately. The manuscript had been found wrapped in a piece of cloth. The rolled up parchment was extremely delicate, and some damage had already been done to it at the time of discovery. A wax seal, worn with age, was still partially intact, and the manuscript had been unrolled far enough to identify its text as Latin.

"Rob, I want this translated, by tomorrow at the latest. And I don't want to be told by some effin' museum curator that it'll be six bloody months before the parchment can be touched. We need any information it contains immediately. Say it's vital to our inquiry."

"Do you think so?" asked a slightly incredulous Robson.

Harris winced, as if questioning the sanity of her own words. "Who knows? Just make them understand it belongs to us and we want it back fast."

*

By the time she left Barnswick Square it was already dark. The evening was bitterly cold. Weathermen were predicting a freeze with a strong possibility of snow. En route to the station, Harris got a call from the custody sergeant.

"He's getting worse ma'am, he's pacing about like a madman … tearing his hair out and punching the walls. I've already called for the doctor."

"Okay, get DS Bryce to organise two armed officers. I'll be there in a couple of minutes."

On arrival Harris rushed down to the custody block. The custody sergeant unlocked the cell block door for her. She opened the door flap to Nicholas' cell and peered in.

Nicholas had become so deranged that he failed to notice Harris watching him as he paced about. Blood oozed from a wound on his forehead, and he was muttering aloud to himself as he stalked back and forth. Suddenly he dropped to his knees as if he was imploring someone to release him from his torture. He scrambled to his feet again, and after a few vague gestures expressing his frustration, flung himself at the cell door. Harris instinctively sprang back. But Nicholas seemed oblivious to her presence, and just went on with his pacing.

Harris felt both horrified and intrigued by what was happening to him. At one moment he held his head in his hands as if a pain was emanating from inside his skull; a second later his fists were lashing at the air or punching the walls. The backs of his hands were raw from the pounding they'd received. Again he fell to the floor, this time lying flat as if in a pose of supplication. Harris made out the words, "Rosemary, make him listen to you. He has to get me out!"

Nicholas got to his feet again, and immediately launched himself at the wall. This time he smashed his face violently into it. Harris winced at the sight and sound of flesh and bone meeting brick. The sheer force behind this self-imposed blow was jaw-dropping. Blood streamed out of his nostrils, spreading like red ink on blotting paper over his white collar. Harris watched in amazement, because apart from the bloody mess visible on his face, the man seemed relatively unharmed. Remarkable indeed, considering the aggression and power he'd employed. By rights, Cureton should have been lying unconscious on the cell floor.

Harris decided to speak, "Hello Nicholas."

He turned immediately. She was convinced by his reaction that he hadn't noticed her before.

"Hello," he answered in a bizarrely conversational way, traces of blood spraying from his lips as he spoke. "It's the police bitch … what can I do for you?"

"A doctor will be coming to see you shortly."

Nicholas laughed. He came up close to Harris, his face only inches from hers. She was trying not to flinch.

"I can see I scare you," he said.

"Keep deluding yourself."

"Oh, I think I do. And you'll be even more scared before I kill you."

"You charmer ... I bet you say that to all the girls," she replied.

"You just don't understand what you're up against. When 'he' arrives ... you'll see."

"Who exactly are we talking about, here?" Harris asked.

"You'll know soon enough," he smiled secretively, then went back and sat on his mattress.

"No-one is coming for you Nicholas. You're in police custody. If you think someone is going to spring you from here, you're sadly deluding yourself."

"Let's see your doctor then," he said, resuming his habitual concentration at the wall.

Harris didn't possess a shadow of a doubt that Nicholas was extremely dangerous. He was physically injured however, and his mental state was decidedly unbalanced. There was no alternative; a doctor would have to see him.

"I'll be back," she told him. Nicholas made no reply, having already entered some dark reverie.

Understaffed, Stan Bryce had nominated himself and a young detective constable, Hughes, to keep Cureton marked while the doctor treated him. Both were firearm-trained.

When the doctor arrived Harris spelled out the danger. She didn't mince her words, "He's a psychopathic killer, give him the slightest opportunity and he'll attack. Make your diagnosis if you can by viewing him through the door. If you do need to treat him directly, please bear in mind the danger we'll all be placing ourselves in. Take no unnecessary risks ... and don't at any time obstruct my men's line of vision." She briefed all three on the procedure they'd adopt if entering became necessary. "Hughes will take up position left of the door while Sgt Bryce cuffs him. Once he's secure the doctor can go in. Don't hesitate to shoot if you have to ... you may not get a second chance."

The custody sergeant opened the outer door to the cell-block for the four going through and locked it again after them.

Harris opened the door flap. Nicholas was lying down on the bed. His eyes were closed and he was sweating profusely, all the while gibbering alarmingly to himself.

"The doctor is here, Nicholas."

Nicholas didn't register any response.

Harris gestured for the doctor to come forward. An involuntary shiver ran through her. She positioned herself behind the man's shoulder in order to observe the proceedings.

"I'm Doctor Charles, Nicholas. Can you tell me how you're feeling?" called out the doctor.

There was still no response. Nicholas continued to twitch and mumble incoherently.

The doctor took Harris to one side. "That gash on his head could be very serious. His mental state clearly isn't good. I'm going to play safe and properly sedate him. He'll be no trouble after that. But we do need to get him into hospital for X-rays. He may have fractured his skull. We have to watch out for any build up of pressure or bleeding on the brain."

Harris called Markland on her mobile and explained the situation.

"Very well, get him sedated, I'll arrange transport and security," he replied wearily.

Harris warned Bryce and Hughes to get ready. They removed the safety catches on their pistols and indicated they were set to go. Harris suddenly wished she'd taken the trouble to arm herself. Despite being a trained firearms officer, she only ever wore a gun as a last resort. However, on this occasion any personal reluctance about carrying a weapon would have been outweighed by circumstance.

Because it wasn't possible to communicate with Nicholas, who appeared to be if anything only semi-conscious, it was decided to keep him covered while Doctor Charles sedated him.

Harris took out the key the custody sergeant had given her, and unlocked the door. Hughes entered first, covered by Bryce. When the detective constable had established a good position to the left, Bryce went in and took up a place at the end of the bed. Harris nodded for the doctor to enter.

Doctor Charles had prepared an injection outside in the corridor. He stood beside Nicholas for a moment. In his left hand was a cotton wool swab primed with spirit. "You're going to require stitches in your head," the doctor explained to Nicholas' unresponsive form.

'No time for bedside manners,' thought Harris.

"I'm going to give you an injection. You'll feel a tingling sensation in your right arm for a second or two."

Nicholas appeared not to hear, he was still jabbering to himself. Doctor Charles transferred the swab to his right hand and began to skilfully undo the cuff button on Nicholas' shirt with his left. He needed to stoop closer to the bed in order to do this, thereby obscuring Davies' view and also limiting what Bryce could see.

Harris' mouth went dry. She was watching the scene from just inside the cell door. She saw Nicholas' right hand flex, possibly in response to the doctor's instruction – or perhaps he was more conscious than he appeared to be? "Could you hurry up please?" she instructed.

The doctor wiped an area of Nicholas' bare arm with the swab then brought the needle into position. The doctor's hand shook slightly, thumb poised at the plunger end of the syringe.

Albeit prematurely, there was a feeling of relief; the task seemed like it was almost done. Perhaps that was why the next moment didn't seem quite real when Nicholas' left hand shot out and took a firm grip on the barrel of the syringe. His speed was phenomenal.

"Shoot the bastard!" shouted Harris.

Stan Bryce was in a position to take a shot, but it was by no means a clear shot. Also, the window of opportunity was very small, and he undoubtedly hesitated. It was understandable, only a psychopathic killer would find it easy to shoot an unarmed man.

Nicholas saw the threat. He freed his right hand from the doctor's grip and drew the man across him as a shield. He was staring up directly into his protector's frightened eyes, "You're looking tense. You should take it easy, doctor," he said calmly.

Doctor Charles, terrified, attempted a placatory smile.

The two armed policemen instinctively braced themselves. There was no longer a shot possible at Cureton without the risk of hitting the doctor.

Harris missed a heartbeat. "Let the doctor go!" she shouted.

"Release the doctor!" exclaimed Bryce at the same moment.

Nicholas prised the needle out of the doctor's hand, then immediately plunged it into the man's chest and began squeezing out its contents. The doctor shrieked with pain.

Stan Bryce made the mistake of rushing forward in an attempt to engage with the situation. He was bowled over as the doctor, propelled by an incredible force, hurtled into him. Bryce, unbalanced, toppled and crashed to the floor beneath the unconscious man. His finger poised on the trigger couldn't prevent the gun from firing. Red spattered from the doctor's chest like a volcanic eruption.

"Christ, shoot!" Harris shouted at Hughes, who was momentarily dumbstruck. Hughes, coming to his senses, loosed a shot into Nicholas' shoulder only a second before he was on him.

Nicholas Cureton's upper chest bloomed red like a flower in stop frame photography. The wound was severe enough to floor anyone; but if the bullet slowed Nicholas at all, its effect was imperceptible.

Nicholas leapt at his attacker. He immediately grabbed Hughes' gun hand. Harris dived at Nicholas' arm to stop him taking the weapon. But Nicholas was incomprehensibly fast. In one fluid movement he had slammed the constable's head against the wall, hooked his fist into Harris' chin and sent her reeling to the floor.

Nicholas took the pistol from the semi-conscious Hughes as he slid down the wall. Bryce, meanwhile, was struggling to free himself from beneath the doctor's corpse. Nicholas smiled at the sight of the unfortunate sergeant and his bungling efforts to get free. Bryce was no longer armed. He'd let the pistol fall once it had gone off.

Harris read the malicious intention in Nicholas' eyes.

"No! He's unarmed!" she cried out.

"Now you've begged, it's irresistible ... I've just got to," said Nicholas callously, a broad grin on his fleshy mouth.

He fired twice into Stan Bryce's head and neck.

"No!" Harris screamed as her sergeant's face was blown apart.

"How about pleading for this one?" Nicholas asked, pointing at Hughes.

Harris would not play this game. At that moment she believed Hughes and herself were both about to die. She struggled to her feet using the wall behind to support and steady her. "Whatever you do, you can't get away ... you can't get out of this cell block ... outside a dozen armed officers will be waiting for you."

Nicholas stepped tentatively into the doorway keeping Harris covered as he assessed the problem. A swift glance along the corridor confirmed what she'd said; the door was locked. He clocked too the numerous faces peering in at him through its small window. Nicholas drew back into the cell.

"Call the key-man. Tell him to open up!"

"There's no way. I'd never allow a psychopath like you to go free. And by the way, your friends aren't coming ... you might kill us but you can't escape."

"Cut out the speech making. Call him, bitch!" Nicholas shouted as he steadied and aimed the gun at her face. The left side of Nicholas' shirt was now drenched in his own blood.

Harris was trying to express an outer calm she didn't feel, "That's why there's a second door, to stop the likes of you escaping."

Nicholas clasped his left hand, dripping with blood from the shoulder wound, around her neck. He applied a lot of pressure. Harris began to choke. He was holding the pistol steady about an inch from her right eye, "If you don't get that outer door open, I'll blow your head away like his," he said, gesturing down at Bryce.

"Go fuck yourself," choked out Harris.

Nicholas pressed the gun into her cheek. He drew his bloodied face in close, "It'll be a shame to kill you … you'd be the perfect gift for Mr Niedermayer. He'd teach you manners."

At that moment Hughes, lying on the floor behind Nicholas, let out a groan as he began to regain his senses.

"I'll make him my hostage then, seeing as you're so eager to die."

Nicholas moved his face away and freed her neck. Harris began coughing and gasping for breath. She felt the gun barrel stiffen against her cheek. She was about to die, she didn't need to look brave. She closed her eyes.

But Nicholas couldn't resist one final moment of sadism as Harris waited for him to pull the trigger.

'He's waiting till I open my eyes. He wants me to see him pull the trigger,' she thought in that interminable moment of waiting.

Unable to bear the agony any longer, she flicked open her eyelids.

Nicholas smiled with pleasure.

Harris was aware of the tension in his hand as it began to squeeze.

For a second after the blast Harris believed Nicholas had fired. Then she saw Frank standing there, framed in the doorway, his pistol smoking, and Cureton falling. Harris collapsed against the cell wall. As the closeness of her brush with extinction dawned on her mind her legs turned to jelly and she started to slide irrevocably towards the floor.

Wain, putting away his pistol, stepped beside her to provide the support she needed to stay upright. He couldn't let her sink to the ground, it was awash in blood.

"Susan?"

She heard her name being called as if from a long way off.

"You're safe. Susan?"

She sucked in breath as though she had just swum a long distance underwater, her eyes flickering about like a radio transmitter being re-tuned. Frank's voice and face became reconciled into one again. She had no words to say to him; just hugged him to her, eyes closed tight, drawing succour from his humanity and warmth.

The words exchanged by the two armed officers in flak jackets who entered behind Wain brought her back to her senses. "Three down, the DP, the doctor and Sergeant Bryce," one of them was reporting into his radio.

"We need ambulances too for DC Hughes and the Chief Inspector," said the other man.

"I'm alright," interrupted Harris. "How are you, Paul?" she asked Hughes, who was still lying at the base of the wall.

"I think my shoulder's broken," he said confusedly. The young man's eyes started to fill with tears as he relived the nightmare, "I shot him, but he kept coming ... he didn't go down!"

"You did everything you could," Harris said in an attempt to comfort the distraught man.

The scene was unimaginably graphic; the walls spattered with brain and blood, the floor a pool of red, the three dead men lying together in a tangled mess. The doctor's staring eyes, his jaw gaping wide, somehow captured the horrific mood perfectly. The hypodermic, still in place, had been stabbed, if not directly into, then very close to the man's heart. Perhaps the doctor had been dead before Bryce's gun had blasted a hole through him. The sight of Stan Bryce, barely recognisable, filled Harris with rage. His torso was drenched in blood and much of his face and neck were shot away.

"Vicious bastard. He didn't need to ... he just killed Stan for the hell of it ..."

"Susan, why don't you come away for a bit?" suggested Wain.

"No!" Harris said emphatically; then more calmly, "I'm alright Frank ... honest."

Harris looked down on Nicholas' corpse, which had ended up in a bizarrely foetus-like pose jammed between the bed and the doctor's ribcage. The contents of his brain cavity had been all but completely blown out of the skull, the walls round about its recipients. Strangely, Harris felt no emotion when she saw her jacket bore spattered fragments of Nicholas' redundant mental faculties. His face was angled up towards her, eyes blank, dumb, staring into nothingness. He had been so terrifying standing there with the gun pointing at her face. It had seemed certain she was about to die. But through some quirk of fate, she was alive and he was nothing. He was no longer frightening, lying in that preposterous death pose with his brains absent; just dead meat, blind, deaf and mute. Somewhere, deep within herself, Harris was dancing on his corpse. Nicholas Cureton had eminently deserved to die.

She could have done without Markland's appearance just at that time.

His face went white, the flaccid jowls of his face quivering at the sight that met his eyes. He had no words of compassion either for those who had fallen in the line of duty or for Harris and DC Hughes, now being aided to his feet by the two officers. Markland's first words were, "This is a hell of a cock-up."

"We didn't stand a chance," Harris retorted angrily.

"Three armed officers failed to restrain one prisoner?"

"Two armed ... I came directly from other duties."

"Why wasn't the prisoner handcuffed would seem a logical question?" Markland was beginning to shout.

"He appeared to be sick. We thought he was unconscious."

"You're trying to say he fooled you!" said Markland contemptuously.

"He looked very ill and had some potentially serious injuries. It was Doctor Charles' decision to sedate him and take him to hospital for x-rays."

"Just admit it, he duped you!" the DCC scoffed.

"What the Chief Inspector says is correct, sir," interrupted Hughes now on his feet supported by the two officers. "The way he moved was incredible, his strength ... I shot him but he didn't go down ... he wasn't like a normal man."

Markland ignored this interruption from a subordinate.

"I was his arresting officer," put in Frank, "We had a hell of a time dealing with him. Read my report!"

Markland had nothing more than a dismissive glance for Wain and his views. There had never been any love lost between them.

"And I suppose this fantastical strength came from the same source as Loxton's eternal youth?"

"DCI Harris was absolutely right to ask for a proper post mortem on the photographer, Loxton," replied Wain. He spoke in a quiet, understated way.

Markland ignored him and continued haranguing Harris. "I want a report on my desk within the hour ..."

"John Loxton probably did look forty-ish," Frank added, not directly to anyone. He was gazing down at Nicholas' corpse like a man away in a daydream.

"And as for your future with this investigation, Chief Inspector ..."

"Sir!" broke in Wain. He spoke assertively now, and this time directly to Markland, "Chief Inspector Harris was absolutely right.

Loxton should most definitely have been re-examined by a pathologist."

Markland, infuriated by Wain's repeated interruptions, said angrily, "How dare you butt in when I am instructing a senior officer. What the hell are you blethering on about, man?"

"There's something very wrong here," replied Wain, still scrutinising Nicholas's body. Wain had everyone's attention apart from the Deputy Chief Constable's. "You see, I'd have judged Cureton to be in his early twenties ..."

"What is it?" said Markland, at the end of his tether.

Harris had begun to see for herself what Wain was getting at.

"That man is no longer young. His hair is turning grey, and look at the skin, it's ageing. He's got older since I shot him."

"What rubbish are you ..." DCC Markland broke off. He clearly didn't find the ageing Nicholas very appealing.

"It's impossible!" was all he could manage. However it was quite miraculous that he could speak at all, with his bottom jaw almost resting on his knee caps.

Frank, enjoying Markland's shocked response, went for maximum mileage. "At this rate," he began, "Another two minutes and he'll be well over retirement age."

Wain's irreverent assessment was, as it turned out, absolutely right. Two minutes on and they were staring at a man of about eighty. But nobody could have guessed exactly how far the degenerative process would go.

Two hours later, all that was left of Nicholas Cureton was bones and dust. And Deputy Chief Constable Markland was very unhappy about it.

Hugh's Tale

XV

Only in those last days did I understand how utterly detestable yet subtle was the mind in him we sought. However much sleep we lost or hard we rode, the vampir and its red-haired parasite remained ahead.

Twenty-seven days on from our channel crossing I came at dawn, Yussuf faithfully beside me, to the lands of my childhood. I approached with grave forebodings. The hard ground frost was glistening in the morning light, scarred deeply by the cart wheels we had relentlessly pursued for nearly a month. But I needed no tracks to show me the way, for I knew full well where they would lead me; directly to my father's house.

I dismounted, handed my reins to Yussuf, ran to the door and entered the hall. Every horror I had known since Acre could not have prepared me for the grim tableau that met my eyes. My father was laid upon a trestle and beside him were three other corpses. The village priest knelt before them in prayer, whilst away in the corner sat my old nurse with a baby in her arms, its shawl saturated in blood.

"What is meant by this intrusion ..." said the old priest as he rose to his feet, glowering at me, before breaking off from his speech. He had not immediately known me, yet the resemblance I bore my father was ever strong. "Why, it is Master Hugh returned I think? M - Master Hugh ... I ..." the priest's words foundered, there was no greeting he could offer me.

I went to my father, took his hand in mine and laying my head upon his breast broke down in grief.

After a time the priest came over to me and placing a hand upon my shoulder, said, "Your father is in the arms of God."

Hearing his words I stopped weeping and asked of him angrily, "Which God, Father?"

The priest, horrified by my reply, said, "May the Lord forgive your blasphemy," then relenting a little, added, "It is only grief that makes you speak so bitterly."

"I am sorry, Father," I said, regaining some composure and rising to my feet, "Did any see what happened?"

"The old woman saw all," replied the priest, gesturing towards the nurse, "Which I fear was more than her mind could bear. She will not give up the child, and speaks to it as though it is still living."

"Whose is the child?" I asked.

"Why Master Hugh," said the priest, "This man beside your father was your sister Melisend's husband Rhisiart, the boys and this little babe were your nephews."

"Melisend?" I asked, staring in turn at the faces of her husband and sons, "Where is my sister?"

"The fiends who did this took her with them," replied the priest.

"Why?" I cried out in despair, "Why were Melisend and her family here?"

"They brought the baby to be christened in your family church," explained the priest, "The christening was to have been this morning. The child has died unblessed."

I looked upon the face of my sister's husband. They had been a handsome match. I asked, "What was this brother in law like?"

"He was an honest man, who treated your sister well. Your father came to love him as a son, though he was uncertain at first."

I saw that he had been killed with a sword. My nephews, nine and seven years old as I learned from the priest, had not been so fortunate. Their skin bore the same grey pallor as my father's, their youthfulness corrupted by the death mask of Jerome's plague. Yussuf himself was much affected by their murders; he took their infant hands in his and spoke some words in Aramaic, the tongue the guardians kept for communion with their god.

"What is the heathen saying?" asked the priest, suspiciously.

"He is no heathen," I replied tersely, "He says a blessing for my nephews in Christ's own tongue, as is the custom with his people." The priest was not assured by my reply, but I had no time for his prejudice and superstition. "Has a search been mounted for Melisend?" I asked.

"The men are too fearful. An old woman saw the fiends approach," the priest swallowed fearfully, "She described a demon driving a chariot."

"What time was this?" I asked.

"The last hour before dawn," he replied.

We had come an hour too late; for want of one hour I might have saved my home and family. I alone was responsible for bringing this destruction upon the heads of those I loved; if only I had gone to Albi to join the others as arranged. It was my own arrogance that was being punished here; Jerome had taken his revenge whilst I had lagged behind. It would have been better had I never left the Holy Land, or had perished in poor Ayyub's place.

"A group of villeins have gone north to Chester to bring the Sheriff."

The priest watched as I inspected the injury to my father's neck. A large piece of flesh had been bitten away leaving veins and sinews hanging out black and congealed; the two boys had similar wounds.

"I have never known such marks," said the priest crossing himself, "Surely the work of a beast."

I stared at the priest's fearful face as he attempted to make sense of the devilry that had descended on his village and its lord.

Yussuf brought me back to the present, saying, "Hugh, your sister may yet live. Let us fight for the living."

I nodded in agreement. I went to Aline, my beloved old nurse, and knelt before her holding my arms out for the child. The old woman was chirping at the baby as though it still possessed life.

"Aline, it is Hugh. Remember. You once held me to your bosom, as you do my nephew now."

Her kindly old eyes looked at mine, then she put out a frail hand towards me and gently stroked my face, saying, "Master Hugh, what a fine man you are become," then returning her attention to the child, said to it, "One day child, you will be a man, tall and fine as your uncle Hugh."

"Let me take the baby, Aline," I said, choking back my tears.

She immediately grew suspicious, "He enjoys being in my arms. See how contented he is."

"Please, let me have him, Aline," I said, "He must be brought to Melisend."

"But she is gone ... they took ..." then a dark memory overwhelmed her mind, she let out a fearful cry and set to wailing as she relived the horror that had come upon the house before the dawn. In that cruel moment she remembered everything as it was, and beheld the infant in her arms in its blood-soaked wrap.

I took the babe off her. So inured to violence had I become, I felt relief when I saw that it had died on the serjeant's sword. I lay the dead child upon its father's bosom.

I raised the stricken woman, who clung to me as if I were her salvation, and gave her over to the priest. I put some coins into his hand and said, "Good father, take my old nursemaid from this place. See to it that she has everything she needs."

The old priest looked confused, "Aline will want for nothing. But what do you mean to do, Master Hugh, will you take charge of your father's estate?"

"I have only come to end the plague that visited here last night," I replied.

"Then you will not return?" the priest asked.

"Go now, Father" I said.

"How was it that you came so soon in the wake of this abomination?" the priest asked.

"To save my family … I arrived too late."

"May God have mercy on you," he said. The old priest turned his attention to Aline, coaxing her gently from the house.

"You must leave too, Hugh. I will do what must be done," said Yussuf.

I took a final look at my boyhood home, kissing my father and the nephews I had never known alive. Then I left, closing the door behind me. I mounted my horse, and followed the cart tracks that led south from the village. When I had gone some distance, the manor out of sight, I dismounted, sat upon a stile and waited.

I recalled the priest's final words to me, "May God have mercy on you." I was indeed in need of His mercy. Wretched, renegade and traitor to the oaths of my order, and henceforth to be remembered as desecrator of my father's house; in this place I cherished most, my name would be despised, forever damned.

The time Yussuf took to accomplish his grim work seemed unbearable. At last he approached along the icy track, his form merging darkly with his horse, like an avenging angel against the slate grey sky that smothered out the sun, a pillar of smoke rising black and thick above the bare trees behind him.

"It is done," was all he said. I mounted up, and nothing more was exchanged between us for a long while.

The pace I set was that of a man possessed by madness.

After two hours of journeying south, we came upon a peasant girl. She lay prostrate upon the tracks we followed. Her skin was blue from the cold, and she was utterly distraught with grief.

We dismounted and between us raised her to her feet.

"What ails you, child?" I asked.

A cry issued from her lips that were quivering with distress and cold.

"My ... baby ... my baby son has been stolen," she replied before breaking into sobs.

"Who, who was it, girl?" I asked, probably shaking her too roughly in my earnestness, though in truth I did not mean to harm her more.

Yussuf took charge, placing a blanket around her shoulders. "Tell us what happened," he asked gently; it was ever his way, for he possessed a kindly heart, "We want to help."

"A man and woman came by upon a cart," the girl answered, "I bade them good morning, for they slowed as they came by me. I thought they wanted directions ..." She burst into tears again.

Yussuf stroked her hair softly. "Did the man have red hair?" he asked.

"Yes ... the pig," she spat upon the ground at the serjeant's memory.

"And the woman?" I asked.

"She was well-dressed, a noblewoman, she did not speak. She only stared ahead of her as though she was made of stone ... I do not think she even saw me. Then the pig got down off the cart and took my baby ..." The rest of her story had to be gleaned through sobs, "He took my baby boy ... I kicked and scratched him, but he knocked me to the ground. Then he said that the good lady had lost her children and my baby could take their place." The girl became inconsolable as she screamed, "But he was mine! He did not belong to her. She hardly noticed him when that pig placed him in her arms!"

The girl told us where her home was; Yussuf put her up on his mare, and we delivered her to her family's hut, for she could not have been left as we found her, or surely she would have frozen to death.

"We will try to find your child," I promised as we left, and for lack of anything better to offer I put a coin into her freezing palm.

As dusk approached we pursued our enemies' wheel tracks across the border into Wales, taking only enough time to rest the horses and take sustenance ourselves. The route was treacherous and our going slow as we journeyed through the night. We were constantly vigilant, never forgetting how powerful Jerome might be in darkness.

We edged along, our mares stoically battling the icy conditions underfoot. Eventually, chilled to the bone, a dim light grew behind us over the eastern horizon as hope of a new day dawned.

Land and sky merged into a grey half-light, with a morning mist that clung like poisonous vapour to the earth. Just visible on the hill's summit ahead of us were the ruins of an abandoned stronghold.

Then I saw him; Jerome's protector, looking about, sat on a stationary cart but a minute's distance from me. When he saw me he folded his arms and laughed. I could see only the front end of the cart; there was no sign of Melisend, which fired up my rage. Yussuf, who rode a few paces behind me, had not yet seen the serjeant.

Then a madness took me, and without taking thought, I reined in my horse and rode at him; him who I had hated for so long, yet whose name I had never known. I galloped across the hillock before me, then down a slope; all that stood between us was a narrow plain, its surface shrouded in mist.

I heard Yussuf cry out my name but I discerned nothing of his warning, my course irrevocably set.

My horse had covered over half the distance when realisation and disaster struck together; the words 'river' and 'ice' only reaching my ears as Yussuf repeated his warning. At the same moment my mare's legs splayed out beneath her on the frozen surface. We crashed onto the ice, shrieks of pain issuing from both man and beast as one of her forelegs snapped and my ankle was trapped beneath her body. We lay for a moment immobilised, the sound of the ice cracking under our weight. Then I was plunged into the icy depths of a furiously flowing river, struggling for breath and life, trying to avoid my mare's hooves as the poor beast thrashed about in terror.

As I came to the surface gasping for air with paralysed lungs, and clinging to the ice's edge, I saw the serjeant jeer at me as he took up his reins and began to move away. At the rear of the cart alongside a wooden crate was Melisend, sitting impassively, blind to my struggle for life and unconcerned by the fiend at rest beside her. She was completely absorbed in the peasant girl's baby suckling at her breast.

My mare reared up in a great effort to free herself; a hoof struck my shoulder and the world of ice and water around me began to spin.

In those last moments, as the freezing water covered my face and poured into my lungs, all striving over, all fighting done, I relinquished my hold upon the ice and my body fell limp. Here at the last I was to be shown merciful forgetfulness; come finally to peace.

Chapter Twenty-Eight

Sunday, 15 December, 1996

Shortly after dawn, on a stretch of road close to the Welsh border, an unremarkable dark blue car was heading east in the direction of Birmingham. The few people about that early paid little or no attention to either the vehicle or its occupant. In any case, it was unlikely that even the most observant driver could have identified Rosemary Hines from a passing glimpse on such a grey winter morning.

Since the murders had come to light, the media, particularly the tabloid press, had been busily exciting their readers' appetite for the macabre. Not even Markland's heavily massaged figures seemed to dampen public interest very much. The story contained the murkiest elements of the darkest fairy tales; cremated human remains discovered in genteel Hove, the hidden assailant's murderous escape and the subsequent trickle of news about skeletons had grabbed everyone's attention. The latest event, the way Nicholas Cureton had met his own death and murdered two others (as yet unnamed) during a failed attempt to break out of police custody, was all over the Sunday papers. Beyond scant details, the police were not prepared to give further information until they'd had time to fully investigate. Even so, hurriedly arranged newspaper front pages, light on facts but bursting with the more sensational elements in the story, were waiting to stimulate the nation's gastric juices over a leisurely Sunday breakfast.

Rosemary's description had of course been broadcast through every form of the media. However, identifying her was more difficult now her raven dark hair had been cut and dyed honey blonde. The shade, together with the thick brown clear glass spectacles she wore, did nothing for her fine aquiline features. Anonymity was on Rosemary's side, and those driving by remained ignorant of her well-deserved notoriety.

A bleary-eyed farm-worker heading south towards Newtown waited at a roundabout while the blue car went by. He observed the driver's striking features, but what he noticed most about her were the tears rolling down her cheeks. Rosemary paid him no attention, her mouth fixed in a hard line with damp eyes set on the road ahead.

'She's got a look to her, that one ... like she means business,' he thought as he crossed the roundabout in her wake, 'I wouldn't want to be in her boyfriend's shoes.' The farm-worker chuckled to himself at his little fantasy about this girl catching the man in her life in the act of some sexual indiscretion.

He wended his way to work, and in five minutes he'd forgotten both her and the soapy storyline he'd constructed, whilst the welfare and management of cows fully occupied his mind until sunset.

*

When Jim woke up he found himself no longer restrained, and immediately experienced a moment of panic.

Ruth, sitting beside him and seeing this, said, "We decided it was the right thing ... to free you. We felt you'd been held prisoner long enough."

"How can you be sure I'm safe ... to be with, I mean?" Jim asked, nervously running his hands through his tangled hair, stiffly matted with his own vomit, blood and sweat.

"Erich says it has to be down to you ... your own sense of responsibility."

Jim drifted off with his thoughts for a moment, "I can still feel his presence inside me ... I sense his rage. You know, don't you, that he'll settle for nothing short of our annihilation?"

Ruth nodded; they had all acknowledged how the score stood. "Friday night was the worst point. We all felt defeated. You didn't look like you'd make it through."

"The pillars," said Jim. There was a childlike look of wonderment in his eyes.

"What?"

"I was in a dark pit. I could feel his foulness all around me. My life was draining into him ... then, I don't know ... it was like a miracle." Jim looked a little embarrassed about this choice of word, but he went on, "Four pillars grew up around me. They were shining ... radiating a golden light. I felt my energy slowly being restored, and the evil slinking away."

Ruth smiled, "You're a lucky man, aren't you?" she said.

Jim got up shortly afterwards and took breakfast with the others in the kitchen. The only one absent was Erich, who was on guard duty.

After eating, Jim asked if he might be allowed to take a walk in the garden.

"I know the morning's not very inviting," he said, looking out through the window at the snow clouds monopolising the sky, "But I'd like to breathe in some fresh air and stand in the daylight. You can guard me if you want. I won't mind."

"Nobody intends guarding you," said Ruth.

"But we'd love to show you our garden," said Millie.

"We could escort you," said her sister.

Jim was given an old cashmere overcoat that had belonged to the sisters' father, and taken on a garden tour. At the base of the steps leading down from the patio that ran across the back of the house, Jim said "I'd like to apologise, for the things I said ... when I was in that madness."

"Sticks and stones," replied Mary.

"Just names," said Millie.

"Say no more about it," said Mary, adding with a smile and a wink at her sister, "We can take it, can't we Mill?"

"Indeed we can," said Millie, "We're as tough as old boots."

"Tougher," added Mary, the sisters' eyes twinkling at each other, "Being little old ladies is just our disguise."

The Thorpe sisters roared with laughter at the idea of this before linking arms with Jim. The trio then set off on a tour of the frosty garden.

They started to the left of the house. On either side of Jim, the sisters were wrapped up in brightly coloured ski jackets that clashed alarmingly. Mary had a peaked cap on her head with mock fur ear flaps, whilst Millie was wearing an Arsenal football club woolly hat that a great nephew had given her as a birthday present.

The perimeter hedge of the sisters' garden was composed of hawthorn and holly, which stood solidly all around. Occasionally, the women described to Jim the plants and flowers he might expect to see there in the spring and summer, but mostly they remained silent, allowing him to experience for himself their labour of love.

The first area, a whole garden in itself, was wild, and Mary talked enthusiastically about the fritillaries, cowslips and cornflowers that appeared at their appointed times. Two large apple trees broke up the uniformity of the meadow and provided shade in summer. Beyond the trees was a frozen stream, with a little wooden bridge leading across it to a rustic archway which led into a more cultivated area.

"In season we grow a large number of aromatic flowers in these borders, like honeysuckle and night-scented stocks; the smell is intoxicating as you brush past," said Mary.

Another arch and trellising brought them to the rockeries set amongst spiralling patterns of raked shingle. Along one side was an old brick wall with a wooden door in it, and through here was the vegetable garden.

Returning in the direction of the house they walked through a place set aside for growing herbs before coming back to the lawned area that had been their starting point. However, there was one more thing to see. At the lawn's farthest end was a beech hedge, and going through a gap in it, they entered the garden's hidden heart. There was a large ornamental pond at its centre.

"The stream we crossed is man-made and should be pouring into it if it wasn't all frozen over," said Millie, "All done with pumps. We really wanted a water feature."

"Both of us are Pisces rising," added Mary, before joining her sister in a burst of laughter.

"Why not stay here a while ... enjoy the peace and quiet," suggested Millie.

"Pa's coat will keep you nice and warm."

The sisters went back to the house. Jim sat on a bench with his back against the wall of the vegetable garden. He couldn't help smiling when a beam of sunlight touched his face as it stole its way out from under the blanket of snow clouds.

No garden looks its best in December, but Jim had a gardener's eye and an imagination to fill in the gaps. He felt at ease with himself. The sisters had created more than just an interesting green space; they had conspired with nature to build a cathedral. The garden was designed to lead its visitors through its chapels, to where Jim now rested, in its tranquil centre. It spoke to him in a language without words that satisfied an inner yearning; he began to see how every church, temple, mosque or synagogue was only an embellishment of an inner design, that the blueprint was archetypal and universal, etched indelibly into the human psyche.

*

The centre of Birmingham was heaving with people taking advantage of Sunday trading to do their Christmas shopping. Perhaps the recent bad weather predictions had driven them into this frenzy of consumerism. Whatever the reason, they had certainly turned out en masse, hunched into their coat collars, on an extremely cold December morning.

On a street corner a Salvation Army band was playing traditional carols, in competition with the Christmas schmaltz being piped out by the department stores. A few people stopped and listened for a while before the freezing wind drove them on. Mostly people ignored the bonneted Army women and their collecting tins, but some paused to drop a coin or two into their boxes.

Only one figure appeared to be absolutely still in the bustling landscape. A young woman with short-cropped honey blonde hair had been watching from the street corner opposite all the time the band was playing. With so much shopping to do and the weather not conducive to standing and staring, nobody gave her a second glance. Had they done so, looked into those chilling deep-blue eyes and witnessed their ferocity, they may have concluded the day was by no means that cold.

Suddenly, Rosemary's face came alive, like a cat that catches sight of a mouse, all passivity gone, only images of the prey inhabiting its mind. Her attention was taken by a Salvation Army woman in her mid-twenties. The young woman had handed her collecting tin to a colleague before crossing the road.

Rosemary could hear the girl humming the tune being sung by her comrades as she passed by. She hung back for a few seconds before following. The Salvationist was walking in the direction of the public lavatories. That would do nicely.

*

Jim was surprised when he caught sight of himself in the bathroom mirror. He had expected cuts or at least some bruising from the vicious handling he'd received from Rosemary. Yet, apart from the beginnings of a beard, he found nothing, no scars or blemishes on his face at all. He called to mind Nicholas's hand, and the swiftness with which it had healed.

"One of the perks," he said humourlessly to himself in the mirror.

The heat of the bathwater had made his big toe flinch on contact, but after he'd eased himself in and acclimatised it was pure luxury. Washing his hair clean of all that matted filth and rinsing it with jugs of steamy water was a delight.

Apart from the twenty minutes spent in that serene spot by the sisters' pond an hour ago, it was the first time he'd been on his own since the cellar in Hove. Actually he was not entirely alone, as Danny was resting in the bedroom next door. The idea of having company nearby was something of a relief. Occasionally he could still sense Niedermayer casting a shadow across his mind, which brought on a feeling of utter desolation.

'Like Erich says, it's still early days. Yesterday I had to be tied up,' he thought, and lowered himself to the chin in the soothing tub of watery bliss. He closed his eyes and let himself drift away. The steam and smell of soap and shampoo filled his head like a narcotic.

He visualised himself in the garden again, by the pond, at the peaceful heart of the sisters' creation. It felt good being there; it was springtime, an added bonus. However, after a few moments things didn't seem quite right, something was missing; there should have been sounds, birdsong, the breeze whistling through branches; it was too quiet, not even a blade of grass stirred in the silence.

Then something fell past his nose and landed at his feet. It was a bird, a blue tit; the head was crushed and its tiny feathered corpse was saturated in blood. A yard away another landed, then two more by his feet again, then another and another; small mangled carcasses were dropping all around him. Soon the ground was littered with them - starlings, thrushes, blue tits, finches, polluting that special place with their rotting stench. He had to raise his hands to protect himself as they fell; literally hundreds were falling now.

Then as suddenly as it had begun, the onslaught ceased. Jim, spattered with blood, went to the edge of the pond to wash it from his hands and face, but the tiny bodies were so numerous that stepping on them was unavoidable, and their bones cracked horribly beneath his feet.

The pond had been transformed into a stinking pool of stagnant filth; dead frogs, squirrels, even cats, bloated and rotten, floated on its surface. He heard someone approach behind him and spun around. He was horrified to see Picton stomping towards him through the dead birds. Panic surged through him. There was nowhere to run; the water was at his back. The red haired man came quickly upon him, leaving a bloody trail of mush in his wake.

Picton raised a hand and tapped one finger on Jim's chest. At first he was surprised by the feebleness of the assault, before realising he was irrevocably toppling backwards. He attempted to regain his balance, hovering in mid-air for a moment with arms flailing. Picton was roaring with laughter at the spectacle in front of him.

Jim fell and was instantly submerged under the slimy waters of the festering pool; the weeds, like tentacles, grabbing him as he scrambled up for air. No sooner had he broken the surface, gasping for breath, than a grey arm clad in chain mail broke through and dragged him under again with irresistible strength.

Jim fought in vain against the force that was holding him down so effortlessly. He could feel the water beginning to pour into his lungs.

Danny ran into the bathroom when he heard Jim thrashing about. He found him lying beneath the surface of the bath, his eyes open, staring fixedly at something before him. His arms were flying everywhere, as if he was fighting off an invisible attacker.

"Shit! Ruth! The bathroom, quick!" Danny shouted.

He tried to lift Jim's head above the water but it seemed to be weighted down. Jim was giving up the fight, his arms and legs were becoming passive. Then a clear thought came to Danny. He plunged his hand into the water and pulled out the bath plug. Mercifully the Grange possessed some fierce plumbing and the bath emptied rapidly.

As soon as the water level fell below the top of Jim's head, the spell that held him drowning there was suddenly broken, and Danny was able to raise him up. Ruth rushed in at that moment and came to assist.

Jim retched and coughed up water for several minutes as he lay gasping on the bathroom floor. When his breathing and panic had eased a little, Ruth drew his head to her chest and stroked his hair.

"Oh God! ... Oh God, Ruth!" he wept, "I'll never escape him."

Chapter Twenty-Nine

Sunday, 15 December, 1996

After his ordeal in the bathtub, Jim had grown increasingly anxious about Hannah and Sophie's safety. Against the advice of the others, he'd insisted on contacting them. He tried to reach them on Erich's mobile. It didn't help at all when the answer-phone clicked in with Hannah's voice, '*Sorry, we're unable to take your call at present ...*'

"Where can they be?" Jim asked, desperately biting his lip as he returned the phone to Erich.

"They've probably gone out. Jim. You're going to have to let it go," said Ruth.

He didn't reply but his look read, 'It's easy for you to say.'

"You know, maybe it's for the best," put in Erich, "If you don't know where they are, then in all probability Niedermayer doesn't either."

Erich was relieved to see Jim nod at this, albeit hesitantly, before slumping despondently into an armchair. After a moment he looked up and said, "He wouldn't have killed me, you know ... least not yet. He was delivering a message, an object lesson in fear and control ... just demonstrating his omnipotence."

"We won't forsake you, Jim," said Millie Thorpe; Mary, at her side, was nodding in solidarity.

Jim found their loyalty touching. And despite his anxiety level running high he couldn't help smiling. There seemed to be no limit to the Thorpe sisters' optimism.

"I think there's a good chance the police will already have Hannah and Sophie under surveillance," said Danny.

Ruth agreed, "They can provide them with far more protection than we ever could."

"Except policemen don't tend to believe in vampires," Jim replied.

"Niedermayer can't get about on his own," said Erich. "If Hannah and Sophie are in any kind of danger at all, then it'll be from his helpers. The police have their descriptions, and after what has already happened they won't be taking chances."

They had of course heard the news about Nicholas on the radio.

"But how long before the police stop watching them? After we're caught and charged as accomplices … or bundled off to an asylum raving on about the undead?"

Jim was to some extent right, and they all knew it. Niedermayer had shown them how far his hand could reach; his body was paralysed in death throughout the hours of daylight, but the intelligence stayed active like a malignant cancer; nobody doubted his determination to be avenged. Jim would need to be protected around the clock. The link with his conscious mind may have been severed, but they had just learnt that Niedermayer could infiltrate the subconscious too. Whenever Jim Latimer's thoughts drifted free, he could easily be attacked.

So far all their efforts had been to act defensively. It dawned on Erich that a change of tactic was called for. Nothing short of Niedermayer's annihilation could ever hope to restore their freedom. The only alternative was a life spent in hiding and fear.

"Where might we find Niedermayer?" asked Erich sounding like he was really eager to know.

The others looked confused.

Erich went on. "Somewhere remote I'd suspect … isolated. A place retained solely for this purpose, the contingency plan ... always ready if something like this ever happened ... perhaps kept hidden away for centuries."

"Nice theory, but how the hell could we ever hope to find it?" Jim asked sceptically, "By looking under V for vampire in the yellow pages?"

"I'd like to ask you, Jim."

"Me?"

"Yes, I believe you may already possess the answer."

Jim looked at Erich uncertainly, although he knew at once what he was talking about. "Past life stuff you mean?"

"Regression … I'd like to take you back to the place you dreamed about. The place you recalled in your dream, when Hart was younger."

"Okay. Let's do it," said Jim.

*

In a ladies' public lavatory in Birmingham city centre, a young woman waits for her friend to re-emerge from a cubicle. She passes the time

358

by combing her hair and attending to her make-up in a cracked mirror that sits above a grimy washbasin.

The friend returns from the cubicle wearing a low-cut, short velvet dress over black tights, pulling at the fabric to get it to cling more smoothly about her hips.

"What d'you think, Shar?" she asks.

"Se - xy," replies Sharon, "Lee won't be able to keep his hands off you. You'll be spending Christmas Eve on your back."

The two girls laugh uproariously.

"Well, it is Christmas. You know, peace and goodwill to all men," her friend Jackie says, and the two girls explode into another peel of laughter. Jackie suddenly points to her feet, absurdly out of place in a pair of leopard-skin Doc Martens, "Don't you think they finish the outfit off?"

They giggle. Jackie returns to the cubicle to change back into her jeans.

Sharon hears her friend let out a gasp. "Okay, Jack?" she calls somewhat distractedly, taking a momentary pause from brushing mascara onto her lashes.

"Get ... get the attendant Sharon, I think someone might be hurt!"

Sharon doesn't respond immediately, watching her friend back out of the cubicle in the mirror, before going to see what has caused the reaction. On the cubicle floor a pool of blood is spreading under the partition wall from the adjacent toilet. Jackie is stepping out gingerly, trying not to get the blood on herself, making exaggerated toddler-like steps in her clumsy footwear. Sharon runs for the attendant. Meanwhile Jackie rescues the bag that contains her clothing from the toilet cistern.

"Someone must be hurt," Sharon is saying to the woman she returns with. The attendant, who resembles a retired eastern European field athlete from the Cold War era, takes a set of keys from the hip pocket of her overalls.

The middle-aged woman taps on the closed cubicle door and calls out in an unlikely high-pitched voice totally at odds with her physique, "Are you alright in there, dear?"

No reply comes back.

"I'm going to have to open the door!" the attendant warns. She places the service key into the lock, stepping back as the door swings open under its own volition. Sharon and Jackie, cowering for protection behind the amply-proportioned older woman, hold onto each other's arms for support.

The onlookers' jaws drop open.

Sitting upright, her legs splayed out, head stretched back onto the toilet cistern, is a young woman stripped to her petticoat. Her mouth has been covered over with a thick strip of adhesive tape, and what must account for a whole roll of toilet paper is wrapped about her neck and folded in piles on her lap to soak up the blood that has poured out from her slit throat.

All together, in chorus, the three women scream.

*

Harris was most definitely feeling the strain. The body count was rising hourly and unimaginable numbers were being retrieved from the graves at Barnswick Square. She had lost a forensic man, two good officers and a civilian doctor, not to mention their detained person. Each line of inquiry her team had pursued was met with a dead end. The hundreds of man-hours already spent interviewing members of Loxton's paedophile network and the Niedermayer & Hart employees had produced absolutely nothing. She felt like she was in charge of an investigation going nowhere.

She was in little doubt that her head was on the block. In such appalling cases, with the perpetrators still at large, someone must inevitably be blamed. The tabloids were having a field day; Frith and O'Malley's killer had gotten clean away, and Cureton's escape bid had made her department look incompetent. She could easily visualise the Shadow Home Secretary, smugly rising to his feet in Parliament to berate his opposite number over the scandalous failings of his police force. Then, after the rhetoric and insults, an inquiry would be launched and a sacrificial victim found. And the one thing for which Markland could be relied on was ensuring that none of the mud would stick to him.

The traffic into south London was bearable, it being a Sunday, and Harris found the street without any trouble. It was close to Clapham Common tube. The house was shabbily prominent, through its lack of care and maintenance, amidst a smart Victorian terrace. The box sashes and period features so elegantly visible on its companion houses had been replaced here with aluminium louvres and stone cladding, probably dating back a couple of decades.

She pressed the doorbell, and was surprised to find from its battered condition that it actually worked. A male voice could be heard shouting muffled instructions from upstairs, followed by the gentle padding of feet along the hallway. As the door opened, stale cooking odours wafted into Harris' face, redolent of a lamb stew left simmering for days.

The open door revealed a tiny woman in her seventies, her shortness accentuated by a curvature of the spine that made Harris' knees her focal point.

"Yes?" enquired the elderly woman. She was dressed in a pink house-coat with pink fluffy slippers on her feet.

"I have an appointment with Professor Quigley ..." Harris started to explain.

A man's head suddenly appeared over the upstairs banister, and peering down enquired, "Chief Inspector?" Allowing Harris no time to affirm or deny this he added, "Do come up!" Then, pronouncing his words far louder as though commanding his pet Doberman to stand down, he said, "It's for me, mother!"

Mrs Quigley shimmied to one side allowing Harris to pass.

"Thank you," said Harris.

"You're welcome," mumbled Quigley's mother.

When Harris reached the top of the stairs Professor Quigley, classics scholar and British Museum expert on mediaeval documents, awaited her.

"Michael Quigley," he said, thrusting out his hand.

"Susan Harris. Thanks for helping us at such short notice, and for agreeing to see me at home on your day off."

"My pleasure. Please, come into the study."

Professor Quigley was in his early fifties, but looked to Harris like one of those academics who had settled comfortably into this age-range before abandoning short trousers.

Quigley's study was a few steps along the landing. The room itself was dingy and densely packed, bookshelves lining the walls, with every available surface including the floor adorned with books and papers. There was no desk as such, but four small round tables had been strategically set around the room, their surfaces awash in scholarly material. It was like entering a literary assault course; you couldn't stride through this man's study, you had to negotiate.

Harris was invited to sit in an armchair next to a standard lamp. The professor took up residence in an ancient office chair displaying more gaffer tape than fabric in places.

"Is the manuscript going to be of any interest to us?" Harris asked, getting to the point at once.

Quigley cleared his throat before speaking, "I can't honestly imagine it's going to prove much help to you, Chief Inspector." He coughed nervously, the cough followed by an excited smile, "But it is a most fascinating discovery. I'd go as far as to say unprecedented. Almost certainly authentic ... although as you'll appreciate the manuscript must undergo tests to be certain."

"When you spoke to DI Robson you told him it was thirteenth century."

"Yes, very early thirteenth, written in the uncluttered Cistercian style."

"It was written by a monk?"

"Monastics were about the only people in the Middle Ages able to read and write. The manuscript was taken down in the form of a letter."

"You mean it was dictated?"

"Yes," replied Quigley, "To a monk named Anselm in the abbey of Valle Crucis."

Harris looked uncertain.

"It's near Llangollen, North Wales. Like all Cistercian houses, the monastery was built in an isolated spot ... Valle Crucis lies at the base of the Horseshoe Pass."

"Is the person who dictated the letter given a name?"

"He refers to himself as Hugh."

"Do you have a translation I could read?" Harris asked.

"Yes of course," he replied. Professor Quigley rose enthusiastically from his chair and began to ferret through a pile of papers on one of the circular tables. "I was looking at it earlier," he apologised as he went fumbling on, "It's quite a treat, a real insight into just how superstitious the mediaeval mind was."

"Superstitious?"

"Aha!" exclaimed Quigley, producing a page of typewritten translation. "Oh yes! There's a little gem here ..." he chuckled, "Sanguinemhauriens daemon." He translated the phrase for Harris as he passed the document to her, "Blood-drinking demon."

Harris experienced a sudden twinge in her stomach at the same moment as there came a timid tap on the door.

"Enter!" commanded the Professor.

Mrs Quigley meekly shuffled in carrying a tray bearing two cups of milky coffee and a plate of four digestive biscuits.

*

Harris and Wain believed that group B, the vigilantes, had gone to ground somewhere near the vicinity of their homes.

"Someone's got to be hiding them ... someone not yet in our picture," Frank had told her. They had been discussing the previous evening's disaster in Cureton's cell prior to the morning briefing. "I'd like to go over their homes again. There has to be something we're missing."

While Harris went off for her meeting with Professor Quigley, Frank met up with Patterson and Thorn at Jim Latimer's cottage. They looked into everything, every drawer and cupboard, even going as far as sifting through the contents of the dustbins. When Frank was satisfied Jim's cottage was hiding nothing, they moved on to Ruth's.

As he searched through the drawer of a writing-desk in Ruth's bedroom, Frank came across a small book of Persian spiritual writings with the inscription inside its cover:

To Ruth,

Friend and fellow traveller,

All our love,

The Sisters

They left the cottages then moved on to Danny Ledermann's studio. There was a plain calendar hanging above Danny's sink that was still on November. Wain flicked the page over and saw scrawled there in pencil the words:

Prune apples for sisters

"Do you prune apple trees in December?"

"Don't know, Frank," replied Patterson, turning to his partner and asking, "Do you prune trees in December?"

"Dunno," said Thorn.

"Any record of any sisters?" Frank asked.

Patterson and Thorn consulted their notebooks. They had come across women during the inquiry who may have had sisters, but nothing more specific.

"What about nuns, religious sisters?" asked Thorn.

363

"Possible. I want you to go through your notes, double check with everyone you've interviewed. Find out if anyone knows anything about any sisters?"

Frank left Patterson and Thorn at Danny's place and went on to Erich's bungalow alone. As he got out of the car he noticed an elderly woman watching him from the bungalow across the road. This was the woman who had given them a description of Picton after she had been woken by the sound of a car screeching outside.

*

"Mrs Wood?" Frank enquired of the wrinkled face that was eyeing him suspiciously over a door-chain, "I'm Detective Inspector Wain, Sussex Police." He produced identification.

"I spoke to two policemen, I told them everything," she replied tersely.

"Yes, my colleagues. I'd like another word with you if it's convenient. May I come in?"

Grudgingly he was admitted.

As Harris was always quick to point out, nobody could schmooze an elderly female witness quite like Frank. Five minutes later, Mrs Wood had the kettle on and the lid was off her Bourbon biscuits.

"So how long have you known Erich Ledermann, Enid?"

"Ever since he moved here ... lovely man is Erich, you know, really genuine."

"What about the son?"

"Danny. Danny takes after his father, lovely young man Danny ... lovely nature."

"Do you know any of the other people who call at Erich's?" asked Frank patiently.

"I don't know his hypnotherapy clients, they just come and go."

"Do his friends call by regularly?"

"Ruth comes every week."

"You know Miss Allinson?"

"Oh yes ... she's a lovely person."

"Can you think of any other friends he has?"

Enid Wood thought hard, really wanting to assist the nice policeman. She shook her head, "No, sorry."

"Not to worry, you can always ring me if you remember something," Wain drained the remaining liquid in his cup and got to his feet, "Thank you for talking to me Enid, you've been most helpful, and thanks for the tea. It's really cold outside, but thanks to you I'm all warmed up."

"Ruth's psychic, did you know?"

"Is she?" he asked innocently, having recently rifled through two shelves of her books on the subject.

"She helped me two years ago when I got shingles."

"How did she do that?"

"She gave me spiritual healing."

"Really?"

"Through the healing circle."

"Circle?"

"The sisters organise it."

"Sisters?"

"Lovely women they are ..."

*

Harris was heading back towards Brighton. It should still have been daylight but the sky was so overcast with snow clouds that she needed her headlights on.

She was feeling distinctly uncomfortable.

Sanguinemhauriens daemon

Professor Quigley had repeated the phrase several times with relish. "I suppose it's a way of saying vampire," he'd chortled.

"Pull yourself together, Susan!" she'd remonstrated with herself and switched the car radio on for the three o'clock news.

'*... Earlier today a woman was found murdered in a public convenience in Birmingham City Centre. The woman is believed to have been part of a Salvation Army band collecting for the homeless. The killer stole her uniform and is still at large. A police spokesman said a murder hunt was underway. The crime was described as vicious and despicable. People in the Midlands area are being warned to be on their guard. The CBI has today released figures that contradict the Government's ...*'

Harris' phone rang. She switched the radio off.

"Susan, I believe I've found the Ledermanns," Frank said eagerly.

"Where?" she asked; her mind was suddenly crashing up a few gears.

"Herstmonceux ... a house called The Grange. I haven't approached it yet. There are three cars in the driveway, couldn't see the number plates, but two fit the descriptions for Ledermann major and minor."

"Whose house is it?"

"Two sisters, Mary and Millie Thorpe. They're friends with Erich Ledermann and Ruth Allinson. They're a couple of latter-day saints, from what I've just been told … hold a healing group in their home once a week."

"I'm going to detour over there," Harris consulted her watch, "I'll be there around four. Just sit tight and watch the house till I get to you."

"Shall I call Patterson and Thorn in for back up?"

Harris considered for a moment. A series of distracting images was coursing through her mind; Frith's puppet-like body emerging from the docking bay, discovering the lead coffin in its secret chamber, and those bite marks on Ian Rice's neck.

Sanguinemhauriens daemon.

"Do nothing Frank. I want to speak with them alone."

*

Frank looked at his watch. It was 4.05pm. Susan was late, but he wasn't surprised, road conditions were worsening everywhere. The snow the weathermen had been promising for days had started to fall. A thin white layer was already covering the road and hedgerows.

Frank had parked beside a gate to a field about a hundred yards from the Grange. From his position he was able to see the driveway clearly.

He saw the trim dark figure the instant she emerged out of the blurring haze and came into vision. She looked rather solemn, he thought, picking her way along the lane, large flakes of snow settling on the shoulders of her overcoat.

"Shit!" he exclaimed, when the woman paused before the driveway. He considered rushing out of the car to stop her, but thought better of it, realising he might blow the whole exercise if he acted rashly.

Anyway, it was only the Sally Army collecting at Christmas.

The woman looked around, and for a second Frank thought she'd noticed him. A combination of the snow, the failing light and the shadow cast by the rim of her bonnet made the young woman's features impossible to make out. A second later and she'd disappeared into the driveway.

Salvation was on its way.

Chapter Thirty

Sunday, 15 December, 1996

Picton was parked-up along the street, a discreet distance from Hannah and Sophie Latimer's house. He'd been waiting for their return for more than four hours. However, Picton loved his work and rarely felt bored by its requirements.

His means of transportation was now a small blue van with squeaky-clean credentials. Unlike his previous 'old reliable' its interior hadn't been fitted out by his own fair hands, and he knew for certain it would prove too cramped for Mr Niedermayer's longer-term requirements. But as was usual in such matters, Picton hadn't been consulted.

From time to time, to keep himself amused, Picton hummed the odd snippet of a song. Over the afternoon, he'd done an uncommonly large amount of thinking, mainly to do with Rosemary's disappearance. 'I wouldn't want to be in her shoes … not when 'his nibs' wakes up and discovers her AWOL!' He'd happily reminded himself of this fact over and over again. The thought of Rosemary in hot water filled Picton with a nice warm feeling inside, 'She's going to suffer for this!'

When Rosemary had left in one of the new cars just after first light, Picton had guessed immediately what she was planning to do. He hadn't tried to stop her.

'Let her get on with it, kill Latimer and his chums. Who cares?' he chuckled. ''His nibs' certainly won't like it though.'

As for any sense of sadness regarding the late Nicholas, Picton had none. In fact, now the brat was gone for good he could hardly believe his luck. 'Disgusting little runt. Wish I could have been there and watched him croak.'

But it was the idea of Rosemary being out of favour with Mr Niedermayer that he liked most of all. Especially as it was over Nicholas, who he'd always loathed. 'It'll be like old times again. I've served him longest … I was there before any of them. I do all the important stuff.'

Picton jealously guarded the position of trust Mr N had long ago bestowed on him and he smiled possessively as he thought of this. 'When he catches her, he'll make her eat her own liver,' he imagined, picturing it with glee.

It was just after 4pm when Hannah and Sophie got home. The road was pretty full and Hannah had to leave their car a good distance from where they lived.

Picton observed the mother and daughter as they walked listlessly back to their house with a few bags of shopping. "Ooh … oh dear, a bit sad, are we?" he said, aloud in mock sympathy. He'd accurately interpreted the body language.

Another vehicle arrived on the street a few moments after Hannah and Sophie entered their house.

'Cop's come back too.'

Picton was skilful at sizing up and reading situations, but then he did have a great deal of experience. Anyway, cop or no cop, it made no difference as far as Picton was concerned.

Occasionally during the last hour he'd started to think that perhaps the wife and daughter might not return today. With heavy snow forecast this could easily have proved a nuisance. But in the end it had worked out fine. 'Things usually do work out if you're patient,' he reflected philosophically, 'Like Rosemary and the brat finally getting their come-uppance!' In fact the Latimer females couldn't have returned at a more convenient time. Because Picton rarely initiated a plan before it was properly dark.

A hefty snow-flake floated down onto the van's windscreen and distracted him for a moment. After this, despite fast falling snow he gave his full attention to the policeman backing his car into a parking space.

"I'll deal with him first."

*

Danny Ledermann reached the front door before the Salvationist had time to knock. Jim's hypnotherapy session was already underway in the library. Erich had asked for them not to be disturbed. Ruth and the sisters were upstairs, taking the opportunity to get some rest.

'I think I can take on the Sally Army,' Danny thought with a smile as he sprinted into the hall. He propped the shotgun up against the wall, safely out of the caller's line of vision. Then he slid back the door latch and opened the door.

The poor young woman looked chilled to the bone. Her cheeks and lips were tinged blue and a fine dusting of snow clung to her uniform.

Rosemary looked the part perfectly; a wolf in lamb camouflage.

"Good afternoon. I'm collecting for the homeless at Christmas," her teeth chattered authentically and she was shivering as she spoke. "Could you spare something?" she asked meekly. The appeal concluded with a warm smile proclaiming an inner godliness.

Danny dipped his hands into his pockets. He should have known from experience what a fruitless search it would be.

"Er ... I ..." said Danny, looking slightly awkward.

"Please don't worry if you haven't got anything," responded the young woman. At the same time Rosemary's right hand clasped the knife handle in her pocket.

Danny suddenly remembered seeing some spare change on the sideboard in the kitchen. "It's okay. I'll get something. Just a moment," he said. He had no inkling this observation had just won him a reprieve.

Once Danny's back was turned, the mask dropped and her eyes re-adjusted to their default setting of ice cold. As soon as he was out of sight, Rosemary crossed the threshold. She spotted the shotgun and allowed her facial muscles to form the semblance of a smile. Rosemary released her grip on the knife then took up the gun and checked it was loaded. She appreciated briefly in her mind's eye the new weapon's potential for harm, especially to flesh and bone.

She heard a voice coming from the room to her right. The accent made it easily identifiable as belonging to Ledermann. She would deal with him soon.

Her reasons for coming were personal. She had been hurt in the only way she could be, through Nicholas. The only surviving droplet of warmth in her whole being had been preserved for him alone. It was the only thing that could make her disobey Mr Niedermayer and be prepared to suffer his wrath. Nicholas, her idol, was dead, through Latimer and his friends' interference. They must pay, and before they died she would see them squeal like pigs at the abattoir gate.

Danny was gone for less than half a minute. He returned with his head down, busily counting a pile of assorted change in the palm of his hand. When he looked up and saw the shotgun barrels staring into his eyes, his mouth dropped open and the money fell to the floor. He had never seen Rosemary Hines before but there could be no mistaking her. She was framed in the open doorway against a backdrop of snowflakes in the fast fading light. It was the most corrupt sight he had ever known; the integrity of the Salvationist uniform contrasting with the malevolent intent written on her face.

"In there!" she spat, gesturing towards the library.

Danny hesitated.

"I'll kill you straight off if you'd prefer," she said, as if she was making a reasonable offer.

Danny complied. His legs were shaking. He opened the door and stepped into the library. Erich, who was sitting on the sofa beside a sleeping Jim, looked surprised by the intrusion. When he noticed the shotgun at his son's back and then saw who held it there, surprise became shock.

"Scared? You should be. Get face down on the floor. Both of you!"

They did as ordered. Rosemary closed the library door behind her. She was clearly infuriated that Jim had managed to sleep through her entrance, and stormed over to confront him.

"Wake up!" she commanded, prodding him with the gun barrel. When this failed to have any effect, she began shouting with more intensity, "Fucking wake up!" She shook him violently and proceeded to kick his shins. He didn't budge.

"He can't respond," said Erich, craning his head up from the floor.

"Did I fucking ask you?" she snapped back. Rosemary, now looking dangerously unhinged lashed out with a foot at Erich's cheek.

Erich shrieked and was momentarily blinded with pain.

"Why then?" she asked.

Erich, his head in confusion following the assault, failed to reply quite swiftly enough. Rosemary kicked him in the ribs. The blow produced a groan succeeded by coughing.

"Vhy? ... Vhy can't he respond?" she asked, imitating his accent.

Erich groaned out, "He's hypnotised. I've put him into a deep trance."

Rosemary squatted beside Erich, resting the gun barrel on the floor. She gripped a handful of the old man's hair and jerked back his head. She was now staring dementedly into his eyes. "You'd better fucking wake him, then!" she said.

Danny seizing the opportunity, with Rosemary momentarily off her guard, sprang to his feet and dived at her. But swift though Danny was, his target responded like an uncoiling spring. Rosemary was out of range a split second before Danny reached her. She then swung the shotgun across her body and jabbed its butt into the young man's chin. The blow sent him flying into the nearest wall. Some shelving collapsed under the impact, showering books and splinters of wood down onto Danny and the floor.

Rosemary raised the gun barrels at Danny's face. Her intention was clear.

"No! Oh God no!" pleaded Erich, "Please no, not Danny! Not my son!"

She held the pose steadily for a moment as if to maximise gratification. Then a change suddenly overtook her, as if Erich's plea for clemency had reminded her of something. When she lowered the shotgun again, there was a look of confusion in her eyes.

"I had a son," she stated flatly. At the same time tiny pearls of moisture appeared in each eye. However, this unexpected display of emotion concluded almost as rapidly as it began. In the very next instant, Rosemary's rage began to simmer up to boiling point again, "It was him!" she shouted, pointing the gun at Jim Latimer, "That bastard's interference ... his fucking snooping killed my love!"

She stepped forward and rammed the shotgun barrels beneath the unconscious man's chin.

"I can wake him for you!" Erich cried out. It was all he could think of to stall for time.

There followed a white knuckle moment of terrible uncertainty.

"Okay," she nodded matter-of-factly before removing the gun from Jim Latimer's throat.

Erich, in some pain and trembling with fear, breathed a sigh of relief. It was short lived.

Rosemary, her deranged face showing only blankness, glanced casually down at Erich on the floor, "I think I'll kill your son first. Then you'll understand what it feels like."

As she took aim at the semi-conscious Danny, Erich made a desperate grab for the gun barrel. He clung to it as any loving father would with a son's life dependent on it. Rosemary, displaying no emotion, clubbed the side of his head with her fist. A stream of blood began trickling from Erich's ear, but still he hung on. She kicked him twice in the abdomen before his strength finally gave way and he fell back to the floor. But Erich still attempted to get up even then. Rosemary put down this final rebellion by smashing the back of her hand across his face.

She looked down contemptuously at the miserable worm grovelling before her, before raising the gun at Danny once again.

"Oh, God no! Please!" Erich pleaded. He was scrambling to raise himself even though his limbs had lost all power.

371

But no begging would stay Rosemary's hand this time. With the gun barrels poised, pointing directly at Danny's head, vengeance was hers.

The weak cry, "Melisend!" that came from a point directly behind her was almost inaudible. But Rosemary must have heard it quite distinctly because her mouth fell open as though a ghost had just whispered in her ear.

The voice came again, and this time Erich heard it too.

"Melisend? Melisend? Is it you, Melisend?"

Jim had now risen to his feet. An invisible veil seemed to be cast across his eyes and he spoke in an altered tone; yet strangely, it was still his own voice. The voice also brought a sense of time and distance; like someone who was trying to be heard from a great way off.

Rosemary's features had drained of colour and her eyes took on a confused look. She lowered the shotgun to her side and turned.

Jim and Rosemary were face to face, staring at each other like a pair of sleepwalkers.

"You could not help it ... I was the one who betrayed Hugh!" Jim cried out, falling to his knees in supplication, "Forgive me, forgive me for being weak ... I might have saved you both."

It was as though a dream from long ago had suddenly pierced the armour plating that shrouded her mind. She began to shake; past memories appeared to be rising up like harpies to overwhelm her. A strangulated sound came from her throat.

"Please Melisend ... Melisend, forgive me."

"Shut up! Shut up!" she screamed.

At that moment the library door crashed open as Frank Wain, propelled by his own force, rolled across the floor. Susan Harris, coming a split second after him, kneeled in the doorway and targeted Rosemary in her pistol sights.

"Drop the weapon!" she shouted, in a voice half an octave above her normal pitch.

Erich couldn't be sure, but he thought as she turned he caught a glimpse of something unexpected in Rosemary's face; a look resembling relief. There certainly wasn't any doubt in his mind that the woman knew her time was come. With cool precision, but with movement far slower than she'd shown herself capable of, she took aim at Harris.

Harris didn't hesitate. She blew a hole directly between the woman's eyes.

Rosemary absorbed the bullet like a statue carved in wood. For a moment nothing happened. Then the shotgun dropped from her hand, her upper body swayed, she toppled, and crashed to the floor face down.

"Forgive me Melisend ... please forgive me!" cried Jim.

Chapter Thirty-One

Sunday, 15 December, 1996

Hannah Latimer jumped when the doorbell rang.

The strain of the previous four days was visible in her face. It was the endless dangling, waiting for news, some word, which made it so damned hard. She knew the man she'd married was no murderer or child pornographer; but inevitably, little doubts crept insidiously into her mind. The old conundrum: how well do we know anyone? In fairness to Hannah, any question marks regarding Jim, Ruth or Erich were quickly dispelled.

The pressure was telling on Sophie too. She had been so upset that she had moved into her mother's bed, but neither of them had managed to get much sleep since Thursday. Hannah found herself making crude attempts to take her daughter's mind off Jim's disappearance. Earlier that afternoon they had probably looked like a pair of stray mourners from a funeral party amidst the bustle of Oxford Street.

Hannah was preparing trout for supper when the doorbell went. For a moment she became uncharacteristically flustered and looked uncertain about how to deal with the slimy wetness left on her hands by the fish. She felt a sudden contraction in her stomach when she heard Sophie's feet pummelling the staircase in descent.

"It's alright, Soph. I'll get it!" Hannah shouted to her daughter, plunging her hands into a bowl of soapy water, and agitating them together in its suds.

"I'm there now," was Sophie's reply.

Hannah didn't want her daughter to answer the door. She feared it might be the police with some bad news, or, as had happened yesterday, another tacky newspaper hack ready to pounce with a gem like, "Did your father ever touch you in a way you didn't like?"

Hannah heard the door being opened and an exchange of indistinct words. She was straining to listen as she shook the drips of water from her fingertips. After a few seconds all fell silent, except for the sound of the front door closing again.

Hannah dried her hands on a tea towel and asked, "Who was that, Soph?"

No reply.

"Soph? ... Who was that, darling?" she called, using a little more voice as she walked through the dining-room.

"Only me, darling," replied Picton.

Hannah leapt back in shock as the stockily-framed man appeared in the doorway. He had a navy blue hat pulled down low on his forehead and looked just like the identikit images in the papers. Hannah felt her whole frame begin to tremble.

Picton smiled; notoriety brought with it at least a few pleasurable advantages. Hannah let out a gasp of horror when she saw him replace the safety cap on a hypodermic needle.

"What have you done to my daughter?" Hannah screamed as she rushed at him, lashing out with her fists at his face in an attempt to get past.

Picton let the syringe fall from his hand in order to contain the woman's flailing arms. He drew her in tightly to him with a muscular arm and covered her mouth with his free hand.

"I like a bit of spirit," he said.

*

Danny's encounter with the bookcase had woken up Ruth and the Thorpe sisters. They met outside their bedrooms and immediately started downstairs. On the staircase they were alarmed to hear a woman's angry voice coming from the library. The front door had been left open and snow was billowing into the hallway. It hardly required the skills of a world-class sleuth to work out what was happening. Exactly what Ruth and the sisters might have done under the circumstances fortunately didn't come to the test. Before the three women arrived at the bottom step, a man and a woman carrying handguns had already slipped into the hallway.

Susan Harris flashed her identity card towards them, signing for them to remain silent and to stay where they were. She proceeded to take a look through the keyhole in the library door before exchanging whispered plans with Frank. He peered through the keyhole himself and cautiously turned the doorknob to check if the door was open. Then with a signal to Harris he charged in, keeping himself low. Harris rushed in a second afterwards and they heard her shout a command before firing.

Unable to remain on the sidelines, Ruth and the sisters entered the library just seconds after Rosemary Hines hit the floor. The three women were speechless at the grim spectacle confronting them.

Frank Wain was checking Rosemary's pulse to make certain she was dead, although there could be little doubt. A red pool was growing about her head like some sort of diabolic halo. Jim was still on his knees weeping inconsolably. Susan Harris was assisting an unusually frail-looking Erich back onto his feet. The sisters, seeing Danny was injured, rushed to help him. He was blinking his eyes, still dazed, probing with fingers for the source of bleeding in his mouth.

Ruth, mesmerised by the sight of the deceased Rosemary, couldn't help stating the obvious, "She's wearing a Salvation Army uniform!"

"She murdered a young woman in Birmingham earlier today," replied Wain. He had heard about it himself from Susan, just moments before their entrance.

Susan Harris settled Erich on the sofa. "Danny ... is Danny alright?" he called across the room to the sisters in concern.

"Danny will be fine," Millie answered as she inspected the wounded upper lip his teeth had bitten into.

"What about you, Mr Ledermann?" Harris asked, surprised to discover she already possessed an inexplicable admiration for this old man.

"I'm alright," he answered, "It's Danny I'm concerned about." Then, taking in the weeping Jim, he added, "And poor Jim of course."

"I heard him mention a name ... a woman's name?" said Harris.

"Something like Millicent or Mellicent I think ... Danny would be dead now if it had not been for that name." Erich shook his head as if to dispel the unthinkable.

Harris took a mobile from her pocket, "I'll get you both a doctor."

"Please wait," implored Erich, reaching out a hand in the direction of the phone, "We have very little time to spare. Danny ... Danny, would you be able to hang on for a bit?"

"I'm fine Dad," understated Danny, who'd just discovered two teeth missing from his upper jaw.

Erich looking directly at Harris said, "This is the best chance we're ever likely to have to catch Niedermayer."

"Niedermayer? Mr Ledermann, there never was a Niedermayer," stated Harris.

"I know ... I know that's probably not his real name," replied Erich before asking, "You are Chief Inspector Harris, right?"

She nodded.

"It was Niedermayer who was hiding in the house and killed your colleagues. We tried to warn you. There was no way you could have stopped him ... Niedermayer is already dead ... he's a vampire."

Wain with a bemused look glanced up at Harris. His incredulity turning to confusion when he realised the only objection she was about to make to this ludicrous statement was an expression of discomfort.

"What's wrong with Mr Latimer?" Harris asked. She desperately wanted to move the subject away from what had just been said.

"I was in the process of regressing him."

"That's to do with past lives?"

Wain could not believe his ears. A question like that, and Harris of all people asking it.

"I think Jim came upon these people in a previous life. It must be why she responded to the name. He also mentioned someone called Hugh."

"Shall I contact headquarters, Chief Inspector?" Frank asked in a deliberately formal and pointed way to bring Susan back to earth.

"What's happening to the woman?" Harris asked Wain, although she could see perfectly well from where she was sitting that Rosemary's hair was turning white.

"Same as Cureton," said Frank.

"Half an hour isn't going to make a whole lot of difference then, is it?" she told him in an unusually dismissive tone. Harris immediately turned back to Erich and asked, "How do you expect a life experience from the past to help you find this ... this Mr Niedermayer?"

Erich nodded. "If you had a really good hiding place, wouldn't you hang on to it? But it's imperative we act quickly, before he realises what we're up to. Jim was quite fearful about his wife and daughter, he thinks Niedermayer will take his revenge out on them."

"I can allay any worries there," said Harris, "Mrs Latimer and Sophie are being watched around the clock. Believe me, they're quite safe."

*

The mother in Hannah resisted her attacker's prodigious strength long after she knew she was beaten. Paralysed by his grip on her upper body, she kicked at his shins with every last ounce of energy she possessed. Picton, seeing his victim was not about to yield, freed the hand covering her mouth and smacked it across her face with brutal force. The weight and power behind the blow sent her head spinning to the brink of consciousness. By the time everything had stopped swimming it was too late to fight. She found herself tied down, her arms and legs spread-eagled on the kitchen tabletop. The ever resourceful Picton carried pieces of polypropylene rope in his pockets at all times. It made harvesting so much easier to come prepared. He prided himself on being imaginative too; improvising a gag from a tea towel Hannah left on the table.

"Coming back to your senses, I see. Now tell me, did all that aggression get you anywhere? I think not," said Picton rhetorically.

Hannah was coughing and spluttering, her tongue paralysed by the dry cotton material packed into her mouth.

Picton was in a jovial mood. He always loved the way terror accentuated eyes.

"Your daughter wasn't anything like so feisty, but then, I don't suppose she knew what hit her."

Hannah's eyes became intensified with fear and despair.

"She's only sleeping," Picton assured, "Just a sedative to keep her quiet. She's not my department. My ... er ... associate," Picton felt proud of himself for choosing such an interesting word, "He'll decide how to use her. He's very partial to the young ... young blood," he added with a chuckle. "Young people have so much life in them."

Tears were streaming from Hannah's eyes. If she'd been able to speak she would have tried bargaining, not for her life, but for her daughter's.

Picton could guess what she was thinking, and her fearful thoughts were like soothing music to him, very satisfying. However, Picton only really obsessed about one thing: the taste of his master's blood. The sadism was vocational.

"Myself I prefer my women a bit older," Picton said. He began to run a hand along the inside of Hannah's leg, his course fingers snagging against the smoothness of her stockings. Hannah braced herself, but his hand came to a stop a few inches above the knee.

"But I forget myself," he said looking about as sensual as a shark, "Business and pleasure don't mix." Picton assumed a more business-like manner for the rest of the victimisation session, "Your husband, Mrs Latimer, has caused our family firm a good deal of trouble, and I was asked by my employer to pay you a visit. He wanted me to pass on his calling card so to speak."

He removed his hand from Hannah's leg and brought his face in close. His bad breath was polluting her nostrils. "I'll come back soon," he whispered in her ear intimately. "But before I go I want to leave you something to remember me by."

The leering eyes disappeared from Hannah's direct line of vision as his face hovered slowly down her neck and shoulder and along her arm. She flinched when the wetness of his lips touched her fingertips. She clenched her fist, but he soon pulled her wedding finger free with his strong hands.

The sensation of his warm saliva as he sucked around the gold band on her finger made her want to vomit. She felt the ring slip up above the lower finger joint. When he bit down, her body exploded in a convulsion of excruciating agony. She very nearly choked on the gag in her mouth.

Picton took the prize from his mouth, its gold ring still attached. His mouth and teeth were livid with blood.

"A memento," he said, dropping the dismembered finger into the breast pocket of his shirt.

Hannah Latimer passed out.

*

Mary Thorpe was closing the curtains in the drawing-room. Outside the snow was falling fast, arranging itself in mounds against the window panes. Frank noticed a handmade cross was sitting on its central bar. He'd noticed one attached to the front door and the library window too. Anyone might assume these were expressions of a devout faith, unless they knew better.

A long list of unexplained details was processing its way through Wain's mind at that moment. Since mention of the word vampire, the secret chamber in the basement at Hove and the lead coffin it contained had loomed the largest. Then there was the forensic man O'Malley, who looked like he had been carved-up by a chainsaw, although there was nothing to suggest any blade or instrument had been used on him. The bullets fired by himself and Robson at Frith's murderer still perplexed him. He had been as sure of his target as Robson was, yet neither shot had brought the killer down.

There was so much more of course: the box in Picton's van, its lead-lined insides greasy and worn from long service and stained dark with body fluids; the severely anaemic girl on the slab in the pathology lab, systematically robbed of her blood; the decapitated corpse of DCI Rice, along with the mould Ashworth had made of those ferocious canine teeth that had torn out a chunk of the policeman's neck. The list, however, didn't end there. There was the decomposing trio of Loxton, Cureton and Hines which just couldn't be explained, the newspaper clippings that Bob Isherwood and his secretary had been murdered for, and all those tragic victims who had been reduced to ash in Niedermayer & Hart's custom-built crematorium. Yet still the list continued, with skeletons dating back almost four generations. When the ground at the Barnswick Square site had reached its saturation point with human corpses, cremation had become the only viable option.

Wain had been over every fact, each tiny detail time and time again. But only now, in this comfortable old house owned by two elderly sisters who had been sheltering a band of the most unlikely vigilantes imaginable, did he feel truly disturbed. There had been vampire jokes going around the locker room, and the press predictably had produced a clutch of sensationalist headlines, but nobody had taken it seriously, not really. Susan was suddenly bothering him quite a lot too. Her response to Ledermann when he pronounced the 'V' word had kicked the legs from under him. Harris was a pragmatist with no room in her life for superstition and touchy-feely claptrap. He was beginning to wonder what the meeting with the man from the British Museum had produced.

Frank was surprised to see Latimer awake. He entered the drawing-room closely followed by Ledermann and Susan Harris. He appeared quite normal apart from the vacancy about the eyes. Jim Latimer didn't notice Wain, or Mary Thorpe, who was plumping up cushions on an armchair in readiness for him.

Jim reached the centre of the room then stood stock still as though his legs had seized up.

"Sit here," indicated Erich. The man complied. "Sleep now."

Latimer's eyes closed immediately, his head slumping onto his chest. It was a bit like watching the instantaneous reaction of a cartoon character.

Ruth came behind Harris, helping Danny, who was holding a pad of cotton wool against his mouth. There was a lot of dried blood staining the front of his sweatshirt, but thanks to the sisters his face had been cleaned up and the bleeding almost stopped. By rights, both the Ledermanns should have seen a doctor. It was an indication of Wain's respect for Harris that he made no complaint, however questionable he considered all this.

Mary put on some table lamps, which helped create a more mellow atmosphere. Her sister Millie had fetched a tape recorder and set it up.

Erich was in the armchair opposite Jim. Harris sat nearby, out of range of Frank's disapproving eye. Everyone appeared to be ready to start. Frank decided he had better take a seat. He opted for an upright chair in the corner nearest to the door.

Erich set the tape to record, and after taking a moment to focus his thoughts he began.

"Jim, I must ask you to leave this restful place. To enter that other time again ... where you answer to another name ... know a different life."

Although the hypnotised man's eyelids remained shut, it was obvious even from where Frank was sitting that a lot of activity was going on behind them. The man's breathing began to display some signs of stress, becoming shallower and more irregular.

"Space out your inhalations ... breathe evenly. There is nothing to be frightened of, you are amongst friends. You need to do this, Jim ... for yourself, for all of us ... for the safety of your wife and daughter."

'That's a bit low. Using emotional blackmail,' thought Wain.

Latimer's breathing began to pace itself.

"Allow yourself to become fully acquainted with the surroundings you inhabit."

Latimer's anxiety level increased almost at once.

"Keep breathing ... breathe deeply. There's no reason to be fearful. You are safe."

Again Latimer grew calmer.

"Take a look around you, at the old but familiar world you are witnessing."

Latimer's eyes stayed shut, his slumped head made small movements to the left and right as though he was taking the instruction literally.

"Familiarise yourself, Jim ... you have a different body ... different life experiences upon which to draw from."

Latimer shifted about like an uncomfortable sleeper adjusting his posture. Then to everyone's surprise he spoke, distinctly enough to be heard, though the voice was muffled by his slouched body shape, "No ... no ... not Jim."

Wain felt his fight or flight mechanism jump second gear and go straight up into third. Wherever this was leading, Wain could not deny the moment was immensely powerful. The vestigial hairs at the back of the neck and along his spine were tingling.

"What is your name?" Erich asked.

A long pause followed.

Frank recalled seeing stuff like this before, in television dramas and pseudo documentaries. He felt a bit foolish at having been momentarily taken in by it. It had to be a con.

"An ... selm ... I am Anselm."

Wain was no longer watching Jim. He caught Harris stealing a surreptitious glance around at him. He could not recall ever seeing her more ill at ease.

382

Chapter Thirty-Two

Sunday, 15 December, 1996

"Tell us about yourself, Anselm."

"I am a brother at Valle Crucis Abbey ... I care for the poor and infirm."

"Anselm, who was ..." Erich paused; he was trying to recall the name Jim had used to get Rosemary's attention; it had sounded to him like Millicent or Mellicent, but which? Tentatively he offered, "... Mellicent?"

Jim looked uneasy; his mouth broke into a painful grimace, "Melisend ... her name was Melisend."

Erich raised an eyebrow. This was a first; being an émigré, he'd often been corrected on his pronunciation, but never by a man long dead.

Jim Latimer's eyes remained closed throughout. He spoke in a strong, clear, voice. However, his speech was at times impaired by the effect of the trance and the awkward positioning of his head as it hung slouched on his chest. Jim's relatively calm demeanour at the very start was noticeably affected by the mention of Melisend. In fact, whenever the name cropped up his anxiety level rose. Throughout the regression, Jim's breathing was regulated by an occasional prompt from Erich; mostly it remained shallow but fairly even; however it could change quickly and dramatically when Anselm was very troubled. During these periods his breathing often became so rapid that he was literally gasping for breath.

From the point of view of the others, believers and sceptics, it was uncomfortable to watch. The sheer ordinariness of the process, lack of any showbiz-style presentation, only enhanced its authenticity and power. Especially coming so soon on the heels of the ordeal in the library with Rosemary Hines; unquestionably linked somehow to the mysterious Melisend. There were times when the regression was very unsettling indeed. When under pressure Jim's face twitched uncontrollably and he had a disconcerting way of opening his mouth and stretching out his tongue as if to sample the air. It was the kind of unflattering look only possible under hypnosis, when a subject is unconscious and not applying any of the normal inhibitions.

Erich allowed Anselm some time to work through his anxiety. Then he asked softly, "Anselm, who was Melisend?"

The effect on the subject's breathing was immediate. "Melisend … was Hugh's … sister …" he panted.

Erich allowed for the man's distress to ease once again before asking, "Who was Hugh?"

"Hugh Apsley was a Templar Knight … a renegade …" Brother Anselm stopped abruptly. He seemed reluctant to proceed.

Erich prompted, "Please, Anselm, continue."

"I gave my word never to reveal the secret matters divulged to me."

"Perhaps you can tell us only those things we need to know," replied Erich.

There followed a disconcertingly long pause. During this time it seemed feasible that their witness from the past wouldn't comply, in which case they'd have made no advance whatsoever. The observers watched and waited anxiously.

Jim's face wore an agitated expression; Brother Anselm was wrestling with a troubled mind; weighing up a promise made to a friend long ago against his own deep-seated need to share the truth.

At least two minutes passed in this uncomfortable limbo. It seemed less and less likely he'd proceed. Then, quite suddenly, without any more discussion or persuasion, Anselm began, "I was asked to attend a blacksmith who had fallen sick. The forge where he lived was about a league to the east of the Abbey. I worked on the man throughout the night aided by his wife, who made up teas and poultices under my direction. An hour before dawn his fever broke.

"I should have listened to the woman and waited until it was light before beginning my homeward journey. The land was frozen, besieged by icy winds that made travelling difficult and paths treacherous. By the time dawn came I had covered only half the distance to the Abbey. I felt miserable as I made my way, regretting the warm hearth I had forsaken for that bitter morning.

"There was a thick ground mist in the valley. I was following the route along the river bank when I suddenly came upon a mare standing alone. She was bridled and heavily laden. The poor creature was cold and very agitated. I stroked her for a time to help ease her distress. As I looked around for signs of the beast's owner I discerned shapes through the mist upon the frozen river. With some trepidation I travelled across the ice and came upon the body of a man. His clothes

384

were soaked and beginning to freeze on him. I took him as dead. Then I tentatively stepped forward to help make out more clearly a dark shape in the mist. In so doing I only narrowly escaped being drowned myself, for the ice started to crack beneath my feet. I quickly sped back some paces. It was then I saw that a great rift had been opened in the ice. Now, as I peered again at the black shape I discerned it to be a horse. The mist drew back for a moment allowing me a clearer view. The poor creature was frozen, its mane and muzzle flecked white with ice. Its head was contorted through torturous death agonies into a most unnatural pose. A movement from beneath the ice then caught my eye, and I saw something was trapped below. I fell to my knees and scraped away the frost from the surface. Imprisoned behind the window of ice floated a corpse. He was little more than a boy.

"It can only have been instinct that caused me to return to the first man I had already pronounced dead. I was surprised to discover not only warmth about the neck but a faint pulse that defied all outer signs. Precariously I dragged him away from the brink and across the ice to the waiting mare.

"By the time I had brought him to the Abbey, his life signs were far weaker. I held out little hope of saving him. But I would try, and enlisted the aid of two brothers for the purpose of assisting me. His left shoulder was badly injured, the collar bone protruding through the flesh. Using what modest skills I possess and my companions' strength, we set the bones to right as well we might. If the man survived, which seemed unlikely, he would never use that arm again, for its tendons were torn apart.

"My patient intrigued me from the start. Although he was outwardly dressed as a merchant, concealed beneath this garb he wore a coat of mail. He also bore the kind of sword and dagger often favoured by knights of the military orders.

"His condition was so poorly that I was given leave from my religious duties to attend on him. The fever raged in him for three days, and for much of this time he spoke deliriously. He talked as if I was his friend, a French Templar by the name of Reynald. At first I paid little attention ... I had often known minds ramble in this way. Yet this man's story was very strange ... I found myself drawn in by it. I acted wrongly, for in my desire to learn more, I deceived him ... pretended I was this Reynald. As the knight's tale unfolded I questioned him, using these deceitful means, to obtain greater detail ... and learned something of the many horrors this poor knight had known ..."

Jim broke off; Brother Anselm was showing signs of great distress. As he confessed how he'd tricked the knight into relating his story he was fighting for breath. Whatever memories were called to mind certainly shook him to the core.

The pause afforded Harris and Wain the opportunity to exchange an uncomfortable glance. They were not at all easy with what they were witnessing; or, for that matter, with just about anything to do with this case. In fact, at that moment, the whole investigation seemed completely insane. Under normal circumstances they would simply have proclaimed the whole regression thing a sham and confidence trick. Science and logic must inevitably pour scorn on it; however, scepticism didn't come quite so easily after witnessing, at first hand, two very unconventional deaths.

Frank's thoughts probably summed-up their individual response to the regression process, 'If Latimer's faking this ... if he's making it all up, the man's wasted as a photographer ... he'd be the most convincing actor who's ever lived.'

Erich spent several minutes calming down and reassuring his subject that it was safe to continue. He repeated the phrase, "You're amongst friends here ..." several times. Erich also stressed how important it was for them to hear Brother Anselm's testimony, "... We mean to help if we can."

"I swore never to reveal what I had gleaned by such unworthy means!" Anselm cried out. He went on, weeping bitterly as he said, "No man should hear such testimony if he wishes to retain any soundness of mind!"

"Please, Anselm ... please tell us what you can," urged Erich.

Jim/Brother Anselm looked hesitant. Somehow he managed to check his tears although his breathing remained rapid and distressed. He was in a highly anxious state.

Erich was required to dig deep, call upon every ounce of experience and skill he possessed as a hypnotherapist to get his subject back on track. "This is vitally important, Anselm. I believe that only you may be able to give us certain information ... this could help save countless lives. There is nobody else who can help ... nobody else was there ... if you're unable to tell us ... then we shan't be able to do anything ... a great evil that has somehow entered our world will be allowed to continue," he coaxed.

"I know ... I know that I must do this!" Jim/Brother Anselm nodded his head in agreement. However, before he would proceed he made a condition, "Yet, I will only tell those parts that need not remain secret."

"I understand. Thank you, Anselm ... please continue."

"In the city of Acre, Hugh, Knight of the Temple ... a man innocent of any crime himself, witnessed a most heinous act ... Jerome, the marshal of his house, was its chief perpetrator ... an appalling act ... an abomination!"

The mere mention of it brought a look of unmistakable terror to Jim's face. Constantly battling to suck enough air into his lungs to enable speech and with fear constricting his vocal cords, he managed somehow to splutter out, "Jerome ... rose from death ... he was no longer able to survive under the sun's light ... to sustain himself he must prey upon the living ..."

The hypnotised man was by now shaking uncontrollably. However, the monk was determined to get everything out. "... Jerome can only survive by imbibing the blood of his victims ... Hugh called him vampir."

There followed a brief pause. Erich didn't comment or interrupt.

Anselm went on, "Jerome passed on the curse to three others ... although in the cellars beneath Acre ... one of their foul brethren was destroyed. Hugh aided by his friend Reynald and one other, joined a party of brave men who swore an oath to rid the world of Jerome's creatures and their evil. After many months in pursuit they were forced to divide. The boy I had seen beneath the ice was called Yussuf. Hugh and Yussuf had followed Jerome's trail for a thousand leagues to England. Jerome had brought only his most faithful servant with him. This man, though outwardly the same as other men, is a cunning wolf within ... once a serjeant of the Templar Order ... a balding red-haired fellow ... his lord's loyal cur.

"Jerome sought vengeance upon Hugh for his persistence. They gave chase to him across the breadth of England until finally they arrived at the manor where Hugh's father was lord." At this point Anselm began to sob, "But Jerome could not be caught ... they arrived too late ... Hugh's father was already murdered ... and worse ... his sister, Melisend and her husband Rhisiart had been visiting with their three small sons ... all had perished except for Melisend ... she was taken captive."

"Breathe ... breathe," said Erich.

After a pause and several deep breaths Anselm continued, "Hugh and Yussuf in pursuit came upon a girl whose baby had been stolen by the serjeant. He had cruelly stolen the peasant's child and given it to

Melisend to take the place of her murdered infants ... Hugh and Yussuf pursued Jerome throughout the night, crossing into Wales. Then, around dawn, Hugh finally caught sight of the serjeant, and rashly charged at him ... In the heat of the moment he did not realise that he was riding upon ice and the frozen river gave way beneath his horse."

There seemed to be a flaw in Anselm's statement. "So it was Hugh then, who fell into the river?" asked Erich, confused by what seemed like a contradiction of the facts Anselm had already given them.

"Yes," Anselm replied, "As has happened on countless occasions, the rescuer bravely saved another's life yet forfeited his own ... in the act of saving his companion, the lad Yussuf, was tragically drowned.

"Hugh, weak from the fever, wept for many hours when I told him the boy was dead ... he blamed himself most bitterly. For several days afterwards this goodly man lay with his face turned towards the wall, barely willing to speak.

"One morning, a few days later, I found him stumbling about, attempting to dress, and I asked him what he was doing.

"He replied, 'There is a pressing matter I must attend to.'

"It was inconceivable that he should leave. The man was barely able to stand and almost fainting from the slightest effort. My conscience was greatly troubled because of my deception during the time of his fever. And I now admitted my secret knowledge to him. 'Are these things true, or were they the ramblings of fever?' I asked after giving my confession.

"Hugh fell back exhausted upon the pallet and shook his head, 'Perhaps some trustworthy soul should indeed know the truth,' he said. 'Sit with me and I will give it all to you. You, good Anselm, shall know everything of Hugh Apsley.'

"Where the details had been scant, I was given a full account. And when his tale was done, I swore that none should ever learn of it from my lips. However, to know the truth in this matter was itself a curse ... far better half-knowing ... to believe it the ramblings of a feverish mind.

"I persuaded Hugh to stay his departure, assuring him that his strength would improve. I knew he intended to pursue Jerome and the serjeant, and a chill came to my blood when I thought of such evil. I made enquiries amongst my companions at the Abbey concerning Hugh's brother-in-law, Rhisiart. Our house had only recently been established; many came and went, for the Abbey was still in the process of being built. Brother Arwain, our provisioner, a Welshman himself, knew this Rhisiart. He described a strong, good-faced fellow in possession of a sizeable holding who had wed an English nobleman's daughter. Rhisiart's house lay three leagues south west of the Abbey.

"I passed on this information to Hugh ... but he seemed unenthusiastic to receive it.

"'Rhisiart is dead, as by now is my sister,' he said.

"'I have given this matter some thought,' I told him. 'Rhisiart's holding according to Arwain is in an isolated place, it would be a perfect spot to hide and remain undiscovered. I have found myself asking why it is that such a fiend allowed your sister to live?'

"Hugh replied, 'Most likely because it was the best means of ensuring that I suffered.'

"'That may be so,' I told him, 'Yet another reason may be that under Welsh law a wife may inherit her deceased husband's property. You said this Jerome was cunning ... do you not think he may have more to gain by keeping your sister alive?'

"By providing this insight, I only succeeded in making my patient more restless. However, he promised to resist leaving the Abbey until I considered him ready. He aided his own recovery by taking up light work around the Abbey. And as his health was restored he undertook some heavier duties, in preparation for the ordeal ahead. The mere possibility that Melisend was still alive brought him renewed vigour. Yet he never thought to consider the price she would have paid in order to survive under such a tyrant.

"After three weeks, he could be delayed no longer and reluctantly I pronounced him fit. However, I had decided that he should not venture forth alone, and resolved to go with him as support. I told the Abbot that Hugh was searching for his sister, and begged leave to accompany him. The Abbot, ever a generous man, agreed.

"When I told Hugh of my intention he would not hear of it. I told him I must go, that knowing his tale demanded it, else I should never again live at peace with my soul.

"'I hoped that if I did not return you might send word on my behalf to Reynald,' Hugh said.

"'That problem is easily solved,' I answered, and fetched some writing materials. I took down a letter and sealed it up, placing it with the Abbot for safe-keeping. It would be despatched to Reynald de Sauveterre in the town of Albi if we did not return within seven days.

"The fierce weather had not abated one jot during the time of Hugh's confinement in the Abbey, and the land was still locked beneath ice. On the morning of our departure we rose many hours before dawn and prayed in the chapel. Afterwards Hugh went to where the mare was stabled, stroking and talking to her as though bidding farewell to an old friend. He had donated the beast to the Abbey out of gratitude for his care.

"He said, 'I am sad to leave her. The brave creature has known many dark days. It is the best I can do for her. Yussuf loved this horse.'

"The treacherous weather made the three leagues before us seem like ten, and some of the ways were so slippery that we were forced to take alternative routes to circumvent them. Hugh's infirmities took their toll; yet he never flagged, and under a foreboding sky we trudged along as best we could. By noon we had lost our bearings, yet still we ventured on, no longer expecting to find Rhisiart's house that day, but hoping at least to come to some shelter before nightfall.

"It was nearing the final hour of the day when we spied a small but steep escarpment. Brother Arwain had described the feature well. He had said that Rhisiart's holding was situated on the slope leading up to it. This proved so.

"The house was a low building of wood and stone, its windows barred tight. As we approached it we came upon a cart that Hugh recognised. We agreed on a simple subterfuge to get us inside. I would go to the door and ask to be admitted, whilst Hugh lay in hiding.

"With pounding heart and doubting my own wisdom for coming on such a mission, I knocked. Within moments, I heard a sound at the window shutter. They did not reveal themselves ... but I sensed someone peering out to see who was at the door.

"I pretended not to notice and knocked again, calling, 'I am a poor brother who is lost, if anyone is within this house I beg them help me!'

"A minute or so passed, and all the time I felt suspicious eyes upon me. I decided to let them believe I thought the house empty. Feigning great weariness I turned and began to walk away. The deception had worked and a moment later the door opened. I was exchanging looks with a short thick-set fellow, his red hair set around a balding head.

"'You're a long way from the abbey,' he said uncouthly.

"'I was called to a man in the Ceiriog Valley who was taken sick. His son escorted me there. But I am not acquainted with these parts and have lost my way. Am I close to Valle Crucis?' I asked innocently.

"'You could never be further from it,' replied the man unpleasantly.

"'May I come inside and shelter from this chill wind?' I asked.

"The man placed an arm about my shoulder in an overly familiar manner and said, 'Come brother. My master will be with us shortly. You will be sweet as wine to his lips.'

"At that moment Hugh rushed from his hiding place, his hatred of the serjeant so evident it was impossible to see his infirmities as he came at him. The red-haired lout, seeing himself tricked, cast me aside and began to draw his sword. But Hugh had the advantage and brought his blade down across the serjeant's skull, forging a cleft from the centre of the man's pate almost to the eyebrows. The serjeant flung up his hands to the source of blood gushing out of his scalp, and fell to his knees. Hugh was preparing to relieve the serjeant of his head when a woman's voice came suddenly from within and checked him.

"'Hugh ... Hugh, you've come,' she called to him.

"As the serjeant dropped face down onto the frozen ground, Hugh rushed inside like a man possessed. I followed after.

"Within the house stood a dark-haired beauty cradling a baby in her arms. I saw emotion swell in Hugh's breast at the sight of his sister alive. Melisend did not look up from the child in her charge.

"'Do you like my baby?' she asked.

"Hugh spluttered out his words through tears, 'Melisend ... our father, Rhisiart your husband, and all your babies were murdered by the fiend who resides here. The child you hold was unjustly taken from a peasant girl.'

"'I know that,' said Melisend, as though these were matters of little importance, 'Is he not truly beautiful? He is fairer of face by far than any of my own children, I think.'

"Hugh fell to his knees and begged her again and again to remember the monstrous events that had overtaken her. Yet Melisend never looked once in his direction. It was as if he meant nothing to her ... and this child alone was everything.

"The light was failing. I reminded Hugh of the task before us. 'Loving care may heal her mind in time,' I said, 'But let us not tarry ... the night is almost upon us.'

"'Where is Jerome?' Hugh asked his sister. Melisend acted as though she did not hear, and began singing a ditty to the baby.

"There was but one door leading from the room. Hugh took a torch from the wall and lit it in the fireplace, I did the same. We opened the door to the side chamber, holding the torches before us to peer inside. There were a few steps down to the room and there in its centre lying upon some trestles was a long box. My heart was pounding as we descended.

391

"'We must be swift,' Hugh warned.

"We prised the lid from the coffin and inside I beheld the fearsome creature that Hugh had described; its face pernicious with evil; a thing more reminiscent of nightmare than of waking. The creature's jaws lay open in its despicable sleep of death, for there were no signs of breathing ... teeth, sharp like those of a wolf, irregular and stained brown from drinking blood.

"'I cannot drive a stake through the mail shirt,' said Hugh, 'You must hold the head up for me, Anselm.'

"I feared to touch the thing though I knew I must. With trembling hands I took the head, and, struggling to support its weight, raised it above the rim of the casket. As Hugh drew his sword, I saw Melisend with the baby slip down the stairs to stand behind her brother. I gestured at Hugh with my eyes.

"'Melisend, go back to the room above, this is no sight for a woman and babe to witness,' he said.

"'No,' she answered, 'I want to watch.'

"There was little time for argument. I held the deathly cold creature by its ears, for there was no hair to grip. As Hugh swept the sword across his shoulder to mete out a blow, Melisend produced the cudgel she had been hiding behind her back and struck at her brother's injured shoulder. He shrieked with pain. The sword fell from his hand as he collapsed to the floor.

"The girl glanced briefly over at me before resuming her song to the baby. Hugh was struggling in vain to raise himself from the ground. I was overcome with terror. I saw all hope was lost. Horrified by our predicament, I let the head drop back into the coffin. In panic I fled from the room. By the time I reached the door to the house my senses had partly returned to me. I understood what I had done and thought to go back. But at the same moment an inhuman growl came from the chamber below. Then I heard Hugh's screams.

"In blind terror I threw open the main door only to stand confused about which way to run. From out of the darkness the red-haired man appeared like a wraith before me. His face was stained red from the streams of blood pouring from his head. He was laughing uproariously at my plight. I ran blindly ... a coward fleeing into the night.

"It was only as I stepped and fell into nothingness that I remembered the escarpment. I knew that I should die ... but I had far less fear of dying than of living to face that thing which lay behind me. I lay quite still. I was still conscious but unable to move ... yet suffering no physical pain, though the bones of my body had been shattered on the hard ground.

"I saw three figures arrive on the brow of the escarpment above. They were lit by the moon. The dreadest of these shapes began to clamber down towards me ... a spiderish creature ... stalking its prey. Terror overtook me as I lay helpless ... in the silence before death comes. As the creature grew nearer, I prayed I should die ... before he took me for his victim ... I called upon all the saints and angels to save me ... and begged and wept for the chance to make amends for my crime of cowardice. Then it came ... sweet, merciful release. ... I slipped into oblivion."

By the end of the account Anselm's vocalisation and breathing was that of a dying man scared out of his wits. In the final moments before he'd passed away, his voice was little more than a hoarse whisper produced in the upper throat.

Erich sounded rather stunned when he finally spoke. "Thank you Anselm. What you've told us may help to destroy Jerome ... rest now, my friend. Nobody blames you for your actions. Be at peace. Drift back into time ... sleep ... sleep ... sleep now."

Chapter Thirty-Three

Sunday, 15 December, 1996

Once Anselm's testimony was complete, Susan Harris called Wain out of the room. They needed to prepare mentally and take a few deep breaths before re-entering the library. This was wise. There was already a good deal less of the corpse lying on the room's wood-block floor. The stolen uniform was now at least three sizes too big for Rosemary's fast-shrinking physique. The halo of blood around her head had decomposed into a patch of brownish-grey dust, while the skin and flesh that still clung to her bones looked like shrivelled leather.

There was an unusual awkwardness between Wain and Harris and they avoided eye contact. Neither of them wanted to broach the subject of the regression.

"Call Patterson and Thorn, Frank ... get them over here. I'll contact headquarters."

Harris' eyes alighted on an ordnance survey atlas of Britain, which she took down from its shelf. As she went past Frank with the book under her arm she took a folded sheet of paper from her pocket and sheepishly handed it to him. "It's Professor Quigley's translation. Take a look. It's almost certainly authentic ... early thirteenth century." She left the room.

Wain began to read.

```
Reynald de Sauveterre,

My friend, if this missive ever reaches your hands
then you may be certain I am dead. With deepest
sorrow I send tragic news of him who was entrusted
to my charge. Yussuf no longer walks amongst us.
His death was needless and I am to blame. Where I
was rash and foolish, Yussuf acted courageously. I
would have gladly died myself to spare his precious
life.
```

We left Gezce and the land of Hungary some eight weeks after your departure. Our journey was peaceful and I became fonder each day of my companion, growing to love him as a younger brother. We had come to the lands of France, when fate brought us again upon the track of Jerome and his accursed serjeant. Unfortunately, they learned of our pursuit, and I see with hindsight how Jerome planned from that time forth to be avenged on me. We chased them across the channel and over half of England until finally they led us to the door of my father's manor. The timing was ill-omened; my sister, her husband Rhisiart and their children had been visiting my father. Jerome took his revenge most vindictively.

Yet my sister Melisend was not corrupted by him but taken as hostage by Jerome's faithful slave. We followed hard upon their heels through the day and night until the following dawn. When I saw the serjeant ahead of me I charged at him in rage. In that moment I knew only madness, not realising I drove my mare over thin ice. I should have drowned, for as I landed in the freezing waters of the river I lapsed into unconsciousness. Yet brave Yussuf saved me, but in so doing sacrificed his own far worthier life.

I was brought to the Cistercian house at Valle Crucis and revived by a brother who possesses great skill at healing. This monk's name is Anselm and it is this same man who pens these words for me.

During days of fever I unwittingly betrayed our cause to him, believing I was in conversation with you, friend Reynald. However, I saw that he was a man worthy of trust and have since taken him fully into my confidence, imparting to him all the details of our tale; how Jerome and the others rose from death to prey on the blood of the living.

Against my counsel he means to accompany me when I leave in the morning. Rhisiart and Melisend's holding is in a remote spot amongst the mountains south of the abbey. It is feasible that Jerome may

be sheltering there, in the belief that he has
found himself a safe haven in which to hide.

If this letter reaches you at our rendezvous, you
may assume my appraisal was correct, and that the
duty has again fallen to you and the guardians to
bring destruction to the blood-drinking demon.

May God sustain you and the guardians always. I do
not expect to receive forgiveness from Aref or the
brothers at my failure to protect their kinsman.
Yet I know that in their great hearts they will
petition their nameless god to show his mercy to my
soul.

On the next line there was a Bible reference.

Matthew XXVI, verse 50.

Professor Quigley had obligingly typed out the verse the numerals
referred to, which read:

And Jesus said unto him, Friend, wherefore art thou
come? Then came they, and laid hands on Jesus, and
took him.

Quigley had made a note below the quotation that a cross was
marked on the parchment at this point, followed by:

Hugh Apsley, penned for him by Anselm, brother at
the house of Valle Crucis, in the month of
December, the year of our Lord twelve hundred and
two.

Wain folded the sheet of paper and slipped it into his pocket. His
first reaction was that Latimer had come across the letter whilst
working at Barnswick Square and that the whole Anselm thing was an
elaborate scam. However, he recalled reading a report about the
parchment's discovery, and how it had been sealed away behind
nineteenth century lath and plaster.

Frank was distracted momentarily by Rosemary's corpse, when an
ear and part of the cheek dropped away from what remained of her
face. They fell instantly to dust on touching the floor. He felt a shudder
run through him and acknowledged that logic appeared to have taken a

holiday on this case. Grimacing down at the body, he took out his mobile and tapped in the number for Patterson.

"It's Wain ..."

Patterson interrupted him excitedly, "Frank, we interviewed a girlfriend of Danny Ledermann's. I was just about to ring you. We've got a description of two elderly sisters living in Herstmonceux ..."

"Save your breath," said Frank.

*

Harris took the atlas into the drawing-room. Not much had changed since she'd gone to talk with Frank. Millie Thorpe was holding an ice-pack to the lump on the back of Danny's head, and Mary was dabbing at his chin with cotton wool.

Erich Ledermann, similarly, was holding an ice-pack to his own cheek. Ruth Allinson was sitting near Ledermann with her eyes closed, hands folded on her lap, in a meditative pose.

'Each to their own,' thought Harris.

Jim Latimer was still fast asleep.

"How long before he wakes up?" she asked Erich.

"Difficult to say ... but not too long I think."

Harris put the atlas down on a coffee table already heavily-laden with books, leaflets and assorted paraphernalia, audio-tapes, bits of rock crystal, a defunct electrical switch and some little brown bottles containing homoeopathic remedies. It was a typical surface in the Thorpe sisters' home.

"Ask him to take a look at this when he wakes."

She left the room and called headquarters from the hallway. She was put through immediately to Markland, who greeted her with the usual mix of veiled aggression and indifference. However, his tone changed immediately once she informed him that Latimer and the others had been found.

"Unfortunately, there's another body ... it's deteriorating in the same way as Cureton's ..."

Although Markland said nothing, Harris heard him sigh.

"... The Hines woman arrived before us. She had a shotgun pointed right at me. I had no option but to shoot."

"Did any of the others resist arrest?" Markland asked eagerly.

Harris understood the question and what was being implied by it. She deliberately chose to misunderstand, "She came alone, sir. I believe it was a personal vendetta. She seemed to think that Latimer and his friends' intrusion into their affairs was responsible for Nicholas Cureton's death ... I still have nothing concrete on the whereabouts of her accomplices."

"Don't be modest, Chief Inspector," said Markland smoothly.

Harris could imagine his mouth smiling unattractively.

"You've captured well over half the gang."

"I beg your pardon?"

"Those people in your custody are in it up to their necks. Surely you can't doubt it?" Markland gave his voice a gentle massage with soft soap before continuing, "Everyone is going to be very pleased, the tabloids will have to ease off, and there'll be a sigh of relief at the Home Office. Everyone's been getting understandably nervous." After pausing for a moment he added, "I think there may well be a commendation coming your way ..."

'What an utter bastard,' thought Harris.

"I'll personally organise a team. We're hard-pressed at the moment because of the weather. A lot of minor roads are blocked and we've got jams on the motorways and some 'A' routes with worsening visibility. I'll try and commandeer a helicopter, but don't expect us for at least an hour ... six-thirty at the earliest."

"We could ask the Eastbourne force to assist?" suggested Harris.

Markland chuckled to himself the way grown-ups condescend to a child's naivety. "After all our hard graft? We wouldn't want them to steal any of our thunder now, would we Susan?"

It felt like a violation of her human rights rather than camaraderie when Markland called her Susan.

"Sir, I don't think we have anything to celebrate yet. We'd be completely in the dark about Barnswick Square but for the Ledermanns and Miss Allinson. They've been helping us all along. The Hines woman actually came here to kill them!"

Harris pictured a vein starting to throb in Markland's temple. The image was reassuring, and helped restore some of her composure.

"If they're innocent, then why were they in hiding?" asked Markland the affability swiftly vanishing from his voice.

"Because they were frightened ... they fear him ... I believe it's the same assailant who murdered two members of my team ... the man they tried to warn us about!"

Markland recalled the warning, as well as his own efforts to obstruct Harris. "And who is this assailant?" he jeered, "Do they give him a name?"

"I believe ..." Harris found herself stumbling over her words, "... I ... I believe his name is Jerome ... they refer to him as Mr Niedermayer."

Markland blew. "For heaven's sake woman, there's no record of any Niedermayer. DS Frith's killer was more than likely the Hart fellow or the driver."

"That's not possible, sir. We have eye witness accounts placing both men elsewhere in the county less than fifteen minutes before DI Wain arrested Nicholas Cureton. There's video footage too. None of the residents re-entered the house after they left on Thursday morning."

"So in other words, you've failed, Chief Inspector. You've got absolutely nowhere with this case?"

"Not at all, I believe Jim Latimer may provide us with some clues as to the whereabouts of the remaining accomplices."

"How will he be able to do that if he's so damned innocent?" Markland inquired sarcastically.

Harris hesitated for a moment before replying, "When we arrived Latimer was in a state of hypnosis. Erich Ledermann believes that Jim Latimer may have some of the answers locked away in his mind." She expected Markland to explode again, but her words were met with an uncomfortable silence. After a moment she said, "Sir?"

When Markland resumed speaking he sounded like he was about a hair's breadth away from an embolism. "I see that you have been taken in completely, Chief Inspector, by their nefarious practices." His voice was seething with rage.

Harris wondered for a moment exactly what he was referring to by 'nefarious practices', before she realised it was the hypnosis. She ought to have known better, having once seen a blacklist published by the kind of church Markland belonged to. The list had put forward all kinds of alternative therapies including hypnosis, reflexology, acupuncture, aromatherapy, Alexander technique, osteopathy and yoga as works of the devil.

"Take my word for it, Latimer had a hand in DCI Rice's murder and the two deaths at his friend Isherwood's office. The Ledermanns and Ruth Allinson are his accomplices. My judgement certainly isn't clouded even if yours is ..."

Harris listened in disbelief as Markland ranted.

"... Barnswick Square is not an ordinary case, Chief Inspector. There can be only one explanation for the number of mutilated corpses uncovered there. Ritual sacrifice. That house was being used as a centre for Satanic worship!"

Harris was speechless. She observed there was a good deal of fear in Markland's tirade.

"As I'm sure you're aware, I have deeply-held religious convictions. I know a very great deal on this subject, far more than the average person. Take my word for it ... these people are devil-worshippers. Hypnosis is not a gentle therapy, as its practitioners would have their gullible clients believe, but an occult practice. I've read in Rice's notes that the Allinson woman claims to be psychic ..." Markland sneered at the idea, "Another of Satan's egotistical works ..."

Harris had had only bad days since Thursday, but this was definitely the worst of all. In one afternoon, she had been offered two explanations for the goings on at Hove: vampires or Satanists.

The Deputy Chief Constable hadn't quite concluded his 'in-depth analysis' yet. Harris wished someone would slip him a valium suppository. He went on, "'Beware of false prophets, which come to you in sheep's clothing, but inwardly they are ravening wolves.'"

Harris assumed it was the Bible being quoted at her. The words sounded too articulate to be his own.

"These bastards are to be charged as accomplices to murder!" raged Markland, "Do I make myself clear?"

"Quite clear, sir."

Markland gave a short cough. "I'll be with you as soon as possible."

The line went dead.

Partly stunned, Harris slipped the mobile into her pocket and returned to the library.

She was grateful to see Frank Wain looking characteristically sound of mind, even with Countess Dracula rotting at his feet. He was speaking on the phone too. She assumed it was to Patterson or Thorn. However her antennae went up when she saw his expression.

"Thank you for keeping us informed, sir. I'll let Chief Inspector Harris know immediately."

Frank flicked back the mouthpiece of his mobile.

"That was the Met ..."

Harris observed an involuntary twitch beneath Frank's left eye. She somehow knew that she was not going to enjoy what was coming.

"The man they lent us to tail Jim Latimer's wife was found dead fifteen minutes ago, his neck was broken. Hannah Latimer's in hospital, suffering from shock mostly ... she lost some blood but she's stable ..."

400

"The daughter?"

"Missing," he sighed, "They found a needle and syringe … looks like the girl was sedated."

At that moment the library door opened. Millie Thorpe was standing there, screwing up her eyes to avoid the sight of Rosemary full on.

"Jim's woken up," she announced.

*

Although Jim Latimer's testimony under hypnosis appeared to authenticate Quigley's translation, it wouldn't have been enough in itself to convince Harris and Wain to adopt the course of action they eventually took. It required a combination of several other factors too – Markland's blind and maniacal insistence on the friends' guilt, the abduction of Sophie Latimer, and the thought of Niedermayer, whoever or whatever, being allowed to continue his unrestrained reign of terror.

Harris and Wain remained fairly sceptical about Latimer's confession as Brother Anselm. Who in their right minds wouldn't have been? However, there was no question of authenticity about the man's distress when Harris informed him about his wife and daughter.

"How did Hannah lose the blood?" was the tell-tale first question he asked.

"She had … had her wedding finger removed … she identified a red-haired man as her attacker," replied Harris awkwardly.

Jim shook his head. He was far too overwhelmed to speak. What he had feared the most was already happening.

"That was Picton," put in Ruth. She was sat on the chair arm beside Jim, stroking his hand. She looked very troubled, as did all the friends, "Danny and I had a run-in with him at Pett on Thursday morning."

"There isn't much time," said Harris, consulting her watch. She reckoned there was about fifty minutes before Markland and the whole Starship Enterprise arrived. "I think I've got the picture up to DCI Rice's visit to Mr Latimer's cottage. It would be helpful if you could fill us in from there."

Erich became the main storyteller, attempting to pull each strand of the tale together. The others joined in occasionally to clarify a detail. Jim was understandably anxious and impatient; even so he recognised the importance of what seemed an interminable process to him, and tried his best to be objective.

401

"You say you were made to drink this man's blood?" said Harris, sickened by what she had heard so far but allowing nothing to show on her face.

"Not a man," Jim answered bitterly, "Like you've already been told … vampire."

"What's his blood supposed to do to you then?" Wain asked.

"You've seen what it does," replied Erich, "The woman in there and I think the man who died in your custody probably too?" He looked at Harris and Wain who were clearly unwilling to comment. Then he went on, "Mostly it keeps you under Niedermayer's thumb and youthful."

"So are you in his power then, Mr Latimer?" questioned Harris.

"No … Christ … yes … yes, to some extent … that's why we have to do something quickly."

Erich attempted to explain, "I believe that Jim's conscious mind is now free of him. That was the main reason we needed to stay in hiding. At first, Jim needed to be restrained, otherwise he would have gone straight back to them. However, the effect of the blood hasn't dissipated entirely - when he sleeps or doesn't keep his mind alert, Niedermayer can infiltrate his thoughts."

"I'll show you how powerful it is," Jim said. He took a penknife from his pocket, and before Ruth could stop him, he'd drawn its blade across the palm of his left hand.

"So what's that supposed to prove?" asked Wain.

"It's the easiest way to demonstrate something," Jim replied, holding his fist clenched to stem the flow of blood.

Erich took a handkerchief from his pocket and passed it to Jim.

At this point the doorbell interrupted them. Frank left the room and let in Patterson and Thorn. He gave them a brief talk about what to expect before showing them into the library.

"You're telling us DCI Harris shot that? It looks like it's been dead a hundred years!" exclaimed a horrified Thorn.

Patterson remained silent but went a bit green about the gills.

"I'll leave the three of you to get better acquainted," said Frank who was annoyed with them both for failing to uncover the sisters' names earlier. "We'll be across the hall. Don't disturb us unless it's something important," he added, taking cruel satisfaction in awarding them this punishment.

"Couldn't we wait somewhere else?" Patterson asked meekly, he looked like he was about to throw up.

Frank shrugged, "Go into the kitchen, if you must."

When he returned to the drawing-room Harris was inspecting Jim's hand.

"Mr Latimer has remarkable healing ability," she told Frank. The wound hadn't completely healed, but in less than two minutes it had stopped bleeding and was beginning to bond.

Erich resumed the role of storyteller. Harris and Wain showed little interest in the psychic defences employed by the friends to combat the dark presence that had apparently stalked Jim Latimer during the nights of siege. However, the telephone calls from Rosemary and Picton over three evenings did cause a ripple of excitement between them.

"I tried to find out where the calls came from at the time," said Danny, "But they'd blocked them."

Harris glanced over at Frank.

"I'll get Patterson onto that right away," he said and left the room.

He returned a few minutes later, by this time Jim Latimer was poring over the atlas.

"It's no use," said Jim, "I can picture the setting in my mind, but looking at this means nothing. I know Anselm said they went south from Valle Crucis," tracing a line with his finger from the Abbey ruins, "I only know it wasn't a direct route. But I can't see anything here that jogs my memory."

"Look for an escarpment," advised Mary.

Every pair of eyes scoured each square of the map for such a feature, but nothing leapt out at them.

"The landscape may have changed considerably in eight hundred years," suggested Millie.

"It's no use," said Jim, pushing the atlas to one side with a disconsolate air.

"I'm afraid I can't promise anything," Harris offered uncertainly, "But I will do my best to get the area searched."

"And will you advise your officers to drive a stake through Niedermayer's heart and cut off his head if they find him?" Jim asked sardonically.

"I think I'm being extremely reasonable, Mr Latimer, in light of ... well ... such unusual evidence."

"How do you explain all the method and dedication put in by the so-called team of Niedermayer & Hart? Forget that bullshit you've been feeding the media. How many corpses have really been discovered at Barnswick Square?" Jim asked angrily.

Harris found herself unable to look directly at the accusing eyes of this understandably distressed man.

Jim went on, "I'm sure you'll be able to come up with sound scientific reasons why Rosemary and Nicholas's corpses decayed so fast, or why Loxton looked half his age until shortly after his death?"

"You can't expect us to act on the extraordinary account you came up with under hypnosis?" retorted Harris defensively.

Jim shrugged his shoulders and began to stare despondently at the floor.

There was silence for a few moments; finally Ruth spoke, her voice was calm. "You don't have to believe, Inspector, just listen to your instincts."

"As Miss Thorpe pointed out a minute ago," put in Wain, "Things would have changed considerably in eight hundred years. Do you honestly believe this Niedermayer would have kept the same hiding place all that time?"

"I'll do everything I can," assured Harris. She was sincere, but she knew there was little hope of a search being mounted on the strength of such a testimony.

Jim looked up at Harris, tears forming in his eyes. He was speaking softly now, "As soon as I fall asleep or let my mind drift, he'll read my thoughts. I've no idea how long I can keep him at bay. If we don't get to him soon, he'll know everything. Then, by the time anyone reaches the place he'll already be gone ... my daughter too."

Jim turned dejectedly towards Ruth after he'd finished speaking. He held out little hope of seeing his daughter alive again, even if the whole national police force was immediately mobilised on her behalf.

Harris and Wain were sharing virtually identical lines of thought, recalling Frith's killer, and how a sizeable show of force, even bullets, had not prevented him from escaping.

Just then a tap came on the drawing-room door. Wain took a slip of paper off Patterson before closing the door again. He read it, then told the others, "They used public call boxes ... three different locations - Chirk, Wrexham and Chester."

Everyone swarmed around the map again. Chester was the furthest from Valle Crucis but only about thirty or forty minutes' driving time.

Anselm's location suddenly looked more promising.

"You have to let me go to Valle Crucis. With Erich's help I'm sure I could find it from the ground," Jim implored Harris.

"It must be worth trying, for Sophie's sake," said Erich.

Harris gestured to Frank with her eyes towards the door.

Outside in the hall it was Frank who got in first. "Don't think about doing this alone," he said. "I'm coming too."

"I can't allow that, Frank. You've got a family to think about ..."

"Shut up and listen for once, Susan. Just suppose that half of what they've told us is true. Do you really think you could take them on between the three of you? You'll need back-up."

"You know Markland will have us crucified."

"Fuck him," said Wain.

Harris nodded her head. She knew any further protests would be useless. At the same time she was deeply touched by Frank's loyalty. She consulted her watch; it was 6.19pm, nearly fifty minutes since she had spoken with Markland.

They returned to the drawing room.

"Very well, Mr Latimer, we'll take you and Mr Ledermann to Valle Crucis."

"If my father goes I'm coming too," said Danny, rising to his feet.

"Oh no, that's absurd. Anyway, you're injured," replied Harris.

"I'm fine," said Danny, "I'm a climber ... I've taken worse tumbles than that. And I bet I'm the only one experienced in survival techniques. Those mountains will be bleak, especially in weather like this. I can easily lay my hands on the equipment we'll need. Don't even think about going without survival gear."

Harris looked at Wain and sighed. 'So what?' she thought, 'My brilliant unblemished career is about to be thoroughly trashed anyway.'

Then Ruth said, "I've foreseen this. Six of us travel there. I must come too."

"Christ, what is wrong with you people?"

Chapter Thirty-Four

Sunday, 15 December – Monday, 16 December, 1996

In light of the national weather emergency, DCC Markland had needed to stamp his feet to get himself airborne. He'd stressed the heinous nature of the crimes and their perpetrators to achieve this. However, despite the great urgency, Markland still found time to call a press conference.

He'd announced to representatives from the various media present, "... I'm pleased to be able to inform you that officers under my direct command are currently poised to make several major arrests in connection with the Barnswick Square investigations ... recently Sussex Police have been criticised, not altogether unjustly perhaps, over our handling of the case ... I'd like to take this opportunity to say on record how personally disappointed I was with the initial progress made ... this in turn has led me to adopt a more pro-active role ..."

The snow was three inches deep by the time Markland arrived in Herstmonceux with an investigation unit. They had received permission to land in a field adjacent to the sisters' property owned by a local farmer. Leading his team from the helicopter, perhaps the Deputy Chief Constable had a boyhood hero in mind as he tramped through the snow, gimlet-eyed, ready to mete out justice and retribution to all transgressors. He also felt quite irritated that Harris hadn't shown up to meet him.

'She must have heard us land. Women ... too touchy feely! Not cut out for this line of work. Too emotive!' he told himself, as his sergeant struggled with the mechanics of a gate so they could exit the field.

When Markland reached the Grange his annoyance was patently visible when he discovered its front door closed to him. He scowled malevolently whilst the aforementioned sergeant rang the doorbell.

When the door eventually opened, DC Thorn nearly choked on the piece of homemade banana bread in his mouth. The unfortunate Detective Constable was immediately struck dumb by the bad combination of Markland and cake. It was plain to see by his fierce expression that the senior man did not feel at all kindly disposed to him. To make matters worse, when Thorn did manage to splutter out a few apologetic words, these were accompanied by a salvo of saliva-loaded crumbs that shot like heat-seeking missiles straight at the DCC's glowering face.

"S-s-s-sorry ... s-sorry sir, we didn't expect ... the Chief Inspector didn't s-s-say you ..."

Markland strode past the blabbering man and entered the room on the left which he could see was lit and populated through its open door. Here he encountered an oblivious Patterson, sipping Earl Grey from a teacup. The man was conversing with two elderly women who smiled charmingly when they saw the Deputy Chief Constable. Patterson, suddenly aware of a dark presence, turned, saw the DCC, then turned white and jumped to his feet. Unfortunately, at the same time he managed to slop a large amount of hot tea into his lap.

Markland's eyes narrowed suspiciously as they roved about the room. He found the Thorpe sisters' friendly faces especially disquieting.

"Where's the Chief Inspector?" he barked at an equally red in the face Patterson, stoically trying to conceal his scalded privates.

"They left about twenty minutes ago, sir," the detective constable replied in a pained tone, "DCI Harris said they had to follow up a lead on Mr Latimer's daughter. We weren't told to expect you, sir."

"Where is Latimer?"

"He went with DCI Harris, DI Wain and the others."

A bad word performed a little mime on the Deputy Chief Constable's lips.

Markland glared at the sisters. "Where have they gone?"

"We're not at liberty to say," Millie Thorpe replied calmly.

The sisters could be extremely uncooperative when they identified a bully at work.

"It won't do you any good interrogating us," said Mary, "Our lips are sealed."

A disturbing vision suddenly assailed the DCC. He pictured the helicopter landing amidst a battery of photographers' flashguns, and himself stepping sheepishly from the machine, with the Miss Marple twins in handcuffs on either side.

Markland's hand inadvertently dislodged a shred of banana cake that had settled on his chin.

*

407

It was decided that Jim Latimer should be taken as far out of Markland's reach as possible. Susan Harris drove him and Ruth, whilst Danny and Erich Ledermann travelled with Frank Wain. Harris took a route north from the sisters' house, then followed the M25 until it joined the M1.

Meanwhile, Frank drove Erich and Danny east. First, they planned on visiting the Emergency Dental Service in Hastings, then the A and E department at the Conquest Hospital, for x-rays and some pit-stop repairs. After this they would pick up Danny's survival equipment. There seemed little point agreeing on a rendezvous time as there were too many unknown quantities, so it was agreed that both parties would meet at the first services on the M1.

Harris' group reached Scratchwood Services just after 10.30pm. The road conditions were very poor and Harris barely achieved more than 40mph at any point during the journey. Visibility was dreadful as the snow drove relentlessly at the car's windscreen. At times they listened to the radio news but mostly they just put up with the repetitive whirr of wiper blades and the sound of rubber impacting on grit and slush for accompaniment. The silent white bombardment appeared to originate from a focal point about two feet from the centre of the windscreen. It created a sense of alienation and gave an impression that their car alone was being targeted.

Jim spoke rarely. He was busy constructing a mental defence between himself and Jerome, aware the monster might easily scan his mind if he let up for a second. The effort proved exhausting and called on everything he knew. He went back and forth through his times-tables, from two times two through to twelve times twelve, over and over again; word games, compiling lists of vegetables and fruit for every letter in the alphabet; the same for capital cities and boys' names. He avoided girls' names, knowing the letters H and S would prove too painful and might cause his wall to crumble.

The motorway services were heaving with people. Harris made no attempt to contact Frank; for security her mobile phone was switched off, as was his. They could do nothing other than to wait, not anticipating the arrival of the others for at least three or four hours.

They bought hot food and secreted themselves away in an obscure corner of the restaurant. The two women talked intermittently but avoided the topics mainly occupying their thoughts because of Jim. However they did touch on some points, like Ruth's initial experiences. This led on to a discussion about psychic ability. For Harris the metaphysical issues weren't at all feasible, although she conceded that Ruth's predictions had somehow been uncannily accurate.

"I believe everyone possesses psychic ability to some extent," Ruth said, "A good police officer might call it intuition."

"But intuition is a product of experience ... it has nothing to with anything other worldly."

"We're still in the Dark Ages as far as consciousness is concerned. And I'm not talking about the brain ... consciousness is an ever-widening circle."

Harris knew the conversation could not go much further after Ruth touched on the idea of some kind of universal consciousness. Even so, she found she liked this unusual character who claimed to possess strange powers. She certainly admired her pluck for taking on Picton with a rolling-pin. At a fundamental level she found the woman was good company, quite remarkably sane and unexpectedly down to earth.

"Why, I wonder," asked Ruth, "Did you and Detective Wain allow yourselves to get involved?"

Harris shrugged, "I don't see myself pursuing a demonic creature out of a Gothic novel," she replied guardedly.

"Nor do we," said Ruth, "There's no similarity between all that stuff and what we're up against here. There's nothing remotely romantic or noble about Niedermayer. I doubt if it can even remember its name was once Jerome."

"Let's just say I came across evidence in my inquiry that can't be explained by following any of the normal rules ... and I don't like unsolved crimes."

"You believe this case is solvable then?"

"It can be brought to a conclusion, whatever we're up against," she replied. Harris was starting to feel uncomfortable. She was the one who generally asked the questions. "Can I get you some more coffee?"

"Please," said Ruth. She saw the policewoman's discomfort and decided it was time to back off.

Harris gestured with her eyes towards Jim. He was staring intensely out into the night through the window beside him.

Ruth stroked his hair, "Jim? ..."

He turned, and managed an unconvincing smile for his friend.

"Do you want some coffee?"

"We have a long way to go," he said.

*

They did indeed have a long way to go. It was 2.15am when Frank arrived with Erich and Danny, and by this time, the motorway services looked like an evacuation centre for Eskimos. There were bodies everywhere. People lay asleep beneath whatever coats and coverings had been salvaged from their cars, on every bit of vacant floor space.

The three long-awaited companions appeared without warning, like bewildered Arctic explorers, entering the brightly-lit restaurant to the incongruous accompaniment of the never ceasing muzak. All were kitted out in windcheaters and ski pants, immune to the liberal spattering of snow on their shoulders and hoods. Frank went a little coy when he saw Harris eyeing him with some amusement; bright yellow and apple green weren't his colours.

"Did you manage to get them fixed up?" she asked Frank.

"Yes ... they were both x-rayed ... no broken bones at least."

"Good," said Harris, relieved to hear it.

Jim's sense of urgency about getting on was immediately apparent to those who'd just arrived. There were after all about a hundred and eighty miles left to travel.

"Did you see a dentist?" Ruth asked.

"Yes, all fixed," replied Danny, his speech muffled by a swelling in his jaw.

Erich, who possessed a black eye and some bruising on his cheek, smiled when he heard his son play down his injuries, and shook his head in disbelief, "Two teeth were broken off at the gum. They covered up the roots with some sort of anaesthetic paste to desensitise the nerves. He has root treatments and crown work to look forward to."

"That must hurt," stated Ruth.

"Not really, they gave me painkillers."

Ruth took his reply with a large pinch of salt. Danny had never been acquainted with the concept of milking sympathy.

Each of the three had carried in with him a rucksack. These were now allocated to the others by Danny.

"Each pack contains clothing and basic survival stuff ... a flashlight, survival bag, sleeping-bag, rope, rudimentary first-aid kit and a flare. I'll give you instructions about how to use the flares once we're on the move. If the boots don't fit, don't worry, there are extra pairs in the back of the Landrover."

"Landrover?" enquired Harris.

"I ... er ... I sort of borrowed it from some people I do a bit of voluntary work for."

"The same source as the other equipment?" she asked.

"No. The friend who lent us the gear hires out ski and climbing equipment. It's a bit old but all quality stuff … he owed me a favour. I have a key for the Landrover," Danny looked a bit awkward as he spoke.

Wain chimed in, "The Landrover's got snow-chains if we need them … and it made sense to travel together and lose the cars. By now Markland will have every division in the country on the look-out for us."

While the others changed, Frank and the Ledermanns bought food and drink from the buffet.

Harris discovered in her rucksack the things Danny had mentioned, but there was more too. Each pack also contained a wooden stake, a mallet to complement it, and a handmade cross. These items caused her to pause momentarily and reflect on her situation. She leaned back against the cubicle wall and took in a deep breath. The cast Ashworth had made from Rice's neck wound and all those canine teeth immediately sprang to mind. Harris sighed and packed the DIY vampire kit back into the rucksack.

Once they were dressed they returned to the cafeteria, collected the others and went outside. The wind was howling; the snow hadn't eased in the slightest and it was now about a foot deep. Danny led them across the car park to the Landrover.

"I'll take the first leg," said Harris.

It was agreed they should drive for an hour apiece, except Ruth, who couldn't, and Jim, who had more pressing things on his mind.

Wain went with Harris to fetch a few items from her car, including a spare flashlight and a couple of blankets.

"Danny Ledermann seems to have thought of everything," said Harris as they trudged back to the Landrover.

"He's a nice lad," said Wain.

"It was a good idea to travel in one vehicle. I don't think I could have driven all night."

When they reached their new means of transportation the others were already settled inside. There were two sets of bench seats in the back; Erich, who had nominated himself to drive after Harris, was in the passenger seat.

As Wain held open the door for Harris to get in, she noticed an insignia partly hidden beneath a layer of snow. She brushed the frosting away, to expose a scouting badge with the words 'Sussex Scouts' beneath.

"Dyb dyb dyb," said Wain.

Twenty minutes later loud snores were coming from the rear seats. The only one still awake in the back was Jim, and he had no intention of drifting off.

Out of the corner of her eye Harris caught something glistening in Erich's hand. She looked across and saw it was a small silver crucifix.

"I'm sorry if I distracted you," Erich apologised, "I find it comforting. The sisters handed it to me just before we left."

A moment went by before Harris stated, "You were born in Austria … your father was a village doctor, and you arrived in Britain as a refugee in 1937. In 1944 you joined a commando regiment, and received a commendation for bravery."

"Crikey! It's like 'This Is Your Life'. You certainly did your homework."

"It's my job. I needed to build a profile of you," said Harris, who thought for a moment before continuing, "Your parents and your only sister died in the Holocaust. You have one brother who like you survived the war and now lives in Denmark."

"That's right," said Erich, "My mother and father were 'last known' in Buchenwald. My sister Freia died from cholera in Bergen Belsen. Shortly after the war ended I applied for compassionate leave and visited it, only to be confronted by the most unimaginable scenes of horror and human degradation. Freia died the day before her sixteenth birthday, just two weeks before the camp was liberated."

"I've spoken to your brother. He sounded concerned about you."

"Poor Hermann," smiled Erich. Neither of them spoke for about half a minute, then Erich continued, "I landed in France with my commando regiment. We were a volunteer company made up mainly of refugee boys and we played our part in the mopping-up operation. We went through Belgium and then on into Holland. I was in Holland when the war ended, and being bi-lingual, as you can appreciate, we were much in demand as translators. There was a lot to be done accumulating evidence for the trials in Nuremberg and I was determined to get my pound of flesh. Even so, I went on to Germany with some trepidation.

"Hermann I learned had been transported from Dachau to Auschwitz. At this point I lost all hope and assumed he'd perished there. Auschwitz could mean only one thing. You can imagine how I felt. There was nobody left … I felt I'd been robbed of everything. It's strange, you know, but I can't describe feeling any real emotion … just bitterness and a terrible emptiness inside.

"I'd joined up as soon as I was eighteen, filled with hate, and with the express purpose of killing Germans, to get revenged. Then, out of the blue a few months later, I received a telegram from the Red Cross to say that Hermann had been exchanged for German POWs and taken to Sweden to recover. I think that was the happiest day of my life. And it was the first time I can remember crying in all the years that had passed since leaving home."

Harris found Erich's straightforward re-telling of his personal history extremely moving.

"But you see, Susan … you don't mind me calling you Susan?"

Harris shook her head.

"For me the war still wasn't over. It took me another twenty years to finally let go of the anger. My wife Jessie was a fine woman … she helped me to look … see the destructiveness of hate and how it can ultimately only destroy its own possessor … regardless of any just cause like I thought I had."

Harris, glancing over, saw that Erich was still moving the little crucifix about between his fingertips. "When did you convert to Christianity?" she asked.

"I didn't," he replied, "I was born a Jew and I'll die one."

"I didn't mean any offence."

"And none taken," he assured her.

"But if you don't mind me asking … how can you gain any comfort from that?"

"You mean because of its anti-Semitic connotations?"

"I suppose so. Yes."

"The cross goes back way before it was adopted as a Christian sign. As a symbol it has very great significance and power, and like the Star of David, it represents every facet of existence. The same grains of truth run through all the world religions, because the need is invariably the same. To understand what we are."

"You think that all faiths are basically the same then?"

"Some might say so, but personally I've always considered that somewhat naive. All faiths are clearly not the same."

"And the cross … what does it represent?"

He was staring down at the little silver crucifix as he replied, "Everything. Spirit, matter, consciousness, the elements, direction … and right at its heart is the point of incarnation. Each one of us lies at the centre of our own cross."

Harris couldn't resist a little flippancy. "Will it hold him at bay ... like in the movies?"

"I hope so ... at least to some extent. You see, he has cheated the cycle of life and death. He wants to continue unchanged for all time - he is a corruption of what the cross actually means. Only by growth and change, through the pain of incarnation, can we transcend matter and become that which we truly are. The cross will have more significance for him because he exists only partly in this world ... during the daytime he's as dead as stone. He only uses our world, this reality, to feed his grossly over-bloated spirit. Niedermayer is mostly mind or spirit which exists in another realm of existence ... symbols work far more powerfully there."

Harris sort of understood what Erich was getting at, but it still sounded to her like a load of spiritual bollocks.

The engine droned on into the night and mostly everyone who could went to sleep. Jim, who dared not sleep, stared hauntedly through the rear window at the snow as it continued to fall relentlessly. He found their snail-like progress interminably painful. In his mind's eye Sophie's face was imprinted everywhere on the frozen landscape. Within himself, he knew only fear and despair.

As dawn came the snow eased, but they were still thirty miles from their destination and off the motorway the roads were even less accessible.

Just before 9am they crawled along the A5 as it struck west through Wales into the town of Llangollen, then onwards. Finally, they reached the ruined Cistercian abbey of Valle Crucis in its dramatic setting at the base of the Horseshoe Pass.

Chapter Thirty-Five

Monday, 16 December, 1996

The Abbey was impressive, and not even the caravans in an adjacent field were enough to mar its ascetic aloofness. They parked the Landrover and started down the slope to the ruins. The snow had stopped but there was a biting chill in the air and they were glad to be kitted out so well, even if they did look like escapees from a charity shop. Theirs were the only tracks down the pristine white surface as they ploughed great ruts into the smooth hill with their boots. All around was still and silent, the surrounding mountains uniformly clad in white, beautiful but foreboding. Their difficulties getting there, together with their secret agenda, fostered a sense of awe in them as they approached the ruins.

The visitor centre, not unexpectedly, was shut, so they scaled the perimeter wall and walked amongst the ruins. All eyes were inevitably focused on Jim. He tottered about the stone remains like a man who is completely overwhelmed. He went around the outer walls, pausing occasionally, trying to picture Anselm there, and attempting to conjure in his mind's eye an impression of how the Abbey might have looked at the beginning of the thirteenth century. The others faked an interest in the buildings to take the pressure off him.

After a time he entered the church. Its west and east walls were still mostly intact. Jim remained out of sight of the others for several minutes.

"What's next, can you regress him again?" Frank asked.

"It would be better if he made the connection himself," replied Erich, looking his age after an insubstantial night's rest courtesy of Sussex Scouts.

"Would it be alright if I talked to him?" asked Harris.

"Yes, of course."

Susan Harris entered through the mostly non-existent north wall of the church. She found Jim kneeling in the snow halfway along what must once have been the nave.

415

Hearing the approach he looked up to see who it was, "I used to claim not to believe any of this stuff. Just look at me!"

"That makes two of us," said Harris. "Is this where Anselm prayed?"

"I don't know," he replied, sounding disheartened. "I keep getting feelings ... one minute it's familiar and then it isn't ... but most of the buildings I don't recognise at all."

"That's understandable," assured Harris, having spent the preceding minutes genning-up on the abbey's history at an information point. "Hugh Apsley came here at the end of 1202 ... but the abbey was only founded in January 1201. It was less than two years old and must still have been in the process of being built."

"How did you get that date?" Jim asked. He meant the later one.

Harris saw the moment had come to own up, to admit that it wasn't just the regression that had swayed her and Wain into coming on board. "We found a letter in the attic at Barnswick Square. It was dictated by a man called Hugh Apsley ... written down by a brother Anselm at this Abbey and addressed to Reynald de Sauveterre in the town of Albi."

Jim nodded as if he suddenly understood a missing link. "Part of me can't believe this is happening," he was speaking in earnest. "That we're hunting a supernatural creature ...a monstrous thing that has killed en masse and cheated death for eight centuries. And that our success or failure today depends on the testimony of a monk from the Middle Ages."

Harris replied, "I'm not the right person to explain the significance of any of this. Whether it's reincarnation, or whether it's some sort of weird mental anomaly ... that somehow allows you to access information from the past ... I don't know. Bloody hell! Through genes or something! But you know what? At this moment, I don't care. All I know is that you people have provided us with just about every lead we've ever had in this case."

"And now it's down to Brother Anselm," said Jim, a note of resignation in his voice, "My daughter ... the future victims he'll carry on taking ... all dependent on poor, terrified Anselm."

"He wanted an opportunity to make amends."

Jim closed his eyes. They both remained silent for a moment.

"Hugh prayed here with Anselm. It was just before dawn on the morning they left."

Jim got to his feet.

"Think you can do it?"

"I've got to. We know they went south … let's start there."

Harris followed him out of the church to rejoin the others, taking in the breathtaking panorama of mountains arranged before her, at once majestic and bleak. If they were to find Niedermayer, then the elements must be contended with first. All of a sudden there was nothing even remotely amusing about her motley band, in their out of fashion ski wear.

*

Nobody really felt like eating, but Danny insisted, so they found a place in Llangollen that served hot breakfasts. While it was being prepared Danny, taking some money from Erich, went off to buy provisions and two thermos flasks that were filled with coffee back at the restaurant. As they ate they studied the ordnance survey map brought from the Grange.

Llangollen nestles in the Dee Valley between the shoulders of the Eglwyseg Mountain and the Berwyn range. Heading south there is a single track road across the mountains, linking the Dee and Ceiriog valleys. This road is reached by heading towards Corwen where it can be easily missed, doubling back on the main road as it ascends. This seemed to all of them the best route to pursue. There were various footpaths and tracks, now under eighteen inches of snow, and a few farmhouses dotted about, in a mostly deserted landscape. Moel Fferna at 2066 feet stood to the west of the intended search area and behind it further south was Cadair Bronwen at 2575 feet; beyond this were the Berwyns themselves. However, studying the map did nothing to refresh Anselm's memory and only increased Jim's sense of desperation.

They reached the start of the road just after 10.30am, reading at once from its undisturbed surface that no vehicle had dared venture up or down it for many hours, or probably would again until the thaw came. This came as something of a blow, as they had not anticipated starting out on foot so soon. There was little else to do but tuck the Landrover in at the roadside and unload their packs. Danny had brought from home some unusual items that he now handed out. Jim took a long-handled shovel with a flat rounded blade, whilst three small axes, two crowbars, a rather nasty looking machete and pair of sturdy boltcutters were divided up between the others.

"What are they for?" Harris enquired of the boltcutters.

"Chain mail," Danny answered.

"I should've guessed," said Harris, raising her eyebrows at Frank.

Every step was a labour as boots sank into the soft white surface before being heaved out again ready for the next plunge. An hour later, still in ascent, Jim felt certain they needed to be further west towards Moel Fferna, and led them beside what according to the map should have been a stream, but was now only an indentation in the landscape. Danny, in possession of a compass, carefully noted each change of direction.

Jim and Danny walked next to each other at the front, Harris and Wain came behind them, whilst Ruth and Erich brought up the rear. Jim no longer had to be careful about concealing his thoughts. He'd needed to keep this up during the night; but the day was different; Niedermayer was helpless. However, Jim was under no illusions, this was the only shot at him they'd ever get. Once Niedermayer awoke tonight from his daily death, he would know everything. 'He's going to be so pissed off with us!' thought Jim.

Occasionally, Jim paused to consider the route. Mostly he despaired as he surveyed the unfamiliar landscape. However, at other times he felt an uncanny affinity with his surroundings and a sense of certainty about his choice of direction. Intermittently he spoke aloud as if to an invisible companion, "Anselm ... I'm lost ... I need you to help me out." And sometimes he could be heard making bitter threats, "When I catch you, you bastard, I'll show you how it feels to be powerless."

Danny got used to the man mumbling beside him. The freezing winds were not doing a lot for his facial injuries, which were hurting like hell. He tossed two more painkillers to the back of his throat and swallowed. He'd already consumed half the pills they had given him at the hospital, which were supposed to keep him pain free for forty-eight hours. He'd have to raid the first-aid kit, if and when the hard stuff ran out.

Susan Harris was nurturing grave doubts and kept wondering how she of all people could have become involved in this. They were attempting to track down the proverbial needle in a haystack. What galled her most was the thought of failing, trashing her career without a result.

Frank's greatest concern was for his family. He knew it would be so easy for them to lose their bearings and simply freeze to death up here, achieving absolutely nothing in the process. 'I don't want my kids to grow up thinking their old man was a lunatic,' he thought. As he struggled through the snow he imagined future dialogues his children might have in the event of his death, 'How did your father die?' And their shamefaced replies, 'He was on a murder case and flipped. He and another policeman went AWOL chasing after a vampire … died on a Welsh mountain along with some new age weirdoes.'

Erich wasn't thinking too much, it was all his mind could do to keep pace with his body. For his age he was exceptionally fit, but the preceding days had told hard on him and the effort of trudging through snow in a seemingly endless ascent would have taxed the hearts and lungs of far younger men. The thought of Niedermayer and his vicious reign being allowed to survive into the next millennium, able to exploit countless future generations, was all the incentive Erich needed to keep going.

As ever, Ruth seemed capable of generating boundless energy. Neither the effort nor the cold seemed to trouble her much. She remained certain, perhaps more so even than Erich, that Jim with Anselm's help would lead them to the creature. And she began to understand why she'd always felt Jim Latimer's life was inextricably linked with her own. To Ruth, the universe was like a gigantic schoolroom which she trusted had coached them well. Each person was there to fulfil a purpose and had been uniquely trained for this particular event. It really didn't matter how they had come together or what as individuals they believed; each was performing as the universal consciousness bid them do; free will was partly an illusion. Yet however strong her conviction was, still some fear remained. And it was important never to lose sight of the fact that Niedermayer had two surviving helpers, and eight hundred years' of preparation behind him. Ruth's gift was powerful but she was not a fortune-teller. The hoped for conclusion didn't come with a cast iron guarantee.

Two hours on, Danny told everyone to rest. He shared out some bread, cheese and apples. Frank Wain poured the coffee. Llangollen and the River Dee should have been visible from their north-facing slope but below all was shrouded under an impenetrable white haze, whilst above and all around ominously dark clouds were gathering.

Wain had a question, "Anselm said this place was three leagues from the Abbey, exactly how far is a league?"

"I think it's reckoned to be about three miles," answered Danny.

"So how far have we come from Valle Crucis?"

"Six or seven perhaps."

"Anselm didn't really know these hills," said Jim. For some time there had been a growing despondency about him, "They got completely lost before getting back on track."

"And are we on track, or lost?" asked Harris, her tone slightly more arch than she'd meant it to sound.

Jim stared at his coffee in its plastic cup and replied uncertainly, "On track I hope. Christ, I hope so!"

Shortly afterwards they resumed their journey. Wain turned to Harris and asked, "Any idea what time it'll get dark?"

"That depends on what you mean by dark."

"When night begins?"

"Sunset is generally about half an hour before civil twilight, basically the point at which the sun's light is no longer lighting up the earth."

"You seem to know a lot about all of this?"

"I made some enquiries last night from the services."

"So which is it that we have to watch out for?"

"Our problems in Hove last Thursday evening started shortly after civil twilight."

"So when is that?"

"Four thirty-eight," she retorted.

Wain consulted his watch, but before he did the subtraction, Harris said, "Two hours, forty-three minutes."

Wain felt a snowflake touch his cheek, "Shit. Here we go again."

*

The endeavour of each one of them became an altogether more insular experience after the snow resumed. Half a mile on from where they had taken their break Jim started to lead them southwards again.

"Moel Fferna was slightly to the west and behind them. I can picture it!" he called to the others in an attempt to justify his action.

Visibility deteriorated and Danny warned everyone to stay close together. He grew concerned for his father who looked quite exhausted, although he knew Erich would never admit to it. Thankfully most of the wind was behind them, but as time passed the cold wormed its way beneath their layers of protective clothing, and each subsequent step seemed to demand more effort than the previous one.

Harris had by this time all but given up hope of finding the place, if indeed such a place existed. Whilst sympathising with Jim and his predicament, what had seemed possible in the light of morning now looked hopeless. She was no longer convinced that Latimer was leading on anything other than wishful thinking.

When Harris looked at her watch again, it was 2.53pm, and she concluded that it was time to save their own skins at least. Danny would be able to lead them across the hills back onto the road, where they stood a better chance of finding shelter for the night. Harris was about to voice this decision when Frank began to point at something only barely visible just east of where they trudged.

"I think it's a vehicle," he called.

Somehow the discovery brought with it renewed energy, as they covered the distance with more vigour than anyone had shown in ages. It was indeed a vehicle, a small blue van. The snow had drifted across the driver's side, where it lay almost totally buried. Frank was extremely lucky to have spotted it.

Wain and Harris scooped handfuls of snow from the windscreen. Frank used the axe blade Danny had issued him with as a scraper to get the ice off the glass. Once he'd achieved a viewing hole, he shone a flashlight into the van's interior.

"There's nothing inside," he told the others, "Driver must've abandoned it."

"Then this must be a track," said Harris, pointing along a gap that ran between two wooded hillsides.

"Which way do you think they went?" Danny asked.

"Probably the direction the van's pointing," replied Wain.

Erich suddenly spoke up in a tone that immediately attracted everyone's attention, although his words were only meant for Ruth. "What is it? What's wrong?" he asked.

Ruth's face had turned almost as white as their surroundings. She looked like she was about to vomit.

"This van … it's theirs. It's the one they used to kidnap Sophie."

"How can you possibly know that?" Harris asked impatiently.

"The vibrations off it."

Harris shot a sceptical glance at Wain.

Jim, however, took Ruth's revelation about the van seriously. He peered into its dark interior, attempting to see what lay beneath its icy cocoon. His eye caught sight of something vaguely familiar that was pressed against the glass on the driver's door. The snow was above the roof here. He utilised the shovel he'd been carrying to dig a hole alongside the window; then pronounced between gritted teeth, "Picton!"

Attached to the window was Picton's private joke; a blood donor sticker that carried the slogan, 'Give blood'.

They dug out and broke open its rear doors. A few filthy blankets were scattered across the floor. Harris climbed through into the passenger seat and checked under the dashboard, where she found a pack of fresh needles and some phials of a sedative.

"Yes. Our man I reckon," she called to the others as she began to clamber out.

Ruth standing nearest to the van door offered Harris a helping hand. The women made eye contact and Harris said apologetically, "I didn't believe you, Ruth. I'm sorry."

Ruth shrugged her shoulders and smiled.

Danny's voice reached them from a short way off, "Over here, I've got footprints."

*

The single set of footprints they followed had been mostly filled in, leaving only a slight depression on the snow's surface. These were deepest at the back of the foot, where Picton's heel had dug in, compensating for the extra weight on his shoulders.

Discovering the van had brought them renewed strength for the final uphill trek. They were moving along what must normally have been a track between two wooded slopes that bore a mixture of coniferous and deciduous trees. It was still snowing heavily, and the light levels were rapidly decreasing.

After thirty minutes of hard uphill slog the ground gradually levelled out. Visibility was far poorer, and everything beyond about twenty feet disappeared into a murky haze. An occasional tree loomed out like a spectral figure from the mist as if to warn them back. An indeterminate distance ahead, a grey line gradually transformed into a stone wall.

Harris and Wain unzipped their coats and took out their pistols. They went first, leading the others through a gap in the stonework.

It turned out to be a driveway of sorts. The wooden gate, which had been left open, was buried up to its central bar. Some distance ahead, hard to estimate through the dim haze, vague outlines of buildings materialised.

Neither Wain nor Harris saw the stout piece of timber being driven at them until a second before it made contact, and by then it was too late. Both police officers were felled like nine-pins, including Danny, who came close behind Harris and took most of her weight as she fell backwards into him.

422

Wain received the worst blow being closest to their stocky assailant. He flew backwards and smacked into the gatepost, although he was protected from far more serious injury on the large nail protruding out from the post by his backpack. Wain's pack was torn open as he slid down the post showering its contents behind him. Harris's pistol had been knocked from her hand but Frank still retained his. He raised the gun at their attacker, but Picton was far swifter. He drove the butt end of the joist he held down onto Wain's wrist in an action like a kango hammer. Frank shrieked with pain as the bones in his wrist shattered. The weapon dropped out of his hand and fell onto the snow.

Jim, raised the shovel above his shoulder and swung it at Picton's head. But once again Picton was ahead of the game and avoided the assault with a well judged side-step. Jim, unbalanced by the effort, toppled to the ground.

Susan Harris, winded and with a fierce burning in her chest, scrambled across the snow to retrieve her lost gun. Before she could get to it, however, Picton had cast aside his inferior weapon and scooped up Frank's pistol.

"Don't bother!" he warned.

Harris came to an abrupt stop as did Erich and Ruth, who were about to enter the fray.

"This is a very funny situation!" laughed Picton. He clearly found the predicament of the defunct band of vigilantes terrifically amusing. "Just like the three little pigs!" he added.

Picton's maths were clearly as piss poor as his choice of analogy, but the imagery worked a treat for him; not only causing him to roar with laughter, but to shed a few mirthful tears.

"Little pigs, little pigs, let me in!" he boomed out in bass baritone, then replying to himself in something akin to boy soprano, he added, "No! No! No! You'll eat us!"

Presumably this chorus was meant to be them.

So appreciative was he of his talent to amuse himself, he needed to take off his woollen cap and fan his red face, overheated from laughing.

Harris observed the white line of old scar tissue running across his bald head from its crown to the centre of the forehead.

"Where's my daughter, you bastard?" cried Jim as he clambered to his feet.

Picton wiped away a fat tear on the edge of his cap before replacing it on his head.

"She's okay … got plenty of blood left in her if that's what you're worried about."

Jim didn't care that the man was holding a gun as he launched himself at him. But Picton was prepared. He jabbed his free hand into Jim's stomach and sent him spluttering to the ground.

Picton smiled inanely. "Ooh! I almost forgot," he said, taking a small padded envelope that was open at one end out of his jacket. "I was going to post it off to you … the weather held me up and I sort of forgot."

He tossed the package after Jim, and as it landed a grey finger complete with wedding-ring rolled out onto the snow.

Jim, overcome with horror and rage, lunged for the shovel and sprang to his feet screaming, "You evil bastard!"

Danny, seeing the gun raised in Jim's direction, immediately dived at Picton's arm. A shot rang out, blowing a two-inch chunk out of the shovel's blade and sending it flying out of Jim's hand. Danny clung to Picton's arm like a terrier, before a savage fist blow to his neck dropped him like a weighted sack onto the snow.

"I'll put a bullet through his fucking brain if you don't behave," Picton assured Jim. He was holding Wain's pistol to the back of Danny's head. "You can creep away from that gun too," he warned Harris, who had taken the opportunity of the diversion to cover a bit more ground. "And what in the name of fuck do you think you're playing at?" he asked Wain, who had risen to his feet at the same time and was now standing less than an arm's length away from him.

Wain offered no explanation but continued to stand his ground, his injured hand protruding at an unnatural angle out from the wrist.

"You're a fucking cripple!" mocked Picton. "You're no use to anyone!" He laughed uproariously, exhibiting in the process a disturbing array of yellow teeth that quite believably hadn't seen a brush in eight centuries.

Wain's eyes, burning cold with hatred, only increased Picton's appreciation.

Wain didn't mind being the object of the man's ridicule. In fact he was gratified by the response, and willing him to laugh some more. Frank wanted him to let himself go completely, and hopefully forget about his other hand, the useful one, behind his back.

"Don't worry," Picton guffawed, "Mr Niedermayer's a real gentleman, he treats cripples just the same as normal people … he's not prejudiced. They all taste the same!"

Picton's last remark was clearly the killer punchline and he subsequently all but burst himself laughing. Frank received the full-on orthodontist's nightmare in Technicolor splendour.

Wain aimed for the tonsils; ramming the flare without hesitation into the man's gaping mouth. Surprise overtook a stunned Picton as his badly arranged teeth bit down onto the tube. Wain steadied the flare's end by an agonising effort that employed his injured hand. At the same time he twisted and tugged the ring pull with his good hand.

"Chew on that, laughing boy!" he exclaimed as the magnesium flare exploded in Picton's mouth.

Picton's eyes bulged like they were about to blow from their sockets. He dropped the gun as he fell backwards, reeling and kicking in the snow. His arms were writhing about his face whilst frenetic hands attempted to draw the scorching tube from his mouth. Its heat was so ferocious that within seconds the tongue, palate and flare became inseparably fused. Only gurgling sounds could be heard coming from Picton's throat as his voice box vaporised. The blinding incandescence pouring out of the man's mouth made him resemble a human volcano.

Most bizarrely, Picton's facial muscles still gave an appearance of smiling, cheeks aglow, like a pumpkin at Halloween.

Chapter Thirty-Six

Monday, 16 December, 1996

By the time the flare was done, all that remained of Picton's head was a blue woollen cap and some tell-tale wisps of gingery hair; most of the face had burned away leaving a smouldering mass of charcoal. Even so, they waited until Niedermayer's delivery boy lay absolutely still before striking off in the direction of the buildings.

Harris led the way, Frank and Jim following closely behind, while a dazed Danny with a sizeable swelling on the back of his neck was helped along by Ruth and Erich.

Frank observed how Jim Latimer's face grew paler the closer they got to the house. At first he thought it must have been paternal anxiety but soon realised it was the house itself or rather its hidden inhabitant that produced such visible foreboding. It was only the hope of saving Sophie that kept Jim moving. He was almost petrified with fear, and each new footfall in the soft snow became an increased agony as he drew nearer to the source of his despair and terror.

As the house came into focus it was immediately clear that only the foundations could have remained since Anselm's time. A variety of outbuildings that wouldn't have seemed amiss around any contemporary farming establishment preceded a house which was certainly old. An upper storey had most probably been added sometime during the eighteenth century. All the windows were modern, with plastic frames, which in a way seemed more incongruous than the iron bars embedded into the walls across them.

Harris marshalled her troops alongside a barn, which was opposite the house's main door. There was a four-foot high wall immediately before them, creating a courtyard between the house and its outlying buildings, conveniently positioned to offer cover. Harris wriggled free of her rucksack and crouched behind the wall; the others did the same.

She consulted her watch; it was 3.54pm.

"Forty-four minutes," she said, hoping Niedermayer played by the Met Office rules, "Any ideas?"

"They certainly take the threat of break-ins seriously," understated Frank.

"A burglar seeing those bars might think there was something inside worth stealing," commented Danny, who was beginning to look and feel a little steadier.

"God only help them if they should find its treasure," added Erich.

"The door must be the weakest point," continued Frank, his voice betraying a note of pain. He was deliberately keeping his right hand out of sight, tucked away inside his windcheater. "We don't know if they're armed, but even if we could get in closer, that door is solid oak. It could take us an hour to break it down."

"Let me see that wrist," Ruth said, fishing out a first-aid pack from her rucksack.

Wain hesitated.

"Let her, Frank," said Harris.

Frank reluctantly obliged. Harris couldn't help wincing at the sight of it. The wrist was highly inflamed, hot and swollen to at least twice its normal thickness.

"I can at least bandage it," said Ruth, trying to be matter of fact.

"Take these," said Danny, handing Wain a packet containing his last two painkillers.

"What will you do?" Frank asked.

"I've just taken some," lied Danny.

Wain guessed the truth but gratefully accepted the sacrifice; the pain was too severe for argument.

"I'm going to take a look around the back," said Harris.

"I can't use my gun," Frank warned.

"Let Erich use it," she replied, adding ironically, "We're not playing police officers any more, remember."

Before she left, Harris caught sight of Jim. During her police career she couldn't recall seeing anyone look more frightened.

"You alright?" she asked.

Her first attempt failed to get through.

"Jim? ... Jim? Are you okay?"

For a moment Jim managed to drag himself free of the darkness which was relentlessly encroaching upon his mind, to stare uncertainly back at Harris, "He's sensed me. He knows we're here. He's confident ... time is on his side."

"We'll see about that," replied Harris. She went off, keeping low, disappearing from sight at the end of the barn.

While she was gone, Ruth bandaged Frank's hand and rubbed some cream onto Danny's neck. Erich, in the meantime, used Wain's pistol and kept watch. Harris was only away for five minutes, but to those waiting it seemed a good deal longer. Now there were only thirty-five minutes left before Niedermayer was due to wake.

"Anything?" asked Wain.

Harris didn't seem optimistic "The rear shows less promise than the front. The back door has an iron gate protecting it. They're certainly well organised. There's another car stashed away in the barn and a tractor too. Do you think we might attach some kind of battering ram onto it to use against the front door?"

"Might be worth a try," said Wain, who knew as well as Harris did that they were clutching at straws.

Jim shook his head despondently. "He'll have thought of that ... he thinks of everything."

"What do you suggest then?" asked Harris, on the verge of losing her patience.

Jim looked at each of his companions in turn as though seeking inspiration from their faces. "I'll ask to be let in," he said distractedly. And before anyone could stop him he'd got to his feet and was heading for the door.

"Christ, the bloody fool!" Harris exclaimed, about to rush after him and drag him back.

Erich calmly put out a hand and stopped her, "Susan, nobody would be a bloody fool if they could help it," he said. "Let him try."

*

Jim began to shiver as he entered the shadow cast by the house. In the centre of the door was a brass knocker, set below a square grille. As Jim's trembling hand reached out, Niedermayer rose up in his mind's eye and he shuddered. He recalled the taste of the creature's putrescent blood in his mouth. The urge to turn and run was very nearly irresistible. In a sudden, spontaneous flashback he saw Anselm, running blindly through an older doorway on the exact same spot.

Jim swallowed hard then let the knocker go, its sound echoing deep through the house's hollowness. He waited a few moments for a response, but nothing came.

"It's Jim Latimer!" he called out, "Mr Hart? I know you can hear me!"

Jim lowered the hood on his windcheater; it restricted hearing and blocked his peripheral vision. He was oblivious to any snowflakes settling on his hair and face.

"I need to talk with you!" Jim was about to knock again when a reply came from inside.

"Come back later, once it's dark ... Mr Niedermayer will see you then."

"I want to talk to you," said Jim. "Your sister, remember her? She's dead."

The silence that followed was a tangible thing; and within its interminable time-span Jim was aware of his own heart beating. When he could bear it no longer, he said, "The sister you loved and sacrificed your own life to save."

No response came back.

"Let me in ... please," he implored. "Let us end this!"

He heard a catch being slipped across on the door grille. As the tiny window was opened Jim saw two keen blue eyes peering back at him. Somewhere within his being he recognised them, not as Jim Latimer but as Anselm had long ago.

Hart was glancing uncomfortably from side to side. Jim felt a wave of pity for the man break over him. He understood now why he had never felt the same animosity towards him as the others.

"What's happened to Picton?" Hart asked.

"He's dead."

Hart's eyes didn't waver, revealing no emotion, as they digested this fact.

"My ... my daughter ... is she ... alright?" The question had been difficult to ask.

"She's unharmed. Picton was delayed by the weather. They got here just after dawn. She's sedated."

Out of relief Jim asked, "Could I see her?"

There was no reply.

Jim knew that Hart retained the remnants of a conscience. Somehow he had to make the man connect with the past, recall his own history.

"Picton was a Templar just as you were. He was a sergeant."

"We've adopted many roles ... far too numerous to recall," Hart replied wearily.

"Rosemary was called Melisend then."

Jim believed he saw something akin to distress flicker across the man's eyes at mention of the name. It was like trying to revive the

429

tiniest glimmer of life in the dying embers of a fire. He was unable to see the lower half of Hart's face, but thought he heard the word 'Melisend' being pronounced softly on his lips.

"I know a good deal about Melisend and about you ... I know how you came to lose the use of your arm."

Hart grew distinctly more uncomfortable every time the name Melisend was mentioned. He seemed unable to comprehend why the name had the effect it did on him.

"I ... I don't understand ... and I don't wish to hear any more." There was confusion and anguish in Hart's tone as he spoke.

Jim couldn't afford to give up. "I know why I dreamed about you. Remember, I started telling you about it in the cellar ..."

Hart's eyes were wavering from side to side. Jim sensed that the barriers in the man's mind, erected over eight centuries and perpetually reinforced by Niedermayer, were beginning to show some flaws; time was the only thing.

"You came here with a monk from Valle Crucis, a Brother Anselm. He'd found you freezing to death on the river and nursed you back to health. Your name is Hugh Apsley and you were a Templar knight. Niedermayer was your enemy, you came here to destroy him. His name at that time was Jerome. You had pursued him all the way from Acre with a man called Reynald de Sauveterre ..."

Hart's eyes stopped roving and began to widen, but if anything, the confusion in them had only increased.

"You arrived in England with a boy called Yussuf, he rescued you from drowning but sadly died himself ..."

Hart's eyes held still for a moment and narrowed; Jim thought he saw, the dimmest glimmer of recollection there.

"You dictated a letter to Anselm that was left with the abbot at Valle Crucis. I think you must have retrieved the letter afterwards ... but you kept it ... then centuries later you hid it in the attic at Barnswick Square. The letter was addressed to Reynald de Sauveterre ..."

"In Albi ..." Hart said. The response was involuntary. The man didn't have any conscious understanding of what had driven him to say it. Yet, this name, long forgotten, brought beads of sweat to Hart's brow. He was visibly shaken.

Jim began to see hope. "You remember?"

"The name of a town somewhere in France ... it means nothing to me," he replied dispassionately.

430

"You came here to rescue Melisend and to kill Jerome. Please try and remember ... your sister ... Melisend. Jerome murdered your whole family ..."

"I must go," said Hart, avoiding eye contact as he spoke.

"Please, wait ..." Jim called to the troubled man as he began to close the grille. He knew he must keep Hart talking. He believed given time he could break through.

"It's no use Mr Latimer. I remember nothing," Hart replied flatly. "It will be dark soon. I suggest you come back then should you wish to take this matter further. I'm sure you're aware of how pleased Mr Niedermayer will be to see you."

The grille was closed and Jim heard a click as its catch was replaced.

"Please. There's more!" Jim cried in desperation. Then, realising the hopelessness and futility of the effort, collapsed to his knees in the snow. He was grimly aware of how he had nursed in vain the improbable hope of re-awakening a spark of light within Hart's long-usurped soul. He banged his head against the door in frustration .Whatever glimmer of a memory he had sought to rekindle in the man had been extinguished long ago. The pain was suddenly unbearable. Not only were his efforts a failure, but invaluable time had been wasted; Niedermayer within his cocoon of darkness would be rejoicing. Sophie's life would soon be forfeit, as well as his own and the lives of his companions.

"Oh please, God! Hugh! Forgive me! Forgive what I allowed him to do to you!" he cried out. "It was my weakness that made you what you are now. I deserted you! I was Anselm!" Jim bellowed through heaving sobs of his despair, "I was your friend, Anselm. Hugh, for God's sake! I betrayed you. I am the guilty one!"

At first when Jim heard the door bolts being dragged across and the sound of a key turning, he thought he was imagining it. Then, looking up from where he knelt in wretchedness he saw the door was open and Hugh was standing there before him with Sophie. She was asleep, her cheek resting against the man's misshapen shoulder, her body gently cradled in his good arm. Hugh no longer kept his deformed arm hidden from view, the shrivelled hand hung limp and lifeless at his side. The man looked older than before, more careworn, his back slightly stooped. He looked cold, in grey flannel trousers and a thin white shirt, as he stood in the doorway with Jim's daughter.

Jim got to his feet and took Sophie in his arms. She looked fine. He could see she was unharmed. The tears streamed out of his eyes as he kissed her hair and hugged her to him.

"She's my only child," he explained to the friend from long ago.

The man observed the father's tenderness for his daughter. An unfathomable depth of sadness and yearning was evident in Hugh's eyes. He was experiencing a lost vocabulary of emotions, just as a man may latch onto the odd phrase from a language spoken with ease and fluency in childhood but long forgotten.

A smile of recognition crossed Hugh's face, "You came back for me, Anselm." At that moment, it was as though Jim Latimer was no more than a cloak Brother Anselm had wrapped about himself. Hugh's words had been spoken without any trace of reproach. "I always tried to resist him," he told the old friend.

"I know."

The two men gazed at each other for a few moments, but nothing more was spoken. No words exist that could sufficiently voice the sorrow and remorse each understood in the other.

Hugh sighed; then turned and began to walk away. He headed towards the opening in the wall, never once looking back. He didn't notice the five crouched figures who stood up as he passed.

Harris raised her pistol in Hart's direction. Wain reached out his uninjured hand to forestall her. But she had already made up her own mind. Harris let the gun hand drop to her side again.

Hugh looked bewildered and frail as he tottered into the blur of falling snow. His torso almost immediately merged into the oblivion. The legs remained visible for a moment longer before they too disappeared into the void of whiteness.

Chapter Thirty-Seven

Monday, 16 December, 1996

The basic layout of the house hadn't altered much since Anselm's time, but of course there had been changes. An open staircase now rose at the back of the reception area to a new floor which had been added above. However, on the ground floor there was still just the one door leading off from its large main room.

They brought the unconscious Sophie back into the house and laid her on a couch. The furnishings, as with the ground floor at Barnswick Square, were charming, a Homes & Gardens centrefold. A combination of snow at the windowpanes, lots of shiny brass and logs burning in the hearth might have conjured up a Perry Como moment, but for the reek of putrefaction. Upon entering the house, Harris had discovered that she was no longer immune to the nauseating stench, so regularly complained of by most of the other officers working at the Square. What's more, she could also confirm the accuracy of Dave Frith's description of the smell as being like 'shit and rotten meat'.

The group, following Erich's lead, quickly discarded any remaining food rations and bulky survival items from their backpacks. None could doubt their close proximity to Niedermayer; which brought with it a deadening sense of ill-ease and physical weariness. Their limbs felt cold, leaden and numb, and although the fire looked appealing to the eye it seemed to give out no heat. Jim, not unexpectedly, was affected the most. He had begun to hyperventilate the moment he crossed the house's threshold.

Observing his powerful resistance to being there, Harris said, "Why don't you take Sophie and wait for us in the barn?"

"That would only be worse," he replied, "I have to be certain he's dead."

"Close your eyes and concentrate on relaxing," advised Erich.

Jim returned an incredulous look. Erich was barking mad if he thought he could close his eyes and relax for a second in that place.

"Stay here with Sophie then," Harris whispered, "You got us in … let us do the rest."

Everyone was whispering and the reason for this was understandable. There was no cast iron guarantee that Niedermayer would oblige by not rising until the time officially calculated for night. In fact, it was already looking awfully dim outside.

Harris consulted her watch: 4.23. There were fifteen minutes left. They switched on their flashlights and congregated alongside her, each holding their breath as she extended a hand towards the doorknob. Erich and Ruth were both fielding one of Danny's home-made crosses. Wain had a stake in his unbandaged hand with a mallet gripped tightly beneath his arm. Danny was keeping a tight grip on the pair of boltcutters he'd brought. Any other equipment they might need was on their backs in the re-organised packs. Harris, not quite able to break with convention, had stuck with her pistol.

She threw the door open. As the five flashlights probed the room ahead there came a spontaneous gasp, it was as if they had all expressed themselves through one voice.

The tension was too much for Jim. He sprang to his feet and rushed over. "What is it, what's wrong?" he asked anxiously.

Harris was descending a short flight of stairs into the lower room. When she reached the floor she swiftly found a light switch.

The problem was glaringly obvious. There was nothing there.

The room itself was a brochure kitchen, complete with brass pans, stacks of expensive earthenware and the obligatory Aga. The earth and straw floor Anselm would have known was laid with elegant flagstones. It was the kind of farmhouse kitchen possessed by senior advertising executives or city bankers; a wholly different type of blood-sucker some might argue.

"Search the house!" cried Harris, "He's here somewhere!"

Her nose told her that much.

*

As the seconds ticked by, pandemonium broke out, and nerves became strained to snapping point. They banged on walls around the house to check their integrity. Upstairs, where just as in Hove the facade ended, Danny used a crowbar to tear an exploratory hole in the ceiling to inspect the attic void.

Only Jim and Ruth remained in the kitchen. Jim was paralysed by terror; while Ruth, though fearful too, attempted to utilise her precognitive gift. However, nothing was forthcoming, and having Jim nearby wasn't helping. He continually let out sighs to express his anxiety, whilst at the same time he shook from head to toe.

He cried out in desperation, "Perhaps we should take the car and get away while there's still time."

"And how far do you think we'd get with all the roads snowed under?"

"Perhaps if we took the tractor then … but once he wakes up … we won't stand a chance. Oh God! Oh God! He's won!" Jim whimpered.

"Will you shut up! It isn't finished yet!" she screeched back, grabbing the front of his coat in an attempt to shake him out of it. "Come on Jim … I know this is really hard for you … but you know him best. My senses are overwhelmed. For heaven's sake, where is he?"

"I don't know!" he screamed at her, "I just know he's close. I can feel him ... so close … he's almost touching me!"

Ruth felt it too; the Niedermayer effect was everywhere, but it was here in the kitchen that his presence was strongest. Her eyes roved about the room until they finally settled on the floor. She stamped down on the flagstone beneath her foot. A brief smile crossed her face at the sound of hollowness below.

"He's down here!" she shouted.

Judging by the sound of running feet it was unnecessary to repeat the instruction.

"Where?" asked Harris, slightly out of breath as she rushed in just ahead of the others.

Ruth pointed to a flagstone that was set before the Aga without any grouting around it. "It's hollow beneath," she explained.

Danny fetched the shovel from the main room, ramming what remained of its blade into one of the flagstone's joints. As he levered it up, Erich and Harris got a purchase underneath with crowbars and prised it out of position. Their combined effort exposed a set of wooden treads descending into pitch darkness.

An appalling bouquet rose on the dank air pouring out from that pit of filth, sharply redolent of festering blood. Harris, clutching her pistol as if it were a good luck charm, went first. She took a final glance at her watch; four and a half minutes till 4.38. Erich went after her, then Frank, Danny and Ruth.

Jim, barely able to move or think, came last. Nobody had expected him to join them, or would even have believed him capable of doing so. But he possessed an overriding need to be absolutely certain of Niedermayer's extermination. His legs and hands shook uncontrollably as he descended with knees barely flexible enough to bend. The sweat was pouring out of him as he clung to the ladder, scared out of his wits, like a vertigo sufferer about to add claustrophobia to his curriculum vitae.

The others didn't exhibit such overt symptoms. However, a deep sense of dread and foreboding was felt by all of them. Fear and malignancy thrived like hybrid cultures in Niedermayer's lair. Entering that noxious atmosphere made every cell in the body feel like it had been contaminated. Just as happened in the cellar at Hove, the flashlights' beams appeared to be weakened by the place's tangible negativity.

Harris, shining her torch around, whispered anxiously to Erich, "I can't see it." 'It' being the anticipated coffin; for a sceptic, Harris had come a long way.

Erich stepped forward gingerly and reaching out a tentative hand drew back a curtain that had not been immediately obvious. It was crudely stitched together out of old grain sacks, rotten and stinking, slimy and unpleasant to the touch. The partition moved haltingly, being looped around a piece of greasy string tied from wall to wall.

The curtain, once drawn back, revealed a long lidded box, made from pieces of roughly-sawn wood, set upon a plinth of loose bricks. This grim pile was Niedermayer's state room, and there, laid out before them was his horizontal throne.

Danny and Erich rested their flashlights against the bricks, angling the beams up towards the ceiling joists. Then taking a deep breath, they prised the lid off the coffin.

The lighting conspired with the sides of the crate to cast Niedermayer's face in stark relief, which didn't make the job any easier and helped play on the imagination. Needless to say, it didn't seem rational to shine a light directly at the monstrous face to check its eyes were closed. The teeth were only too graphically depicted by the spill of light. They were pointed, sharp and unappetisingly stained after long adherence to an unwholesome diet.

Danny, using the boltcutters, began to cut away the chain mail, starting at the neck. The mediaeval armour, in the latter stages of advanced metal fatigue, offered the kind of resistance butter shows a knife. Beneath the mail-coat were the threadbare remnants of heavily malodorous undergarments, mostly in tattered shreds. Here and there patches of bare skin were exposed, grey, cadaverous, the colour and texture of Portland cement. There were two distinct holes made by bullets in the upper chest of the mailshirt, these had punctured and singed the rags beneath, but below this the skin was unmarked. Wain and Robson had both hit their mark.

As Danny's hand reached the waist it unintentionally brushed a patch of Niedermayer's cold, dead, skin, coarse yet slimy, most reminiscent of the scales of a fish. He felt his stomach begin to heave in reaction.

"That's enough," whispered his father.

Danny gratefully backed away and immediately threw up onto the wall behind him.

Erich, steady-eyed, drew back the flaps of the cut hauberk. He placed the stake's finely honed point lightly on the chest directly above the heart. Then he brought down the mallet with every ounce of strength contained in his old but wiry arm.

Erich looked perplexed. The stake had moved, but only imperceptibly.

In the very next instant the true horror dawned on all.

Mr Niedermayer was no longer their passive prey. His long fingers were wrapped around the point of the stake, explaining the disappointing lack of downward movement. The time calculation had been correct. The blow had been struck a mere second late. Nobody felt prompted to check their watches for accuracy.

Erich gasped at the monstrous eyes observing him, yellow and translucent in the semi-darkness. He released his hold on the stake. The creature's hand lunged out from the coffin and grabbed Erich's wrist. Then, deftly turning the stake around in his other hand, Niedermayer re-directed its point up towards his would-be slayer. Erich, seeing what was intended for his own heart, tried in vain to break free of the vice-like grip.

Niedermayer began to rise; eyes burning with malice, lips peeled back from slavering jaws.

Harris, like everyone else, had been shocked to witness such an awakening, but recognising the need for action, she stepped before the coffin and fired three shots in rapid succession at the hideous face. Three holes in a neat line were blasted into the creature's forehead, but only seconds after the wounds appeared they began to close. Harris, wide-eyed and open-mouthed in disbelief, let the pistol fall.

Frank, a stake in his useable hand, dived at the coffin aiming straight for the creature's chest. Niedermayer, caught off guard, relinquished his hold on Erich and dropping back into the coffin kicked a mailed foot into Frank's shoulder. Frank cried out in pain as he was hurled backwards into Susan Harris. Niedermayer swiftly recovered, ramming the stake's point into Erich's back as he attempted to flee out of harm's way. Erich let out a deep groan and dropped to his knees gasping for breath, the furniture leg his son had sharpened protruding from his side.

Danny rushed to Erich, dragging him over to the wall and out of immediate danger.

Niedermayer began to rise again; then, pausing for a moment as if in reflection, distractedly drew a long black tongue across the back of his hand where some drops of Erich's blood had spurted. When Niedermayer stood, towering above them on his altar of bricks, he bore the look of an assured victor, disdainfully surveying his would-be slayers in their pitiful disarray.

Harris lay crushed and winded beneath the incapacitated Wain, whose collar bone was smashed, effectively making both his arms redundant. Jim, unable to move or think, was utterly consumed with terror. He continued to clutch onto the base of the ladder where he had remained transfixed throughout, passively watching as his nemesis defeated his comrades. Ruth, seeing it had fallen to her to do something, began to advance with a home-made cross held out before her.

Niedermayer, eyeing her with malevolence, growled low as she approached.

However, the next attack didn't come from Ruth but from an enraged Danny. He ferociously swung the axe he'd taken from his rucksack at the back of Niedermayer's neck. Its blade dug deep into the flesh and sinews and the creature's blood oozed out thick and black from the wound. Danny withdrew the blade and immediately struck again. This time the neck was severed almost halfway through and the blood began to spurt out faster. Niedermayer was severely wounded, and emitted something between a growl and a scream as he collapsed onto the coffin, which shattered into pieces beneath him. Danny standing above him, axe raised, was ready with a third blow which might easily have completed the job, had it reached its mark. Niedermayer, infinitely resourceful, expert and wily in the art of prolonged survival, had calculated his own nefarious salvation in the split second it took Danny to prepare the final assault. He caught the axe's handle as it swung for his neck and sent both weapon and assailant somersaulting across him. Danny smashed into the wall, which he met with irresistible force, and fell to the ground unconscious.

Even though Niedermayer was hurt, he displayed a predator's instincts and immediately sprang to his feet, using a hand to staunch the leaking of his precious blood.

Ruth, the only one now left, and displaying extraordinary courage, leapt onto the plinth of bricks, with the cross held out before her; Niedermayer, spitting and snarling at the sight of the despised object, flung out an arm and knocked it flying from her hand.

Then, seeing only a helpless female before him, he gave a most terrible cry; a victory call. It was unlike anything known in either the animal or human repertoire of sound. It grew from the depths of his despicable being and rose to a frenzied note proclaiming his glory and omnipotence. The battle was over; this night, as every night, was his.

Yet the puny female audaciously remained. He glared at her through his luminous eyes and growled, exposing his grotesque teeth. Standing well over a head taller than Ruth, he viewed her with contempt. Perhaps there was a little something of the old Jerome left in him after all. He shifted his neck from side to side to assist the healing process, although the wound itself had all but vanished.

Just as conceit and arrogance had led to Jerome's downfall, it was Niedermayer's folly too. During his long reign he had grown accustomed to watching souls quake helplessly before him. His disdainful expression seemed to pose the question, 'What do you dare do to me?'

It was to prove his costliest mistake in eight hundred years. Niedermayer's eyes widened at the sight of the stake in Ruth's two hands and saw by its momentum that he was already too late to deflect its course. All her strength was invested behind that blow, directing the stake's-point directly up at his heart. She felt the resistance of muscle and rib beneath the force of her arms as the stake invaded his flesh, cutting its path deep.

Niedermayer flung back his head to expel an agonised howl. An instant later his fist struck out at Ruth, catching her unawares, hard beneath the chin with a blow so powerful it raised her bodily into the air. It was accompanied by a sickening crack at the moment when her neck snapped. Her head lolled unnaturally to one side as she crashed to the floor. Ruth had died before she hit the ground.

Niedermayer grappled with the stake in his chest, blood gushing from the wound. Its effect had greatly depleted his strength but, little by little, with agonising effort, it was being withdrawn.

Harris, momentarily stunned by Ruth's death, determined that her life would not be sacrificed for nothing. She knew this was going to be her only chance, and indeed the last chance for all of them. It took a massively painful effort to draw her leg from beneath the semi-conscious Wain. Her face broke into a sweat from the agony in her ankle as she finally extricated her foot. Niedermayer would soon free himself and then quickly recover. Harris tried putting weight on the foot; she knew time was beating her.

Harris had forgotten Jim Latimer. The man had been too petrified to move the last time she'd seen him. He had stood helplessly by watching his friends fall, clutching desperately to the ladder, unable to flee or fight. It was Ruth's death that finally roused him. If he still feared Niedermayer, it was impossible to see it then as he charged at him, enraged by his tyranny. He leapt at the stake, driving it deeper into the creature's chest. As Niedermayer tumbled backwards to the ground, Jim clung on and landed on top of him.

Niedermayer lashed out in attack, tearing viciously with his hideous fingernails, long and brown with filth, at Jim's face and neck. Jim cried out in pain, but he hung onto the stake and attempted to force it in further. Niedermayer was snapping ferociously with his jaws at his attacker's face. Jim managed to keep clear of the teeth, but couldn't avoid the reek of decayed breath filling his mouth and nose.

Harris hobbled her way across the cellar floor. She supported her body by leaning against the bricks, raised her left boot, and hammered its heel down onto the stake's end. Niedermayer shrieked.

Jim felt the creature's power weaken. He managed to pin down its arms to offer Harris an easier target. Despite the seriousness of Niedermayer's injury, it still demanded every bit of strength Jim possessed to hold him.

Harris picked up a loose brick and dropped down beside them. She hammered the end of the stake with half a dozen frenzied blows until it would go no deeper, and only a small stump was left protruding from the creature's chest.

Niedermayer was finished. He remained conscious but all his strength had drained away. No perceptible sound came from him as his body twitched and contorted in its death throes. The silence added a dimension of eeriness to his final moments. Blood was gushing from the chest wound, and he began haemorrhaging from the nose and mouth, then finally his ears and eyes began to bleed. The yellow luminosity of his eyes drowned in pools of the stinking blood that collected in their sockets.

Jim fetched the axe which lay beside the half conscious Danny, and with four ferocious blows severed Niedermayer's head from its neck.

Then, taking an earlobe, he raised the hairless veined head, its face and teeth streaked in blood, and flung it with disgust into the darkest corner of the room. Niedermayer's ignominious end seemed appropriate. The head bumped into the ground then rolled and met the wall with a concluding thud.

Jim helped Susan Harris to her feet and over to the pile of bricks. She sat down stunned and exhausted, breathing rapidly for a moment before fishing under her jacket for the mobile phone.

Jim went to Erich first. He'd lost a lot of blood and had passed out, but it was a relief to find a pulse still beating in his neck. Danny he saw was beginning to come around. Frank was sitting up, dazed and clearly in a lot of pain, but he nodded at Jim to let him know he was okay.

Finally, Jim knelt beside Ruth, and raising her head in his arms, stroked her face and wept.

Chapter Thirty-Eight

March 1997

When he discovered the ticket office was closed, Jim re-traced his steps and went through a side gate onto the railway platform at Robertsbridge. It was mid-afternoon, nobody was about and he was early. He ambled along thinking about nothing in particular. Finally, he settled on one of the oddly curved benches, a kind of latticework in red-painted metal. It proved to be incredibly uncomfortable.

'Most likely won an award for design and a letter of grateful thanks from the British School of Osteopathy,' he thought as he lit up a cigarette.

The sun was pleasantly warm on his face. He closed his eyes and soaked in its rays; spring was already underway. He loved this time of year and its wonderful light.

The winter had been tough; each time he had gone outside to fetch logs for the fire, Ruth's home had been there gazing back at him. Sophie had cried inconsolably when she'd first visited, and seen the cottage of her childhood's greatest adult ally sitting empty and dark.

Sophie had been spared the truth about Niedermayer & Hart. Although she knew she'd been drugged and abducted, this was about all. She believed it had been an act of revenge against her father for exposing them as killers. This came as close to the truth as Jim ever deemed was necessary.

Susan Harris had brought help swiftly. An air ambulance had lifted them to hospital in Wrexham where Erich underwent emergency surgery to remove the wooden spike that had pierced his right lung. For thirty-six hours his survival had been touch and go.

Sophie was discharged almost immediately, collected and taken home by Hannah's parents. Jim was glad; judging by the police presence around them, there would be a lot of questions needing to be answered.

Susan Harris was never actually admitted to the hospital. Immediately after the helicopter landed she'd disappeared and three days were to pass before they would see or hear from her again.

They were placed under a kind of unspoken house arrest, watched over by two surly plain-clothed police officers, but not formally charged with anything. During this time they were allowed to sit with Erich while he remained in intensive care.

Danny Ledermann, who'd broken a spectacular number of bones, would remain in plaster for weeks. Frank fared slightly better, with one arm in plaster and the other hung in a sling. The deep, ugly lacerations Jim had sustained to his face and neck, however, proved to be something of a medical enigma. Within a few hours, scabs had formed, and by the third day nothing remained but rapidly fading scar tissue.

The Thorpe sisters mysteriously arrived in time to be with Danny and the others when Erich came around. They sat on opposite sides of his bed, each holding a hand.

When he first opened his eyes his first response had been to search out and tick off their faces in a kind of mental roll call.

He looked troubled as he asked fraily, "Susan Harris?"

"She's fine," Wain assured him.

Erich nodded his head, satisfied by the answer, managing a smile before settling back to sleep.

They felt relieved that Erich hadn't asked about Ruth, thinking it best to break the news gently when he was a little stronger.

Erich wept of course when he was told. Somehow he could take a philosophical view about her sacrifice, but her friendship was an enormous personal loss to him.

"We've lost a dear friend …. a fine human being," he said through his tears, "God alone knows how many lives she may have saved."

The others were relieved at the way he received the news. They had feared that it might set back his recovery. A few days later when Erich was stronger and alone with Jim, he told him, "You remember when I first came around and I asked about Susan? That was because she was the only one not present."

"Except Ruth," Jim replied.

"No, Ruth was there, in fact she winked at me. If you remember, I smiled."

It was Thursday when Susan Harris eventually re-surfaced. Wain had been able to glean nothing about her whereabouts from their guards, who had obviously been instructed not to discuss anything about the case with him. However, he wasn't the only one without a clue as to her whereabouts. This had become crystal clear when Markland had stormed into his hospital room. It was late on Monday, shortly before Frank had gone down to surgery to have his wrist and collar bone fixed.

"Where is Detective Chief Inspector Harris?" a furious Markland had demanded.

Wain, blissfully floating along on a gently lilting raft of pre-med at the time, and not much taken with the senior officer's intrusion, replied, "Go shove your head up your arse!" At the disciplinary hearing he would deny all knowledge, and blame the medication.

What Wain knew for certain was that Harris wouldn't have disappeared just to save her own skin. That wouldn't have been her style at all. And after the Thorpe sisters turned up unannounced at Erich's bedside, he'd guessed that Harris was somehow behind their appearance.

Initially, Mary and Millie had been arrested at Markland's insistence. They had spent two nights in a cell. Later on, Robson told Wain how the sisters had driven the DCC quite dotty during his interrogation of them. They had politely declined to give away any details about their friends' whereabouts. Whenever Markland had inferred guilt they had calmly but doggedly re-asserted their innocence.

About the same time as the sisters arrived, the number of guards around them dramatically reduced. The two taciturn officers were replaced by a cheery young uniform from the local constabulary. Wain gathered from this that the list of possible charges against them was being reconsidered.

Neither Frank nor the others were at any time questioned about their activities in the area to the north of the Berwyn range. On Thursday morning, a grey man in a suit arrived with copies of the Official Secrets Act for them all to sign, except Wain of course, who had already signed up when he joined the force. He also produced a document, which Wain did sign, guaranteeing immunity from prosecution as long as they never discussed with anyone what they knew about the firm of Niedermayer & Hart.

Erich and the sisters had no hesitation about putting their signatures on the dotted line. It was Jim and Danny who questioned the integrity of doing so.

"Shouldn't people know the truth?" Danny enquired of his father.

Erich said, "Do you think people really want that … to know the truth? Would knowing the truth about Niedermayer really help anyone?"

"Anselm said there were two more like Jerome, what do you think happened to them?" Jim asked.

Erich shrugged, "Who knows? I think we've played our part. Let's close the book and get on with our lives."

Shortly after the man from the Home Office left, Harris showed up. Her foot was bandaged and she was using a stick to help get about. They had been in hospital three days by then and Wain had just heard he could go home.

"Where the bloody hell have you been?" he asked her, feigning anger.

"There were a few loose ends that needed my attention," she answered with a grin.

Wain grabbed his senior officer as well as he could for plaster and bandage, and gave her a long hug; both hoped the sudden accumulation of moisture in their eyes would be put down to a freak dust outbreak in an otherwise speckless ward.

"Christ Almighty, Susan, I'm glad to see you."

"You must've been bored stiff sitting around on your backside without me to keep you on your toes. How are the injuries?"

"The collar bone's okay ... the wrist ... it's fifty-fifty," Wain looked anxious, "I might be pensioned off."

"Not bloody likely," replied Harris, "You don't get away that easily."

Frank smiled, "So Susan ... what exactly have you been up to over the last three days?"

"Fighting our corner ... didn't seem right that Sussex police were about to lose two of their best officers. Let's just say I did a bit of lobbying on our behalf."

And this was all Frank Wain got from her on the subject. He concluded that she must have gone extremely high up the ladder of command to make her points. She would have put their case unambiguously, without any doubt taking the opportunity to stress how embarrassing the real death total for Barnswick Square might be, let alone the panic and outrage that would follow if the true story was ever told. It amounted to blackmail of sorts, and Wain applauded her temerity.

After the elimination of Niedermayer the next best result as far as Harris and Wain were concerned was to do with Markland. The powers that be were apparently furious over his handling of events. Almost overnight, poor Markland's health deteriorated, and by Friday morning he'd opted for early retirement. It was clearly the right decision, because his diminished health soon miraculously improved, again almost overnight. He could be seen most days, except Sundays, on the local golf course, sanguine and bombastic as ever. On Sundays he climbed the pulpit in his role as lay preacher and gave sermons on sin and damnation.

Ruth's cremation was attended by all of them. The sisters had organised it, asking Ruth's many friends to read something they treasured or to say a few words in memory of her. This ranged from the sisters' reading a text from the Bhagavadgita, to old art students like Danny bidding simple but heartfelt farewells. Jim with Sophie beside him was too distraught for words himself.

Erich took a long time to recover and it was considered doubtful whether he would ever regain his former vigour. The injury to his lung had repaired but the wound in his side seemed to resist healing. Erich believed the stake's point had actually pierced Niedermayer's flesh and that he had been poisoned with its foulness.

Nevertheless as soon as Erich was able, he and Jim began to work. They met every day for almost six weeks, working up to three hours at a time. Bit by bit through hypnotic regression, Anselm's memories were pieced together.

"Do you think the Holy Grail stuff is true," Jim asked Erich after one of their later sessions, "Or do you think Hugh embellished his story a bit for Brother Anselm?"

"You can answer that better than any man alive. Did Hugh Apsley strike you as a liar?"

Jim was brought back to the present by the sound of a train approaching along the track. The train itself was still out of sight. Jim got to his feet, excited but a little nervous too. Sophie had already visited him for weekends but this was the first time for Hannah. Her ordeal with Picton had left her deeply scarred and for a long time afterwards she had suffered panic attacks whenever she was alone. Because of this, they had moved out of the house in Clapton and were living with Sophie's grandparents, and Hannah was currently undergoing a course of psychiatric treatment to help her cope with the trauma. This was to be the first time she had left London since the experience, and Jim wanted it to be alright.

"Do you think Hannah will ever be herself again?" Jim had asked Erich the day before.

"Give her time. Time heals," Erich replied sagely.

'Never ask the mystic pixie anything,' Jim thought, 'You never get a straight frickin' answer!'

The train came into view. He remembered the cigarette in his mouth and quickly dashed it to the ground. Sophie hated to see him smoking. He had started again on the morning of Ruth's funeral. He was resolved to ask Erich for another course of treatment. It was over a year by this time since Jim had taken his last drink.

'Oh hell!' he thought, as he looked down at the offending article before extinguishing it beneath the heel of his shoe, 'The worst thing a cigarette can do is kill you.'

*

The snow had lasted for four days before the thaw set in.

A few miles downriver from Llangollen, two men out walking their dogs spotted what looked like a body on the opposite bank. The local police were alerted and an investigation immediately begun. The body turned out to be a skeleton, mystifyingly dressed in a white shirt and grey flannel trousers.

After being examined, it was found to be a male, who in life had been paralysed down his left side. Later, tests proved conclusively that the bones were at least seven or eight hundred years old.

The North Wales police scratched their heads for a bit before concluding they had been the object of a practical joke.

THE END

If you enjoyed reading Niedermayer & Hart and would like to find out what

Martin is currently working on, then join him on his blog and website:

www.mj-johnson.com